Praise for Asia Mackay

'Sexy, stylish, thrilling and funny. Asia Mackay rips up the rulebook in this wildly original, razor-sharp tale of marriage and murder, mundanity and mayhem. I loved it.' Chris Whitaker

'Murder has never been so funny. If you liked *Mr & Mrs Smith*, you'll love this original and darkly funny thriller.' Clare Mackintosh

'An invaluable manual that I return to again and again' Hugh Grant

'I ABSOLUTELY LOVED IT!!! It's so new and different and refreshing and I found it such fun (also loved the feminist message)' Marian Keyes

'Certain to be your sassy, twisted must-read of 2025' Janice Hallett

'I absolutely gobbled up this darkly funny and clever thriller about one of the most dysfunctional marriages to ever make it onto the page. Loved it.' Katy Brent

'Huge fun with a dark beating heart, a game of cat and mouse with sharpened tooth and claw. You won't dare to put it down.' Harriet Tyce

'A riotously fun read. Asia Mackay puts the sass in assassin as it's never been done before' L. S. Hilton

'With a slick plot, pin-sharp prose and an authentic feel, this fiercely feminist and witty thriller will keep you gripped . . . and rooting for a rather wonderful heroine' *Sunday Mirror*

'Funny, fast and full-tilt!' James Swallow

'Mackay's debut is fresh and fun, and adroitly combines social and parenting comedy with detail-rich derring-do' *The Sunday Times*

'With dark humour, a twisty plot and a healthy dose of genuine emotion, this unique novel is a thrilling ride' *Heat*

'I loved it. Really entertaining, good fun and captures the mum juggle/guilt perfectly' The Unmumsy Mum

'Witty . . . fun . . . clever. BRILLIANT!' Sophie Ellis-Bextor

'This might be the best fun I've ever had reading a book. Funny, observant and proper adrenaline inducing thrills' Georgia Tennant

‘What new mother can’t relate to murder? This is the funny and thrilling story of how one woman does what all women do all the time – manage every single thing – and throws in a bit of efficient killing. Brilliant, wish I’d done more of that . . .’ Arabella Weir

‘I really think it deserves to be read as a feminist rallying cry to all of those mothers doing such a lot of emotional, as well as physical, work to keep their families happy’ Stephanie Butland

‘This fiercely feminist and witty thriller will keep you gripped – and rooting for the really rather wonderful heroine’ *Sunday People*

‘Hilarious, clever and refreshingly original’ *Lancashire Evening Post*

‘Exciting and very funny’ *http://bookoxygen.com*

‘*Killing It* is lighthearted, funny and very easy to read . . . I couldn’t put this one down’ *The L Space*

‘Smart, funny and pacy’ *Better Read Than Dead*

Also by Asia Mackay

KILLING IT
THE NURSERY

ASIA MACKAY

A SERIAL KILLER'S GUIDE TO MARRIAGE

WILDFIRE

First published in hardback in 2025 by
WILDFIRE
an imprint of HEADLINE PUBLISHING GROUP

3

Cataloguing in Publication Data is available from the British Library

Hardback ISBN 978 1 0354 1966 1
Trade paperback ISBN 978 1 0354 1967 8

Typeset in 12.76/15.95pt Sabon LT Pro by Jouve (UK), Milton Keynes

Printed and bound in Great Britain by Clays Ltd, Elcograf S.p.A.

MIX
Paper | Supporting responsible forestry
FSC® C104740

Headline's policy is to use papers that are natural, renewable and recyclable products and made from wood grown in well-managed forests and other controlled sources. The logging and manufacturing processes are expected to conform to the environmental regulations of the country of origin.

Headline Publishing Group Limited
An Hachette UK Company
Carmelite House
50 Victoria Embankment
London EC4Y 0DZ

The authorised representative in the EEA is Hachette Ireland, 8 Castlecourt Centre, Dublin 15, D15 XTP3, Ireland (email: info@hbgi.ie)

www.headline.co.uk
www.hachette.co.uk

For Rebecca Thornton
My oldest and best friend
I couldn't do any of this without you
('this' being life not just writing)

PROLOGUE

Maybe we should've tried marriage counselling. Or planned a proper mini-break somewhere, just the two of us, as soon as the cracks started showing. If this relationship was worth saving, why didn't we do more to try and make it work? I couldn't help but wonder: if we'd had more date nights, maybe we wouldn't be standing here right now, in a Berkshire nature reserve at 1am, circling each other with a pair of hunting knives.

I stared at my husband; his lip was bleeding, his usually perfect, tousled hair wild.

A summer storm was brewing. The unbearable heat that had been suffocating us for the last few days was finally about to break. I shouted at him over the warm wind that was whipping both our faces, 'Do you even still love me?'

'How can you ask me that? Of course I do. I would've killed you in your sleep months ago if I didn't!'

He was right. He would've.

I touched my jaw and ran my tongue over the back of my teeth. One of them had come loose. A familiar metallic taste was filling my mouth.

'What about me?' he shouted back. 'Do you still love me?'

Marriage was a gamble. We all knew that. You were cashing in your chips on someone you hoped you didn't hate twenty years down the line. We all change; we just had to hope that we would change in sync, in parallel.

'Till death us do part.' I spat blood onto the ground.

He tightened his grip on his knife. It was engraved and had a leather handle – a present from me for his fortieth. I'd presented it to him in a red velvet box as we were curled up on a four-poster bed in a suite with a view of the Amalfi Coast.

We had been perfect together. Totally fucking perfect.

He did this. He killed us.

The sound of thumps carried over the wind. We both turned to look at the black SUV. The noise was coming from the boot. Someone was awake.

'We need to make a decision,' he shouted. 'You or me?'

I couldn't let him do this.

I always knew our life together would involve bloodshed. I just never thought it would be ours.

Part 1
Honeymoon

'The honeymoon marks the very beginning of your marriage. You can look the decision you made right in the face and say yes! This is us! Forever! It's blissful. Everything is so fresh and new. You are your best selves, and you must promise each other to keep that energy going for the rest of your lives.'

– Candice Summers, number-one bestselling author of *Married Means Life: How to Stay Happy, Fulfilled and Together Forever*

'Soak it up, bitches – it ain't going to last.'

– Hazel Matthews, married woman

1

Three months earlier

Haze

I really was very lucky.

I looked around our brand-new, expansive kitchen. Bespoke wooden cabinets, marble countertop, an electric five-door Aga. A family painting of three stick figures holding hands stuck to the stainless-steel fridge doors.

I grew up in many different places, but I never had a home. I grew up with many different people, but I never had a family.

Now I finally had both.

Don't fuck it up.

I stared at the wall nearest the window as I chopped grapes at the island. Four different shades of white were painted on it. The paint codes for each option underneath. Decisions, decisions.

'Neeeeowwwwwwwwww!' Fox walked into the kitchen, holding a giggling Bibi with her arms out like an aeroplane. He was in the suit he was wearing when we first met. It was thirteen years ago this June. The American stranger who came to my rescue in Paris. I felt a stab of something. I wasn't sure what.

'And crash landing!' Fox dropped Bibi into her highchair at the oak dining table, where a bowl of porridge and banana was waiting for her.

'Pawgee!' said Bibi as she picked up her plastic spoon.

'Porr-idge,' Fox corrected, sitting down next to her. 'She's twenty-nine months old, she should be up to two hundred words by now. At last count, she was only at a hundred and seventy-three.'

I shrugged. 'She'll get there.'

Fox observed me slicing. 'Don't forget: to stop the risk of choking, the grapes need to be cut vertically. Not horizontally.'

I paused. And altered my slicing direction. The knife was sharp. I was cutting them faster and faster.

At forty-three, Fox was only six years older than me, but he had aged much worse. Yes, his dark blond hair still had no streaks of grey. Yes, he was still annoyingly handsome and wrinkle-free. But . . . Jesus. He kept sounding like an old man. Maybe the passport I thought was his real one was also fake. Maybe he was actually a youthful-looking sixty-year-old.

'She's definitely behind on her talking.' Fox cleared his throat. 'Studies show a baby sibling can help toddlers develop faster.' He looked up at me over his cup of coffee.

My knife faltered and slipped.

'Fuck!' I lifted my left index finger, a streak of blood now colouring the end of it. I stood there staring at it as it dripped onto the white chopping board.

'Fuccck.' Bibi laughed.

'Language, Hazel!' Fox slammed his coffee down on the table. Wow, using my full name – he really was mad.

'What?' I shrugged. 'Now she's at a hundred and seventy-four.'

Our home was a four-bedroom detached house in a gated community in Sunningdale. Here, the nice mummies, whom I mostly managed to avoid, had many ways to deal with the stress of running a perfect home and raising perfect children. They focused on Pilates, day-drinking, Net-a-Porter, and the local spa, where Jonas and his tight shorts massaged away any tension in their upper backs.

I had my own way of dealing with stress, but that was not allowed anymore.

It had been one thousand, one hundred and sixty-nine days.

Tonight, we were having a few of the neighbours over for dinner. We had somehow joined a rota of entertaining one-upmanship and tonight was our turn. When Bibi was at nursery, I went grocery shopping. I always went to the same smaller but slightly out-of-the-way independent shops. Supporting local businesses and killing more time. I remembered the names of all the people behind the counters and granted each one an inane pleasantry about the weather. A smile was so fixed to my face, my cheeks began to ache.

I picked up Bibi, dry-cleaning and flowers for the table. Once home, I put Bibi down for a nap. I stood over her crib, stroking her hair as she fell asleep.

'I love you more than anything in this world.' I leaned closer to her. 'I'll never let anything happen to you.'

Don't fuck it up.

Next to Bibi's room, a spare bedroom had been converted into a makeshift art studio. Sheets covered the beige carpet. I sat on my stool, paintbrush in hand, as I stared at the blank canvas in front of me. Eventually, I dipped the brush into the red paint and did one little line in the centre of the canvas. And then another and another, until a stick figure looked back at me. I drew a sad face on it. I stared at it for a moment and then pushed it off the stand. Picking up my phone, I accidentally lost an hour watching Instagram reels. Then another fifteen minutes editing photos of myself to see if fashion's latest choppy fringe would suit me.

When Bibi woke, I got her out of her cot and held her close, breathing in her sleepy neck.

I let her loose on my abandoned canvas. I took photos of her as she handprinted black and red all over it: #mummybondingtime. When we got bored of that I parked her in front of Peppa Pig as I prepared dinner. This involved placing clean baking trays onto the drying rack, spreading crumbs onto a chopping board and ripping the deli and patisserie boxes into little shreds to go into the bottom of the recycling bin. Faking it in the bedroom – unacceptable. Faking it in the kitchen – commendable.

The three couples arrived within minutes of each other.

I watched Fox slice the beef fillet. It was very rare. He cut it with precision. He barely even seemed to notice how the bright red of the steak gently wobbled as he sliced into it.

I took Mark by the arm and brought him over to Fox.

'Isn't he perfect?' Fox looked up at us, large knife in hand. I waited a beat as he took in Mark and his fine suit and large, gaudy Rolex. 'He brought us your favourite red.'

'Perfect is a bit much,' guffawed Mark.

Fox wouldn't meet my eyes as he chuckled with Mark over the expense of having such a fine palate. There was no hint he remembered what the two of us used to do with men who looked like Mark.

Dinner followed the usual script. I sympathised when Raquel droned on about the difficulties of getting planning permission for their basement extension. I nodded along with Nick and Caro at the horror of interest rate rises affecting mortgage payments. I crossed fingers with Georgie for little Arthur getting a coveted school place. I sneaked a glance at the clock: 10.37pm. The final home run before the chorus of, 'Oh, look at the time!'

'I do worry that there are three Florences in Florence's class,' sighed Raquel. 'You're lucky Bibi is such an unusual name.'

'She's named after my grandmother Sabina.'

'How lovely. Were you close?'

'Oh yes.' I took a glug of wine. 'She was the only member of my family who wasn't a total cunt.'

Raquel's mouth dropped open.

I stood up. 'Anyone for more raspberry pavlova?'

After the last couple was air-kissed goodbye and the dishwasher was fully loaded, we collapsed onto the sofa. Fox was a little drunk. I was a lot drunk. I put a hand on his thigh. He smiled and pulled me to him. I reached for his belt buckle. He stopped me with his hand.

'What?'

'Bibi plays on this sofa.'

'I'll clean it,' I murmured as I pushed him back on the sofa.

'It's . . .' He sat upright. 'It's dry-clean only. So you know, bit of an effort to—'

I unbuttoned my silk shirt. 'We could put a towel down.'

He pressed at the sofa cushion. 'And it's quite soft.

Probably not good for my back.' He patted my arm. 'Our bed is just upstairs.'

By the time the routine of locking up, checking on Bibi, removing make-up and getting undressed had been completed, Fox was asleep. I got into bed beside him and stared up at the ceiling, listening to the sound of his light snores. I wanted to scream.

2

Haze

I looked around at the rabble gathered together in our village hall. My daughter was clearly the best of this sorry lot. Felix could barely pincer-grip the castanets. Sienna had no rhythm. And don't even get me started on Lottie's pitiful attempts with the triangle.

Today was my first session of Music Is Magic: '*Sing the song, bang the drum, high octave fun for you and your toddler!*' I was here because my husband thought I needed mummy friends. He thought if I could find women I wanted to have lunch with, could enjoy frothy cappuccinos with while our children played, that I'd be happier. He thought that was all that was missing from my life. Yes, darling, eating avocado toast while bemoaning the lack of Montessori nursery options within a ten-mile radius: that was exactly what I needed to get my spark back.

Did he even know me?

One thousand, one hundred and seventy days.

Don't fuck it up.

I watched as Sienna's mother rocked to 'The Wheels on

the Bus' with her eyes closed. Nope. No way were we going to be friends – unless she was actually asleep. That, I could relate to. Then I spotted her lips moving. She was singing. A definite no. Too keen.

Lottie's mother was in a trouser suit and had one arm snaked around her daughter's waist while she scrolled manically through her phone with the other. Too corporate. Too busy.

A father dragging twin boys by their hands came crashing through the doors. 'Sorry!' He sat down on an empty playmat, pulling the boys down next to him. They sat still for precisely twenty seconds before they got up and ran in opposite directions. 'Sammy! Sit down. Oh, are you Sammy? Or Tommy?'

Too male. Too incompetent.

Felix's mother looked like she'd got dressed in the dark. A misbuttoned flannel shirt and jeans with questionable stains on them. Sally, the perky teacher (although, what was she actually teaching anyone?) had asked everyone to say a little about themselves. Felix's mother had been chattering about her single-motherdom, her *gawgeous* son, her life, her maternity leave, for nine minutes. Even Sally's grin was looking a little stale now. Felix's mother was called Jenny. I'd worked out that much before I drifted off. I watched her looking round at each of us, her eyes practically pleading, 'Like me! Please like me!' Too needy.

Jenny finally came to a stop, and I realised it was my turn to talk.

I wondered what they'd think of me. Too bored? Too bitchy? Too hot? I wasn't being arrogant. I knew my incredible metabolism really pissed off other women. I thought back to the last mum group I'd faced – our National Childbirth Trust group's first meet-up with our new babies. I could now see that rocking up in a tank top and skinny jeans with a four-week-old Bibi on my hip, while everyone else was in tracksuit bottoms and milk-stained hoodies, was probably a little galling. Telling a room full of new mums that the baby weight just fell off without any effort – that definitely felt like the closest I'd come to dying. Which really is quite something, considering.

'I'm Haze. I'm an artist.' I wanted to add that I was a real artist who'd had three exhibitions with reviews in high-end culture supplements describing my paintings as 'raw, exquisite takes on female rage'. But I was trying to make friends, wasn't I? So I'd have to let them assume it was a hobby I enjoyed while hubby was at work.

'This is my daughter, Bibi. She enjoys the guitar the most. And we're thinking of piano lessons soon.' Bibi was sitting perfectly upright, the guitar in her arms. Now and then, she strummed it in perfect time.

Everyone in the circle was looking at me, but no one was really smiling. Where was the warmth they were doling out for everyone else's intro?

I was a fearless champion of women, but I really struggled to get them to like me. Ironic?

Sienna's mother leaned forward to Bibi. 'Darl, could Sienna have the guitar now, please?' She had an Australian accent. She looked up at me. 'The kids are meant to only have a few minutes with each instrument.'

And then she plucked the guitar out of Bibi's hands and handed it to her own daughter.

What. The. Fuck.

Bibi spun round to look at me, her eyes already filling with tears.

I dug my nails into my hands to try and stop the rage overwhelming me. I stared at Sienna's bitch mother and imagined maiming her. Taking my time. Starting with a one-by-one nail dissection.

'Felix is done with these. Sienna might want them instead?' Jenny leaned forward and handed the castanets to Sienna, who immediately dropped the guitar.

'Clack clack clack,' she squealed.

Jenny took the abandoned guitar and gave it back to Bibi. 'Here you go.'

She'd solved the problem quickly and quietly, while I'd merely stewed, thinking bloody thoughts. 'Thank you.'

Jenny smiled. 'No problem.' A pause, and then: 'Coffee after?'

Definitely too needy.

3

Haze

Jenny was currently living at her parents' house. She told me how Felix slept in a little bed at the foot of hers. I found her set-up depressing, I didn't know what to say.

'I'm hoping to move out eventually,' she said, as she stirred her mocha. 'I just need to get back to work, find a flat I can afford, and just generally get life back on track. You know, minor things.' Jenny giggled as she put her mousey brown hair up in a mum-bun. Anyone with an experienced eye could tell her hair was crying out for highlights and a decent cut. Although yes, it did sound like she had bigger problems than finding the time and inclination for a makeover.

We were in a café round the corner from the village hall. It was always busy whenever I walked past. I now realised this was because of the soft-play area, where Felix and Bibi were happily jumping around, and not the quality of the coffee.

'Have you and your husband lived here long?' She motioned to the ruby and diamond ring on my wedding finger.

'We moved in just before Bibi was born. We were in Knightsbridge before.' God, how I missed our gaudy, anonymous flat.

Constantly absent neighbours. Designer goods on my doorstep. Restaurants that served food I actually wanted to eat.

'Everyone moves out for the kids, don't they?'

'Fox insisted.'

From the minute we were stabbed by the two pink lines of a pregnancy test, he became someone I didn't recognise.

I looked over at Bibi, building blocks with Felix. Her little frown as she concentrated. The blue bow holding back her shoulder-length curls.

I had never regretted having her, not for one second. But I missed the old me. I missed the old Fox. The old 'us' was a fuck of a lot better than this one.

'Haze and Fox. Such glamorous names. I'm not surprised; I mean, just look at you.'

I nodded. 'Thank you.' I never bothered with effusive denial of any compliment. I'd never understood the point.

'What did you think of the class?' she asked through a mouthful of almond croissant.

'Sally is shit. And I really hope the instruments are cleaned thoroughly. One of the twins had the recorder down his pants.' I took a sip of my coffee and winced. 'But Bibi loved it.'

'So you'll go back?'

'Yes.' I had resigned myself to it. Seeing Bibi happy was like crack. I'd do anything for a fix.

'That's great. I know I'm meant to be doing it for Felix, but really it's for me too. I've had a difficult few years and, well . . . I think it'd be good to have some new friends to talk to. You know, people who understand how tough it all is.' She looked down at her mug. 'I'm just trying to work out how the hell to be a good mum when I don't even think I'm a good person.'

'Aren't we all?'

Oh God, we were bonding. Needy Jenny was going to become my friend, wasn't she? I guessed it had to happen at some point. And it would shut Fox up about my total lack of effort. '*You're miserable because you won't even try.*'

Jenny looked up at me. 'I've not met anyone like you.' She smiled. 'Normally, people would blat on about how of course I'm a good person.'

I shrugged. 'We've known each other three hours. You could be good or you could be fucking terrible. It's none of my business.'

'There was an incident at work. It made me question myself.' Jenny started folding creases in her paper napkin. 'The way it all went down was pretty bad but, you know, that's all behind me now. And I'm on some great new pills.'

I nodded in what I hoped was a comforting way.

We all had secrets, so who was I to judge?

Especially as my secrets were fourteen dead men.

Yes, you read that right.

Fourteen.

But you know what?

They all deserved it.

4

Haze

I may have questioned many things in my life, but I have never questioned whether the men I killed deserved to die.

There was no lying awake at night feeling bad that they were no longer of this world. My beauty sleep was only affected by early-morning visits from a two-year-old who was 'just not tired, Mama'.

I am well aware an ability to end multiple lives and not be affected by it is an unusual character trait. Fox was always telling me a therapist would have a field day over me and my childhood traumas. This is why you kill! You've been hurt! You're acting out! Blah blah blah. But they wouldn't get it, not really. I wasn't doing it because I was fucked up from being fucked over (repeatedly). I was doing it because I was providing a service. To womankind.

When it came to who I wanted to die, I had a very specific type.

Straight. White. Men. Ohhhh, a therapist would say, hurting the exact demographic who hurt you, interesting. Okay, yes, you could think of it like that – or you could think of it as more of a strong feminist statement. Hear me out.

Who gets murdered the most? Women. Who kills the most? Men. Here I was, doing my absolute best to try and even the scales. And straight white men were the pinnacle of the food chain. The most privileged, entitled, unworthy. Why should they hold all the power?

I wasn't smashing the patriarchy; I was killing it.

Literally.

One by one.

While there were women out there in public, demonstrating and shouting #metoo, I was hiding in the shadows, killing and whispering #youtoo.

My brand of feminism may have been a little more niche, but who do you think they were more afraid of?

None of my victims were innocent. Take my word for it. I analysed the evidence and decided their fates.

I was judge, jury and executioner, saving the taxpayer money by avoiding a costly trial and simply ridding the earth of one more scumbag. I was an incredibly efficient, moderately controlled, killer with an agenda.

I always thought no man was worth letting into my life. No man was worth the effort or the risk of them hurting you before you could hurt them. Until I met him.

My wild Fox.

A dark alleyway in Paris. The city of love. He appeared out of nowhere. God, he was beautiful. Tall, blond, piercing baby-blue eyes. A loosened Hermès tie, a well-cut suit. I was captivated. And that was before I saw the clip point-bladed hunting knife with a pearl handle he was holding. It had made me cringe at the off-the-shelf kitchen knife that was sticking out the pink-shirted gut of the drunk man I'd just pinned against the alleyway wall.

I had followed Pink Shirt out the restaurant we'd both been in. He'd made a scene inside; groping a teenage waitress, making her cry. Halfway down the alleyway, he had noticed me. Mistaking the hunter for prey, he punched me in the face.

Fox had come to save me.

Until he saw I could save myself.

We fucked right up against the wall, the man's life blood draining out by our feet.

After, as we walked off together down that alleyway bloodied hand in bloodied hand, I felt sure this was it. This was something special.

We were married within six months. A small registry office ceremony followed by the honeymoon of our dreams – and our victims' nightmares. Sex, bloodshed and room service. All my favourite things. I loved calling him my husband: 'My husband will be right back,' 'My husband is just paying the bill,' 'My husband is going to make you bleed.'

For better, for worse; for richer, for poorer. He was a part of me now. We were a team and together we soared. We had years and years of flying high. We got so much work done. So many bad men finished. So many good times enjoyed.

And then everything changed. *He* changed. I wanted to have it all; he wanted to give it all up. The passion that had peppered our early years quickly drained away. There was no spice there anymore. Forget fifty shades of grey, it was death by a thousand shades of Farrow & Ball white.

Whenever I thought about my knives being packed away – my wings clipped, my fun banished, my mission ended – I'd always presumed it would be down to a stranger in uniform armed with a gun, handcuffs and evidence of my crimes.

I'd never thought it would be down to the man I loved firing a baby into my belly, a house in the suburbs, and a whine about doing the right thing.

Yet here I was.

Trapped.

Caged.

Bored.

So.

Fucking.

Bored.

5

Then

Haze

When I was eight, my most treasured possession was a notebook with a sparkly unicorn on the front. It could've been from a well-meaning foster parent or a shrink who wanted me to write down my feelings. Or I could've just helped myself to it from a WHSmith. I just knew that one day I had it, and I took it with me everywhere. It was blank for months. It was so special that I didn't want to ruin it. I could never decide what was worthy of being inside such a pretty book. And then one day, one really bad day, it didn't seem to matter so much. I started drawing in it, copying the unicorn on the front. I knew the image so well I barely needed to check back to it. I wasn't that happy with the finished result, but what I was happy with was that for the hour it took me, I thought of nothing else except how to get the hair just right and the hooves just so. And that was it. I was hooked.

I got lucky in that school number four had an art teacher who actually noticed me. She got everyone off my back and let me hang out with her in the art room at breaktimes rather than suffer the canteen alone. Making friends had never come easily to me. I wasn't completely sure I liked people. I mean, understandable. I'd mostly met really shitty ones.

By eighteen, I'd aged out of foster care and crashed out of nearly all my exams, but I'd got into an art school in Kingston and that was all that mattered. I was soon living in my own tiny flat and had financial support covering my tuition. The councils and systems that had let me down for so many years were finally helping. I had nothing so foolish as actual expectations for how my life was going to turn out. But at least my art was taking me in the right direction.

Men continued to disappoint me. With their conversation, their character, their bedroom performance.

There were flashes of hope. Two, to be precise. A tutor at art school who seemed to really want to take my art to the next level, with talk of my unique talent and promises of introducing me to galleries. And I finally made a friend, a best friend: Matty. To manage to be outsiders at art school, a place where everyone prides themselves on being different, was quite an outstanding achievement on our part. But that's how we found each other. On the fringe. Eye-rolling at the pretending-to-be-wild normality of those around us. It felt good to finally let someone in. I shared the horrors of my childhood and the men who hurt me, and he shared the horrors of his dating life and the men who hurt him. I had no family, and he'd repulsed his, so we leaned on each other. We were loners who suddenly weren't alone.

We revelled in each other and despaired of everyone else.

Matty came bounding up to me in the hallway one day. 'Oh my God, did you see Crystal's latest piece? Do you think anyone is going to tell her that the Confederate flag is racist? Even when it's covered in sequins?'

'I nominate you. I think you'd do it so tactfully. And to thank you, she might deign to actually look you in the eye.'

Matty laughed as he ran a hand through his peroxide-blond hair. 'No fuckin' way. We're totally beneath her. Shall we break it to her that those trustafarians are never going to invite her to one of their fancy parties?'

Art school was cursed with a group of rich kids who, after under-performing academically, had been persuaded to pursue their (questionable) artistic talent. It pained us to realise they were the ones most likely to get their own exhibitions thanks to Daddy and his friends. They were always so loud when showing off their superiority. I had no trouble imitating their accents.

'Bunty, darling! You simply must join us in Hampshire for the weekend. Pimm's and croquet time!'

Matty howled. 'You're too damn good at that voice!'

'How did your tutorial go?'

Matty was an incredibly talented sculptor. He worked mostly in copper. Large pieces that spoke to me about pain in a way that words couldn't.

'She loved it. I can't believe it.' He smiled.

'Of course she did.'

'You know what it's like: one day you think it's a masterpiece, next it's a hunk of shit.' Matty closed his eyes. 'It's exhausting.'

I didn't relate. My art was my quiet space. If I was happy with it, I wasn't so worried what anyone else thought.

'Let's get ice cream and sit in the park and try and get some colour in you.' I squidged his pallid cheeks.

'I am an English rose. White or red. There is no in-between.'

'If you're the rose, I'm the thorn.' I linked arms with him as we walked outside into the sunlight.

Matty laughed. 'Yes! You can't get one without the other.' He kissed the top of my head. 'You're a prickly bitch, but you're *my* prickly bitch.'

It was us against the world, and I felt I'd finally found the family I'd been so missing.

Throughout art school, we were the duo who didn't care about anyone else, because we had each other. We each learned everything there was to know about the other. I knew he was weird about certain foods. *'I got you those noodles you like. Don't worry, I've eaten all the mushrooms out of it; no, I still don't believe they come from outer space.'* And he knew I needed a little guidance when it came to talking to people. *'Babe, it would've been better to say, "That's my backpack, I'll move it." I just think, "Why the fuck are you touching my stuff?" might be seen as a little too confrontational.'*

When it came to tapping into my violent side, Matty was the very first to see my potential. One night as we were leaving the pub, a lanky teenager charged at us. He figured a woman and a scrawny guy were easy targets. He pushed Matty to the ground and reached for my bag. But I wouldn't let go. We tugged on it back and forth, and then I punched him in the face.

I didn't think, I just hit. And I kept hitting. At some point, he was on the ground. But I wasn't done with him.

Matty calling my name jolted me out of it, brought me back to reality for a second, just long enough for the teenager to scrabble away from me. I made to go after him, but felt Matty's hand on my shoulder.

'Leave him!' Matty was up and dusting himself off. 'You're crazy. He could've really hurt you! What were you thinking?'

'It was just . . . instinct?' Growing up, I'd learned to always be prepared. Braced for whatever could be coming my way. 'If it'd been your bag, I'm sure you would've done the same.'

'I could never! I'd be too scared to throw the first punch.'

I didn't want to tell him that the problem for me wasn't starting, it was stopping.

The next day, I joined a boxing class a local gym was running. I also found a self-defence class at a women's hostel. I wanted to learn how to fight. Properly fight. To make sure I could protect myself. It was easier telling myself that than admitting it was because I had liked seeing the teenager bleed. I'd liked hearing the crack of my fist colliding with his jawbone.

Matty was bemused by this new hobby. He accepted it just like he accepted all parts of me. He'd stay late at the art studio, and finish in time to meet me outside the gym, usually holding fatty fast food to make sure I wasn't going to 'waste away and become a super-skinny bitch'.

I'd had relationships before. Well, I guess you could call them relationships; men I'd have sex with and then kind of just made plans to have more sex with. But I kept them at arm's length. They never got to know me like Matty did.

He had his own troubles. Sometimes I wouldn't see him for a few days. He'd come back to me eventually. Hollow-eyed. Even paler than usual. He felt things deeply and sometimes it became too much, he just wanted to hibernate alone in his flat. I used to try and help; bang on the door bearing treats I knew he liked. Until he told me it was making things worse.

'Just let me do my thing, babe. Okay?'

And so I did. We respected each other, acknowledged each other's damaged bits, and loved each other all the same.

I finally understood the saying 'Friends are the family you choose.' I'd seen it once written in pink on the front of a greetings card, back when I was a lonely teenager. Awesome, I'd thought – I've struck out on both counts. No fake family. No real family.

I'd never met my father. I didn't know his name. Or even his heritage. A problem for me only when it came to forms that wanted me to tick a box for mine. I'd draw a new one. 'Mixed Unknown' I'd scrawl next to it. My mother wasn't much help when it came to answering my questions. She didn't love me – only the bottle. When I was finally relieved of her, the day after my eighth birthday, I didn't feel sad. I didn't feel much about it other than resigned to what came next. I was lucky that social services found my mother's estranged mother – my grandmother Sabina. For three months, she fussed over me, held me close, fed me nothing but mashed potatoes, as it was all she could really cook, and then died of a heart attack.

The bouncing around foster families was bad. But at least there were moments when I got to be a kid. Food appeared at the right time. I had clean clothes. Social services used to tell me my mother was working on cleaning herself up, that one day we'd be reunited. I never dreamed of her coming back and claiming me. I didn't want it. I didn't need her. I had no idea where she was now or if she was even alive. She'd had her chance with me, and she blew it. She didn't deserve another go.

In our final year, in the run-up to graduation, Matty and I would work late on our art, and then he'd come with me to my evening job as a cashier at an all-night petrol station. It was easy money. He'd sit eating crisps with his sketchbook while I flicked through all the latest fashion magazines.

'God, look at that dress.' I turned to show him a red Valentino dress. 'One day I'll have a wardrobe full of this shit.'

'Focus on your art, my thorny one.' Matty stretched as he stood up.

'I can do both.' I smiled. 'Wear the designer dress to my very own exhibition.'

'That's my girl. Aim for the stars. You're a total fuckin' princess.' He leaned over the counter and kissed my cheek. 'I've gotta sleep. Love ya.' He walked out and waved at me through the glass. I blew him a kiss.

That was the last time I saw him.

Two days later, Matty killed himself.

Just like that. He left me. With no goodbye. That part stung nearly as badly as the whole choosing to die thing.

I lost three days in a blur of vodka, tears, and screaming into my pillow. One night, I broke into his art school studio and stole one of his sculptures – the only one that could fit into the palm of my hand. It was a bird with a broken wing. I figured he wouldn't care that I was depriving his parents of it. And really, something beautiful to remember him by was the least he owed me.

I didn't go to his funeral.

I hovered by some trees in the graveyard and watched. Grim-faced relatives in black. A few people our age I didn't recognise; friends from school, I guessed. All were greeted by a couple by the church door. His parents. They didn't look evil. They just looked grey. I didn't need to meet them to understand why my Matty didn't belong to them. I could've made a scene. Gone in there shouting that they were to blame.

That their rejection of him was a part of it all. But I was too tired. No one ever warns you how exhausting grief is. There was no fight left in me.

He'd always told me he loved me. Just clearly not enough to not top himself. He used to joke it was his job to protect me from heartbreak, and then he went and broke my heart more than any lousy, irrelevant boyfriend ever could. He went from being the best friend I'd ever had, to just another man who'd let me down.

I waited until he was in the ground and everyone had left him alone before I went to say my own goodbye. I scanned the discarded order of service I'd found by the church door. *'All Things Bright and Beautiful' . . . 'John 14:1–3. Do not let your hearts be troubled . . .'* There was nothing Matty about it. A generic goodbye from people who didn't really understand him. I held tightly to the paper bag I'd got from the florist and thought of her frown at my request.

I lay down on the ground beside him, like I had so many times before, except this time he was beneath it. I was nothing but a ball of grief, rage and guilt. I could've saved him. I'd known it was bad, I just hadn't realised it was that bad. I had finally opened my heart, and look what it had got me. I wiped my tears with my sleeve. I didn't know it was possible to love someone and hate them at the same time.

'Fuck you, Matty. Fuck you very much.'

I opened the paper bag and took out six headless rose stems. Thorny stems for my rose beneath the ground. I lined them up against the headstone.

I got up and walked away.

The happy chapter of a shitty life so far was over. Dead and buried.

6

Haze

I woke to the sound of the coffee machine going downstairs. I looked at the clock: 7.35am. Right on schedule. It must be a weekday then. It took me longer than it should to remember which one. Thursday. I was pretty sure it was Thursday.

The vast expanse of a day ahead used to fill me with excitement. All the things that could be achieved in it. And now . . .

I looked over to the empty side of the bed. He had always been so diligent at not leaving a trace of his DNA anywhere – yet he failed to execute that same care when it came to the inside of my womb. I worshipped Bibi. I would never regret having her. But I missed me. Who was I without my art? Who was I without my kills? Did being a mother really have to take everything from you?

'Mamaaaaaa.' Bibi came in with a running jump. Right on top of me.

'Morning, baby girl.' I held her close and smelled her.

'Not baby.' She frowned at me and stuck her tongue out.

'Always my baby.'

This bit came easily to me. Loving her. I didn't have to do

anything. It was just there. It was everything else I struggled with. Our glory years before pregnancy had spoiled me. I had become inherently selfish, and so much of parenting was doing stuff you didn't want to. Who actually enjoyed dragging themselves out of bed at 7am for soggy leftover cornflakes when they could be lying in and brunching at The Wolseley? I wanted to be an amazing, awe-inspiring mother . . . without doing any of the actual work required to be an amazing, awe-inspiring mother.

'Come on, let's get you dressed. We've got music class today.'

'Yesssss!' Bibi bounced up and down on the bed. 'And then play Felicks?'

'I'm sure we can.' I had a feeling I didn't need to ask Jenny if she was free.

'Morning, my girls.' Fox was at the cooker. He was wearing an apron emblazoned with 'Life Is What You Bake It!' and flipping pancakes. BBC Radio 2 was playing through the digital radio on the island.

He looked so happy. Was he faking it so hard he'd started to believe it? Or maybe this was the real him. Maybe his darkness was always a blip that didn't fit in with the perfect Ken-doll package.

This was the longest I'd ever seen him with his natural blond hair. Our disguises were long-since packed away. There was no need for them now our European weekend touring had ended. Besides, hair dye had been banned as soon as Fox heard the baby's heartbeat for the first time. He had read an article questioning whether the chemicals in dye were safe for use during pregnancy.

He was always reading articles. All the work and research he'd once put into helping us to kill was now focused on helping us keep her alive. Just as he'd once thought he was destined to be the world's greatest serial killer, he now believed he was meant to be the world's greatest father.

I watched as Bibi went running up to him and wrapped her arms around his leg. The smell of the pancakes cooking, the soft rock of a Bryan Adams song on the radio. The matching smiles of two people who loved me. It was homely perfection.

I had a hot husband, a happy daughter and a healthy bank account. Why couldn't I just be fucking happy? Every TV show, every wretched woman's magazine, had told me this was the ideal. What to aspire to. I was winning at having a perfect life and the only thing ruining it was me.

I took a deep breath. Maybe I should just try letting go of wanting more and embrace what I had.

Right on cue, my phone beeped. A message from Jenny. It was a hand-waving emoji, then a guitar emoji, a two-women-and-two-children emoji, and a coffee emoji, followed by a big question-mark emoji. I wondered if, at any point while searching for each relevant emoji, it had occurred to Jenny that just typing 'Coffee after music?' would've been quicker. I sighed. And sent back a big thumbs-up emoji.

'Bibi, I just got a message from Felix's mum. We're going to go back to that play café after music.'

'Hurrahhhh!' Bibi did her little happy dance.

Fox turned around from the cooker. 'You've made a new friend?'

'She's called Jenny. She seems . . .' How could I describe Jenny? Unhinged? A little broken? Unstable? Trying too hard? Both depressing and depressed? '. . . Fine.'

'That's great. Really great.' Fox grinned at me.

This was all I had to do to make him even happier – play nice with some locals and look like I was embracing suburbia. I could do this. The benefit of never fully belonging in one world, fitting into one box, meant I wasn't confined to one either. I could be anything, and I excelled at it. I was the master of adapting to what I needed to be. Of all the different roles I'd played over the years, normal middle-class mother shouldn't be so tough.

7

Fox

The problem with growing up in a family where everyone swore by therapy, was that sometimes I felt like I really, really needed therapy. Who wouldn't want to be their best self? I took pride in making sure my body was in peak physical condition – I wanted to be as diligent with my mind.

But therapy wasn't an easy option when I couldn't just search for 'therapists near me' and get talking to whoever had the highest ratings, as nearly everything I needed to talk about would get us arrested. It was totally unfair. How was I meant to look after my mental health when I couldn't trust a therapist not to run screaming to the nearest police station?

Haze said I talked about therapy too much. That I needed to stop being 'so fucking American'. She thought my obsession with it was as much of an 'other side of the pond' quirk as calling trousers 'pants' and spelling 'color' wrong.

I saw her point, but I didn't know what else to turn to. How was I meant to understand myself if a professional didn't get to see inside my head? I wanted someone to tell me what I needed to do to make myself a better man, a better father, and a better husband. If I was going to be a family man, I wanted to do it properly.

I knew therapists always liked to start at the beginning. To understand the man, you must first know the boy, etc. But what was there really to know about the childhood of Nathaniel Foxton Cabot II? A deep dive into my immensely privileged upbringing would show nothing that explained the real me. I might have grown up in cosmopolitan New York, but we lived within a very small bubble of the Manhattan elite.

Our house was the largest one on a much sought-after street on the Upper East Side. By the time I was eight, I had a schedule so packed that at one point there was a debate over whether my snack break could be five minutes shorter if I was given food that was easier to swallow. My brother Julian was two years younger than me, and at six he still had a scheduled thirty minutes for 'developmental play' after school. I'd bite my lip at the sound of him whooshing himself around the playroom down the hall with a rocket ship as I was drilled on times tables by one of my many stern-faced tutors.

It could be argued that my parents were grooming us for greatness. They wanted to use their limitless resources to help us become the very best versions of ourselves – and it was just an added bonus that doing this meant we were out of the house as much as possible. I'd often questioned whether my parents ever really wanted children, or if they'd just had us because it was 'expected'. I guess there was also the knowledge that if they died without offspring, all their money would go to siblings they didn't really like, or cousins they'd always sneered at.

Even though everything about me should've fit in, I'd always known I was different. Everything in this world had its place, while I had yet to find mine. I tried many different paths, but nothing felt right. Medical school was a learning experience, but my talents were not appreciated there. The family business, a large pharmaceuticals corporation, was too boring to ever seriously contemplate. A dabble in real estate did give me the chance to make the most of unoccupied properties, but as an industry it felt too crass for me.

I was a lost boy without a calling, and then I was a lost man without a home.

Banished from American soil once Ma and Pa got bored of covering up yet another 'unfortunate incident', I had no choice but to make Europe my playground and hone my craft. Here, I didn't have the luxury of well-connected family members to make things go away.

For the first time, I was free of my parents and their suffocating world. Being alone forced me to grow up and take responsibility for my actions. And I really did. When I first moved here, I started a spreadsheet. A carefully detailed account of every kill. These were not random victims. They were carefully vetted and then selected for the crimes they had committed, or were planning to commit. Paedophiles, rapists, wife-beaters, thieves, fraudsters, blackmailers . . . None of them deserved to live.

Who knows how many people were saved by my actions? Prowling the nights, helping keep others safe, with no thought as to the danger I was putting myself in. Actively seeking out harm, in order to protect others.

I'm not saying I'm Batman or anything.

Well . . . I mean, if the cape fits.

I always took the precaution of arranging an alibi for each kill. Just in case I was ever accused of having been in the vicinity, I made sure I had a ticket stub for something somewhere else.

This safeguarding started when I was a solo crusader and continued after Haze sashayed her way into my heart. My partner in life. My partner in crime. My stubborn, ferocious queen.

From the moment I saw her, in a darkened Parisian alleyway, her knife deep in the gut of a man who'd dared to try and touch her, I recognised a kindred spirit.

Fearless. Bloodied. Beautiful.

My other half.

She was home. It didn't matter where we were, as long as we had each other.

She never seemed to understand that she needed protecting – not from the bad guys she was more than capable of handling, but from herself. She worked in a flurry. A whirlwind of rage and retribution that was never thought through. I was the ice to her fire. The methodical planner she needed to make sure she was never caught. She left it all to me.

Our heroics may have been what brought us closer together, but couldn't she see they weren't worth the risk of tearing us all apart? Surely she wouldn't wish a childhood like hers upon our little Bibi? We had to do whatever we could to keep her safe. And if that meant keeping our heads down and our weapons sheathed, then so be it.

Of course I missed our glory days, back when the bloodlust ruled our lives. That side of me was still there. Poke me hard enough, and I would roar . . . Although my darling wife said I was not so much a sleeping lion but a neutered one in a coma. That was what my queen thought of me now. Just because I was putting our safety first. I loved my wife. I loved my daughter. We were a family. Why couldn't that be enough for her?

8

Haze

All my earlier good will was seeping out. I couldn't do this. My ears were bleeding at the sound of four adult voices half-heartedly singing a George Ezra song about a shotgun. As they smacked their hands down onto playmats, out of time, I was left in desperate need of the real thing.

'Come on, Haze!' shouted Sally. 'Join us!'

Bibi turned to look at me. I smiled down at her, pretending I hadn't heard dumb Sally. I clapped Bibi's hands in time with the music. My living, breathing puppet. I deeply wished I could be anywhere but here. I mean, how essential was all this socialising and bonding with other kids? I certainly never did any of it and I turned out just . . . Okay. Right. I gritted my teeth. I guess this *was* a necessary evil to make sure she wasn't . . . evil.

As I suffered through the last fourteen minutes, I was helped by the knowledge this was one of the many sacrifices I needed to make to help prevent our daughter from developing our killer instincts. I had no misgivings about who I was and what I was capable of. I've never wanted to be any different. But what parent didn't want better for their children?

The very first time I held Bibi in my arms, I stared into her big blue eyes and promised her I would do anything for her. I grew up with nothing, but she would have everything. I never had my own bedroom. I moved around clasping a bin bag with donated clothes – my name scrawled in marker pen on the labels. I smiled every time I walked into Bibi's room. The pale blue canopy with little yellow stars hanging over her bed. Her penguin duvet cover. A wardrobe full of pretty dresses and cardigans neatly hung up. A doll's playhouse that Fox had constructed last Christmas. I didn't care if she was spoilt. I wanted her to always carry around with her that heady confidence I used to notice in other kids at school. That feeling of being so loved you felt invincible.

I kissed the top of her head. I just needed to focus on my love for her, and not my hate for everybody else.

Sally started the 'tidy-up time' song, and we obediently started clearing away the instruments. Sienna and her Australian guitar-stealing mother and the twins and their incompetent father were back again. Lottie was also here, but this time with a mute nanny who was holding a mobile phone with Lottie's mother on FaceTime, barking commands from the office – 'Rosa! You need to hold it up a bit more, I can't see her expression.'

'That's one way of trying to have it all,' said Jenny, as she leaned towards me. 'How's your work going?'

I shrugged. 'It's hard finding the time with her. I miss my art, but I guess it can wait until she's older.' I couldn't explain I needed to wait for my husband to change his mind, rather than for my daughter to grow up. My creative process was a little different from other artists'.

'Maybe you could keep things going by decorating her nursery,' Sienna's mother butted in. 'You know, painting little Beatrix Potter animals on the walls. I saw something like that on Pinterest and it was just the cutest.'

'Oooh, you're an artist, are you?' cooed Sally. 'You could upcycle old furniture. There's a real market for that. Get some ugly stuff off eBay and transform it. You could resell it and make some nice spending money.'

I dared not speak. Equating my art. My masterpieces. To crafting hobbies. I chewed on the inside of my cheek. I knew it wasn't their fault. They clearly had simple minds and couldn't understand that my art was not just a need to fuck around with some paint. It was the way I expressed myself, channelling everything I had into a creative outlet. When it flowed, it came to me as naturally as breathing.

What came out was pain, suffering, love, hate, trauma, rage, joy, all captured on a canvas to stand the test of time. Not just shit to flog on Etsy.

'Shall we go?' Jenny suggested. Perhaps she'd noticed my murderous look and was more astute than I gave her credit for.

'And what do *you* miss most since becoming a mother?' Jenny stirred her coffee as she looked at me hoping I'd offer up an answer as honest as hers ('a pelvic floor').

'Travelling,' I lied. 'That's what I miss most.'

'Where did you used to go?'

'All over Europe. All the best places.' I looked around the café and its brightly coloured plastic tables.

'Your favourite trip?'

'I'll always love Saint-Tropez, and Lake Como is up there. But my best trip was probably San Gimignano. This artist called Francesco Argento is one of my heroes. He had a special exhibition there and I got to meet him. It was incredible.'

Jenny looked at me. 'Francesco Argento? I've heard of him. Did he have many exhibitions in San Gimignano?'

I was surprised. Jenny was more cultured than I had unfairly presumed. 'No, that was the only one he's ever done there.'

Jenny nodded to herself. 'Where else did you go on your travels?'

'Wherever was the best party. Greece, Switzerland . . . We got around.' I took a gulp of coffee. I desperately wanted to relive my glory days and take her through every glamorous location we'd ever been – the poor love was probably more of a staycation gal. But I'd had enough lectures from Fox about keeping details on our adventures quiet. It was easy enough for him. Travelling was a non-event that had always been a part of his life. He got his first frequent flyer card when he was six. When I met him in Paris it was my very first time abroad. A confession that had surprised him – he often remarked I slipped into his lifestyle so effortlessly it was as if I was born for it. My sweet husband. He made it sound as if you needed blue blood to know how to order room service in a fluffy robe, or that only those of noble birth could wear oversized Gucci sunglasses on a restaurant terrace and mutter 'thank you' in the local language. Fitting in with the rich was easy compared to being invisible with the poor.

Marrying him gave me entry into a whole new world, but I never walked around pinching myself, thanking the heavens above for my good fortune. I just rolled with it, like I did with everything life threw at me. Good or bad, I never knew how long what I was going through would last. I just had to stick it out or soak it up. The stakes were higher now; I could adapt to whatever was thrown at me, but my daughter couldn't. She was used to having everything, and I was here to make sure she always did. And that was why, no matter how much I wanted to relive our European highlights reel, I would abide by Fox's rules of discretion.

Jenny was frowning at me. 'The Argento exhibition in San Gimignano was in 2015, wasn't it?'

I laughed. 'How on earth do you remember the year? I was there, and I don't!'

'I just remember reading about it.' Jenny dropped a sugar cube in her coffee.

'We travelled a lot all around that time, right up until I got pregnant with Bibi. Doesn't feel so glam once you're in elasticated waistbands with swollen ankles.'

Jenny looked over at the kids playing. 'I hated my pregnancy. Pretty much spent all of it in my parents' shed wondering what the hell I'd done with my life.' She turned back to me with a small smile. 'Onwards and upwards, though!'

What the hell was she doing in a shed? What did it say about me that the one mum friend I'd made was someone like her? Maybe that's why we'd been drawn to each other and left the nice normal mums to it. She put people off with her neediness, and I put them off because I didn't need them. My usual vibe at the playground was sunglasses on, regardless of weather, steadily eating crisps as I watched Bibi like a hawk and assessed any potential threats to her safety.

'So, Felix's dad? What happened?' Might as well cut the small talk and get to the true root of crazy.

Jenny's eyes widened. 'I . . . well . . . A lot happened.'

'Spill.' I moved my chocolate brownie towards her.

'I guess I could say Bill is a complicated man.' Jenny started picking at the brownie. 'We met at work. When we first got together, it was good. He was nice; sweet, even. We moved in together and he had some problems, but he was, you know . . . okay.' Jenny bit her lip and looked away.

'And then you got pregnant?'

Jenny nodded. 'He said he'd never wanted kids. Drove me to the clinic, told me to deal with it. I just . . . I wanted my baby.' She looked down. 'I came back to our flat and he'd changed the locks. All my stuff was outside the door in bin bags. He wouldn't answer my calls. Blocked me on everything.'

'What a total shit. Who owned the flat?'

'A friend of his. We were renting it off him. Bill had had some trouble at work, got laid off, and it was a while before he found a new job. So for six months, I'd paid for everything. And then he kicked me out.'

'He's never met Felix?'

'Never. He owes me fourteen grand from the money he borrowed off me, and has never paid a penny in maintenance. He's got a job now, so he's making more money than me.'

I shook my head. 'You need to go after him for everything.'

'I know, it's just . . . he has a temper.' She pulled off a large bit of brownie. 'And I don't think I can face him coming after me. It wouldn't be safe for Felix.'

I clenched my fists. I had a pretty good idea of what kind of man this Bill was.

'Jenny, the law is there to protect you. Hire a lawyer, go

after him for everything he owes you. And get a restraining order.'

Jenny spoke through a mouthful of brownie, 'You're right. It's just . . . it's a lot.'

'You're a mother now. You need that money for you and your son to start over. You're in some kind of shitty limbo until you move out of your parents' place.'

'I'm a mother.' Jenny nodded to herself. 'I need to do what's best for Felix.'

'And for you. Don't forget you. How are you going to get laid when you've got to add "single mother living with her parents" to your Tinder bio?'

Jenny laughed. Her whole face lit up, and for a flash she looked less grey. 'I've given up with all that.'

I didn't know this Bill, but I enjoyed the thought of making him pay. Old me may have been able to do that with violence, but new me had to make do with encouragement and litigation. This was new for me. Helping women with words, not weapons.

The PG-13 version of revenge. Yawn. I was betting the pay-off was not as significant or as satisfying.

Jenny shook her head. 'All this talk on the car crash of my life is depressing.' She leaned forward. 'Tell me more about your travels.'

9

Fox

To kill or not to kill. It made me feel like I was waiting outside an emergency room, with a grave-faced doctor before me saying they could only save one. Who to choose? Your wife or your daughter?

It was an impossible choice. But I had more faith in the belief that Haze could be happy without our pastime than I did in the idea of Bibi growing up in foster care because we were both incarcerated.

Right now, Haze and Bibi were at a music class with their new friends. Haze might not have wanted to admit it to me, but she was acclimatising. My little one was acclimatising. Maybe this was the first tentative step towards us becoming what we once were. I smiled to myself as the train rattled into Waterloo. How long I'd hoped for the return of my old sparring partner. The Haze with a fire in her belly and without disappointment in her eyes.

I knew all she'd wanted these last few years was for me to hold her close and murmur, 'Let's go hunting.' I knew she longed for those words like other women longed for *'I love you', 'Marry me', 'Let's have a baby.'*

But I wouldn't say it. I wouldn't give us a recall to arms. I wouldn't give her what she wanted. And it felt like every day, she hated me for it a little more.

We'd become like those other couples. The ones we used to look down on. The civility masking an underlying resentment.

Before, we had been the couple everyone wanted to be. The annoying ones who, even in smart restaurants, couldn't keep their hands off each other. The ones who didn't notice anyone else existed, as they were so involved in soaking each other up.

Now we didn't even go out. Not properly. Not further afield than the occasional neighbourhood dinner party. I'd tried. But Haze had yet to find a babysitter she didn't think was weird/untrustworthy/obnoxious/stoned/obviously a child kidnapper.

She may have slept next to me every night, but I missed my wife.

Every time I thought I couldn't take it anymore, and how, with just a few words, I could get that spark back in her eyes, I looked at my daughter and knew I couldn't do it.

An attractive woman in a trouser suit smiled at me as she got on and sat down opposite me. I stared down at my phone. My screensaver was a photo of Haze and Bibi, both wearing sunglasses. My cool girls. They were worth all the sacrifices I had to make.

I never envisaged a life where I was just another suit commuting into the office.

This was never the plan. Not long after our honeymoon I

had found work at UBS as a Director in Private Client Stockbroking – a position granted by a fellow American who knew nothing about my CV, but enough about my surname to know he wanted to be in my family's good graces.

Perhaps because of how I got the job, my attendance at the office didn't seem to be expected. I flitted in and out, muttering things about big meetings and tip-offs. There was also the fact my numbers were good. Astoundingly good. My instincts were apparently impeccable. But then, not many had the tools that I did, and the balls to use them.

Choosing victims who might have inside information that could help my investments had been a genius masterstroke. Thankfully, there was an abundance of badly behaved straight white men working in finance. Follow them for long enough, and they'd slip up enough to justify a death sentence. These kills were all the more enjoyable when I was working towards a goal – getting them to spill their guts before I spilt their guts.

I had a very healthy trust fund that I was always in fear of being cut off from. I wouldn't put it past my parents to one day tire of supporting a son they'd never really understood. Especially when they had Julian, my younger brother, the WASP without a sting, who had never put a loafered foot wrong.

At first, working at UBS had allowed me to continue living the free existence I had always so enjoyed and brought in enough money I could keep Haze in the designer clothing her body so cried out for.

It was meant to be a temporary flirtation with employment, but it'd been over ten years and I was still there – now as an MD and earnings were not what they once were. A worry I couldn't share with Haze. She was having trouble enough adjusting to our new life, without the idea of having to actually rein in her effusive spending. I had once questioned whether Bibi really needed six different winter coats – for which I got a withering look and a declaration of how no child of hers would ever have to feel the cold like she did.

I looked around the train carriage. Everyone suited and booted. Most staring down at their phones. A couple with newspapers. One twenty-something-year-old, head down on the table, a half-eaten bacon sandwich next to him.

No longer did anything set me apart from the rest of them. The cape was packed away. Bruce Wayne full-time.

I was nineteen when it came to me what my true calling was. At college in Dartmouth (of course, as it was where everyone in our family went), I was walking home from a party when I heard a woman scream down by the library. I charged to her rescue to find that two burly men had her down on the ground. They clocked my youthful looks and my Ralph Lauren suit and tie and laughed. Right up until I knocked them both out.

I had a black belt in Krav Maga. I wasn't sure why my parents were so enthusiastic about me taking it up aged six. It could perhaps have been down to their social competitiveness with the other Upper East Side parents. Or the fact that it was the only class that ran three-hour sessions on Sunday afternoons.

The woman's profuse thanks rang in my ears for weeks. I was a good man. A saviour. I wanted to do it again. The crunch as my fist collided with cheekbone. The warm superiority of knowing I had done the right thing.

It was my first brush with morally acceptable violence, and I wanted another fix.

Despite my best efforts I had to wait months for it. A hot summer evening in the Hamptons. A college kid in a Cornell sweater outside the country club picked a fight with my friend Brandon. I stepped in to break it up, and when he came for me, I floored him with one punch. A dumb fight between drunk college boys. If he'd left it alone, that would've been it. But he followed us back, and waited until I was alone – smoking a cigarette outside the boathouse. He had a knife. His was an ego so fragile that with the giggles of strangers still in his ears, he'd been angry enough to track me down and try to kill me. In three moves, the knife was in his gut, not mine.

Even I could not have predicted how naturally I would take to killing, from that first time to the many that followed. It made me feel special. I had the means, skills and stomach to track down bad men and do what needed to be done. It was a public service I was undertaking to make the world a better place. I deserved to be judged not by a line-up of the lives I'd taken, but a line-up of the lives I had saved. There had been no doubt in my mind that eliminating evil was what I was put on this earth to do.

I looked down at my phone, at the photo of Haze and Bibi. That was how I felt before. Now I realised that keeping these two safe was my true vocation.

I had learned to adapt, maybe Haze could too. Maybe today would be different. Maybe when I got home tonight it'd be to the Haze I'd been waiting for.

10

Haze

As soon as I heard his key in the lock, I went to the front door. Fox smiled at me and then tilted his head. I was in my running kit.

'You going now?'

'It's still light.' We both turned to the window. Dusk was undeniably creeping in. I shrugged. 'The joys of a safe neighbourhood.'

I left the house before he could offer up anything else. I didn't know why he looked so disappointed. I'd been stuck here all afternoon waiting for him to come home.

I'd started running last year, not down to suddenly caring about my fitness, but purely to give me an excuse to get out the house.

I craved time alone.

Away from my daughter.

I was clearly a monster.

Fox would never understand it. He didn't see her all day, so every minute with her was therefore a novel delight. While for me, apart from a few hours of nursery here and there, she was always in my orbit. When Fox was home, if I told him I wanted him to keep Bibi away from me so I could sit in our bedroom with the door locked and read a book or watch Netflix, he would think I was mad. And selfish. A madly selfish monster who didn't care about our daughter. But if I said I needed to get out and go for a run, that was acceptable. Looking after yourself and your health was part of being a responsible parent. So I started running. Very slowly. Sometimes I even walked. I always had AirPods in, so I could pretend to be on an important phone call if I had the misfortune of bumping into a neighbour who wanted to talk.

I set off at a slow jog, Dr Dre blaring in my ears. I wondered if as well as being the only resident wife who'd killed before, I was also the only one who listened to rap music. The vanilla vibe in this neighbourhood was very much Adele and Ed Sheeran only. Although there was Mrs Bird at number four; she had a look in her eye that suggested maybe she rocked out a little when she was alone.

I normally did a few circuits round the neighbourhood and then headed out onto Cobham Common opposite. Twice round and then back. When I got to the common, I started to pick up my pace. I spotted a man by the gate. He was wearing a ripped black T-shirt and tracksuit bottoms. He was lingering. I felt his eyes on me before I even approached. I only gave him a fleeting glance as I jogged past, but I saw him. Really saw him.

I knew what he was.

I assessed the situation as I kept running. I could report him. But for what? Trying to explain that I knew a bad man when I saw one wasn't exactly a sure-fire way to get the police to help. I bit my lip. I couldn't have a man like that hanging around my neighbourhood, a place where my daughter lived and played. Next time I came running I'd be prepared. It was totally understandable for lone female joggers to arm themselves against potential threats. If I saw him again, I would deal with him. For Bibi. For her safety. I picked up my pace. I liked that idea. I liked that a lot.

Graduation Piece: *Betrayal* by Hazel Matthews. July 2007.
Mixed media, 30cm by 20cm

A woman is the central figure of this piece. We get strong projections of conflict, sadness and anger – all powerfully and masterfully executed. There is great potential here. Perhaps a little more fire is needed. This is an artist who, as she grows in confidence, will surely revel in her natural talent for exploring the female psyche. I will be personally recommending her to all my contacts, as I have great faith in her ability. Tutor – D. Richards.

11

Then

Haze

A few weeks after Matty's death, I dragged myself back into class. I wanted to finish my final graduation piece. I had to finish it, otherwise my whole time there would have been for nothing. My art could do what it always had done – give me an escape from everything I was living through.

Dan, the tutor who'd been such a champion of my work, said he'd help me with some of his last thoughts before I made my final touches.

It was late. We were the only ones still in the studio. We'd drunk a couple of Coronas from the shared fridge as we sat facing my canvas.

'It's so nearly there. I think maybe the addition of another element would help finish it off.' He reached towards me and kept talking. 'If you could find something inspirational, something that could tie it all—'

I held eye contact with him as I picked up a Stanley knife by my easel and flicked its blade across the back of his right hand, which was between my legs. He jumped up. His hand was bleeding.

'Fuck!' He reached for a rag on the table behind us and held it against his hand. 'I'm sorry, okay! I—I—'

'Just leave.' I turned back to my easel.

'Haze, please. I didn't mean anything by it. It was a mistake.'

'I said *leave*.' I held up my Stanley knife without looking at him.

He dropped the rag on the table and left. I took a deep breath and reached for it. I cut out the bloodstained middle and dabbed the back of it with industrial glue. I stuck it onto my canvas and started painting. At least I'd found my missing piece.

It was laughable, really.

Matty was dead. Dan was a dick.

The universe had given me a break for a couple years, allowed me a holiday from the horror show I'd been living, and now it was back with a vengeance.

And I was furious.

I carried it around with me. This rage. This anger. It kept me awake at night.

I was going to make my mark on the world. I was going to show everyone.

But before I could do all that . . . I needed money to live.

A popular bar on the high street was advertising. I walked in and talked to the manager. The salary wasn't great, but with the right level of flirting I knew the tips would supplement it enough to make it worth my while. He told me to come back for an interview the next night. The bar was rammed. He spotted me on the other side of the bar and motioned for me to follow him. His hair was scraped back in a man bun, and he had on a tight black T-shirt and jeans. He led me into a small back office and checked his reflection in a gold-framed mirror above his desk when we entered. We had an innocuous ten-minute chat, which he spent mostly talking to my chest.

'You've got the job.' He smiled at me. 'A lot of people applied. But I like you.'

'Great.' I stood up. 'When do I start?'

'How about a little shot to celebrate?' He motioned towards the bottle of tequila on his desk. The cheesy fucker had his own little mini bar set up there.

'No, I'm good.'

He gripped my arm. 'Don't worry. There are no cameras anywhere back here.'

I looked at him blankly.

'No one will see anything.' He ran his hand up and down my arm.

Ah. He wanted to fuck me on his desk, and he thought the only reason I'd possibly not want to was because some security guy might jerk off to it.

'Come on, I know you want me.'

'No, I don't. And now I don't want the job either.' What a waste of time.

A flash of rage crossed his designer-stubbled face. He wasn't used to being told no. He reached out and clutched my right breast. Hard.

I pushed away his hand. I felt the beginnings of a hot flush of rage. He didn't get to touch me. How dare he think that he could?

He grabbed both my arms and shoved me up against the wall.

'Fuckin' tease.' He licked the side of my face and put his mouth against my ear. 'I told you. No cameras.' He sniggered. He had done this before.

The rage was burning now.

Fuck him.

Fuck him and every man before him.

My father, for never giving a fuck. The foster fathers who didn't understand the father part. The many boys and men somewhere along the way who assaulted me with their hands, their words, their eyes. Dan, the tutor who'd fooled me into thinking he liked my talent, when really, he just wanted what they all wanted.

And then Matty, the boy who'd made me believe in goodness and hope, before he took it all away.

Enough.

This was the day I stopped just accepting it all. Bad men. Bad luck. Bad things. It was time to carve my own fucking path.

He dropped one of his hands to undo the top button of his jeans.

I punched him in the face. And then two jabs to his stomach as he stumbled back. His eyes wide in shock. And then he hit me back, right in the jaw. I felt the pain spreading and shook it off.

I grabbed the corkscrew from his desk as he came at me again, and plunged it into his gut before he even saw it. I twisted it once and he gasped as I pulled it out. He went very white and dropped to the ground. I knelt down next to him and put my head by his ear.

'You're a rapist.'

He slowly shook his head.

'How many?'

He was shivering, going into shock.

'You heard me.' I pushed his shoulder. 'How many have you raped?' I enunciated each word.

He shook his head again.

'Stop fucking lying!' I took out my mobile and waved it at him. 'Come clean, and I'll call an ambulance.'

He looked me in the eye. 'Three,' he breathed out. 'Three.'

I nodded. I put my phone back in my pocket and plunged the corkscrew back into his gut. I pulled it out and plunged it in again. A third time.

It was nice and symbolic, but we both knew he'd raped more than three. Of course he was going to lie about his body count.

I watched him bleed out. It happened fast. The whole time, I waited to feel something. And it never came. When I eventually stood up, I looked down at his torn-up body and all that came to mind was: *one less fucking asshole.*

I remembered how one of the therapists I'd been forced to see, before I was old enough to refuse to go, told me how it was always better to let the rage out, let it *allll* out so it didn't stay inside you, so it didn't ruin you.

What better way to do that than letting rip on a man who deserved to die?

It was self-care.

You could argue I was saving myself.

I kept waiting for the police to turn up at my door, ready to play the traumatised in-self-defence victim. But the knock never came. I'd got away with it. And that was another high.

My second kill was equally as opportune. I'd been on a couple of dates with a man. He seemed normal. Nice, even. He offered to cook me dinner. I'd laughed when he spilled a bottle of salt. Called him clumsy. And he hit me. Twice. A skull crushed by an iron skillet was the price he paid for being a bad man with a bad temper. Again, I walked away with zero repercussions.

No wonder I started to think I was invincible.

I had a clear mission plan now. I'd use my newfound bloodlust to kill villains, bad men who deserved to die. And then it hit me: I should start with those who'd directly impacted my life.

I looked up where Matty's parents lived. If they'd shown him the love and acceptance he'd so desperately wanted from them, maybe he would still be alive.

I decided I would kill his father.

The man who couldn't love his son just because he wasn't straight. I would kill him, avenge Matty, and prove what a strong ally I was.

I had no plan at all; one day, I just rang their doorbell. His mother opened the door to me and exclaimed 'Haze!' before bursting into tears. Through her breathless sobs, I worked out that she knew who I was because of Matty's Instagram. I was all over it, as we'd spent most of our time together. They'd tried to find me after he died, but couldn't get through on my mobile or Instagram. I didn't explain that I stopped paying my phone bill for a few months as there was not a person in the world I wanted to talk to.

Their house was a shrine to Matty. He had been an only child, and there were photos of him everywhere. His mother rang his father and got him to come back from work. We sat and talked for three hours about every Matty story I could think of. We all cried. They told me they'd never rejected Matty for being gay; he had rejected them for trying to force him to take medication for his depression. He had told them the pills made him so numb he couldn't create his art, and that without that, there really was no reason to live.

I was glad he'd never told me the truth. I wouldn't have known what to say to him – I understood more than anyone how much it was a part of who we were. I couldn't imagine a life without it.

His dad seemed like a nice man. He held my hand and told me how glad he was that Matty had had me in his life. If they blamed me for Matty dying, they hid it well.

It was a therapeutic afternoon for me – and life-saving for his father.

I decided I wouldn't kill him. The pride and love in his voice when he spoke about Matty were real.

Instead, I tracked down a foster father who didn't deserve to live. Walking away from his bleeding body, thinking of all the girls I'd helped by ending him, was the best high I could hope for. I knew what I was doing was risky, and yet still I killed with carefree abandon.

I was an avenging angel. Punishing them for all the women they'd hurt. Maybe that's why I wasn't getting caught. Because I was on the right side. If there was a God, he was high-fiving me for sending these sickos to hell.

It was easier to live without fear of consequences when you felt you had nothing to lose. Without Matty, I was miserable. If ending a bad man ended up with me in prison, I could take it. I wasn't really living anyway.

After years of feeling powerless, I suddenly felt powerful. The high I got from the moment in which the men realised that they were done for. At the hands of a woman. When they'd never contemplated, not for one second, that they could be weak enough or unfortunate enough to become victims themselves.

Their deaths were wonderful for my mental health.

And they helped my work, too.

I soon realised I was at my best creatively after a kill. Sparked on by the adrenaline, the rush, the buzz of bloodshed. These men were my muses. They just never got to know it. They should be happy; their deaths became art.

All of this, it made me blossom. I finally became the butterfly I'd always known I could be. I didn't need anyone else. I had my art. I had my kills. I could spread my beautiful, colourful wings and finally feel free.

12

Haze

It was an unseasonably warm spring day and, like so many others, Jenny and I had felt forced to take advantage of it. We were in a park, Bibi and Felix happy in the playground.

'All this fresh air and sunshine! So great for us all.' Jenny had repeated this enough times that I could tell she too was wishing we were on a sofa inside, and not on a rickety bench overlooking a tired climbing frame and a large bush that was unofficially known as 'poo corner' due to the modesty it offered those toddlers who 'had to go'.

I was eating prawn cocktail Walker's crisps. Jenny was holding a soggy-looking cucumber sandwich. Why did even her sandwich look sad? We'd already covered nursery small talk, and I was getting bored.

Jenny seemed to be one of those classic nice people we're all encouraged to be like. But surely even those who were good had a limit when it came to someone who'd wronged them.

'Would you be sad if your ex died?'

Jenny's mouth dropped open. 'I . . . I . . . Really, Haze, you shouldn't ask things like that.' She took a nibble of her sandwich. And then I heard it. A small quiet 'No.'

'That doesn't make you a bad person. It's totally understandable.'

'I might feel more forgiving if it was just my personal life he trashed, but he ruined my career too.'

'How did he do that?'

Jenny pulled off a bit of crust and dropped it into her lap. 'Bill was accused of flashing someone at work.'

I grimaced.

'I told our boss that he couldn't have done it, as he was with me when she claimed he did it.' Jenny kept staring at her sandwich.

'Was that true?'

Jenny sighed. 'He forced me to say it. Told me if I didn't, he'd get the sack, and if I loved him, I wouldn't let that happen.'

I bit the inside of my cheek. This man. This bad, bad man.

'But it turned out they had CCTV of him doing it. He got fired and I got a disciplinary warning. I said I'd got confused with the timing. Grovelled. They all accused me of being a misogynist, of not being part of the sisterhood. By the time I realised I was pregnant, no one in the office was talking to me. I took an early maternity leave, and I've been getting the impression they're hoping I'll never go back.'

'Ouch.'

Jenny continued looking down at her sandwich. I wasn't one for physical affection with semi-friends, but if I was, I definitely would've given her a hug.

'Did Bill ever hit you?'

Jenny remained quiet.

'Did you ever think about going to the police?'

Jenny wrung her hands together. 'I couldn't . . . I just couldn't.'

She looked scared at the thought. I got it. Some people just didn't trust the authorities.

'Your office can't fire you for being intimidated by your live-in partner. You need to go back there, with your head held high, and tell everyone everything.'

'I don't know if I can.'

'The woman he flashed. Is she still there?'

'She moved abroad. Not because of . . . I don't think because of what happened.'

'Remember what I said about going after Bill for the money he owes you?'

'I'm a mother. It's for my son,' Jenny repeated it dully back to me.

'It's the same with this shitty office job. You need to go back.'

I'd gone from multi-man-killing avenger to one-woman self-help guru. And Fox thought I couldn't do wholesome.

'I wasn't always like this, you know.' Jenny bit her lip. 'I was a competent, capable person. My job was important. I was good at it. Really good. Years of being with Bill – it changed me. I kind of hate myself. I have for a while.'

Fuck.

Matty came into my head. I really couldn't have another person I hung out with top themselves. It wouldn't help my insecurity that I was a toxic influence who made people want to die.

I took a page from Fox's book. 'Are you in therapy? Taking medication?'

Jenny nodded. 'Yes and yes. Don't worry, I know I need to take care of myself for Felix's sake!' She plastered on a smile.

Why hadn't I listened to my instincts? She was needy because she was in need. Of a whole new life. And now . . . I was invested. Involved. Thankfully she had what was hopefully a seasoned professional helping her with her mental health. But there was one area where I could help.

'Let's start with some basic training.'

Jenny frowned. 'What?'

'I'm talking about getting fit, learning how to beat the shit out of someone. All of this is going to help. Trust me.' I scrunched up my crisp packet. 'Sometimes violence *is* the answer.'

13

Then

Fox

Waking up the morning after my first kill, I couldn't be sure I hadn't dreamt it. Was there really a dead college boy in a Cornell sweater in the lake? Or was it just a drunken fantasy? I got through a pancake breakfast with Brandon and his family where everything felt so normal I started to believe it to be the latter.

It was only when I got back home that reality crept in.

'Nathaniel, please come in here.'

I had been trying to creep past the open drawing-room door, but my mother heard my squeaky sneakered footsteps and summoned me inside. I walked in to find my parents sitting by the fire. Each had a glass of red wine in hand. It was eleven-thirty in the morning.

'Please sit down.' My mother was not smiling.

'What the hell do you think you're playing at?' my father barked at me, before I'd even sunk into the plush armchair opposite them.

'I told you I was staying over at Brandon's. Surely that's not an issue?'

'Do you think there's no issue with what happened at the boathouse? Devon reported everything straight to us.'

Devon was officially our driver. Unofficially, he was the family's spy/fixer/bodyguard.

I took a deep breath and braced myself.

They would call the police. Tell me my life was over. I was picturing a future now committed to a different kind of institution, one that my grandfather had not donated a library to. My life was over, and it had barely begun. But I understood. This was paying the price for my actions. I was surprisingly calm. Maybe I was in shock?

'I'm sorry. I've let you down. I understand what comes next. Are you getting me a lawyer, or do I need to find one myself?'

'A lawyer? What the devil are you talking about?' My father leaned forward. 'We've already cleared up your mess. No one will find any trace of him. And Devon paid a witness to say that they saw the boy leaving the area at two in the morning, so drunk he could barely walk.'

My mother huffed. 'It's cost us a lot of money and totally ruined our morning.'

There was no mention of the life lost. Of the man I'd cut down in his prime.

They were just annoyed about the hard-earned inherited dollars it had cost them to cover it all up.

Were they sociopaths?

And then there was the fact I wasn't exactly cut up about the dead man either.

Was *I* a sociopath?

I had always known we were a little different to most people. Our wealth, our privilege, it set us apart, gave us different, warped ideas of what was normal. Until that moment, though, I'd had no clue that we were all also lacking in humanity.

The signs were always there, if I'd known to look for them. Several years before, I'd commented to my nanny on the coincidence of all three of the gardeners we'd had in my lifetime being called Carlo. She had told me that only the first one was, and that once he left, my parents just kept calling the subsequent ones Carlo as it was easier than learning a new name to shout whenever they noticed a rose that needed pruning.

It was an important lesson to learn. You start to consider those in menial jobs as too unworthy to bother learning their names, and next thing you knew, you were rolling your eyes at the inconvenience of a dead twenty-year-old. A slow but steady descent into having less and less regard for human life, until you reach the point at which only you matter. No one else. Not for the first time, I wondered how they would feel if I died. I guessed after all they'd piled into my education, they would be irritated at the poor return on investment.

I often wondered if things might have gone differently if I'd faced repercussions after my first foray into taking a life. After only sitting through one stern but brief talking-to and then being told to get changed for lunch, I was hardly to be blamed for killing again. Now I had a taste for it – and, clearly, a skill for it – I wasn't exactly about to let it go.

Saving the girl, killing Cornell: I was on a path of no return. I had been sleep-walking through life and now I finally felt in control.

My life until now had been spent training to be the perfect successor to our family business. If I stayed on course, it would be an easy cruise to retirement age – token appearances at the office, more money than I could spend, and vanilla socialising with people I had grown up with. A perfectly privileged bubble to keep me safe from all hardship.

But I wanted more. I needed more.

I knew I wanted to save people; I knew I could kill without remorse. I didn't want to just rely on bumping into bad men, so I started doing research.

It made for an interesting fall semester.

Rather than being impressed that I'd found the time to kill a paedophile and a rapist while keeping up my 3.9 GPA, my parents were furious.

Devon was all too good at sensing when I'd made a mistake, but I had got better at covering my tracks, having learned from my brush with Cornell.

For the first time, I looked at the privilege with which I'd grown up and realised that I'd been given the perfect tools to become a covert killer. I was a well-educated, attractive, rich white man. I was predisposed to win. Doors everywhere would open to me without me having to do anything. In my every interaction, I was already at an advantage, having done nothing except be born this way. Minimum effort, maximum return.

In the dark and criminal words I scoured to find my targets, I was just a tourist. The authorities would never believe I had anything to do with the dead men I left there. They would find no link between us, because there wasn't one. I had hunted them down.

'After everything we've done for you!' I heard this from my

parents a great deal. They eventually threatened to cut me off. I shrugged and said they were welcome to. It wouldn't stop me. I'd drop out of college and get a job to support myself. There was, however, a chance that this would make me sloppier, meaning there was a higher chance I'd get caught . . . and the only thing worse than having a son who was a murderer was having one who was a murderer *and* a college dropout.

This was the dance we did constantly in the years that followed. The threats were ongoing until finally, when my body count was nearing double figures, they called me in for a meeting. They had put together an offer for my future. My inheritance had always been tied up in a trust fund with many rules and regulations, but now they were willing to make some changes. Gone was the requirement of having to eventually work for the family business. Gone was the requirement to do any type of work at all. I was to be given free rein over my money. Scanning through the document, it became clear I didn't have to give up anything – except America.

Once I had emigrated, there was only one stipulation: if I did anything to bring the family name into disrepute, I would be effectively disinherited. Booted out of the trust fund.

I signed my name with a flourish, packed up and left without a backward look.

Europe soon felt like home, and my very own playground. In addition to those I was monitoring, I'd also occasionally take the time to visit the worst areas of a town. Sometimes it didn't go so well for me. But I got better. I trained harder. And the weapons I fashioned, they helped too.

I was Mr All American. The bright white smile, blue shirts and perfectly ironed chinos. No one saw danger; they just saw money. I stayed in the best hotels, ate at the best restaurants. I was the charming good tipper they were happy to have.

I knew the normal – the expected – thing to do would be to pick a city and build roots. But this was the problem with having a large trust fund, luxurious tastes and an illegal pastime. There was no reason to stay put; there was so much out there to explore, so much to enjoy. Why be normal when I didn't have to be?

Art ReviewED Magazine, November 2011
Midnight in Paris by Hazel Matthews
Mixed media, 100cm by 200cm

This striking painting depicts a couple entwined. The bright red of her dress encircles him and then flows through him, flying out into the sky and down onto the ground. The broad brushstrokes contrasting against the starry night sky make for a dramatic setting. With the moon shining down on them, nature's spotlight, we see them elevated on a dark stage, only on closer inspection do you see it's a heap of fallen men they're standing on – the woman's right high-heeled foot on the throat of one of them. This is a couple in charge of their destiny, and they don't care who they've had to crush to get there. The use of fabric and jagged pieces of stainless steel bring a 3D quality to the piece that makes it feel more alive. It's a vibrant piece and further establishes Matthews as an exciting new talent.

MATTY MOBILE *Sent 2 January 2011 02:08*

How could you not say goodbye? Twat.

MATTY MOBILE *Sent 29 May 2011 23:22*

I finished off another one. I have a mission now. Losing you gave me the anger I needed to do this. You helped set me free.

MATTY MOBILE Sent 11 June 2011 04:32

Fasdsnd grate partyyyyyyy. Saw guy looked like youuuuu. But not youuuuu as youuuu deaddddd.

MATTY MOBILE Sent 29 August 2011 22:49

I have a boyfriend. He's perfect. Totally fucking perfect. Totally perfect fucking.

MATTY MOBILE Sent 3 October 2011 15:18

I'm thinking of all the times I told you what a croc of shit marriage was and how I'd never tie myself to any man. And now look at me with the sparkly handcuff on my ring finger. If you met Fox you'd understand. There's no way in hell we'll end up one of those boring couples in suburbia who never fuck and don't have anything to say to each other. Hah. Laughing at the thought.

14

Then

Haze

It never failed to amaze me how much life could change in such a short amount of time. Just as spring was blossoming, I went to Paris to see two of my paintings displayed in a high-end gallery. It was one of those evenings where it all felt worth it, as if everything I'd been through had led me to this moment, my talent getting me praise and accolades I'd never dared to dream of.

I never could've known that following a drunk man into an alleyway would lead me to the best discovery of my life: my Fox, my other half.

And now here we were.

Wed.

In bed.

'Good morning, Mrs Cabot.'

We had married six months after meeting. One perfect honeymoon later, and now we were waking up in our flat in Knightsbridge, facing a rainy London autumn together.

I was in a state of wedded bliss that the old me would've mocked mercilessly. I was a strong, independent woman, but when he called me 'little one', I got weak knees and an overwhelming urge to do whatever he said. I could literally feel the feminism seeping out of my body whenever he stared at me with that knowing, crooked smile. I just wanted to fall into his arms and tell him to take care of me forever.

'Good morning, Mr Cabot.' I sat up, stretched and clapped my hands. The electric curtains opened in response, exposing the tops of the trees in Hyde Park. When we first rented this place, we had imagined using the expansive balcony to have a leisurely breakfast overlooking one of London's best green spaces. England's famously shit weather meant we had yet to use to it.

Fox had no ties to anywhere in Europe and he understood that although no people bound me to London, it was the city itself I was tied to. The polluted air, the dirty streets, the crammed tube. All of it felt like home.

Knightsbridge was new to me, though. Fox chose it as he felt it was the best place for us to be anonymous. We'd been here over a month and we'd yet to lay eyes upon a single neighbour in this exclusive block of flats.

The doorbell rang.

I stretched again. 'It's your turn.'

Fox groaned and pulled a pillow over his head. 'I'm too cosy.'

'Fine. I'll go. Like this.' I hopped out of bed. I was naked.

'Stop!' Fox threw back the covers and got up. 'You win. I'll go.'

He reached for his dressing gown and headed to the front door.

I got back into bed with a smile. Today I'd go to my studio. I'd started on a new piece. It was going to be my best yet, I was sure of it. My studio was a ten-minute walk from our flat. It was bright and airy with big windows and high ceilings, a dream come true for someone who'd previously only ever painted in a cramped living room.

Fox walked in with a tray of fresh fruit, pastries and two freshly made coffees. Deliveroo-ing the easiest meal of the day was the epitome of luxury. He laid it on the bed in front of me. I popped a strawberry into my mouth. 'Plans tonight?'

'There's a party at Loulou's we could make an appearance at.' Fox sat down on the bed and took a gulp of his coffee.

'We could, I suppose.'

Invites to everything the capital had to offer came to us without being courted. We had many friends who might not know our surnames but knew what we liked to drink. Flick through a glossy magazine looking for us, and you might spot us in the social pages, in the background at some glamorous event. People just loved us. They thought we were a couple to die for; they'd never guess we were a couple to die from.

'A new Mexican restaurant opening in Mayfair?' Fox reached for a croissant.

I shrugged. 'Maybe.'

'A preview screening of a new artsy film in Soho?'

'Perhaps.' I reached for my coffee. We observed each other over our polystyrene cups.

He smiled. 'Got the itch already?'

'Is it that obvious?'

'Well then, little one.' He drained his coffee and stood up. 'Let's go hunting.'

My man, my king.

I was always meant to find him. I was sure of it.

To find someone who shared my passion, who understood me, who really saw me. We both understood this darkness in us needed an outlet, and that it was one that could be used to make the world a better place. There were plenty of men capable of killing, but Fox was one of the good ones. He killed calmly. And only men that deserved it. No vulnerable women alone in darkened car parks for my *real* man.

Fox wanted to kill bad guys. But he particularly wanted to kill bad guys with money.

Luckily, my type of straight white men were also the ones that were most likely to be rich.

Sympatico.

Fox would select the victim, making sure to abide by our required remit. And then we followed a simple formula: snare, capture, rupture. Our very own overture. Sweet, sweet music.

We were a partnership, a team. One hell of a duet. With the utmost respect for each other's talents and abilities.

Our playbook was simple.

My job was baiting these men to get them alone. It was easy. The merest hint of a blow job, and they'd follow me anywhere. I mean really, it was ridiculous. All the things us girls are taught: avoid dark places, don't have headphones on, wear modest clothes, be on the lookout, view every man as a threat. Men had never been given any such lessons; they'd blindly follow a strange woman anywhere, such was their desperation to get their rocks off and their deep-seated belief they were invincible. There could be a sign on the door saying 'Torture Chamber', the sound of rattling chains and knives sharpening, and they'd still skip in there, unbuckling their belts.

They didn't know fear, as they'd never had to face it.

The world was theirs for the taking. Women were the ones who had to be careful – to not put our safety at risk, to not take up too much room, to not make our voices too loud.

Fox and I might have been the ones who ended their lives, but it was their privilege that let us. If they'd been just a little more cautious, a little more modest, they'd still be driving their flashy penis-extension cars and getting off on their girlfriends' faked orgasms.

When it came to how we'd kill them, that was where Fox was the real artist. Sometimes he'd take days. He was interested in how the body worked, what the body could take. While he played with them, I'd check Instagram, bookmark dresses I wanted to buy, hotels I wanted to visit. He'd take his time and then I'd swoop in for the grand finish.

It made me laugh, the way these men would see me and their eyes would light up. A woman! She'd scream and run for help, be horrified, be kind enough to want to let them go! All this presumption that we're the weaker, fairer sex. So foolish. I'd make them pay for that in extra pain, and I'd get extra high thinking about how good a job I was doing to subvert the stereotype.

Hunt, kill, hold hands. That was our love language, and we knew exactly how to keep the passion burning bright.

Our date nights weren't like other people's date nights.

Marriage has been the making of me. I'd never been happier. I'd never thought I'd be able to trust a man, but this was no ordinary man. This was my Fox. And he was magnificent.

I got out of bed and walked to the bathroom. Pausing at the door, I turned back to him. 'Why aren't you following me?' I put my hands on my naked hips. 'Is the honeymoon over already?'

He threw his phone onto the bed. 'You are insatiable.' Fox grinned. 'How did I get so lucky?'

15

Fox

Bin juice. Of all the terminology I'd learned since making England my home, this was probably the grossest. It described the slosh of stuff that dripped out of the bottom of a leaking trash bag. The stuff that was currently all over the kitchen floor, leading out to the side door.

I sighed and told Bibi not to get down from her chair. When Haze finally entered the kitchen, I was on my hands and knees, in my bespoke Savile Row suit, spraying disinfectant on the floor and scrubbing it with paper towels.

'Bin day?'

'Yep.' I grimaced as I continued. I tried to ignore the jolt of irritation that she had no idea what day it was. Just like she had no idea about how to fill up the car with petrol when it was running low, or where the spare light bulbs were kept, or even where the keys for the window locks were. '*You need to open the window, I don't know how to.*'

'Morning, baby girl. You full now?' She stroked Bibi's hair and took her empty bowl to the sink.

'Full full. Down?'

Haze lifted her out of the chair and carried her across the room, avoiding me and the bin juice spots. The TV was tuned to Sky News. I heard the volume rising and saw Bibi slumped on the sofa, her eyes already transfixed by the screen.

'You know she's not meant to have screen time in the morning,' I called over to Haze. 'And especially not the news – she might see something inappropriate.'

She rolled her eyes as she walked back to me. 'We're meant to be at the Thompsons' tonight. Can I bail?'

I stopped scrubbing. 'Why? It'll be fun. Mimi's already booked.' Mimi was another neighbour's nineteen-year-old daughter. She claimed to love kids, but then insisted on only arriving once the kids were actually in bed.

'She smelled of weed last time she babysat.'

I understood why Haze had trust issues; when the worst had happened repeatedly, it was hard to expect goodness in people.

'The Thompsons are three doors down. You can check on Bibi every fifteen minutes if you really want to.'

I knew my wife, and I knew Mimi's ability to be responsible enough to look after our sleeping daughter for two hours while we were so close by, was not the real issue.

Haze tightened the belt on her dressing gown. 'Why do you want to go? It's not like it's going to be fun.'

And there it was.

'They're our friends.'

'Do they really know us? Do we really know them? You know I'm still not totally sure who's married to who.'

'It's not that hard if you pay attention. David and Georgie are the blondes. Caro is married to Nick the baldie. Raquel the redhead is married to grey-haired Mark.'

She nodded but I could tell she did not take it in.

'Do you know who Mark reminds me of? That guy in Saint-Tropez. The one who was . . .' She cast a glance at the oblivious Bibi, who was seemingly enraptured by a story about a Tesco staff walkout over pay conditions '. . . R-a-p-i-n-g his stepdaughter. Remember him?'

'Just because Mark reminds you of a bad man doesn't mean he is one.'

'How do we know? Who really knows their neighbours? I bet if we dug deep enough, we'd find we—'

'Haze, stop it.'

'I don't think they recycle.'

'Haze, this is—'

'Pretty sure I saw him kick a dog the other day, I—'

'We're not killing him!' I hush-shouted at her. 'We're not killing *anyone*. Remember?'

She stared at me, her face impassive, then spun on her heel and left.

16

Haze

The hushed talk over canapés was that the Hartnetts at number twenty were about to get divorced. *'The signs were there – have you seen his new car? Totally impractical for a family man.'* Simone at number sixteen was on everyone's shit-list, as she'd poached Frederica at Chorley Lane's nanny. *'Can you imagine? That's even worse than screwing her husband!'*

I was standing with the wives in the sitting room. The men were by Nick's *'it's cheesy but in an ironic way'* home bar. They were undoubtedly talking about work as we gossiped about the shitshow lives of people we knew so that we could feel superior.

I looked around and realised we had become our cover story.

Haze and Fox, the wild, bad-man-killing duo had become Hazel and Nathaniel, respectable parents and affable neighbours.

This temporary blip was becoming our life.

This was fucking *it*.

I downed my glass of champagne in one. Oh God, even

developing a drinking problem would be too clichéd. *'I could see it coming, she was having her first glass way before Mummy's wine o'clock.'*

I stared at my empty glass. I could control myself. I'd be damned if the one gift my mother passed down to me was alcoholism.

The doorbell rang and Georgie rushed to the front door. 'I'll get it, Caro, it's David!'

We watched as they kissed a long hello and held each other.

'Has David been away?' asked Raquel.

'No, he's just getting back from the office,' said Caro.

We continued to stare at their elongated greeting.

Was he actually cupping her face? 'Are they always like that?'

'Oh yes.' Raquel laughed and took a glug of champagne. 'It's weird, right?'

'Fucking weird.'

Caro leaned closer towards us. 'I saw them the other day at Waitrose. They were holding hands in the frozen food aisle.'

Raquel squinted at them. 'Maybe he's got cancer? Or something else terminal?'

'Yes. That would make sense.' I nodded my agreement.

We continued to watch them talking and smiling to each other.

'Or . . . they could just be . . . happy?' offered Caro.

We paused to take this in.

'No. Nope. They can't be.' Raquel shook her head. 'They've been married nearly ten years and have three kids. He's probably fucking her younger sister and is so nice to her because he feels guilty about it.'

'Oh yes, that makes sense.' Caro nodded. 'Her sister is really hot.'

We were all silent as we strained to hear what they were saying.

'God, you're looking beautiful.' David smiled. 'I love this dress on you!'

Caro frowned. 'Last week Nick was working from home. We spent the whole day together, and at five o'clock I realised I had toothpaste smeared on my cheek. He said he hadn't noticed as he hadn't looked at me.'

I winced.

'Yeah, that's normal,' said Raquel as she patted Caro's arm.

Maybe this was what life in the suburbs was like. Anyone who looked too happy was about to die or clearly cheating.

I wanted to be one of those couples people were jealous of again. I looked over at Fox, now earnestly nodding at Mark while holding a wilting canapé. But he was just too annoying. Maybe if we had more sex. That might help. I tried to think how long it had been. The fact it wasn't memorable or recent was not a good sign.

What had happened to us? Was there something in the water here? Something that dulled sex drives and killed energy levels? Or was that just a long-term relationship and parenthood? I had no 'normal' barometer when it came to happy couples and happy families and I wasn't about to open up to neighbours whose names I could barely keep track of. Fox was no help as he was the person I wanted to talk about – not to. It was fine. I was sure I wouldn't be the first person to google 'how do you know if your marriage is shit'.

* * *

When we got home, Mimi the babysitter was already waiting by the door with her coat on.

'How was she?'

Mimi shrugged. 'Haven't seen her, so still asleep, I guess.'

'Let me walk you home.' Fox was ever the gentleman.

'Whatever.' Mimi headed out the door as I gave Fox eyes that said, *Why should I allow this idiot teen the privileged responsibility of looking after our beloved daughter?*

I'm not sure if he chose to receive that message, as he gave me a thumbs-up.

After checking on Bibi and tucking her blanket back over her, I headed into my makeshift studio. I stared at the canvas on my easel. The pitiful attempt I had been working on today. I'd received an email from Hamish at the gallery earlier. A friendly 'just checking in' with strong undertones of 'WHY HAVEN'T YOU PAINTED ANYTHING?' Matty's bird sculpture was on a small table next to my easel. I picked it up and rubbed the broken wing. The smoothness of the copper, the detail in the feathers. He would've done so many great things. He didn't want to live if he couldn't create; it was so much a part of him that he couldn't see life without it. I understood now how intrinsic my art was to my happiness. I wasn't *me* without it. My love for Bibi helped fill the gap, but goddammit, it was tough.

I heard Fox returning, the front door closing. I put the bird back on the table and went through to our bedroom.

'Was that really so bad?' Fox asked as he joined me in our expansive his-and-hers dressing room.

I assessed the evening. 'A total waste of make-up. And vintage Dior.' I slipped off the green silk jumpsuit I'd been wearing and dropped it on the back of my dressing-table chair. I sat down and started wiping at my face.

Fox came up behind me. I looked up at his handsome reflection in the mirror.

'What can I do?' He put his hands on my shoulders. 'To make this better?'

'You know what.'

'Apart from that.' He sighed. 'Remember, nothing is more important than keeping Bibi safe. This is what parenting is. Sacrifice. I know how hard it is for you.' He squeezed my shoulders. 'We just need to be strong and think of how much we want her to have a perfect childhood, with both her parents here for her.'

I knew what we were doing it for. It didn't mean I had to like it.

I locked eyes with his reflection.

'I want you to help me remember what it feels like to be alive. To feel powerful and beautiful and invincible.'

Fox nodded. 'Okay.' He kissed the top of my head and walked away.

17

Haze

It had been over a week since I reached out to Fox and asked him to help me regain my lost power. And nothing. No whisper of what plans were afoot. No grand gesture. Not even an attempt to lift my mood with sex. How long had it been now? Was his sex drive inherently linked to his kill drive? He'd succeeded in completely suppressing both?

I'd dropped Bibi at nursery and had an hour before I was due to meet Jenny at the workout class I'd found at a nearby gym. I figured listlessly driving around was better than arriving early and potentially having to talk to people.

I drove down a quiet residential street. All the houses here looked the same. They were nice. Better than I could have ever dreamt of growing up. Back then I'd walk past streets of houses like this and think, *Look at those happy homes.* I'd see the lights on and the warmth radiating from inside. I wouldn't have noticed the cracks in the paintwork.

Maybe I had never wanted my own family because I wanted to keep the perfect dream alive.

I'd asked Fox to help me feel good again. To feel strong

and invincible. To try and recapture everything I'd lost thanks to my forced retirement. And he had ignored it. Pretended I'd never said a thing.

Dick.

Why did I struggle so much when it all came so easily to him? He had downed all our many tools without a second thought. He could stop killing, just like that. He could become a father, a dedicated, loving, perfect father, just like that. He knew what needed to be done and he made sure he excelled at it. He had numerous parenting books, all with highlighted and bookmarked pages. He studied them with the fervour of a man preparing for an exam that, if failed, would see his child taken away. Back when we were trying to get her to sleep through the night, he'd log how many ounces of milk she took, what sleepsuit she was in, the ambient room temperature, all to see what variants encouraged maximum sleep time. He channelled the same dedication into her sleep data that he'd once given to his now-defunct killing spreadsheet.

I got to the end of the road and slowed my speed. Up ahead was a large oak tree hanging over a small grey house.

I recognised it and then remembered why. Without thinking, I'd driven to Matty's parents' house. I hadn't even realised I still knew the address.

As I stared at their house, I thought of how I'd felt leaving it that day all those years ago. I was just starting out on my one-woman-mission to rid the world of scumbags. The power I'd felt when I debated whether Matty's father would live or die. In my life up until that point, nothing had ever worked out for me in the way I wanted it to. I had never taken charge of my destiny; I'd just bitched about the shitty hand I'd been dealt. I was always reacting to what happened to me, not making things happen.

That day, walking away from Matty's house, having given his father a stay of execution, it had all clicked for me. I was choosing who got to live, who had to die. I was finally in control.

But, all these years later, I was powerless again.

The loud house music kicked in. The perfectly honed man at the front of the class was wearing a headset. 'Good morning, ladies! I'm AJ, and I'm here to get you fit and keep you safe.'

There were titters from the two women next to us. AJ was an undeniably hot twenty-something-year-old. He looked like he'd be more at home at the front of an LA spin class where everyone he was leading was an equally attractive out-of-work actor. He shone a little too brightly for a tired studio in Berkshire with middle-aged women in support leggings.

Jenny was staring at him, her mouth agog. She leaned towards me. 'I can't sweat in front of him!'

I looked over at AJ. He was now encouraging everyone to warm up. We were marching obediently along with him.

'It's his job to make people sweat. He chooses to work around sweat. You really think he's going to be horrified at yours?'

Jenny tugged at her baggy T-shirt. 'Why are we here again?'

'To learn important self-defence skills, increase your feelings of self-worth and gain an understanding that when it comes to your personal safety, you can't rely on anyone but yourself.'

'Oh. Right.' Jenny looked around the room.

'You've never done anything like this before?'

'I know the basics, but I'm very out of practice.' Jenny shrugged. 'Pregnancy, new baby, then . . . just a general feeling it was all pointless.'

'Where did you learn—'

I was cut off by AJ giving a loud whoop. 'Okay, ladies, follow me.' He was now lunging with his right leg. 'Fifty reps and then switch.'

'Jesus,' huffed Jenny. 'This'll get me ready for the summer.'

I tutted at her. 'Forget beach body, this is about battle body.'

'My. Body. Is. A. Weapon.' She fired out a word with each lunge.

Half an hour later, I was impressed. Not with Jenny's fitness – that was abysmal. But with the class. It was a good build-up of cardio, some core strengthening. All helping areas of weakness. I hadn't been to anything like this since before my pregnancy. It felt good to be training again. Except, I realised with a jolt, I now lacked a mission to be training for. I'd never been in it so much for the self-defence, more the man-attack.

AJ stopped the music and motioned for us to gather round the large mat he was standing on. 'Now we'll move on to more specific active response techniques. Do we have a volunteer?'

Everyone's eyes dropped down.

'I know it's intimidating, but—' He trailed off as my hand shot up. 'Great. Come forward, please.'

I stepped onto the mat. He looked me in the eye and furrowed his brow. 'Imagine I'm an attacker. It's dark. You're alone. I'm coming towards you, I'm holding a knife, what do you—'

I kicked out AJ's knees. He stumbled, and then I body-slammed him to the ground, leading with my elbow. I landed on top of him. He was very solid. AJ blinked repeatedly as he tried to process what had just happened. A couple of the women had shrieked. One had started clapping and then stopped.

I got up and leaned down to offer a hand to AJ. To his credit, he smiled and took it.

'Now that's how you do it!' He turned to me. 'You must've had some training before?'

'I take protecting myself very seriously.' I knew more than anyone it could be life or death. I did what I needed to do to make sure I was always the one walking away.

'If you don't mind, I'd like to block through some moves with you for the group to see?'

'No problem.'

'So first of all, if the attacker reaches for you here' – he grabbed my waist and pulled me to him – 'what you need to do is . . .'

'This.' I motioned digging into his baby-blue eyes with my thumbs.

He nodded in approval. 'Exactly. And now your instinct will be to feel trapped because I've got you here.' He ran his hands up and down my waist. 'But you have to remember your hands are free.'

I tried to ignore the tingle of his hands on my body.

'Okay, so next, imagine you've been flung to the floor.' He motioned to the mat. I lay down on my back. He straddled me and pinned my arms above my head.

A woman gasped and tried to turn it into a cough.

'This is a position of power for your attacker. You're vulnerable like this, and he can do whatever he wants. What you need to focus on is planting your feet.' He nodded down at me. I pulled up my knees so my feet were flat on the mat. 'And now you . . .'

I gave a big thrust with my hips and the motion propelled him forward, releasing his grip on my arms.

He smiled down at me. 'This is exactly what you need to do.' He turned to the gathered women. 'Now her arms are free. What's important is she doesn't waste this chance.'

I took this as my cue. I clamped on to his arms, slamming my feet down on the mat. I gave another big thrust, using the momentum to roll him at the same time. Now I was on top.

AJ turned his head towards the watching crowd. 'See? With a few practised moves, you're back with a fighting chance.' They started clapping.

He looked up at me and held eye contact a moment too long. I knew that look. I used to live off that look. The double-takes, the lingering glances. I thrived off knowing the power I had over men, and how simply they were taken in by a symmetrical, conventionally attractive face and a slim body. All that had faded away since pregnancy, since pushing a pram. It felt good for someone to notice I was still a woman. My husband certainly didn't.

I leaned back and got to my feet.

AJ bounced up next to me. 'Now, who would like to volunteer next?'

All hands shot up.

'That was amazing. You were amazing.' Jenny had not stopped gazing at me with stars in her eyes since the class ended. We were attempting to drink some undrinkable green juice in the studio's adjoining café.

'They're just simple skills that, once learned, you don't forget. And they'll help make you feel in control if you ever find yourself in an uncontrollable situation.'

Jenny nodded to herself. 'I'm glad I met you.'

I wasn't used to having female friends. Correction: I wasn't used to having friends.

I had gotten used to not letting anyone in. Matty showed me the joy of friendship and then he took it all away. It was hard to believe you were a good friend when someone chooses to die on your watch. Every time I picked up his little bird sculpture it reminded me of what I had lost and how much I never wanted to feel like that again.

Fox steamrolled his way into my heart and didn't give me the chance to push him away. He tore down the defences I'd spent years carefully building and our big shared bloody secret made us so entwined he felt a part of me.

But things were different now.

We weren't there for each other in the way we used to be. That created space for others. Especially when my days had vast expanses of time to fill. It didn't take a genius to work out that was why I'd let Jenny inch her way in. She had a child the same age as mine, and chit-chat with her was helping me reduce my screen time on my phone, which had previously been my go-to when faced with hours alone at soft play. As friendship requirements went, it was a pretty low bar.

18

Fox

'Cabot, my good man, how are you doing?' Hugo Sinclair was waiting for me when I stepped out of the elevator. He must want something.

'Great, I—'

'You have a contact for the Chester account? Harry's away and I thought I'd better check in on them.'

Trying to steal a colleague's client. Sinclair was nothing if not predictable.

'I'll send it to you,' I lied.

'Good stuff. Group of us are hitting Annabel's tonight. You going to join us?'

'Afraid I need to get home.'

'Don't worry about missing the last train. Just stay in your club for the night. You must have one? Tell the old ball and chain it's a work thing. She can't argue with that, can she?'

I knew how these nights went. Wedding rings left in the top drawers of their desks. The good old boys back-slapping, coke-snorting, champagne-quaffing, female-fondling.

'I like to see my daughter before she goes to bed.'

'Ah.' I loved silencing these guys with honesty. 'Such a modern man!' He gave me an awkward thumbs-up and slinked off.

I walked through the office, nodding at the colleagues I knew, a small smile for those I didn't.

I flung myself into my chair and leaned back. My desk was very tidy. Everything perfectly positioned. Nothing personal except a framed photo of Bibi. I purposefully didn't have one of Haze, as I didn't want the inevitable leery comments from my male colleagues. It might be 'just banter', but I would struggle to not be violent in response to jokes about jerking off while thinking about her.

I turned on my computer and checked my portfolio updates.

Our income had taken a hit since Bibi was born. This was not just down to the inevitable expenses a baby brought. My colleagues enjoyed laughing at how becoming a father had knocked my golden touch, my innate ability to pick winners. And they would be right. But they would never guess the real reason why.

Haze didn't seem to understand I was working harder than ever to make up for this shortfall. She thought I was choosing to be here while she battled on the home front. I knew she was frustrated. Her work had suffered since Bibi too. I'm no creative, but I could see how difficult it must be when something you loved no longer gave you any pleasure. Whenever I walked past our spare room I'd only ever see her staring at a blank canvas holding Matty's little bird sculpture. Her lack of artistic inspiration had also hit our finances. One of her beautiful works of art could command a lot of money. But she hadn't finished a piece in three years.

I didn't want to worry her, but things were precarious. If

my parents ever cut the apron strings, all I would have access to was what I had saved – and it wasn't enough, not for the type of life I wanted us to lead. I wanted to give Haze everything she never had growing up. I wanted to give Bibi everything she could ever want. I knew it was a tragic throwback to hunter-gatherer days, but I felt fully responsible for providing for our family. This was why I suffered through the inane office chit-chat, the enforced laddie comradery and the distinctly average Pret A Manger sandwiches.

I stared at the numbers swimming across my screen. I kept thinking of how Haze had asked me for help to feel powerful again. It felt like a breakthrough. She was accepting that this was our life now and had come to me wanting me to find a solution. I never loved her more than when she let herself be raw unfiltered Haze.

She was so used to being different people she didn't even notice when she was doing it. Her upbringing had made her astute at understanding what and who she needed to be to get herself out of a bad situation; at a flick of her hair, she could change character and accent. A talent born out of self-preservation. She was the ultimate social chameleon – when she considered it worth the effort, which was rare. I was at least grateful she deemed that presenting a united, normal front to our neighbours was important for both our safety and our position in the social hierarchy. She might have attended their dinners grudgingly but when it came to hosting, the food she faked as her own was masterfully done. I always pretended I believed it too. Even though when we were alone, the most she'd ever made herself was cheese on toast – and even that she microwaved, as she hadn't worked out how to use the grill.

I had taken her request for help seriously. I was working on something that could be the answer. I hadn't risked telling her about it as I didn't want to get her hopes up when it might not pan out. All I wanted was for her to love this life we had built together. I hated watching her sleepwalk through it.

19

Haze

It had been over two weeks since our first session with AJ, and we'd been back several times. Jenny was already looking better for it. She looked less deathly pale. Nothing like occasional exercise and abject lusting after a hot man to bring a bit of colour into the cheeks.

'I definitely feel better.' Jenny was nodding vigorously as she forked a salad. 'Though I'm not sure I could kick anyone's arse just yet.'

We were having lunch at the café near music class. I was not surprised to learn the food they served was as bad as their coffee.

'It's about feeling empowered, not necessarily being able to beat someone up. That's what weapons are for. You just stab them.'

Jenny laughed, and then stopped when she saw my straight face.

'Have you spoken to that lawyer?' I'd given her the details of someone Fox had recommended. Full credit to Fox, he had not enquired why my new friend needed legal advice.

'She's amazing. I've sent her all our messages and emails, and she was so encouraging about our chances that I'm starting to have hope.'

I might not be able to punish this particular bad man physically, but it was a bit of a kick knowing I had set the wheels in motion for punishing him financially.

'It's just as well he has zero interest in custody. My lawyer was saying if he did, he'd start coming after me, questioning my mental state, which would be unthinkably awful.'

'What have you got?' I asked through a mouthful of bacon sandwich.

'Bit of depression, bit of anxiety. I'm just a bit all over the place.' Jenny rolled and unrolled her paper napkin. 'I can't tell what's life and what's just a chemical imbalance in my brain. I know I'm meant to be happy, but things are a bit shit. So is that depression, or is that just feeling bummed out at my lot in life?'

I got what she meant. Maybe depression was easier to diagnose when life was perfect but you still felt down. Shit. Was that me? Was I depressed?

I shook it off. No. I was more pissed off than depressed. And that was down to my husband being a stubborn fucker.

'How's Fox?' Jenny was moving her fork through her salad, hunting for more croutons.

'He's good. Weirdly happy.' I pictured him humming to himself at the cooker in his ridiculous apron.

'You haven't really told me much about him. I just know he's American and works in finance.'

'Doesn't that say it all?' I'd gathered from our interactions with our neighbours that the key factors in getting to know each other seemed to be learning what jobs everyone did.

'Where did you meet?'

'Paris.'

'Oh, of course you did. How romantic.'

'It was. Very.' I sighed as I thought of the beauty, blood and passion of the moment. A lifetime ago now. I looked around the tired café.

Jenny put down her fork. 'How well do you know your husband?'

I frowned. 'That's a strange question.'

'I know more than anyone that how a man appears at first can be very different to how they really are.' Jenny was looking at me steadily.

I shrugged. 'Of course I know my husband. He's great. A great, great guy.' Even to my ears that sounded a little hollow. But how could I really explain Fox? A man who was a perfect contradiction. A rule-abiding, cold-blooded killer. Gentle and kind, ferocious and methodical.

Jenny paused. 'I guess it's just you've been so good at helping me with dealing with Bill, I just wondered if you'd had first-hand experience with a . . . difficult partner.'

Wow. She was worried about *me*?

'Fox has never laid a hand on me. He never would.' The very thought made me want to laugh.

I watched her as she continued to dissect her salad. I'd written her off as a flaky sad case. Maybe that was premature. Maybe I had to be a little more careful around her.

'How well do you know your husband?'

It rang in my head as I tried to sleep next to a snoring Fox. I could feel the gulf between us. Ever expanding.

Did we actually know each other? It had been easy to be

happy back when we'd had money, time, and a desire to pursue anything that we wanted to. Lunch at Scott's that turned into dinner as we had discovered a particularly good rosé and a thirst for oysters . . . Finishing off a skiing holiday with streaks of red snow after coming upon a bad man on a dark night . . . Dancing on a yacht until the sun rose, having become best friends with a couple we'd met in a bar and would never see again after that night . . . That was how we'd lived. We were so busy having fun and being happy that we never took the time to work out if it was the life we loved or each other. Once you stripped away the glitz and the glamour and the blood, was there even anything left of us?

20

Fox

'I'm Nathaniel, and I'm an alcoholic.'

I am not an alcoholic.

I looked round at the group of strangers I was standing in front of. We were in a rundown, damp-smelling church hall, a twenty-minute walk from my office. Although there were five AA lunchtime meetings closer than this one, I had chosen it in the hope that it was far enough away, in an unappealing enough venue, that I'd never bump into anyone I knew. I'd heard of some contacts using AA meetings as networking opportunities. Imagine faking a drinking problem just to get friendly with someone whose company you wanted to buy stock in. Some might say I'd lost the moral high ground on this issue by also faking a drinking problem. But it was the closest I could get to getting help.

I had an addiction.

It just wasn't to alcohol.

I figured the principles were the same. Learning to live without it. Doing it for the sake of my family. And really, as I had given up something that gave me great joy, didn't I deserve a little tangible something to mark every milestone by which I'd succeeded in not slitting someone's throat? I still had in my sock drawer the bronze chip, awarded to me for my one year of 'sobriety'. Last summer, I'd been upgraded to the black key tag for three years or more. It hung proudly on my silver Tiffany's keyring, along with my house keys. Haze had noticed it once and asked what it was. She'd smiled when I said it was just a memento I'd kept from some dead man.

'I've been sober for just over three years now.' I paused for whoops but received none. Sometimes I did miss America. 'It has changed my life for the better. I'm not saying I don't miss it. I think about how much I want . . . to drink . . . every day.' I took a deep breath. 'But being able to go to sleep at night, without worrying that something I've done could lead to me being torn apart from my wife and daughter, is a great feeling. Whenever I get the urge to drink, I just think about them, and how I don't want to let them down by endangering their safety.'

I sat back down in my plastic chair. There were a few half-hearted claps. Of the group of seven of us, six were men. Pam, the lone woman, was in her seventies, and I'd never heard her speak in all the years I'd been coming here. She always looked like she was half-asleep.

My sponsor, a bearded man in his sixties called Griff, was the next to speak. He was also the group leader and had been sober for ten years. I wasn't fully versed in drinking problems, but I would've thought by now he could just chill. Griff liked taking newbies under his wing and telling them all about how drinking had lost him his marriage and damaged his relationship with his son. I think this was why he had always taken such a special interest in me.

Griff and Pam were the only ones of this group who'd been here since I started coming. The others seemed to rotate on a regular basis. I had a feeling this was less because they were cured of alcoholism, and more because they had found a better venue (perhaps one that offered such amenities as a Nespresso machine and mould-free walls), or their court-ordered time had come to an end and they didn't need to keep pretending they wanted to stop drinking.

When Griff finished talking, no one else wanted to take the floor. He read out a little from *The Big Book*, which he always had on his lap, and I nodded along as he talked through the twelve steps. I wasn't so keen on all the God stuff, and the eighth step – 'Make a list of all the people you have harmed and make amends' – didn't really work for me. I couldn't exactly bring them back from the dead.

Griff wrapped things up and invited everyone to help themselves to a bitter, lukewarm coffee from the Thermos dispenser and stay for a chat. I caught his eye and motioned towards my watch with a grimace. That was the joy of lunch-time meetings: always an office to rush back to.

'You must be Nathaniel.'

I looked up from brushing Pret A Manger sandwich crumbs off my silk tie. A tall blonde woman was standing in front of my desk.

'I'm Suzanne. Just transferred from Washington. I was directed your way as I asked who the fellow Americans here were.'

'Great to meet you.' I stood up and shook her offered hand. She was wearing a slinky white shirt and tailored trousers. She had an empty ring finger and a firm handshake. She didn't let go as she looked me square in the eye. There were forty-three Americans on this floor. I wondered how many she was taking the time to introduce herself to. I extricated my hand.

'Are you free tonight? I was thinking drinks and you telling me everything I need to know to acclimatise myself?' She gave me a little smile as she played with the gold chain round her neck. I could see the top of a black lace bra peeping out from her shirt.

'Sorry, I'm very boring and always need to get back to my wife and daughter. We live out in Berkshire.'

Suzanne wrinkled her nose. 'Where is that?'

'It's to the west of London, in the M4 corridor. It's a pretty easy commute. Takes about an hour to get in. The Jubilee line is a—'

'Just tell me if you ever change your mind.' Suzanne continued to hold eye contact. 'About drinks, that is.' She spun around on her heels and walked back through the office. The line of desks may have had people busy shouting into their headsets or tapping wildly at their keyboards, but most heads turned as she walked by.

She looked back and clocked me still looking. She smiled to herself and kept going.

I noticed women. I wasn't dead inside. It didn't mean I wanted to do anything about it. I could observe attractiveness as one might observe a particularly nice painting. Or a well-tailored suit.

I was used to women hitting on me. I'd even had a few men give it a go. I always politely declined. I was faithful because I loved my wife. Not because she might slit my throat if I wasn't. I didn't expect medals for resisting their attention. I was never tempted. I always told Haze about it. We used to laugh off the more overt come-ons together. But nowadays, she'd just roll her eyes and say they were probably only staring because I had something stuck in my teeth. Sometimes I wondered if she even still liked me.

My phone pinged. An email from my father, requesting a call. I stared at it for a minute and then pressed delete.

My phone pinged again. Now a message from my beloved: *'Don't forget need more bin bags.'* A beat and then: *'And milk.'* Another beat. *'Broccoli.' 'Kitchen roll.'* The pings kept coming. *'Dishwasher tablets. Must be Finish ones.' 'Avocados. But only if ripe.' 'Alpen – no added sugar. If don't have, then porridge (non-jumbo) oats fine.'*

I turned off the volume and did a silent scream at my phone. Why don't *you* go get everything, you lazy . . . Deep breath.

My phone vibrated. Another text. This time an unknown number. *'Just read your excellent review on the Grimaldi stock investment. Very impressive, Cabot. Good to show these Brits how it's done.'* It was signed off with a winking emoji and an S. Suzanne had already tracked down my cellphone number. And read up on me.

I'd seen many a man before me succumb to the lure of cheating. I was disapproving.

Especially so of the cliché of doing it with someone at work. So what if a man had left a tired, grumpy wife at home that morning, and arrived at the office to a bright young thing fluttering her eyelashes and hanging on every word he said? Even if he had a long, dreary commute every day and worked very hard, with no thanks or appreciation, it was no excuse for having his head turned by someone who still believed in the importance of sexy underwear. What kind of man would betray the woman they'd vowed to stay faithful to for the rest of their lives?

Buzz. Haze. *'Downstairs toilet blocked. You need to buy a plunger.'* A beat. *'And rubber gloves if you're going to be a pussy about it.'*

21

Haze

'Do you ever think there's more to life than this?' I was sitting next to Jenny as we watched Felix and Bibi splashing about in the leisure centre's over-populated pool.

The smell of chlorine was unbearable, and I felt like I could catch a verruca through my shoes. Being here was not helping my mood. I'd left the house in a rage, having spent two hours staring at a blank canvas trying to create something, anything, that could bring me back to remembering I had any form of artistic talent.

Jenny shook her head and said something unintelligible through a mouthful of crisps.

'What?'

'I've always wanted to be a mother.'

This I understood; if it's something you've always dreamed of, perhaps worried would never happen, you appreciate everything all the more. I was the spoiled ingrate who, one unplanned pregnancy later, was mother to a child I worshipped and worried I wasn't good enough for. I was lucky that all I was suffering from was boredom. No thrill of kills.

Missing out on nights out. No art, no inspiration. This normal life was simple, steady, quiet – and not what I wanted.

I thought of the brief frisson of excitement at AJ and his incredibly toned, hard body – his lingering look and how he had touched me, having first got my consent. Was this what lay ahead? The cliché of an affair with the personal trainer? Or would it be a kids' tennis coach? Or whatever other man in my limited orbit as a married stay-at-home/frustrated-artist mum? Decades of only getting kicks from being eye-fucked by random men? Would it stumble over into getting felt up by someone's husband at a god-awful charades night? Was this the kind of stuff people did to feel alive? Did they get so bored they blew up their lives by rubbing up against someone inappropriate?

Could any of them see I was different, or had I got too good at playing the game? I could adapt so easily to what was expected of me – make the right face, say the right thing. We all hid the bits of us that people wouldn't understand, the parts that were too complicated to allow the world to see. At least my thoughts were mine. Unpoliced and all mine. No one would ever know what I was really thinking.

I knew when to make a scene and when not to.

'Nice parking, love!' The builder who'd scoffed at my attempt at a parallel park. My head might have been raging about where I'd cut him first, how I'd tear him to pieces. But all he got was a gritted-teeth smile and a *'I did my best!'*

The patronising dick at a dinner party: *'Digital detox is the only way. You women are just too connected to your phones.'* I imagined plunging a fork into his eye. But: *'That's such an interesting idea!'* and a gulp of wine were all he got from me.

Roll over and play nice for those with whom it wasn't

worth the fallout if I bit back. But underneath it all, I was still me. Those thoughts, those screams in my head, were still there. I was still different to them. Better. Stronger. More fucked up. It depended how you looked at it.

Jenny offered me a crisp. I took the bag.

Recently, I'd been finding my rage harder to control. My thoughts had been getting progressively more vicious. After years of having no outlet, I could feel it bubbling.

One thousand, one hundred and ninety-six days.

Don't fuck it up.

But how long before it spilled over into me stabbing scissors into the neck of some loser who stole my parking space? Knifing the delivery driver who always left a 'Sorry I missed you' slip without even ringing the doorbell?

I realised Jenny was talking to me.

'Sorry, what?'

'I think I've met someone,' she repeated.

'That's great!' After all she'd been through, she deserved some happiness – or at least to get laid. 'Where did you meet?'

'Morrison's. He asked my opinion on whether Wagon Wheels were better than Tunnock's Teacakes.'

I looked blank.

'He's French,' she explained. 'Wanted to know what us Brits enjoyed more. I went on about how superior Wagon Wheels were, and outside he presented me with a packet of them and asked for my phone number!'

I tried to muster enthusiasm for this meet-cute. 'Asking you out with chocolate. Very romantic.'

'We're going for coffee next week.' Jenny wrung her hands together. 'Felix wasn't with me, so not sure when I mention the whole kid thing.'

'Don't stress about it. If you just want sex, don't say anything. If you want a relationship, just drop it in casually. If he runs for the door, you know it's not an option.'

I finished the crisps and handed her the empty packet.

There was a clap of thunder from outside. We turned to look out the small window above the bleachers. Torrential rain. Of course, it had to happen on the day the only parking space I'd been able to find was a ten-minute walk away.

22

Fox

I got home early, bearing flowers. Not because I had done anything wrong. Or thought anything wrong. But because I wanted to show my wife that despite everything we had going on, she was still special to me. The house was empty. I texted Haze, asking where she was.

'*Just leaving swimming with Bibi,*' she replied, along with a face-palm emoji and a gun emoji. The 'kill me now' subtext clearly illustrated. A beat, and then: '*You should know her schedule by now.*'

I might have been the one bringing home the pay cheque, the one out in the office all day while she stayed home with Bibi, but yes, of course, I should still be fully up to date on everything they did. I was a feminist. A modern man. My daughter's daily routine mattered to me. And it was quite right for my wife to pick me up on any failings. I just wished she'd sometimes acknowledge that I did as much as I could with Bibi. If I was ever home from the office in daylight, I always whisked her out somewhere. It wasn't out of duty, but because I wanted to. I could never get enough of the feeling of her little hand in mine, and seeing how when she was happy, she didn't just walk, she skipped.

I did what I could, but still it wasn't enough. Haze expected so much from me. It was quite a burden – to try and be the one good man in her whole world, to show her that not all of us were bad.

I am exactly her type. I would think of that on our darker days. If I put a foot wrong she would take that as resounding proof that I was bad after all. I would be relegated to the huge scrapheap of men she'd encountered and been disappointed by.

Being on the right side of her felt more important than perhaps it would do in more traditional marriages. If I dared to wrong her I knew her broken heart would lead to my broken limbs. And that was best case scenario. I know lesser men would be scared off at the thought of living with someone who saw the world in such black and white terms – right and wrong, alive and dead – but I knew Haze loved me. She'd never killed anyone she loved before. We had a strong, beautiful, life-affirming relationship based on mutual respect and understanding. And I knew she sure as hell didn't want to be a single mother.

The doorbell rang. Inevitably Amazon. Haze seemed to have an addiction to buying any 'parenting hack' gadget she saw advertised on Instagram. Storage solutions to make you forget plastic toys were cluttering up your house! Bedtime audiobook-reading nightlights that would make sure your child never left their bed! I had tried gently telling her she couldn't one-click her life back to how it was before.

I opened the door and had to stop myself from crying out in shock.

* * *

Twenty-two minutes later the inside door to the garage opened. I quickly stood up.

'Fucking fuckety fuck, what a fucking day,' shouted Haze from the hallway. 'Where are you? Bibi zonked out in the car. That's fucked—'

I leaped into the hallway with a finger over my lips.

'Why shush? And why do you look so weird?'

'We have company, Hazel.'

Haze frowned at me. She hated it when I used her full name.

'Come on through.' I took her by the arm and led her into the sitting room. 'I'd like you to meet Reginald and Sarah-Anne Cabot.' They remained seated with gritted teeth. 'My parents.'

'Oh.' Haze stared at them.

There was a beat as they took each other in. I looked at my usually beautifully put-together wife, who today resembled a bedraggled rat.

'How lovely to meet you. If you just excuse me a moment.' She smiled at them, death-stared me, and went straight out of the room.

I knew my wife.

And what I knew best was that she was unpredictable.

She'd either rally and come down immaculate and the epitome of sweetness and light. Or she'd stay up there with the door locked, watching Netflix until she heard them leave.

Once I'd got over the shock of my parents standing right there, on the doorstep of a house to which I'd never given them the address, I'd done my best to rally. They'd rejected my offers of refreshments and had sat themselves down on a sofa, leaving me the armchair opposite them. It was not unlike an interview.

They had been mid-attack before Haze interrupted us, and were quite happy picking up where they'd left off.

'The pandemic was no excuse. I don't understand why you haven't brought the child over to see us,' huffed my mother.

'And the way you announced it?' continued my father. 'Just a vague email that you'd had a baby? No formal mention in the papers?'

'Bibi was a blessed surprise. It all happened very fast. And we weren't really in touch, so I didn't want to feel like—'

'What on earth?' scoffed my father. '*Bibi?*'

'Sabina. It's Hazel's grandmother's name.'

My parents exchanged looks.

I had seen them only a handful of times since I had packed up and left America. A dinner in Provence back in 2009, while they were there for some socialite's wedding. A lunch in Tuscany in 2015, as they'd travelled over for a business associate's seventieth. Apart from my father recently reaching out, we'd had no contact at all in the intervening years. Now that I thought about it, I realised I had not missed having them in my life.

'What was wrong with an American name?'

I had not missed them at all.

It was also with a jolt that I realised they seemed genuine in their outrage that they'd only found out about Bibi from my email. No Devon reporting back on my big life events? They really had washed their hands of me. Or was there an edict declaring that he should only inform them if I'd got myself into a fix that could ruin the family name? I guessed that made the most sense. They weren't interested in me when it came to my actual life, only how it might affect their lives.

Haze re-entered the living room. Her wet hair was scraped

back into a chic bun, her make-up was reapplied, and she was wearing a black dress with a white Peter Pan collar I'd never seen before. She looked completely beautiful, even though she didn't look like herself.

'Please let me introduce you to your granddaughter.' She motioned towards the empty door. 'Bibi, darling.'

Bibi walked in slowly, wearing a flowered dress I knew she hated.

'She is a pretty little thing, isn't she?' My mother looked over at me. 'And Hazel. It's very nice to finally meet you.'

Bibi came up to me and threw her arms around my leg. I stroked her hair.

'Hazel, what is it that you do? I know mothering is a full-time job in itself. But I've always kept myself busy beyond the home.'

'I'm an artist.'

'Lovely. Good to have a creative in the family, isn't it, darling?' Mother turned and smiled at my father. Then she turned her attention back to me. 'We've been thinking. Now that you're . . . settled. Maybe you could come back home. There's a position in the family business waiting for you.'

I glanced over at Haze, who stared back at me.

'I'm not sure that's something—'

'Julian is sadly getting divorced,' announced my father.

Aha. The perfect son, letting them down. It was with some pleasure I imagined the loaded looks from friends at the country club. The whiff of scandal, the hint of blood, and they would circle.

My mother shook her head. 'Not his fault, of course. Martha seems to have been completely unreasonable about everything.'

'I really expected better of her,' said my father.

I saw my mother nudge him. He cleared his throat. 'It's been over fifteen years; a lot has changed. You've clearly changed. Coming home would be the right thing to do.'

'The right thing for whom?' Haze took a step towards them.

Uh oh.

'For our family.' My father straightened up and looked her in the eye.

'I think you'll find it's *my* family now.' Haze crossed her arms. 'How many Christmases and birthdays have you spent with your son in the last couple of decades? How many phone calls have you made to see how he's doing?'

'That's not—'

'We are not uprooting our family just because you now decree it's time for him to come home.' Haze pulled down her hairband and ruffled out her bun. 'Now, would you like a cup of lovely English tea before you leave?'

23

Haze

A flurry of insincere goodbyes, and Fox's parents were once again out of our lives. I parked Bibi in front of the television and went into the kitchen, where Fox was drinking a large whisky. Hard spirits at 4.55pm was unusual for my husband.

I went to the cabinet and got a glass for myself. 'Jesus, what a relief that's over with. How ridiculous—' I stopped when I realised he was frowning at me.

'Before you lose it, just let me say . . .' He took a deep breath. 'It is something to think about.'

'What the hell are you talking about? You can't be serious?'

It was bad enough he wanted us to live out our normality here, but to take me to the other side of the world to do it? Forget it. Over his dead body.

'America is home for me. You can't forget that.'

'You hated it over there. You hate your parents. Why would you want to move back to be closer to them? To be their walking sock puppet, giving good face at the family business, sucking up at the country club?'

'I'm not saying we live anywhere near my parents; I'm not

saying I work for the company. I'm just saying America could be an option for us.'

'It's fucking sad. After all these years away from them, making your own mark on the world, doing your own work, great work, and all you still desperately fucking crave is the approval of those fuckers.'

Fox ran a hand through his hair and gritted his teeth. 'Do you have to be so . . . crass?'

'What the fuck? Is that what we are now? Not equals, but instead I'm the little woman who can't swear too much as it's unseemly? Get fucked, you fucking fuck.'

I stormed upstairs to our bedroom and changed into my running gear, throwing my perfect daughter-in-law dress on the floor.

I'd given up so much, and he dared to entertain the thought of making me give up even more? What the hell was wrong with him? What the hell was wrong with me? How had I ended up here?

We fell in love, we got married, we had a kid. For two unconventional people, we'd followed one hell of a conventional path. Like everyone, we'd been told in subliminal and overt messages that this was what we needed to do, but what was it for? We'd been brainwashed into feeling that a life of security and predictability was something to aspire to, that it was really living, when actually it was the *end* of living. Now we were just painting by numbers. There was no deviating from the path set out for us. We'd fallen into the trap laid by parenthood. There was no being our true selves now; we had a dependant to think about. We'd had to give it all up, to protect her, to protect our future.

I thought of the year ahead. Nothing but playdates and

dinners with people talking shit about their boring lives as I talked shit about my boring life. Was this it?

I wanted to blow it up and burn it all down.

I wanted to live hard and fast and have no regrets.

I wanted everything. I wanted a happy, healthy child who was well-balanced and grounded and grew up to cure cancer because she was just that fucking spectacular. I wanted to be my real, true self, the one who could hurt bad men, make good art, and get home for a hot dinner and hotter sex.

I needed a partner who'd lift me up, who'd love me so hard he'd make me my best self. Someone who would challenge me when I needed to be challenged, and hold me close when I needed to be held.

I'd thought Fox was that man. But look at him now: he was holding me back. He was crushing me. Why should I put up with it?

He had always been the ice to my fire. I had thought that we balanced each other out. I'd never thought of the fact that he didn't just temper my flame, he extinguished it.

I ran downstairs and out the front door fast, before he could call my name. I wasn't ready to talk to him without losing my shit so completely I might never be able to take it back. Dusk was hitting. I put my AirPods in, pulled my baseball cap down low and set off. I found my pace and settled into it comfortably, my rage helping me reach a quicker speed than usual. What the hell was wrong with him? This was what I hated about no longer being alone. Having to factor in someone else's wants and needs and awful family. How could I feel in control of my life when I had to deal with him wanting things I didn't?

When I reached the edge of the park, I saw a flash of black

by a tree. The bad man. He was here. Again. Was he always here, just waiting, hoping for a lone woman to attack? I felt my heart race a little. Anticipation, not fear. My sheathed knife was digging into my back. Let's see if he'd make me use it. Let's see if he was what I thought he was.

I picked up my pace as I ran through the park. It was near empty. A dog-walker and a teenage couple were all I spotted as I did my first circuit. By the time I came back again, to the tree where I'd seen the bad man lurking, the park was empty. I couldn't see him. Maybe he'd gone.

I felt his presence behind me just seconds before I felt his hands on me. He clasped me by the shoulders and pushed me roughly into the undergrowth. I fell back onto the ground. As he walked towards me, I pushed myself backwards, further into the trees and bushes. He thought I was backing away; he didn't realise I was drawing him in. He flung himself at me. I felt him scrabbling at me, touching me, and then the rage took over, just like it always did. It didn't matter how long it had been. It all fell away, it came as naturally to me as breathing. The red mist came down and I worked in a flurry.

Every man that had hurt me, every man that had wanted to hurt me, every man with a leer and a wink, with a rub and a grind, every man that had touched me without my permission. I wanted to punish them, make them hurt, make them bleed. This empty vessel, this sorry excuse for a human being, he would take it all for them.

An offering from the gods: a bad man to pay the price for all the bad men before him. It was beautiful. It was what I needed. It was what this world needed. One less scumbag.

When it was over, I looked down at my handiwork.

I took a deep breath out. I felt better. A deep-seated three minutes of peace and elation. And then the dread started to creep in.

I'd broken our deal.

I'd cheated on my husband.

Part 2

Honesty

'Honesty is everything! Your man is your other half; together, you are one. You need to hold him close and tell him everything, because open communication is the only way to keep you truly aligned. How can you be soulmates if your souls have secrets?!'

– Candice Summers, number-one bestselling author of *Married Means Life: How to Stay Happy, Fulfilled and Together Forever*

'Honesty is fucking overrated.'

– Hazel Matthews, married woman

***Fine Art, Big Words Magazine*, May 2015**
***Flying High* by Hazel Matthews**
Mixed media, 100cm by 200cm

This piece features a woman in armour, her black hair flowing, as she stands at the peak of a mountain. A bow and arrow are raised to the sky. Crawling up towards her are giant rats with the heads of men. Some have arrows piercing their bodies, their blood flowing down towards the others beneath them. It's disturbing to look at, but you can't take your eyes away. She is the lone warrior, halting these monstrous beings. From her stance and the look in her eyes, you know she is very much the hunter, not the hunted. Hazel Matthews is getting bolder and taking greater risks – and the pay-off shows it's working.

MATTY MOBILE Sent 3 May 2015 18:34

I might have a husband, but I still miss having a best friend. Who will I complain to when he drives me nuts? This honeymoon of ours surely has to end. I can't be this happy forever?

24

Then

Haze

'I need to know how you do it,' sighed Hamish. 'Why can't all my artists be this prolific?' He turned to Fox. 'Your wife is one talented lady.'

We had dropped into my gallery to go over my upcoming exhibition. Hamish, the curator, was more than a little impressed by the vast quantity of new works I had created in the last year.

'I was just feeling particularly inspired.'

We walked around the stark gallery space. Blank white walls and white resin floors: the perfect showcase for my works.

'Tell me about this one.' Hamish motioned to a blue-and-black painting I'd titled *Creep*.

'What are these made of?' Hamish pointed at five metallic spray-painted molars positioned in the shape of a flower.

'Clay.'

'I love it. Gives a real grittiness.'

'Oh yes.' I smirked at Fox. 'A certain bite.'

Fox shook his head. He was deeply disapproving of my insistence on using little mementos from our kills in my works of art. I knew it was potentially risky, using evidence that linked us to grizzly crimes, but I couldn't resist. They grounded every piece. Gave me a focus for what I was trying to achieve. Showcasing my two greatest talents: art and death.

'I think this one's my favourite.' Hamish took a step towards a red-streaked white canvas. *Perception* was the title. Two dark figures were facing each other. 'I just love it. The battle with your own inner self.' Hamish tilted his head. 'The hairs?' There was brown hair speckling the bottom of the canvas.

'Dog hair.' I smiled. 'To represent the animal within all of us.'

'You're really making a name for yourself, Haze.' Hamish rubbed his hands together.

'It's all I've ever wanted to do.' I looked around the gallery, my art adorning its walls, and my handsome husband holding my hand. How was this my life?

We went from the gallery straight to lunch at Le Caprice. Then a lazy, mostly naked, afternoon at home before glamming up for a party at Kensington Roof Gardens that neither of us could remember who invited us to, or what it was for.

'Darling, you look amazing. Who are you wearing?' The red-headed girl was filming me on her mobile phone. Judging by the many small, fragrant pink bottles dotted about, it must have been some kind of perfume launch.

I struck a pose, opened my arms wide and pouted at the camera. I was in a tight, bright blue halter-neck dress. I'd accessorised with big gold jewellery and killer heels. 'Dress is Versace, shoes are Jimmy Choo.'

'Of course. You're fucking fantastic.' The redhead lowered the phone. 'What's your handle? I'll tag you!'

Fox came up to me and swung me round, nuzzling into my neck.

'Oh, I don't have Instagram. We're not on social media. We want to be in the moment.' I smiled over at the redhead.

'And each other,' said a muffled Fox.

'God, you two.' She clicked a few more photos of us together. 'And who—'

'Tom Ford.' Fox brushed at the lapels of his perfectly cut suit.

'I'm calling you the hottest, best-dressed mystery couple here.' Her fingers were in a flurry over her phone. She didn't notice us slink off.

We walked over to the bar, arms entangled. I soaked up the double-takes from people along the way. It was always fun trying to work out if it was because we had the look of potentially being famous, of being somebodies, or if they just thought we were hot. For me, just the fact we mattered was enough.

Fox reached for two of the glasses of champagne, laid out and waiting, and handed one to me. He ran a hand up and down my back. 'You having fun, little one?'

I felt the throb of the loud music, the flashes of photography, the clink of glasses and the laughter of the happy and pretend-happy people all around us.

'I'm in the mood.' I flung my arms around his neck and leaned right up against him.

'Now, now. You know the rules.'

I made a sad face at him. 'Couldn't we just—'

'We have it all, baby. You don't want to ruin it, do you?'

I sighed.

My mighty Fox enjoyed being both the brain and the brawn of this operation. I guess that left me as the fun and the fury. Whatever we were, it made for an excellent team.

I had found my Mr Right to help me take out all those Mr Wrongs.

The power I felt walking into a room with him by my side, knowing we could have anyone there, any way we wanted. The arrogance of a man thinking he could fuck any woman was nothing compared to the arrogance of a woman who thought she could kill any man.

People often think about 'the one that got away'. I know I did. Pre-Fox, there was the man who very literally got away, on his hands and knees, bleeding from a stomach wound. We were in a wooded area right by a motorway, and I turned my back on him for just a few seconds to check a text message. He made a crawl for it . . . right into the path of an oncoming truck. His body was so mangled, no one seemed to clock he'd been stabbed first. I was very lucky.

Fox had so many rules to keep us safe. I had gone from being a haphazard stabbing solo artist to being part of a well-oiled, well-prepared killing duo. His golden rule was no shitting on our own doorstep. We had to steer clear of London. No matter how tempted we were to break it, this was something he was always strict on. It wasn't worth the risk.

We kept our killing solely to European tours. We'd make fleeting visits. A man here, taking in a sight there.

Someone at Interpol had started a dossier on an international serial killer. The Backpacking Butcher. It made me laugh. The very idea of *us* backpacking. Some genius had come up with the theory these men were being killed by a broke loser who robbed wealthy targets before packing up and moving on to the next location. The only time I saw Fox get really angry was when some hack mentioned that due to the incisions the killer had made, they felt he was someone who'd flunked out of medical school.

Fox checked a lot, but there was never any mention, any theory that it could be a couple working together.

I was confident that even if there was a whisper about a killing duo, it would never lead the police to our door.

We didn't fit the mould. We weren't quiet and we didn't keep to ourselves.

We courted attention. We partied hard. The invites never stopped. It was the privilege of the attractive. It made people naturally want to befriend us. Oh, and the money. That helped too. We were rich and pretty. Who wouldn't want us on their guestlist?

When I was single, I grew used to dealing with cringey come-ons from strangers. My heritage always seemed to be considered a good conversation-starter. 'You're so beautiful! What are you?' My response was always 'Someone you can't ever have,' blowing a kiss as I walked away. Even as a clearly besotted couple, there were those who'd try to break us apart. Phone numbers scrawled on anything to hand, slipped into our pockets when they thought the other wasn't looking. We'd compare beer mats, matchbooks, tissues and laugh. I'd never been tempted to cheat. Fox knew everything about me, he really knew me, and he wanted me, he wanted every part of me. Ours was a connection of such intensity it felt as if our very bodies, souls and minds were interwoven for eternity.

How could I go back to being wanted by someone who was just turned on by a pretty face and open legs? It was so primitive. So basic.

Growing up I was someone who didn't belong anywhere or to anyone – whenever I came across groups of people it was as an observer. Watching and judging from the outside. I never felt lonely, until I realised how complete I felt with Fox by my side.

The world was our oyster. We cut it open and drained it. Used it up for everything we needed to be living our best lives. And throughout it all, we got to feel superior. We were doing the world this secret service of getting rid of those bad men who didn't deserve to live. We might never be able to tell anyone, and could never post about it, but we were unsung heroes #vigilantepowercoupling.

25

Then

Fox

'Woooooohoooooo!' Haze was in the driver's seat of a red 1961 Jaguar E-Type Roadster. I was the passenger, trying to soak up the view, but finding it hard to not keep one eye on the road. Lake Como careened into view.

'Hands on the wheel, Haze!'

We'd come to Italy for a party. It was for Holly Something-Double-Barrelled's thirtieth birthday. Holly was a sweet girl with a bad cocaine habit.

Haze screeched down a road until we saw the outside of the Mandarin Oriental. I held on to the side of the car, confident that, thanks to her large sunglasses, she wouldn't see how white my knuckles were. She pulled to a halt and turned off the engine, then clapped her hands together as she looked up at the beautiful hotel building.

'You're not going to park?'

'I'm sure they have valet.' She was already getting out of

the car. Accepting the hand of the doorman, who was leading her up the stairs to the grand reception.

My wife was born for this life.

It was a thought I kept repeating to myself as I watched her navigate Holly's party. She was wearing a tight floral Dolce & Gabbana dress that made her look like a screen siren from the 1950s. We walked out onto the hotel's sweeping terrace, soaked up the view of Lake Como, and felt the warm breeze on our faces. At our first sip of pink champagne we were accosted by a few familiar faces from one of the private members' clubs we often frequented.

The brunette touched Haze's arm. 'Darling, where were you at school again? I'm sure you know Minty and Bella from Ascot?'

'Who doesn't know Minty and Bella?! But I was at boarding school in Switzerland. Mummy insisted, as she wanted me to be fluent in French, German and Italian.' Haze shrugged. 'I actually fucked one of each, but it did nothing for my language skills.' The girls howled.

Haze had a good ear. She could clip her accent to sound just as privately educated as the rest of them. She snaked an arm around me. 'America's home. Everywhere else was just for visiting.'

The girls duly cooed. We were adorable.

'Hello, beautiful people!' Sophia joined us. She was American and Botoxed to such a degree it was hard to determine her exact age. She held up a large pink cocktail. 'I'm back on the booze! Six doctors have told me my husband has a better chance than I do of getting pregnant.'

'Oh babe. You could always adopt?' offered the blonde.

'Ewwww. I don't do second-hand clothes, and I don't do second-hand kids.'

There was a tinkling crash as Haze knocked her champagne glass. It broke on the stone balustrade she was leaning against. She was gripping the jagged stem with a certain look in her eyes.

'Darling, we must go see Lara and Samuel, they're waving at us.' I took her arm and led her away, gently taking the glass stem out of her hand.

The night flew by in a blur of excess, and it was decided sometime around midnight that Como was now done. A jet was booked, bags were packed, and by the next day, Haze and I were sunbathing on the deck of a luxury yacht owned by a Russian friend of a friend of a friend about to dock in Corsica. With enough money anything was possible and the party never needed to end.

Throughout it all, the noise, the screaming laughter, the music, Haze and I would look at each other and find quiet. That evening, when we spotted a bad man on the streets, with one squeeze of our hands, we knew what we would do.

We were watching the sunrise back in Cannes before his body was even discovered.

I made sure we behaved ourselves in London so we could really let loose on our European tours. That holiday feeling everyone gets when they're abroad, where the rules of real life don't apply, we always really took that to heart. Champagne before 12pm? A dead man by teatime? Anything went.

We used fake passports and an array of disguises to mix it up. A redhead and a brunette in Paris, two blonds in Saint-Tropez, two brunettes in Gstaad.

By the time our kills were hitting double figures, I took it a step further. We'd leave our cellphones at our apartment when we went away, taking only untraceable pay-as-you-go ones instead. I'd even download movies to our home Sky box to make it look as if we'd spent the weekend holed up together, having movie marathons.

Throughout, I kept detailed encrypted records. It was a risk, but I needed to remember what disguises we'd used in which location, what cellphones we'd used, the names we'd booked hotels under, the ways in which we'd made them die.

I did aim for us to use different kill methods within one country, to prevent our victims being linked together. But it was tricky. In the heat of the moment, it was difficult to keep on track. It was a failing that Interpol finally picked up on and they were hunting for a serial killer they named 'the Backpacking Butcher'. It didn't worry me. As long as they were looking for a budget-conscious solo man, a rich couple were safe. They presumed that to steal from victims, the killer must be poor, not thinking about how even people with money never feel like they have enough.

I kept an eye on all the relevant channels. I kept clearing my internet search history. I was constantly thinking of what I needed to do to make sure we were protected. I thought of everything so she didn't have to.

No matter how hard I planned, there was always the risk I'd overlook something. That there would be something I was unprepared for. A security guard deciding to change his nightly routine. A nosy neighbour jotting down a number-plate. People were everywhere. And people were unpredictable. How often had I stayed awake at night worrying that we could be foiled by something as random and simple as a man looking for somewhere quiet to take a piss on the stumble home from a club, a woman storming off into the night after a row with her boyfriend, a taxi driver taking a wrong turn . . . Strangers' lives, their decisions, their last-minute choices, could ruin everything for us. Things had got even harder with the dawn of influencers and selfies and everyone wanting everything recorded. How easy it would be for us to be captured on a recording at the wrong moment.

We'd never talked about it, but I knew neither of us could ever justify killing an innocent whose only crime was witnessing us in the act. If we were seen, that was it. It would all be over for us.

Every high, every joyous kill, came with dread that it could be our last.

I planned everything with military precision. It didn't just stop with the act itself, but the clear-up, the after-effects. Long afterwards, when Haze was post-bliss and passed out, I'd be out patrolling. Revisiting our steps. Looking for mistakes, looking for weaknesses. It was hard, relentless work, but it was all worth it whenever I saw how happy my wife was. She didn't need to say it, she didn't need to thank me, but I knew she couldn't do this without me.

26

Haze

Staring down at the dead man, I couldn't let myself get overwhelmed. I needed to focus on what I needed to do now. This was usually Fox's area. He'd have a detailed plan. Maybe even a checklist. I was still gripping my knife. It was covered in the man's blood. I leaned down and wiped it on his T-shirt. A bit of the fabric got entangled in the blade. I pulled at it and a tear formed. I gritted my teeth and disentangled the knife. A small rip of fabric came away with it. I tucked it into my leggings pocket.

My hands were bloody. I splashed them with water from my bottle, rubbing them together as best I could. I took out my phone and switched it to selfie mode. No blood on my face. I checked the rest of me. Blood-free. It was dark now. I wasn't worried about people on the way home spotting any – I was afraid my husband would.

I needed to move fast. I lugged over a few loose branches and manoeuvred them onto the body. I checked myself over one more time and crept to the edge of the path. There was no one in the park. I set off at a fast jog, pulling my baseball cap further down.

All the way home, I kept replaying everything that had happened. No one had seen me on the way there, had they? It had been quiet. The dog-walker and the teenage couple were far enough a way that I don't think they'd clocked me. I'd been so raging at Fox I may not have noticed anyone else.

I saw just one person on my run back home – a man with a mobile phone clamped to his ear. He didn't even look at me. A total of three cars passed me by. I kept my head down all the way until I got to my front door. I took a deep breath and let myself in quietly. My sheathed knife was tucked into the waistband of my leggings. I could feel it digging into my back.

I could hear Fox and Bibi in the kitchen. 'Let's go flyyyy a kite!' Fox was singing along to the Mary Poppins song on the radio, his voice out of tune. I could hear Bibi's squeals of laughter.

I took off my trainers at the door and held them as I tip-toed upstairs to our bedroom and headed straight into the ensuite. I stripped off as soon as the door was closed, leaving my trainers, clothes and running belt in a pile on the floor. I took my knife to the sink and unsheathed it. I covered it in antibacterial handwash and ran it under the hot tap. By the time I'd finished scrubbing it, there was not a spot of blood I could see – but what about DNA? Were there invisible traces still there?

I should throw the knife away.

That'd be the safest thing to do. But it was one of my favourites. I'd picked it up in a Moroccan market and it had this beautiful engraving on the handle. Now I understood why Fox always insisted we use standard kitchen knives. No sentimental meaning, an undistinguishable blade. Maybe the dishwasher? Would that be enough? I could google it – but then wouldn't it save a search to the Cloud that could later be used to incriminate me? Fuck. It was one thing killing someone and trying to hide it from the police, but quite another trying to hide it from my husband. He knew what to look for. And he knew me.

I looked up at my naked self in the mirror. There was a small smear of blood on my neck that I'd missed earlier. I hid the knife inside my empty water bottle and turned on the shower. Feeling the hot water rush over me felt so good that I had to keep reminding myself I was in a rush. I scrubbed at every part of me with the soap. I lathered up my hair and rinsed it twice.

Once I had changed into a soft cotton tracksuit, I picked up my pile of running clothes and trainers and dropped them into the laundry basket. I chucked the water bottle on top, ignoring the rattle of the knife inside. I just needed to get everything into the wash, and it'd be like it had never happened. Simple.

The utility room adjoined the kitchen. I could hear the radio still playing; it was now on to 'The Hills are Alive' from *The Sound of Music*. I walked in to see Fox bouncing Bibi round the room in his arms. They were half dancing, but mostly laughing. He saw me and put Bibi down.

He came right up to me. 'How was your run?'

'Good.' I tightened my grip on the laundry basket.

'I'm sorry.' He touched my shoulder.

I clenched my jaw and tried not to look down at the basket.

Was there a spot of blood on my clothes? The water bottle? Why hadn't I put everything at the bottom?

'We can talk later. I—'

'I'm telling you I'm sorry. I don't know what I was thinking.'

He was surrendering on the America idea already?

'I just got a little nostalgic. Thinking of everything back home. But that's my past. You, Bibi, England – that's my future. I would never do anything to jeopardise that.'

My mouth felt dry. He was staring at me, waiting for a reply. Julie Andrews was singing her heart out over the speakers.

I managed a 'Me too.'

He leaned down and gave me a kiss, the laundry basket pressing into us both.

'Dada! Dance!' Bibi shouted from the other side of the room.

He whirled over to her and lifted her back into his arms.

I walked quickly to the utility room and leaned back against the door as soon as it was closed. I put the laundry basket on the floor and piled all the clothes inside it into the washing machine, including my trainers. I picked up my running belt and removed my phone and AirPods case, before chucking the belt in too, along with a laundry capsule. I threw another three capsules in for good measure. The machine went on, and only when the water had filled the drum did I start to breathe normally again. I was clean. My belongings were about to be clean. It never happened. I was never there.

Except for the knife.

I stared at the water bottle on the countertop. Where could I hide it?

Above the washing machine were shelves housing a whole

array of items from old vases to a basket of odd socks and bulk-bought supplies of toilet roll. I climbed up onto the countertop and dropped the water bottle into a large, chipped vase we had never used. Until I worked out what to do with it, here was as good a place as any.

I had done all I could.

By the time we were in bed, I was feeling quietly confident it was going to be okay. I stared up at the ceiling and tried to calm my thoughts. The man had attacked me. It was self-defence. In my experience, men who attacked women never did it just once. If they had it in them, it didn't take much to set them off. He was a bad man who'd deserved to die. It was a righteous kill. Surely the knot in my stomach was only there because I was hiding it from Fox?

'You okay?' Fox turned over to me. 'You seem . . . wired?'

I pulled him towards me and kissed him hard. I needed to distract us both.

27

Fox

I was running late for my AA meeting. I was cycling fast on one of those London rental bikes that Haze enjoyed mocking. Her main objection to them was that she thought they were deeply uncool. I'd once tried to get her to use one so we could make it to the cinema in time for the start of a film, and she'd point-blank refused. She said she'd rather miss the movie than be seen on something so unsightly.

I hated fighting with Haze. Despite my apology last night, she'd still seemed out of sorts this morning. My parents had made an appearance in our lives for barely half an hour, and had still managed to cause trouble. Years of ambivalence, and suddenly they cared enough to turn up here? I paused. Of course, they didn't come all the way here just to see me. If I looked hard enough, I'd find some high-society event, some big-ticket reason. I was just a small detour while they were already here. Julian, for the first time in his life, had let them down. They were big Republican, big Godly squad, big deals. Divorce was frowned upon, both as a breaking of what the Lord had brought together, and due to the underlying belief that you were less of a man for failing to keep your little woman in line. I wondered what had pushed sweet gentle Martha into making the split official and not just toeing the expected line of turning a blind eye and leading separate lives. It must've been something pretty huge for the vacant blonde I'd thought was more mouse than woman to have the balls to stand up to my family.

It wasn't just that Julian had let them down, but also that I hadn't. They clearly thought that whatever darkness had been in me, I had grown out of it. The fact I was here, married with a child, no conviction, not even a police interview besmirching my record, must mean I'd stopped. They had such little faith in my ability that they didn't consider I might just have got better at getting away with it. Always underestimated.

'You're still desperate for their approval.'

Haze's words stung because I knew she was right. I didn't like my parents, I didn't understand them, but I still wanted them to value me. No matter how terrible they were, I wanted their approval. Was that something ingrained in us all?

Everything they'd done wrong, I would do right for Bibi. I would find my own brand-new way of messing her up. Of course, there was always the worry that this dark side that Haze and I both had, might be something Bibi inherited. But then, who better to guide her than us? We knew the signs to look out for, and we could teach her how to suppress it. We had been doing admirably at holding ourselves back from our true calling, our true selves. Weren't we proof that your dark side didn't control you, but you controlled it?

I arrived at the meeting just in time for the end of Griff's welcome. There were only five of us today. Griff, Pam and two twenty-somethings I'd never seen before. I gave Griff a thumbs-up as I sat down.

'And a welcome to Nathaniel, who I'm proud to say has been sober for over three years now.' Griff raised his eyebrows at me. I nodded back in response. 'And he is going to speak.'

I stood up. 'Hi all, I'm Nathaniel and I'm an alcoholic.' I'd said this enough times now, I nearly believed it myself. 'As Griff said, I've been sober a while now. I stopped doing something I loved for the sake of my daughter. Some days are tougher than others.' I paused. 'My parents visited me a couple of days ago. I hadn't seen them in many years, and it was, as you folk' – I nodded towards the twenty-somethings – 'would say . . . triggering'. They both looked back at me solemnly. 'I remembered how a lot of who I became was down to how they treated me. I can see now that . . . drinking . . . was what I'd do to feel powerful. To remind me that I was the one in control of my life, not them.'

Griff started clapping. 'Man, this is a great breakthrough, Nathaniel. I'm proud of you.'

'Thank you, Griff. That means a lot.' I sat back down in my chair. 'They might be horrified by how much I like to drink, but really, it's their fault I do.'

Griff nodded. 'A great deal of us with drinking problems can link it back to childhood abuse, and—'

I held a hand up. 'Sorry, no – that's not really it. They didn't actually touch me. I didn't mean it was difficult in that sense.'

'Oh right, I see. It was a difficult childhood in that you worried about having enough to eat, ending up on the street, how—'

'No, nope. I was meaning more in terms of ridiculously high expectations, a crushing pressure to get into an Ivy League school, being forced to learn ballroom dancing. You know, stuff like that . . .' I drifted off.

Griff opened his mouth and then shut it again. 'All our experiences are valid.'

It was the way he said this – through slightly gritted teeth – that made me wonder if this really was the safe space it was meant to be. I knew on the surface it sounded like I'd had a very privileged childhood, but did I not get sympathy or understanding just because I was crying myself to sleep on 800 thread-count Egyptian cotton? Why even be a fake alcoholic if I couldn't speak my slightly altered truth and be embraced as a survivor?

I knew that nothing I'd been through could compare to what Haze had suffered. But that was why I came here. I couldn't share with her some of my deepest traumas. How can 'Mama never hugged me' compare to 'Foster fucker number three was the worst, as he used cigarettes, and they scarred much worse than foster fucker number two's knife cuts'? I was the big, safe, good man for her so she could let herself be vulnerable with me. I had to be strong and infallible enough for the both of us. But where did I get to be the damaged goods who needed a sympathetic shoulder?

I looked down at my phone just as I was leaving. A missed call from Petra. Every marriage had its secrets. I thought of Haze. My beautiful, complicated wife. If I was keeping things from her for her own good, then that didn't make me a bad husband. Just because we were married didn't mean we had to know everything about each other.

28

Haze

Five days.

It took five days for the body to be found. And even then, it was a smaller announcement than I'd thought it'd be.

I was having breakfast with Bibi and Fox, and trying to keep my breathing even as I flicked through *The Times*. Fox insisted on having it delivered every day, along with glass bottles of milk. When he signed up for the suburbs, he really signed up.

It was an article on the second page: '*Murder victim found on Cobham Common.*' An understated headline for what, by my own experienced eye, was a violent killing. Where was the horror of a murdered white man in a good neighbourhood? I read every word twice. '*The victim had recently been released from prison and was residing at a halfway house outside Slough. Police are currently trying to contact his next of kin . . .*' I'd killed an ex-con. I felt a weight lift from my shoulders. My instincts had been right – clearly trying to hurt me wasn't his first offence.

'Do you want any porridge?'

I realised Fox was talking to me. 'Huh?'

'Porridge?' He motioned to Bibi, who was shovelling hers down with an admirable focus.

'No, thanks.' I stretched and went back to the article as nonchalantly as I could.

'*. . . record of a previous altercation between him and a homeless man over a tent the victim had erected in Cobham Common . . . Looking for witnesses . . .*'

I let out a breath, then looked up at Fox. He was staring at me. 'You okay?'

'Yeah, just really tired today for some reason.' I gave a big yawn and turned the page. I'd have to wait until he'd gone to re-read it properly.

'Mama, look!' Bibi showed me her empty bowl.

'Clever girl.'

It looked like I had got lucky.

I'd managed to kill someone who no one was going to get up in arms about. The way the article was written implied an ex-con had gotten into a turf war with a homeless man. This could wallow in 'unsolved' for years. There'd be no one marching in the streets demanding that the police hurry up and find the killer. A murder so close to home might be deeply unsavoury for the local well-heeled residents, but there would be no pearl-clasping, no '*It could've been me.*'

I could . . . I could actually get away with this. I might have escaped police attention, but what about my husband's?

I looked up at him. He was drinking a coffee as he tapped away on his mobile. The newspaper had been laid out on the table by the time I came downstairs. He must've already read it. Did he glance over the article without a second thought, or were alarm bells now ringing?

For the last week, Fox had been nothing but kind and attentive. Clearly he was still feeling guilty after his parents' meddling. He was always very good at admitting when he was wrong. Just holding a hand up, apologising and moving on. I was more of a grudge-holder. But if he had any inkling that the dead man in the bushes was down to me, surely he'd have confronted me? At the very least, he wouldn't be being so nice. Or was it all an act? Was he planning on whisking Bibi away to America when I least expected it as punishment for me breaking our pact?

Fox stood up. 'Right, my girls. I need to go.' He drained his coffee mug, then leaned down and kissed Bibi's head before leaning over the table to kiss me. It seemed like a normal kiss, not a secretly seething, angry kiss.

'You back for dinner?'

'Of course.' He smiled and picked up his coat and bag from the chair near the door. 'Be good!' he said as he left the kitchen.

I tried to remember if he always said that.

As soon as I'd dropped Bibi at nursery, I read and re-read the newspaper article in the car. I had near memorised every word. Then I went into a Sainsbury's and flicked through every newspaper there. I had got so paranoid about Fox's constant lecturing about a digital footprint that I did not dare search for anything about it on my phone. I learned nothing new from the four different papers I skimmed – the police were seemingly working on the assumption that the victim setting up a tent in Cobham Common a couple of weeks ago had upset a local homeless man, leading to an altercation. The police were interested in finding this man but there was no real description of him, so members of the public wouldn't be able to help locate him – and I highly doubted he was likely to come forward.

Could I really start to relax?

I'd put the knife through the dishwasher three times and then I'd buried it, still inside the water bottle, in a deep hole at the back of our garden. I'd marked it with a large rock. I didn't know at what point I'd feel safe enough to have it back in the house, but I was glad I hadn't thrown it away. Call it speaking too soon, but it did feel like the worst was over.

When I got back home, I started painting. And it went well. Really well. It was hard not to believe that death inspired me when now, finally, after years of aborted attempts, I had started something I believed in. I'd forgotten how much I loved it; being so immersed in what I was doing that nothing else came in, no other noise. Just me and this canvas and the paints I held.

Everything went by in a blur. When my alarm went off reminding me to go and pick up Bibi, I left the house in a daze. Only when checking myself in the rear-view mirror on the way there did I realise I'd got paint along my cheek.

I gave Bibi a quick lunch and put her down for a nap, then got back to it. I loved this. I didn't want to be anywhere else.

When my alarm went off again, reminding me to wake up Bibi, I chewed on my lip. I was meant to be meeting Jenny so the kids could try out Tiny Gym – it had opened last month to great neighbourhood fanfare. I wasn't sure exactly what a session there involved, but I really hoped there were mini running machines and mini dumbbells. I leaned back and stared at my canvas. I hated leaving when I was in full flow. But I had Bibi to think of. I couldn't just lock myself away and stick her in front of a three-hour *Peppa Pig* marathon, no matter how tempting it was. I took a deep breath and put down my paintbrush.

Bibi woke happy, and bounced around so excited to go that she didn't do anything she needed to get ready.

'Wee! Shoes! Clothes!'

I was barking orders at her, to no effect. We were running late now. I rushed around the house, locating my wallet and my AirPods. I stuffed them into my handbag. I'd call Jenny from the car to let her know we were going to miss the fun-filled introduction.

'Shoes, Bibi!' I shouted up the stairs again. 'Bibi! Now!'

Bibi finally came down the stairs, brandishing her shoes. She was dressed as Elsa from *Frozen*.

'It's a Tiny Gym session, sweetness. So maybe something a little less flouncy?'

She stared me down with her arms folded.

'Okay, don't worry, let's just get out of here.' She sat down on the stairs as I pulled her trainers on her. 'Right, let's go!'

As I opened the door to the garage, I flicked open my AirPods case.

The right one was missing.

My heart skipped a beat. What the fuck? I had definitely used them since the dead man – right? I thought back over the last few days. I only really used them for talking in the car – which I hadn't done recently – and going on a run . . . That was it. Killing that man really had been the last time I'd worn them. I must've checked? Surely, I must've checked. I tried to think back. He'd attacked me while I still had them in. I'd stabbed him and then . . . Didn't I put them straight back in their case? Or did I just run off with them still in?

Did one fall out when we were fighting? Or did it fall out on the run back? The man I saw on his phone – did I hear him talking or just see him? I closed my eyes and tried to picture running past him. I definitely didn't hear anything he was saying. But that didn't mean I still had my AirPods in – it could've been because I went by him so fast, or the adrenaline was making my ears buzz, or because I had just fucking killed a man I had a lot on my mind and wasn't paying attention. I had no idea.

Was a lone AirPod currently sitting in an evidence bag at a Berkshire police station? Did earwax have DNA? I could google— fuck, no, I couldn't google it.

Everyone lost AirPods. Wasn't that their whole business model? Make them so small that people would lose them anywhere and have to buy new ones? I was just a yummy mummy worried about her weight, going for a run, and I'd lost one. Yes, if it was found by a dead body that would look bad, but what would my motivation be? It didn't matter. The moment the police turned up here asking questions, Fox would know. They might not have enough to ever prove it was me, to lock me up and throw away the key, but he would know. And my life would be over in a different kind of way.

Bibi climbed into the car and I strapped her in. I got into the driver's seat and took a deep breath. I reached for my phone and typed out a message which contained a series of expletives and frustration over how I'd potentially ruined everything thanks to my lack of both self-control and attention to detail. I hit send and started the engine. I tried not to think about how texting a dead man about a different dead man was a pretty pitiful state of affairs. Sending Matty rants and life updates was a habit I couldn't seem to break. Especially in the last year. The more I confided in him, the more I realised how far apart Fox and I had grown. I looked down at my AirPods case. And things could be about to get even worse.

29

Haze

Jenny was acting weird. She had a stinking cold and sounded like she was talking through a blocked nose. But she was more hyper than usual. Bouncing up and down, jiggling Felix around on the huge plastic mat. She kept leaning towards me like she was about to say something, then stopping herself. It could've been my grimace at being so close to her germs.

Tiny Gym was hot and unpleasant. My bare legs kept sticking to the matting. Bibi had shed her *Frozen* dress within five minutes of arriving and was now undertaking the session in her vest and pants. It must be nice to have no judgement over what you were wearing. I mean no judgement for the individual; clearly, *I* was being judged. One mother kept looking at Bibi and then me with a wrinkled nose.

I was sitting cross-legged and trying to focus on forgetting about the missing AirPod. *It's fine. It's all fine*, I kept repeating to myself. I stared at my happy child as she balanced on a beam and jumped off, cackling to herself as she rolled over. Sadly, there were no mini running machines or dumbbells – just a lot of matting and the encouragement to fling themselves around.

If Fox somehow found out about the dead man, I'd have to deal with it. Brace for the fallout. Marriages had their ups and downs. It was normal. I mean really, who hadn't got angry at their husband and stormed off in a rage and done something they shouldn't have? There were undoubtedly many women before me who'd done the same, except perhaps instead of killing a man, they'd just fucked one. And really, when you looked at it, which was the bigger betrayal? Wedding vows contained no mention of promising to never kill a man, but definitely something about not having sex with one. Just in more flowery language. Something about forsaking?

I smiled at little Bibi, who was now spinning herself round and round. It was going to be okay.

'Did you hear about the man who got killed on Cobham Common?' Jenny burst out with it the second the kids were ensconced in the soft-play area of Tiny Gym's expansive café.

My heart nearly stopped beating.

I was stupid to think it wouldn't register on the local mum radar. Of course it would. A murder in a nice neighbourhood was always going to spark interest.

'I . . . I think I read something about it, yes.' I looked at her face. She was buzzing with excitement – and something else. Why? Was she one of those true-crime obsessives, happy to have a neighbourhood murder to get her amateur teeth stuck into? 'Aren't the police saying it happened during a fight?'

'The victim was an ex-con and there was one report of him having a fight with a homeless man. Police seem to believe he was the one that came back and killed him. But—' Jenny sneezed. She pulled out a skanky-looking handkerchief from her sleeve and wiped her nose. 'I don't think that's what happened.'

I motioned for the waitress. Before she was even halfway over to us, I shouted over our order: 'One cappuccino, one mocha.' She gave me a thumbs-up.

'You a bit of an armchair detective, then?'

Jenny smiled. 'No. More of a real one.'

My ears started ringing. Everything seemed to be happening in slow motion. 'What?'

I stared at Jenny as her lips started moving. 'It's like I told you, I've been on maternity leave for the last couple of years. So I guess I'm still a detective, just an out-of-work one.'

I nodded and tried to think. Jenny. Her job. What had she said about it before? I would've remembered the police bit, wouldn't I? She'd never said police. She'd just complained about the flasher ex who'd ruined it all for her. A flasher. A flasher who worked for the police. Things started to click into place.

I leaned forward. 'Your ex is that police officer who made the news? The one that everyone made memes about?' I remembered all the lurid headlines. 'Officer Flash! Isn't that what they called him?'

Jenny looked down at the table. 'Sorry. I know I should've told you the full story, but I was so embarrassed. It got a lot of press coverage, and I thought you'd be so disgusted with me that you wouldn't want to be friends.'

The waitress put our coffees down on the table. I stared at the steam rising from my mug.

How the hell had it not clicked for me sooner? I recalled the grainy CCTV footage that someone had leaked. 'Wasn't he, like, swinging it at her?'

Jenny picked up her mug. 'His penis is very small, so he probably had to wave it around to make sure she could really see it.'

I winced. 'You should've told me it was him. I would've said to ask for double the money for all the humiliation. What a total shit.'

'Talking of bad guys.' Jenny put her mug down on the table. She cleared her throat. 'I don't think this Cobham Common victim was killed by a random homeless man. I think it's the work of a serial killer.'

I attempted a laugh. 'Jen, we live in a nice neighbourhood. I know it's a shock when someone gets murdered, but there have been no other killings around here.'

She leaned forward. Her eyes were focused. 'The other victims weren't from around here. They were from all over the place.' She took a deep breath. 'Have you heard of the Backpacking Butcher?'

The ringing in my ears got louder. I looked around the room. I tried to find Bibi and locked on to her jumping up and down on the corner trampoline. Bibi. Oh God. What had I done? This couldn't be happening. Focus, Haze. Focus. I could hear Fox's voice in my ear. I needed to talk. I needed to say something. Anything.

'That's a funny name!' I took a large gulp of coffee and burned my tongue.

'A few years ago, he was getting a few headlines. Killing men around Europe, using similar kill methods.'

I tried to keep my breathing normal. 'I think I remember reading something about that.'

'Do you remember the locations where the victims were found?'

I looked off into the distance. 'No . . . nothing ringing any bells.'

Jenny took a deep breath and looked me straight in the

eyes. 'One of his victims was knifed to death in San Gimignano. Police found evidence at the scene that the killer had attended the Francesco Argento exhibition.'

I attempted a look of surprise. 'The one we were at! How terrifying.' I tried to think back. Had we been careless, dropped a ticket or something else that could link us to that exhibition?

'You previously mentioned Saint-Tropez and Lake Como as places you'd been to during your travels. I'm betting Gstaad, Paris, Mykonos, and Corsica might all be places you went to, too?'

I tried to ignore my creeping heart rate. 'I'm not so sure. I guess maybe.' What the hell was this? Was she interrogating me? Was it better to deny it and risk being caught in a lie? She was police! She could check! What passports did we use for those locations? Damn it, where were Fox and his spreadsheet when I finally needed them?

'Mobile phone records at the locations where his victims were found all show a UK mobile being in the vicinity at their time of death.'

What. The. Fuck.

I shrugged. 'I'm not surprised. You'll find Brits in every European country. The challenge is being somewhere there isn't one!' This was all a bad dream. This couldn't be happening.

'The man on Cobham Common. The way he was killed. Stabbed repeatedly with a knife. I'm waiting for a contact to get back to me, but I'm betting it will show similar stab patterns to those used by the Butcher.'

Fuck. Fuck. Fuck. She was right. I always got carried away and stabbed to a pretty distinct pattern. Why hadn't I sliced him up or done something weird? Fox would've done. If Fox had done something as dumb as killing on his own doorstep, he would've made sure the body looked nothing like any of our previous kills.

God, I'd become so reliant on my man that I couldn't do anything right by myself.

'Oh, I don't think we have anything so exciting as a serial killer around here!' I motioned around the neon plastic seating of the café. At the table next door, a three-year-old was howling over wanting a third blueberry muffin. 'This is a nice neighbourhood. And didn't that killer stop years ago? Why would he go from all those glamorous places in Europe to Berkshire suburbia?' I chuckled to myself.

Jenny reached over the table and gripped my hands. 'I couldn't sleep last night. It's hard breathing' – she motioned to her blocked nose – 'so I was up thinking about it all.' She took a deep breath. 'I really believe the Backpacking Butcher is back. And I don't know how to tell you this, but I think you might be married to him.'

30

Haze

'Jenny, you are just hilarious!' I laughed and laughed to the point where the noise shut up the tantrumming boy at the next-door table.

Jenny sat watching me for a moment. 'I know it's a shock. I know it sounds insane, but I—'

'Okay, Jen. Right, let's have a think about all this. I know things have been tough for you and that you've got a lot of time on your hands, but really, thinking my husband – the gentlest, sweetest man imaginable – could be involved in murder just because the killer went to the same exhibition as us? And that victims may have turned up in some of the holiday destinations we went to? You must realise you sound crazy.'

Jenny shrugged. 'I know it's a lot. But don't you think it's just too much of a coincidence? Francesco Argento has this one exhibition in this Tuscan town, which only eighty people went to? And then other victims turn up in places you travelled to in the same time period? And then the killer just happens to stop, just when you get pregnant?'

I shook my head. 'Jen, when I got pregnant, we were still in the midst of a global pandemic. There were all kinds of travel restrictions that might stop a Backpacking Butcher from actually backpacking?'

'Shit. I had kind of forgotten all that.' Jenny pinched her nose.

'Look, I get the exhibition thing is weird. But then who's to say for sure that the killer was even there? They might have planted a ticket stub or whatever it was linking them to the exhibition. Or maybe the victim himself went to it? It was the biggest event on in San Gimignano that week – all the tourists went there!'

'But what about the other locations? Lake Como and Saint-Tropez are also places where victims were killed by him!'

'All the places you've mentioned are the most popular destinations in Europe. I'm sure if you did a poll, hundreds if not thousands of people would've gone to those very same places in that time frame.'

'Surely not? It's such a long list!'

'In our circles' – I motioned towards my general hotness – 'it's really very normal.' I patted her hand. 'There's the ski season, when anyone who's anyone will hit Gstaad or Verbier . . . and Paris is so close, it barely counts as being away, so that's a standard go-to for a pick-me-up weekend. And Saint-Tropez, Corsica, Mykonos – they're where our crowd tends to hang out in the summer, usually on a yacht, chasing the best parties.'

Jenny was staring down at her coffee. 'But who can really go away that much? What about holiday allowance?'

'Oh, Jen. Think about it. We're talking about people so rich they don't have nine-to-five jobs. They have their own billion-dollar companies or never-ending trust funds. The world is your playground if you have enough cash.'

Jenny was chewing on her lip. 'So you're saying the Butcher could be a rich guy.' She looked up at me. 'Like your husband.'

Shit.

'If Interpol or whoever else in power is investigating and gave him the name the Backpacking Butcher, they clearly have evidence he isn't a rich guy.'

Jenny stared at me for a beat and then let her head drop onto the table. There was a muffled, 'I'm sorry.'

I'd brought her back from the brink. Now to go in for the kill.

'You've got nothing linking this dead Berkshire victim to the Butcher other than the fact he was stabbed? Have you seen any proof or any other similarities?'

Jenny's head swung up. 'My contacts on the force aren't exactly on good terms with me. I've left messages, but no one's calling me back.'

'So all this is you. You alone?'

'When everything with Bill kicked off, I was put on leave. Before they could even tell me whether I'd be allowed back, I found out I was pregnant, so it just turned into maternity leave. I had a lot of time to myself and one day, I watched this TV show on the Backpacking Butcher. I knew that Interpol had been in touch with UK forces because of the whole theory that the killer had a British mobile.' Jen chewed on her thumbnail. 'I don't know. It kind of sparked something in me. I became really into finding out everything I could about him. I was one of the force's top detectives. And now everyone hated me. I thought if I could unmask this Butcher, it'd be a return to glory.'

I could picture it all too easily. Pregnant, slumped on a sofa, watching too much TV. I had been there myself. But while I was watching true-crime shows because I was missing being out there killing, she was missing being out there *solving*. Clearly, seeing the Backpacking Butcher programme had reminded her she wasn't just an armchair detective, but a real one – who needed a maternity leave project.

'You keep talking about how desperate you are to get back to work.' I remembered she'd mentioned her office calling her in for a meeting to discuss her coming back. 'But don't you see, if you go to them with this hare-brained theory, that could delay your return even further?'

'Only if I'm wrong!' Jenny was wringing her hands together. 'I've got copies of all the case notes, of the autopsy descriptions. If I could just see the state of the Cobham Common body, I'd know for sure!'

I was now picturing one of those proper conspiracy walls of crazy in a disused room in Jenny's parents' house.

'As your friend, I need to say this . . . Drop it. You want to get back to work, but do you realise how stacked the odds against you are? You think anyone is desperate to have a single mother working for them? Especially one who backed up her creepy flasher boyfriend?'

'You really think they don't want me back? I've already done my time out for lying for Bill. That must count for something? And I had the best case-solved ratio of any detective there!'

I internally gulped at this information. 'You know that saying: a woman has to be twice as good as a man just to be treated the same.' I wasn't totally sure I hadn't just made that up.

Jenny frowned. 'Is that really a saying? Twice as good at everything? How are we meant to—'

'I'm saying it's going to be hard enough as it is. You're going to have to be there proving yourself, proving that you're not going to rush home every time Felix has a sniffle, proving that you can be trusted to believe women, and not provide false alibis for sex-offenders. It's a lot, Jen. It's a lot. And none of it will be helped if you swoop in there ranting about a case you actually have no official right to investigate.'

Jenny leaned back in her chair. 'You're right. I just— I just need a good night's sleep.'

'Yes, definitely.' I took a sip of coffee. 'And when was the last time someone checked your meds?'

31

Fox

Smithfield Market was busy. I passed through the crowds with my head down. Leaving work in the middle of the afternoon was something I tried not to do too often but I needed this. Club Astaga had a small unmarked door. I rang the bell. There was a crackle of the intercom, and I was buzzed in. Within minutes, after two separate swipes of my private member's card, I was in Astaga's hidden back room with a tray of £50,000 worth of casino chips in front of me.

This was a high-stakes poker game – the type where the organisers didn't just need to know who you were, but also needed to have proof of address, funds and assets.

Poker had always been a hobby of mine. In the last few years, it was something I had become increasingly reliant on. Stopping our little killing enterprise had left me missing the adrenaline high I'd grown so used to. It had also dented my pay packet. High-stakes poker helped fulfill both these shortages. The size of the figures on the table made it a good opportunity to replenish depleted funds. I got a buzz out of it: not only from gambling with such big numbers, but also from the chance of potentially getting my head kicked in. I might have had the occasional bad night, but I did seem to have a natural skill at poker – I found it just as easy to hide a good hand as I did a dark side.

The poker table took up nearly the whole room. A low-hanging light shone above it. Round the table, four players were already seated along with Az, the dealer, who was wearing a nifty red bow tie. He gave me a small nod. I'd never heard him say more than a few words. A small bar was set up in the corner, staffed by a short woman in a black dress. The walls were wood panelled. It gave the room a more refined feel and hid an exit, as well as a door to a security office. Rumour had it they were very efficient at swiftly ending any unfolding dispute.

'Oh, lookie look, it's Captain America.' Robbie Whitmell was a hard-faced East End gangster with white-blond hair. He may have been unoriginal with his nicknames for us all, but he was fairly original with his poker playing. He was hard to predict and dangerous to cross – he had a hot temper and the henchmen to follow through. 'Come to claw back some cash?'

My last night here had not ended well.

'Evening all.' I looked round the table. I had done background checks on each of them previously. Getting to know your poker opponents was just as important as getting to know potential victims. Research was key when it came to finding weaknesses and avenues for attack.

Tonight there was Dan McCartney, an Irish man who was curt, to the point and not a big risk-taker. Next to him was Tessie Pritchard, a glamorous woman in her late sixties. I'd only played her a few times, but I knew by now that she over-played the old lady card and tried to get us to underestimate her. She was a shark. The final player was Shizu, looking stylish in a black turtleneck and oversized blazer. Shizu was Japanese, and all my research had turned up was that they had more money than they knew what to do with. A difficult opponent was one who really didn't care about losing.

'Just sit down and let's get on with it,' sniped McCartney.

Az started dealing as I motioned to the waitress for a whisky. I only ever had one, and I drank it slowly. Enough to take the edge off, not enough to make my head remotely fuzzy.

Within six hours of starting the game, both McCartney and Shizu had busted out. Tess, who was down to her last £10,000, was hanging on by a thread. I looked down at my stack, which, thanks to Shizu's courageous attempt an hour earlier to bluff me at exactly the wrong time, now totalled chips amounting to £130,000. Robbie was just behind me on £120,000.

With one look at his newly dealt cards Robbie made his play. 'I raise five grand.'

Tess looked between the two of us, chewing her lip. 'Fuck! Fuck this. Fucking fuck.' She threw her cards down. She only ever dropped the sweet granny act when she was down and out.

'It's just you and me, America.' Robbie eyed me over his hand. A small grin was forming. A simple tell he was convinced he was on to a winner.

Everything in the room seemed to go quiet. Time seemed to speed up and then stand still. It was a back and forth of raising and re-raising until . . . The final card. This was it. What it all came down to.

'I'm all in,' said Robbie.

There was now £240,000 up for grabs. Robbie and I stared at each other. He was chewing the inside of his cheek.

'I call,' I said, pushing my stack towards the centre.

'Gentlemen,' said Az, looking between us, 'let's turn them over.'

Robbie went first, turning over the ace and king of spades. The nut flush. He put his arms behind his head as he grinned at me.

'Very nice, Robbie. Very nice.'

I turned over my ten of clubs first. And then my ten of hearts. Full House.

Robbie's grin disappeared. He jumped up and pounded his fist against the wall. 'Fuck!' He shook his hand. He had forgotten that behind the panelling was a concrete wall. 'I know you, America! There's no way you had that hand from the start!' He came towards me. 'You hiding cards in that stupid suit?' He swung to Az. 'Why the fuck aren't you searching everyone as they come in?'

'Don't embarrass yourself.' I stayed seated. 'Take the loss like a gentleman.'

The security door opened and a man who must've been nearing six foot seven entered and gave Whitmell a hard stare. 'Do we have a problem here, sir?'

There was silence as Robbie observed me. 'No problem.' He stood up and swiped his card at the exit door before storming out.

I looked up at the security man. 'I'd like to cash out, please.'

Coming out of the depths of Club Astaga and back into Smithfield Market I scanned the street ahead of me for

Whitmell and his men. No sign of them among the people still strolling the streets and sitting outside drinking.

I checked my watch. Only 10.13pm and I was buzzing from my win. I looked around at the bright lights of the bars and restaurants. Warm weather made Londoners forget about work the next day. So many of our old haunts were a short walk away.

But that wasn't my life anymore.

I needed to get home. I tapped into my phone and ordered an Uber.

'Cabot?' I turned to see Suzanne standing there. She walked towards me. 'Where are you off to?'

I took in her clinging pencil skirt and white shirt. Her top button was undone flashing a glimpse of her red lace bra.

'Home,' I managed to get out.

'I just finished at a client dinner. I'm in the mood for celebrating. Come for a drink?' She started playing with her gold necklace. The oval pendant kept dipping in and out of the swell of her cleavage.

My phone beeped. *Your Uber is arriving.* Saved by a Toyota Prius.

'My Uber's here.' I looked around and waved at the driver parking up just opposite us.

'Cancel it.'

'Don't want to ruin my 4.96 star rating.'

Suzanne held eye contact. 'Let's make plans for another night then. Team bonding is very important, apparently.'

I smiled. 'You're not on my team.'

She smiled back. 'Inter-team bonding, then.'

I tilted my head. 'You know, I keep thinking how you look familiar. Are you sure we never met before? Back home?'

Suzanne flicked her hair. 'I would've remembered you, Cabot. You're just wishing you met me earlier as we could've had a lot more fun than we're having now.'

She spun on her heel and walked off before I could reply. Judging by the way her hips were swaying, she was expecting me to be watching.

I hadn't clocked it before, perhaps too distracted by her very obvious charms – but I was now positive I knew her from somewhere. Maybe I should take her up on her request for a night out. Get her to drink a little and see if she slipped up. It was important for my family's safety to investigate people in our orbit who might be hiding something. I had to be thorough.

32

Haze

I had managed to befriend a police officer.

Of all the fellow parents in a toddler group, I had managed to befriend the one who was a police officer. What did that say about me? That I was instinctively drawn to danger? To damaged women? And she was both.

I'd thought I had all the power in this friendship. How naïve I'd been.

I had to fix this. This was my mess. It was down to me to save us.

I'd spent the last month building up Jenny's confidence and making her feel better about herself, and now I was going to tear her to pieces.

I needed to make Jenny think she was crazy.

That was all I had to do to save my family. It wouldn't be too much of a push, surely? She had confided in me how she was already on an array of different medications from her shrink. She had form. I just needed to push her over the line.

No one at her office trusted her. She was single. She lived with her parents. They might believe everything she had to say, but then they were her parents. Hardly unbiased observers. She seemingly hadn't seen anyone recently apart from me and this French guy who liked eating. But then, she surely wouldn't confide in him about her crazy theory about a serial killer. Not if she was trying to get laid. Although Jenny's ideas of what made for appropriate date chat might be slightly different to everyone else's.

I could handle this.

I had lost control and now it could ruin everything. Images came to me in a flash. The police at our door. Taking me away as Bibi screamed. I felt sick.

You don't realise what you've got until it's gone. In that moment, being bored, unfulfilled and feeling like my marriage had gone to shit suddenly seemed like a dream. It only took the thought of facing a life in prison and Bibi growing up in foster care to make me see the light.

Fox was no longer my jailor, the one who'd ruined everything. He was the one who'd tried to protect me. I saw it all now. Too late.

I wanted to go back to 'one week ago' me and slap her around the face.

But it was going to be fine. Jenny had confronted me and crumbled at the slightest questioning of her theory. I just needed to keep on at her, make her realise how ludicrous it all sounded. And to do that, I needed to be around her as much as possible.

The next morning, I rang Jenny. I never rang Jenny. The most she usually got from me were a few text emojis in response to something she'd suggested.

'Haze? Everything okay?'

'Hi Jen!' I had to tone it down. Too perky. 'Just calling to see if you're around today. Park trip?'

'I think so. Yes, that'd be lovely.' There was a pause as she blew her nose. 'Is there anything else? You don't usually call.'

'I just wanted to check up on you. You kind of freaked me out yesterday.'

'I'm sorry. I don't know what came over me. Must be all this flu medication. Some drug-induced haze made me think I was seeing things clearly, but really it was probably just the pills.'

'I mean, yeah. You did accuse my husband, whom you've never even met, of being a serial killer.' I gave a strangled chuckle.

'I am sorry.' She half laughed, but it quickly turned into a cough.

'You can buy the coffees today.'

I watched Fox eating his breakfast as he read the newspaper. He was completely oblivious, with no idea how close we were to being ruined. And it was all my fault.

I'd thought I would feel better. That killing a bad man would help release all the pent-up frustration I'd been dealing with for the last couple of years. But all those good feelings, all that joyous buzz of ending someone, had been ruined by the fear that I'd also potentially killed my marriage. If Fox found out, that would be the end of us. I'd broken our deal, and I'd broken his trust. And even worse than that, I'd put Bibi at risk. Thanks to my double whammy of killing a man in our neighbourhood and befriending a fucking detective, we were the closest we'd ever come to being unmasked.

Fox looked up at me. 'All okay?'

I bristled. 'Your parents have definitely left the country?'

He turned a page of the newspaper. 'Safely back in the good old U S of A.'

'Then yes, everything is okay. I'm just bracing myself for a morning in the park.'

'Park! Park! Felicks!' Bibi bounced up and down in her highchair.

'Aha, with your friend Jenny?'

'She's not my friend,' I said quickly.

Fox frowned at me.

'I mean . . . I guess she is. It's not like we put a label on it.'

Fox laughed. 'I forgot how rubbish you are at understanding how friendships work.' He put the paper down. 'You don't need to announce that you're friends. You keep in touch, you meet up, you tell each other things.'

'I don't tell her anything!' I got up from the table.

'Of course you don't. But she probably confides in you?'

I took Bibi's empty porridge bowl from her. 'Yes, she has a horrible ex. So we talk about that. I'm making sure she chases him down for the money he owes her.'

'See?' said Fox. 'You're a good friend.'

I bit my lip as I washed up Bibi's bowl.

The park was blissfully quiet. I had forgotten how much nicer everything was when there were fewer people around. Less jostling. Less queuing. We watched Felix and Bibi taking it in turns on the slide.

'How's it going with Bill?' Talking to Fox had reminded me that the psycho ex could be a useful player in all this. He sounded like the type of beast that if you poked him, chaos would ensue. And that's what I needed. 'Any positive sign you'll manage to get money out of him?'

'My lawyer has sent him a letter officially informing him we're pursuing him for the money he owes me.' Jenny scrabbled in her bag and handed me a piece of paper. It was a copy of the letter that had been sent to Bill. I skim-read it and memorised his address at the top.

'She said we had a particularly strong legal case, especially with the loan I gave him for the flat's rent.'

'You've heard from him since he received it?'

'Three abusive voicemails. Which I've saved.'

'You'd think as an ex-copper he'd try not to leave evidence.'

Bill was the lowest of the low. A creep masquerading as someone there to help, to protect and serve. He was protecting no one and only serving himself. A police badge never magically made a bad man good – it made him worse. He'd use it to help him do more, get away with more.

Jenny shrugged. 'When his anger takes over he can't think straight.' She looked down at her coffee. 'I know I need to do this, but hearing his voice again – it brings it all back.'

'I know it's tough, but it's the right thing to do.'

Jenny attempted a smile. 'We're all going away this weekend, so at least a change of scene might help.'

'Where are you off to?'

'Bedfordshire, to see my aunt. She lives alone, so we presume she likes us visiting, although she always does all she can to make us feel unwelcome – she's already complaining about Felix's hamster.'

I thought about how their house would be empty all

weekend. 'I can help with the hamster. Why don't you leave him, and I can go in and feed him? All that stuff.'

Jenny frowned. 'I couldn't ask you to do that. It's a real pain.'

'No, it'd be great. We're considering getting one for Bibi,' I lied. 'Good to see what kind of upkeep it involves.' Hamsters were domestic rats. They creeped me out.

'Are you sure?' Jenny leaned forward. 'It really would be a big help. His cage takes up half the boot and my mother has always been incapable of packing light.'

'Absolutely.' I nodded. 'Just leave me a key, the alarm code, and detailed instructions.'

'Thank you, Haze. You're amazing.' Jenny smiled at me. I smiled back.

Friendship was a wonderful thing. It was so much easier to destroy someone when you had all the inside info you could hope for.

33

Haze

Bill was a loser. How anyone had let him become a police officer was beyond me. For a start, it was incredibly easy to break into his house.

I'd decided I needed more intel on him. Considering I'd been encouraging Jenny to hammer him for money, I had to make sure I hadn't potentially endangered her life. The man was a walking red flag, and I wouldn't be able to live with myself if Felix lost his mother because of me. Being a good friend was hard work; it came with so many responsibilities.

After dropping Bibi at nursery, I'd changed into my running gear, pulled on a baseball cap and driven over to Bill's house. I'd parked round the corner and, having scoped out his back garden and noted the lack of any security cameras, I'd niftily jumped over his fence. His back door wasn't even locked. According to Jenny, he'd inherited the three-bedroom house from his mother two years ago.

The kitchen had piles of dirty plates stacked up, alongside numerous empty takeaway containers. There were enough half-crushed beer cans lying around that I kind of regretted not having a bag with me – Bibi's nursery would've loved them for their big 'Recycle!' art project.

In the living room, the abundance of China figurines and a bulky television set from the early 2000s made it clear that Bill had done nothing to the place since he'd moved in. Next to the reclining chair in front of the TV was a large box of tissues and a tub of lavender hand cream. I grimaced.

I went upstairs to the bedrooms. He'd turned one of the smaller bedrooms into a makeshift office. On the desk there was an old desktop computer. No password. This lack of security did not surprise me – no thief would bother lugging it out of there.

I scrolled through his internet history. He was a frequent commentator on a bookmarked website about 'men's rights'. I flicked through; it was just a lot of ranting about 'the world gone woke', with them all giving reasons why they hated women and liberals and really anyone who wasn't a white man. There were a couple of token searches relating to his current legal woes – although 'how to stop bitch ex getting me for child support' may not have brought up the educated advice he really needed. Unsurprisingly, there were also numerous visits to extreme porn sites. His searches on there were a little chilling. I remembered that studies had shown flashing was the gateway starter crime to a whole heap of nasty. I knew if I looked hard enough, I would find numerous reasons that qualified him for death. In fairness, his treatment of Jenny alone was enough.

But I wasn't going to kill Bill. I had learned from my park indiscretion. I did not have Fox's eye for detail. All the shit I'd gone through trying to cover it up was enough to put me off doing it again. I missed killing, but I didn't want to do it alone. I mean, I *could* do it alone. Girl power, etc. It just . . . wasn't as fun. How could I be expected to enjoy the act itself knowing all the stress of the aftermath and the clear-up was coming? It was kind of how I felt about cooking.

I opened the cupboard. There were three pairs of women's pants laid out on the bottom shelf. One black lace, one white thong and a green silk pair. I did not check if they were used. A few pictures of women were tacked up all over the inside of the wardrobe; some were cuttings from magazines, some looked like pictures he'd taken himself while the subjects were unaware. The good news was that none of them were of Jenny.

Inside the overflowing bin were the letters from her lawyer, scrunched up into little balls. I rummaged around under the bed and tried not to gag when my fingers brushed a pair of dirty boxer shorts.

I looked through the other two bedrooms. No sign of illegal weapons. No sign he'd been following Jenny. Plenty of signs he was a grubby human being.

I was about to head back downstairs when I heard the rattle of a key in the front door. Bill was back from his shift already? I moved fast into the empty spare bedroom and hid behind the door. I could hear him on the phone in the hallway.

'Hello, pal! . . . Yeah . . . Sacked it off. Fuck them making me work so hard this week . . . What now? . . . Hah . . . Too right. Those skanky bitches drive us to it . . . Okay, okay. Order me a pint. I'll be there in a minute.'

I heard him coming up the stairs. The corridor floor creaked as he walked across into the master bedroom. A few rustles, a cupboard door slamming shut. And then he was heading back down the stairs. The front door closed a few seconds later.

I waited a few minutes, and then made my way back out to his garden and over the fence. Once I was in my car, I drove slowly towards the pub around the corner from Bill's house.

Bill was approaching the entrance. He'd gained a bit of a gut since his Officer Flash days. I watched him back-slap a big man who had his back to the road. The man flinched. Just for a second. He adjusted himself and nodded at Bill, and together they walked in. Even his drinking buddies didn't like him.

Bill was a hot-tempered, bad man, but he was no threat to Jenny. I didn't think he had the balls to try and harm her, not when he'd be the number-one suspect. If he did go for her, I was confident that even with Jenny's limited fitness, she could fight him off. She clearly had more of a spark than I'd previously given her credit for.

My phone pinged. Fox telling me he'd be home late. This was happening more and more. He must've forgotten how much he'd slagged off evenings with clients before we had Bibi. *'All that pointless schmoozing. If they don't trust my instincts, then that's their tough luck.'* Not trusting Fox had never occurred to me before. He was mine. He knew that. Screw another woman? He wouldn't fucking dare. Would he?

Last month I'd made the mistake of reading one article on the ever climbing statistic of workplace affairs and now the internet kept recommending me more items on the topic. *'Offices the world over are a hotbed of wanton lust'*, *'Our eyes met across the boardroom table, I was powerless to resist'*. Thinking about the sorry state of our sex life it now felt like I was waving off a loaded gun each morning. I'd been so busy focusing on covering up my actions, I had lost sight of how maybe I needed to start looking into his.

34

Fox

Haze didn't understand how hard I was working. She seemed to think everything happened by magic. When was the last time she'd put in a full day of actual work? A schedule packed with commuting, meetings, staring at my computer, doing deals. Yes, I'd made it harder for myself, fitting in drinks here and there that were outside company remit. Petra was also taking up more and more of my time. Everything I was doing was important for my wellbeing. I needed the distraction, I needed to try and stop the itch, the need to be out there doing what I was born to do. All the things I did were part of my process, part of how I tried to keep our pact and protect our family.

At least I felt like I was handling the sacrifice we'd had to make better than Haze. She was a coiled spring, always ready to pick a fight. She'd told me off for breathing too loudly the other day. Did she want me to just stop? Would that make her finally happy?

Maybe all the clichés about husbands and wives are clichés for a reason – everyone felt the same. Playing at being respectable, dedicated spouses but really, we were all the walking dead, waiting for the chance to get our freak on.

I looked around the office. All of us here working hard to pay for everything in our lives. The treadmill that doesn't end until we do. No wonder we all had to do what we could to get our kicks from somewhere. It was too depressing otherwise.

I reached for my wallet and flicked through the notes inside: £120. I was seeing Cal later. That wouldn't be enough. Not for the first time, I was glad Haze never bothered checking any bank statements that came through our door. Even in her little self-obsessed bubble, she might wonder about all the cash I'd been getting out recently.

I missed the days when we'd had no secrets from each other. We'd been lucky we had enjoyed such a long extended honeymoon period. Nearly a decade. I'd always thought we were so perfect together because we were meant for each other. Was that naïve? We'd had years and years of doing whatever we wanted. We'd chased pleasure. Of course we were happy, because we were doing wonderful things and we had each other to share it all with. A bad day was having a disappointing starter. A bad day was the blade chipping on a favourite knife. A bad day was being stuck in a traffic jam in between parties and feeling that perfect booze buzz wearing off. But when I looked back on it now, I realised it wasn't real life. We'd had lots of money and no responsibilities. Of course we got on. If parenthood and the suburbs were our very first hurdle, we were failing.

I checked my watch. One hour until I needed to be at The Connaught hotel. I'd have lunch at the Italian round the corner. I was going to need my energy.

* * *

When I got home, Haze was pacing in the kitchen. She was holding a piece of A4 paper.

I kept my breathing level. 'Where's Bibi?'

Haze jumped at the sound of my voice and spun around. 'In the garden.' I peered past her and saw Bibi sitting on her little push bike. 'We were in the park but she wanted to come home because there were too many dogs.' Despite our best efforts to encourage her to be fearless, Bibi remained terrified of even little pooches. She'd cried at a small spaniel last week.

Haze was still staring at the paper in her hand, biting her thumbnail.

'What have you got there?' I tried to work out which one of my secrets she'd potentially uncovered.

'Hamish forwarded it on. It's a letter from my art school.' She looked up at me. 'They've asked me to come in and speak about my work to the students.'

'That's incredible!'

Haze shrugged. 'It's not like I've done much recently.'

'But look at all you *have* done. You're a success, Haze. All your exhibitions, the rave reviews. Of course they want you to come and talk! Are you going to do it?'

Haze looked at the letter again. 'I want to go back. It feels important to.'

'For Matty?'

Haze nodded. 'We used to sit through guest lectures together and dream about it being us up there. A sign we'd made it.'

'You should feel really proud of yourself.' I took a step towards her. 'Can I come? Be there for you?'

'I'd like that,' she said quietly. 'I hate speaking in front of people.'

My wife, my warrior queen, had weaknesses too.

'When is it?'

'Next month.' She showed me the letter.

'Consider it in the diary, underlined in red.' I put my arms on her shoulders. 'I'm your number-one fan, you know that, right? If something's important to you, I'll always be there. We're a team. You and me against the world.'

She turned to look at Bibi outside. 'You need to teach her how to actually ride that thing.'

I went out to our daughter, and tried not to think about how, throughout my impassioned speech, my wife had seemed to avoid looking me in the eye.

35

Haze

It was finally the weekend. I hammed up period cramps and let Fox take the lead with Bibi. As I lay in bed, clasping a hot water bottle I did not need, I waited for them to leave for the day. Fox was taking Bibi to the park. He'd hired pedalos and was bringing a picnic lunch.

I waited until I heard his car leaving, then got out of bed. I was already fully dressed. This was an important reconnaissance mission. I had the run of Jenny's house. I was going behind enemy lines.

When I got downstairs, I heard the washing machine beeping. I opened the door and pulled out the sheets. As I transferred them to the dryer, something fell to the floor. I picked it up. My missing AirPod. I kissed it and put it in my pocket. In my rush to chuck all my running clothes into the machine, it must've got mixed in. How many rounds in the machine had it done? It was undoubtedly ruined beyond repair, but it was not at the scene of the crime, and it was not sitting in a Berkshire police station.

I just needed to neutralise the Jenny threat and I could

start to believe I was on the home stretch once again, getting away with murder.

Jenny's parents lived in a semi-detached house in a small cul-de-sac about fifteen minutes from us. I disabled the alarm as I let myself in with the spare key in their hidey gnome. All along the hallway were framed photos of Jenny as a girl, as a teen, then it jumped to ones of Felix. Ones of them together. Her parents looked nice. I mean, everyone tried to look nice in photos, but they looked like the real deal. I walked up and down the hallway, watching the chronicling of Jenny's life, and felt a pang that our house held hardly any photos of Bibi. I hadn't grown up with any of this. I knew this is what you were meant to do, but for some reason I hadn't done it. I saw Bibi every day. I felt lucky I lived with the living, breathing version of her, not the grinning, glossy one in a frame.

I went up the stairs. The large bedroom on the right was clearly her parents' room. Next to it was Jenny and Felix's bedroom. A single bed and a child's cot bed made an L-shape. There was just about enough room for a wardrobe and a bedside table, which was empty except for a copy of a detective thriller. There was no room in here for anything else. I got down to my knees and looked under the bed. There was a pull-out storage box that contained nothing but Jenny and Felix's winter clothes.

Jenny must have a laptop, but she'd probably taken it with her. Seeing as I had zero hacking skills, that wasn't a big loss. There was a small bathroom on the landing. I went to the cabinet above the sink and opened it. Inside were an array of toiletries and— bingo. Three different prescription pill bottles in Jenny's name. I took photos of them with my phone. One I recognised as an anti-depressant. I opened the bottle and pocketed one of the pills. I had an idea that was pretty dark, but it might work. The other two names I wasn't familiar with. I'd look them up later. If things got bad, really bad, I was going to have to get creative.

Back downstairs, Popcorn the hamster was asleep in his cage in the kitchen. I wrinkled my nose as I passed it. I looked out at the small garden and saw there was a large shed at the end of it. A shed . . . Hadn't Jenny made some comment about spending a lot of her pregnancy in one? Right by the door out to the garden was a hook with a key hanging on it. I took it with me as I headed outside.

My phone rang. It was Fox.

I answered on the second ring. 'Hello?' I used my weak, woe-is-me voice.

'Where are you? We're home. Bibi pooed herself.'

'What? Why? She hasn't had an accident in weeks.' Could I not even have one day to myself to snoop around a friend's house? 'I'll be back soon . . . I . . . I ran out of Tampax.'

'I got you a new box yesterday.'

'Do you know how quickly we go through these things?' I needed an excuse. If it meant making my husband think women changed tampons every hour, then so be it. 'Just leave the dirty pants and leggings, I'll deal with them when I'm home.'

'Oh. I already threw everything in the bin.'

Of course he did.

I hung up and put the key into the lock on the shed door. It fit. One turn and I was in. I looked around and smiled.

I had found it.

Jenny's wall of crazy.

Along the back wall of the shed was an array of pinned articles, highlighted with notes, crime scene photos. There was even a map with coloured pins showing the locations of the places suspected Butcher victims had been found.

Although the Butcher took up the bulk of the wall, he wasn't the only killer she was interested in. There were articles about other unsolved murders, all much closer to home. These must be crimes she'd been investigating before she was put on leave. All still unsolved. There were even what looked like surveillance photos of a man with a shock of white hair. Next to him was an article about a paedophile teacher who had absconded before he could be charged. Six victims had come forward. Did Jenny think this was him?

Underneath the shed window was a small rickety desk and chair. On the desk was a battered A4 notepad. I flicked through it. Pages and pages of handwritten notes. There was a large section on the Butcher and four other sections on other cases she was looking into.

I took photos of everything in the notepad and on the wall. To tear apart her Butcher theories, I needed to work out exactly what she thought she had. From the look of things, I also had plenty of other avenues I could lead her down if she was wanting a crime to solve. Maybe I could distract her with a glossy different bad man to find?

I looked around the shed. I could picture Jenny here, her bump ever expanding, her brain bursting with thoughts and ideas, while she was trapped at home with nothing to do. I imagined her avoiding her well-meaning parents by hiding out in her only private space, trying to find her way back to a career that a bad man had torpedoed.

Looking through her notes, I didn't doubt she was good at her job. Neat, ordered handwriting. Clear research. Bullet points to back up her ideas.

And she had great instincts. For all my scoffing at her piecing together of a theory with flimsy evidence, the fact of the matter was, she was absolutely right.

Once I was back home, before I got out of my car, I changed the passcode on my phone. Just in case Fox happened to want to scroll through it, looking for adorable snapshots of Bibi, and instead came across how close we were to being found out.

I walked into the kitchen to find Fox and Bibi having their picnic lunch at the kitchen table.

'Mama, I poo pants,' said Bibi through a mouthful of cheese sandwich.

'Not while we're eating, Bibi.' Fox grimaced, then looked up at me. 'How are you feeling?'

'A bit better. The Nurofen is kicking in.'

'We can all have a nice lazy day at home.' Fox looked at Bibi and shuddered. 'I've had more than enough excitement already.'

Bibi sniggered.

'Great. I'm just going to head back to bed for a bit.'

I spent the rest of the afternoon scrolling through everything I'd found in Jenny's shed. I could hear Fox and Bibi's movie marathon going on downstairs. The strains of *The Little Mermaid* became the soundtrack to me staring at crime scene photos, descriptions of victims' injuries, and long lists of sexual predators living within a forty-mile radius of our home. It seemed that as well as looking into cold cases, Jenny also wanted to keep an eye on anyone who could be deemed a threat to children. Some might see that as extreme, but as someone who understood better than most the depravity human beings were capable of, it was a type of helicopter parenting I approved of.

That night as I drifted off to sleep, I thought about how lucky it was that I'd been able to get in there and see it all. At least now I could forensically pick apart everything she'd found on the Butcher and work out how to fix whatever mistakes we'd made. I had left no trace of having been out in the shed and there were no CCTV cameras positioned anywhere. Nothing would give away that I'd done anything other than what she'd asked me to.

Shit.

I sat up in bed. The hamster. I forgot to feed him.

I quickly picked up my phone. I could only sleep after having extensively googled it. I was pretty sure he would survive until morning.

36

Fox

Haze was staring at something on her phone, her brow furrowed. Bibi was down for her nap. It was a quiet Sunday afternoon. I'd hoped to relax, potter around the garden, maybe even read a book, but Haze had handed me a list of chores. A man's work never ends.

'Are you painting again?'

'Nope. No. Why?' Haze didn't look up from her phone.

I reached out and touched the back of her wrist. A streak of green paint.

'Painting with Bibi doesn't count.' She shrugged and stood up. 'I'm going to lie down. Cramps are bad again.' She disappeared from the kitchen.

It was the ultimate trump card. I could never question a cramp. I would be an insensitive man who didn't understand a woman's suffering. I just had to accept that it was a free pass to both lounge around in bed and scream at me for even the slightest infraction. Her PMS had definitely gotten worse since Bibi – I'd once had the bravery to comment on it and her response was if I wasn't going to let her stab people then *'what the fuck did I expect?'*. I looked at my chore list. I'd better get on with it. I didn't want to poke the bear.

The first item was: 'Replace batteries (3 x AAA) in extractor fan remote control. Spare ones in the drawer or my handbag.'

I rooted around in the drawer of crap in the kitchen that housed all the random items in the house we weren't quite sure where to put. String, stamps, an Allen key, eight envelopes, but no AAA batteries.

Haze's Louis Vuitton tote bag was on the island. I opened it up to find the usual Haze mess; it was crammed full with anything she'd thought to shove in there. I emptied it onto the countertop. There was everything from parking tickets to crumpled receipts, a half-eaten chocolate bar, a leaking biro and a pair of Bibi's mermaid pants. I did not check to see if they were clean. There were also baby wipes and a pink plastic toy phone whose ringtone was Peppa Pig snorting. I found an open pack of AAA batteries with only two left inside. I found a third stuck to what looked like a squashed Starburst sweet. I unstuck it and put it back in its rightful place inside the pack.

I started to return the items to her handbag. The parking tickets I tucked into my back pocket. I didn't want to look at the dates of when they were issued; the deadline to pay a smaller fine had undoubtedly passed already. I binned anything that looked too damaged and unsavoury, and used the baby wipes to clean down the stickier items. Next to her Stella McCartney wallet was a small white pill. I held it up and saw it had a small line in the middle of it, with an E and L stamped on each side. Haze with pills? She never took any vitamins (*'Don't be a dick, that's what food's for'*), she took only Nurofen at the slightest ache ('*It's a painkiller and I have some pain*'), and had laughed her head off when I'd once offered her a breath mint ('*If your breath stinks, just eat some toothpaste, you weirdo*').

I went to Google. As expected, there was a website that claimed it could identify any pill. I took several photos of the pill and then uploaded it. Was Haze ill? Was she a secret drug addict? I waited until the ping came in. Cipralex. An anti-depressant. Jesus. What was she doing with this? I ran it over in my head and couldn't think of any reason why prescription medication would be in her handbag unless she actually had a prescription for it.

I felt bad. All the times I'd thought she was grumpy or crazy or had PMS, perhaps she was actually depressed. Maybe I really needed to start being more understanding. She was a complicated woman; it was only natural to be after everything she'd been through.

37

Haze

'How are you? Feeling okay?' Fox rubbed my shoulders as he passed me on the way to our coffee machine. 'It's so good to be home all together. Don't you just love Sundays?'

Fox had been weirdly nice to me all week. Clearly last weekend and my enforced bed rest had made him freak out after seeing what life as a single dad would be like.

Or he knew about the dead man and was trying to pretend he didn't know about the dead man by overcompensating and being extra nice? Jesus, this was why keeping secrets was a bad idea. All the overthinking and trying to work out whether or not someone knew was exhausting.

I had a lot on at the moment. The week had gone fast.

Whenever I'd spent time with Jenny, I'd made sure to keep subtly reinforcing how nice and normal my husband was, while also showing concern for her mental well-being:

'I came home to find Fox sobbing in front of The Sound of Music. *He said "Edelweiss" gets him every time. He's such a softie.'*

'When's your next check-up with your doctor? You feel

like the meds are working okay? It's just you seem a bit . . . No, no, forget I said anything.'

'We had quite a drama last night. Bibi was screaming as there was a spider in her room. It took ages to get it out because Fox refused to kill it. He just insisted on this really humane method of a cup and piece of paper, and it took so long to get a hold of the little blighter. He's living happily in our garden now, and he taught Bibi such an important lesson about how every life is precious.'

Behind the scenes, I was working on figuring out which of Jenny's cold cases had the best chance of heating up and distracting her with a potential breakthrough. The more I delved into her notes, the more nervous I became about succeeding in throwing her off our scent. Jenny was meticulous. Her research on her potential suspects was far superior to Fox's research on our potential victims. The only comfort I had was that she was held back by her insistence on doing things within the law. With all the cases she'd been investigating, she'd hit a brick wall once she'd exhausted all legal options available to her. I could get her to the finish line.

Apart from the Butcher, she'd focused on a suspected rapist and sex-trafficker, the ex-teacher paedophile and a serial hit-and-run killer. I had to commend her on her choices; all of these people deserved to be brought to justice. If I could ever get Fox to sanction a return to our former life, they'd all be top of the list. They were criminals who'd slipped through the cracks – her notes talked of botched investigations, missing evidence, lawyers jumping on a technicality. It was all infuriating enough to make me want to dig up my knife. But no. I was trying to get us out of a mess, not into another one.

I zeroed in on the rapist and sex-trafficker. His name was

Nicky Blaine and, according to her notes, he lived a mere twenty miles from us. This made him the number-one choice from a convenience point of view, as he was the only one I could fit in stalking while being a full-time mother and loving, totally normal wife.

Blaine was fifty-one years old and owned a couple of nightclubs in Slough. The way these establishments were decorated was a crime in itself. The police reports named several reported rape victims who had all dropped out of testifying in the run-up to his trial. From Jenny's notes, it was clear that the rape trial was meant to be the start of going after him for the bigger charges of sex-trafficking. His downfall would've torn down a whole international operation that led to the kidnap and rape of vulnerable young women.

Looking through it all, I actually felt sorry for the police. To have to spend all that time building a case, gathering evidence, talking to witnesses, going through a trial. All that time-consuming work, with no guarantee that it would end with the person locked up, that they could even stop them.

The way Fox and I had worked was so much more efficient.

Research. Find. Kill. Next!

And a lot of the time, we didn't even need to research, we just came across them. Instant elimination.

'You haven't been for a run in a while.' Fox handed me a cup of tea I hadn't asked for. 'Exercise is so good for us all. Helps clear the mind. And just your mood in general.'

'Right.' I took a sip of tea. What the hell did he know?

'I'm going to take Bibi to the playground. You could go for a run while we're out?'

'Sure. Thank you.'

He was being nice, considerate, helpful, selfless. Did he

know what I'd done wrong, or was he making up for something he'd done wrong? I bit down on my lip and suppressed the urge to grab him by the shoulders and ask him outright.

Having hauled myself back from a run I didn't really want to go on, I came home to find Fox cooking dinner for us all.

'Where did you go?'

'Just to the park and back. Nothing very exciting.' I'd made a point of avoiding Cobham Common. I also didn't mention I'd got a stitch and had to walk back. On the way, I'd checked out Nicky Blaine's nightclubs on my phone. Labyrinth was advertising a Masquerade Party Night next week. A perfect chance for me to check out the club without being seen. 'I'll go up for a shower and give Bibi a bath.'

'Are you sure? I can do it later.'

What the hell was going on? If he started offering to do the laundry, then I'd know something was really up.

I had filled Bibi's bath with so much bubble bath she was now wearing a bubble beard.

'Was the playground fun?'

Bibi nodded. 'I go weeeeee'. She flew her sailboat in the air. 'Dada talking woman.'

I wondered why Fox hadn't mentioned seeing anyone he knew. 'What woman?'

'Nice woman.' Bibi swung her head from side to side. 'Chat chat chat.' Her usual response to adults talking too much.

Once Bibi was in bed, happily fed and having had six stories from Fox, I went to help him with the washing-up.

'Who did you see in the playground?' I took a clean bowl from him and dried it.

Fox frowned. 'No one. It wasn't that busy.' He stared down at the sink as he scrubbed a plate.

'Bibi said there was a woman. A nice woman.'

'Oh, her . . . I bumped into a friend from work.' Fox carried on scrubbing the already clean plate. I watched him for a moment, then went to switch on the TV.

He didn't tell me her name. He'd never mentioned anything about the women at his office – he only ever complained about the men and all they did to annoy him. I looked over at his phone lying on the kitchen table. I knew his passcode. I'd wait for the right moment. If he wasn't going to tell me his secrets I'd have to find them out for myself.

38

Fox

I was back at The Connaught. I headed straight to the Terrace Suite's private elevator, walking swiftly with my head down. The problem with knowing so many people in London was the risk of seeing someone who knew me when I most wanted to remain unseen. On this occasion, I reached the door of the suite without any shouts of 'Cabot! Fancy seeing you here!'

I took a deep breath before I opened the door. Time for Round Two. And it was going to get ugly.

My parents were sitting on a yellow velvet sofa.

I knew why they always chose this suite. Its mahogany furniture and silk cushions were exactly to their taste. I noted the large, empty vases. Flowers were always banned in my mother's proximity due to her hay fever.

'Good morning, Nathaniel,' said my mother.

'Good morning to you both.'

My father gave me a small nod but remained quiet.

By the time I had sat down in the armchair opposite them, a butler had appeared proffering a cafetière of coffee. With a flourish, he put a small silver jug on the table. 'Oat milk, as requested.' Neither of my parents acknowledged this with even eye contact.

I thought with a flash how strange it was that I didn't know they had given up dairy. I wondered how long ago this dietary requirement had been introduced. It had been eighteen years since we had even lived in the same country. I'd seen them only a handful of times since. They were the people who had made me, raised me, and we were strangers to each other.

We sat in silence as the butler poured us each a coffee.

'Thank you,' I said as he left the room.

As soon as the door latch clicked, my father started speaking. 'Considering you left so abruptly last time, we didn't have a chance to talk properly.'

Not long after their visit to our home, I'd been at the office when John Perry, the managing partner who'd introduced me to UBS, stopped me in the lobby to tell me how nice it was my parents were in town. He'd mentioned plans to see them for lunch next week. I had immediately rung The Connaught and asked to be put through to their suite. They were creatures of habit and very few establishments made the grade.

When I had made it over there, the conversation had ended before it began when they refused to explain why they were still here, and both made some incredibly derogatory comments about Haze. I had wanted to sit there and be the controlled, reasonable grown man I knew I was. But when it came to rudeness about my wife, I found it impossible to keep calm. I doubt it was a power move that impressed them; the best I could hope was that it gave them a scare. They knew better than most what I was capable of when angry.

'If we could please speak calmly about Hazel.' My father took out a thick, brown A4 envelope and dropped it on the table.

I was prepared for this. And to be honest, surprised it hadn't happened earlier. Presumably, when I'd simply been a disgraced son on the other side of the world, with them having no hope or desire for me to re-enter their polite society, there was no need to find out about the woman I'd chosen to marry.

'Makes for one hell of a read.'

'I already know everything.'

He guffawed. 'There's no way you know—'

'Everything.' I leaned forward. 'I don't know why any of this is relevant to you. I've made a life for myself here. I've already told you I am not moving back to America. This is my home now.'

'We are delighted you're happy here, Nathaniel,' said my mother. Was it the Botox or her lack of human emotion that meant her face remained rigid? 'But even though you are not back home, you still bear our name. You are still our eldest son.'

'What does that even mean? You're worried I'm going to somehow humiliate you? You really think the painful middle-class normality of my suburban life is going to make you look bad?'

My father leaned forward. 'We wanted to believe you'd changed, and for a while we did. We built a picture in our minds. That you'd married a nice English girl. That she'd calmed you down and made you want to live a decent life. A normal life.'

'The baby was the icing on the cake,' sighed my mother.

'But when we met your wife, we realised things were clearly not quite as right as we'd hoped.'

'From what we've seen of her.' Her nose pinched in disgust. 'And read of her . . .' She motioned towards the envelope. 'There is no way that someone of her upbringing can give you the stability you need. What do you even have in common, apart from a shared bloodlust?'

I gritted my teeth. Of course, one look at the fine spirited woman I'd married, and they'd judged right there and then that she was unworthy. And summarising the righteous kills in our past as just 'bloodlust', where was the acknowledgement of the fact those men did not deserve to live?

'Is it still Devon? Is that still who does all your dirty work?'

It was textbook. A phone call as soon as they were out of our front door. His reconnaissance would've begun immediately. I wondered if he'd been flown over especially to make sure he got everything he could on my wife's sorry upbringing. Had he since left? Or was someone watching me even now? Watching Haze?

Haze and I may have grown up worlds and millions apart, but toxic family was something we both shared.

'Devon does invaluable work for our family. If someone is going to ruin the family name, we need to know about it.'

Time for cards on the table. Let's see if Daddy dearest would play ball. 'Do you have evidence of anything I have done to bring you into disrepute?'

'Yes,' said my father.

My heart skipped a beat. 'Since I have been in Europe?'

A pause. 'We'll find something eventually. I know we will.'

Thank God. I wanted to believe I had been as careful as I thought I had been. If I'd done enough to keep our activities hidden from Devon, I knew I didn't need to worry about the police.

I looked between them both. 'Just tell me what you want from me, and we can get this family reunion over with.'

My father bridged his hands together. 'There's an issue with the company. I know you don't like to trouble yourself with information on the family business that has allowed us to always live like this.' He waved an arm around the suite. 'But the long and short of it is, we need your vote. We're trying to stop a hostile takeover. Your shares give you the right to have a say.'

And there it was.

The whole reason they were here. Why they were still here. Of course they didn't give a shit about me, about their granddaughter. They just wanted my vote to save the company.

I took a moment to work out how I felt about this. And it was clear: relief. That was the overriding feeling. Relief that they didn't actually want to be a part of my life.

'And if I don't vote the way you want me to?'

'As if you need to ask, Nathaniel.' My father tapped the envelope on the table. 'Between the two of you, we have plenty to keep the police busy.'

'If you let the family company slip away, we have no desire to protect you. Or your wife. And there is no statute of limitations on murder.' My mother took a sip of her coffee.

'We spoke to a family lawyer,' added my father. 'Did you know that if the parents are incapacitated or incarcerated, then the grandparents have the best chance of taking custody of a minor? And your daughter has no grandparents other than us, does she?'

I looked down at my hands. I was clenching and unclenching

my fists. I wanted to throw everything in reach of me around this perfectly designed room. I wanted to watch the coffee stain the velvet. I wanted to smash every piece of china, and throw a chair through the window. But what would be the point? Staff would tidy it all up. My parents' credit card would be charged, and no matter how high the amount, they wouldn't even notice. It wouldn't even make a slight dent in what they had, and all I would get is an eye-roll rebuke for being so unseemly with my emotions.

'Come on now, Reginald. You make it sound as if taking that little girl away and giving her a life of luxury beyond her wildest dreams is a bad thing,' my mother said. 'She'd be very lucky to come and live with us, wouldn't she?'

I focused on my breathing. I would not allow myself to picture Bibi anywhere near these people. 'I'm not setting foot back in America.'

'There is no need for that.' My father leaned back in his chair. 'We now realise that having you back there would be risky. Seeing as you are not as changed as we'd previously thought.'

Their dream of replacing Julian with me as the prodigal son had quickly evaporated. I couldn't be trusted not to let the side down. It also meant their threat to give the police Devon's evidence on me was not an empty one. If I didn't do as they wanted, if they lost the company because of me, things would be so rock bottom, they could suffer through an estranged son being arrested for historic murders. Another thought hit me, now they had evidence on Haze, what was to stop them coming after her to get back at me? A perfect revenge, and one that would leave the family name relatively clean – better for them to be whispered about for my questionable choice of wife, rather than my own questionable actions. After everything I've done to keep Haze safe, I wasn't going to let my parents be the ones to take her down. They could come for me, but never her.

'Send me the paperwork I need to sign. And stay the hell away from us.'

39

Then

Fox

I was going to be a father. Every time I thought about it, I couldn't help it – a little smile would start to form. Haze would always wallop me on the arm. Without me ever confessing it to her, she knew what I was thinking.

I had never realised how much I wanted a baby until Haze came running at me, pale-faced, brandishing a small white stick, howling that she was pregnant.

I was always thinking about our future. I had to. I was the planner, the organiser, the spreadsheet-inputter. I was the grown-up. I knew the life we had couldn't last forever. The more men we killed, the greater the chances of us being caught. I think Haze genuinely believed this beautiful, wonderful extended honeymoon would never end. But it had to. One day, we were always going to have to hang up our tools and change our ways. We were just two people trying to do our best, to eliminate bad men before they could hurt innocent women. We had a purpose, a mission objective, that had got us through this last decade, but maybe we needed to realign while we still could.

Haze had never really contemplated the risk of what we were doing. How one mistake could lead to a lifetime behind bars. I often thought of the night we'd first met. She'd done no scoping out of that alleyway. She didn't know there was no CCTV there. She hadn't factored in the two entry points and how easy it was for someone to approach her and her victim from a blind spot. It was extremely fortuitous for her that I was the one who came across them. And that from that night on, she'd no longer need to rely on luck to not get caught.

It was when I was thinking about our baby growing inside Haze that it hit me.

Maybe there was more to life than death. Maybe if we just tried hard enough, we could be a normal family. Maybe this was always what I was meant to do.

I wasn't a big believer in a higher power, but the world felt crazy right now, nothing felt normal. Maybe this was the sign we needed to change our ways? The threat of an unknown deadly virus. No one seemed able to predict what would happen next or what the following wave could bring. We were home. Locked down. And throughout, our little bean inside Haze was growing. New life. A different life.

I thought of our future with our little one and all I knew was that I didn't want to keep looking over my shoulder. Lying awake at night worrying about what detail I had forgotten, what clue could lead the task force to our door.

Haze slept soundly. She had her fun. She made her art. And she trusted me to keep us safe. A baby raised the stakes.

The more we had to lose, the more pressure there was to not get caught. If anything happened to us, our little one would be all alone in the world. Or even worse; sent to live with my parents.

I couldn't let that happen.

40

Haze

I'd just put Bibi to bed when the doorbell rang. I raced downstairs before they buzzed again, and opened the door to two uniformed policemen standing on my doorstep.

My heart skipped a beat and then nearly stopped all together.

I needed to be calm. Icy calm. I was going to give the performance of my life. I wasn't going to let them think they had anything on me.

What would a normal person think when seeing police there? I looked between the two of them.

'Oh my God, is my husband okay? Was he in a car crash? Is it—'

The taller policeman held up a hand. 'Madam, please calm down. We don't know who your husband is. We're just here to ask if you've seen anything recently that's given you cause for concern.'

'Oh. Thank goodness. You scared me!' I gave a small smile that was not returned.

'We've had a couple of complaints from neighbours that homeless men have been having altercations around here.'

Was this a bluff? Were they wanting to see what I knew? Or was this just unbelievable good fortune that would help reiterate their working theory about who had killed the dead man?

I tapped a finger to my chin. 'You know what, I have seen a couple of homeless people here and there recently. I mean, it's so sad, that they have nowhere to go. But yes, I was surprised, as we never used to . . .' I put a hand to my mouth. 'Wasn't that man who was stabbed killed by a homeless person?'

'It's an ongoing investigation, but yes, that is what witness accounts have led us to believe.'

'Are people around here feeling worried?' It seemed that the police paid plenty of attention when upstanding residents were fearing for their safety. They were seemingly a lot less concerned when the victim was an ex-con. Not that I was complaining.

'As we said, there have been a couple of complaints.'

I could picture the buried knife in our garden. It felt like it was emitting a signal that would somehow magically draw them to it. I could feel my heart rate rise at the very thought. How close they were without even realising.

'I've had no direct contact with any of them myself. But of course, I do worry' – I clasped my hands to my chest – 'as a mother.'

'We understand, and we just want to reassure the neighbourhood we're doing what we can to clamp down on the problem.'

'Thank you, officers. We all really appreciate everything you do.' I gave my best winning smile.

* * *

'Haze?'

I woke to Fox calling for me from downstairs. I checked my watch. It was nearing midnight.

'Dada talking woman.'

I headed out onto the landing. 'Shhhhh! You'll wake Bibi,' I hush-shouted at him.

'Come down to the kitchen!' he hush-shouted back.

I walked in to find him with the freezer door open. He turned around, clutching a bag of peas to his face.

'What the fuck happened?'

'I got knocked off my bike. Some idiot didn't see me.'

He insisted on riding those stupid rental bikes around London.

I went up to him and took the peas away from his face. His cheekbone was bruised and swollen. 'Were you wearing your helmet?'

'My head's fine. This' – he motioned to his cheek – 'is from colliding with the tarmac.'

I checked him over. 'Anything else hurt?'

'Ribs are a bit sore. Winded hitting the ground.'

'That's what you get for riding a bike.'

I looked him over. No tears on his Turnball & Asser shirt. No dirt or gravel on his bruise. No marks on his suit. He didn't look like he'd fallen off his bike, he looked like he'd been punched in the face. Which made me question exactly who had done it, and why the fuck he was lying to me about it.

41

Fox

I stared at my reflection in the mirror in the kitchen. It had been a week and the bruise on my cheekbone had faded enough now that it was barely noticeable. I turned my head from side to side.

I think Haze had bought my story about a bike crash. That excuse was definitely helped by her hatred of two-wheeled vehicles. Not only would she refuse to get on one, but 'Move out the fucking way, you prick!' was always her instinctive reaction upon seeing any cyclists when she was out driving.

I thought back to the fight. I'd remained in control, despite being outnumbered. I didn't like to think how it would've ended if I hadn't had my switchblade and knuckle-duster with me. I had purposely aimed to make sure I didn't wound any of them badly enough to warrant further retribution. Throughout the onslaught of three men doing their best to hurt me, my overriding thought had been not how to stay alive, but how to get away without any injuries that would spark Haze's interest.

Lying to your wife really did make things more difficult.

I looked down at my phone. Another email had come in from my parents' lawyers, asking for a tracking number for the company papers I was meant to have signed and sent by now. I still had them in the envelope they'd arrived in, inside my desk drawer in my study. I knew what was at stake if I didn't play nice. I just couldn't bring myself to do it just yet.

My parents were, at least, definitely back in America. I'd checked and there had been enough sightings and photos of them at various local social events that I did not have to worry they were still physically here. Although they had made sure that their presence was still felt.

In the last few days, I'd noticed someone had been following me. A tall man in a suit. The fact the man had made it so obvious he was following me was undoubtedly because my parents wanted me to know I was being watched. To remind me of their power. They might be back on the other side of the Atlantic, but their spies were everywhere.

I often think their disappointment at my little killing habit was not just about the money it cost to cover it up, but also because of the fact I'd chosen to get my hands dirty when it was something that could've been outsourced.

If I could talk to a therapist, I was sure they would say that my parents' micromanagement of my life made me feel so emasculated that killing men was what I needed to do to feel validated. To show that I was still a big man, a threat. That I had control there that I didn't at home. Maybe I was never born to kill, they just made me this way.

I would sign the papers. I needed them out of my life. I'd just make them wait a little longer.

I thought back to the fight. I flexed my hands. It had felt good. I needed more nights like that. It helped take the edge off the relentless grind of being a working father. Although in fairness I had hardly been in the office this week, both Suzanne and Petra had taken up more time than they should. My head was ringing with all the things I was having to keep from Haze. Juggling everything I had on and making sure she remained blissfully clueless was pushing even my organisation skills to the limit. Today, I'd got home early to come clean on at least one secret. The hope was this would help our somewhat floundering relationship. Although there was every chance it could make things a hell of a lot worse.

The doorbell rang and I took a deep breath.

42

Haze

Bibi was finally in bed. I was in the bath, hoping that enough bubble bath and a lavender-scented candle would ease the tension in my shoulders. I was worried Jenny had been avoiding me. Normally so keen to hang out, she hadn't been in touch for three days. I didn't want to look suspicious by texting her first. So now I was just constantly checking my phone, hoping for it to ping with one of her usual emoji-ridden playdate requests. I felt like a lovestruck teenager waiting for my crush. It was a new level of tragic.

I heard the sound of Fox moving around downstairs. He'd come back early a couple of days ago, and barely said hello before he whisked Bibi off to the playground. He'd seen that woman there again. He didn't tell me. But my innocent daughter had. 'Nice woman chat chat.' Who was this fucking hussy? If he was cheating, why was he so bad at it? Who brought their daughter to an illicit date? I hadn't yet had the chance to go through his phone as he never seemed to have it out of his hand. The other night enroute to the bathroom I'd looked for it on his bedside table. There was no sign of it. Locked somewhere in a drawer? Underneath his pillow?

I got out the bath. It was going to take a fuck of a lot more than lavender to make me forget about how my mum friend could be bringing about our downfall, and my husband could be cheating on me.

I pulled on my dressing gown. I could hear him pacing in the hallway, and then the doorbell went. The front door opened and shut, and then I heard the strains of low talking.

This, I needed to investigate. I tightened my dressing gown. Whoever it was, they could judge me all they wanted for being ready for bed at 7.30pm. I was a mother.

I walked down the stairs. Fox was alone in the hallway.

'Who was at the door?'

'I don't want you to freak out . . .'

'That's a terrible way to prepare me for freaking out.' A thought hit me. 'Oh fuck, it's not your parents again?'

'I know things have been tough for you. I can see you're struggling.'

'Well, struggling's a little—'

'I want you to be happy, little one. I love you. You know that, right?'

I felt prickles on the back of my arm. What the hell had he done?

'It was just the two of us for so long, and I know all these changes have taken some adjusting to. But I think it's time to add someone else into the mix. Someone who will help take our marriage back to where it should be.'

Was he planning a threesome or saying we needed a shrink?

The downstairs toilet door opened, and out walked a heavyset woman I'd never seen before.

'This is Helga.'

'I'm here for you,' she said with a thick Eastern European accent and a smile.

I looked between the two of them. My mouth may have dropped open a little.

Fox clicked. 'No! No, not . . . She means she's here to help you. She's here for Bibi. She's a nanny.'

I let out a deep breath. Okay. He hadn't gone completely deranged. But a nanny?

'Isn't this something we should've discussed?'

Fox turned towards Helga. 'Please go help yourself to a glass of water in the kitchen.' He waited until she was out of sight, then turned back to me. 'I read somewhere that trying to find help is nearly as stressful as not having help. So I thought I'd do it all for you. Helga has excellent references. And Bibi has already taken to her. She's met her in the playground a couple of times.'

Okay, so he wasn't fucking someone else. Well, he still might be. Just not the imagined playground hussy.

'I don't know.' I shook my head. 'You can't just give the job to the first person you interview and hope—'

'Twenty-three.'

'What?'

'I've interviewed twenty-three people.'

'Right.'

'She was by far the most qualified. You should've seen her reaction when I got Bibi to fake a choking fit.' He leaned towards me. 'She might be big, but she was like a ninja.'

My mind raced. A nanny. Someone hanging out in our

house. Knowing our business. Someone Bibi liked. What if she liked her more than me?

'You asked me for help. To make you remember what it felt like to be powerful. Remember?'

That was after the dinner party at the Thompsons'. Well over a month ago. I had reached out and he had seemingly ignored it. I had cursed him for it. Hated him for it. But he'd heard me.

'You miss painting. I know that it's such a huge part of who you are. Having someone around to help will let you focus properly on getting back to it. I just want you to be happy. I want us to be happy. I know you've given up a lot. For Bibi. For me. And I want you to know how much we appreciate it.' He reached out and squeezed my hand. 'I just want to feel like we used to. Back in sync. Together.'

'And how do we do that?'

'We start by going out for dinner. I've made a reservation at Scott's in Richmond. We used to love the one in Mayfair, remember?'

He was being amazing. So amazing. And kind and understanding. Wanting to fulfil my emotional and practical needs. Being the type of partner who fully understood what I needed, perhaps even better than I did.

It all became clear.

He must know about the dead man.

43

Haze

Scott's was full. It was a little more garish in the decoration than its Mayfair counterpart but considering the last time we'd been out to eat it had been to a chain restaurant with sticky floors and an extensive kids' menu, this was a marked improvement.

With a flourish, we were shown to our table and seated in our velvet chairs.

'So, what do you think?' Fox leaned forward. 'As good as the original?'

'Are you talking about the restaurant, or us?' A declaration of war.

Fox paled and motioned to the waiter. 'We're going to need champagne.' The waiter bobbed his head and rushed off.

We sat observing each other. I was sure I'd read somewhere silence was an excellent tool for eliciting a confession. I waited for him to speak.

He took a deep breath and leaned forward. 'I know things are different from what they were. But life moves on. We're older, wiser, we have Bibi. We have a good life.' He reached over and squeezed my hand.

The waiter set down two glasses of champagne.

I drained mine in one. 'Another one, please.'

The waiter swiftly disappeared.

'We want Bibi to have a normal life. This is us setting the building blocks for a good foundation.'

I frowned. 'She's a human child, not a house.'

Fox sighed. 'I know you miss our little sideline. I know it's been hard on you. But by the time she's eighteen, I'm sure we can look at revisiting it.'

He had decreed that until Bibi was a legal adult, our tools should remain downed. Over fifteen years. A prison sentence. Being forced into a life you don't want for the good of your child. Now I understood what it must feel like to be in an unhappy couple feeling they had to stay together for their kids, waiting for them to be old enough to be less fucked up by a divorce. It was all a balancing act. Right up until the moment you realised your kids were being more damaged by you staying together and hating each other. Would Fox realise that holding us back, stopping us from enacting our true calling, was making us shittier, unhappier people?

'We'll be in our fifties by then.'

'None of this is easy. But we're doing what's best for Bibi.'

I remained silent as the waiter placed another glass of champagne in front of me.

Fox charged on. 'We should toast your success. The call-up to go and talk at your old art school. That's really something.' He raised his glass, and clinked it to mine. 'You made your dreams come true. Never forget that. You did it all alone.'

I took a large gulp of champagne. 'I'm dreading it. All those people looking at me.'

'It'll be intimidating for the first few seconds, and then you'll get into a flow. I'll be the familiar face in the crowd, reminding you what you're capable of.' He smiled. 'Front-row seat for my clever wife.'

I had squeezed into a navy Victoria Beckham dress that clung in all the right places. My hair was freshly washed and blow-dried. I had a glass of champagne in my hand, and my handsome husband opposite me. But things did not feel any-where near as goddamn perfect as they should have.

He'd tried to do a nice thing tonight. He'd hired a nanny, booked a decent restaurant. He was trying to remind me of what it was like before. But didn't he see? That was the prob-lem. We were nothing like we were before. And trying to be like the Fox and Haze we once were just showed us how far we'd sunk.

Did he know about the dead man? He must fucking know. How could I have been so blind? Who'd punched him in the face? What was he really doing on those supposed late nights at the office? I had so many questions I wasn't going to ask him. I wasn't going to show my hand.

And then it hit me.

We weren't on the same team. We were on opposing sides, circling each other, waiting to see who was going to crack first.

I had my secrets, he had his.

What had happened to us?

How did we descend from peak adorability to this farce of a marriage?

Familiarity breeds contempt. So how the fuck were you

meant to live with someone, know their every quirk, their every annoying habit, and not hate them?

Where was the man I'd married? The one with the dark sexiness bubbling away underneath the clean-cut package? Back in our glory days, him being the organised, efficient planner was counteracted by our adventures where he'd let rip – literally. I'd see him in beautiful full flow, indulging his every screwed-up whim on his very own human canvases. But that artiste had gone. He was now just a hard-working wanker banker who liked spreadsheets. Another nerd without a nerve.

'I think I'll have the cod.' Fox looked up at me from his menu. 'What about you?'

'Steak.'

He chewed his lip. 'I like the sound of the potatoes. But I really shouldn't.'

He'd lost his spark, his *joie de vivre*, and he hadn't even noticed.

The waiter came and I placed my order. I looked round the restaurant as Fox continued to debate the menu. At a table in the corner were a couple in their twenties, side by side, arms entwined. The man reached over and cupped the woman's face. Their food was untouched in front of them as they spoke softly to each other.

'And is there a lot of cream in the sauce?' Fox was still deliberating.

The man's hand dropped from her face, to under the table. She closed her eyes and moved closer to him. I remembered those nights. The ones where you didn't want to wait until you got home. The ones where any place was a good place to reach a discreet O.

Even if we were getting on well enough to suggest having a go ourselves, I knew it would lead to another one of those 'You're a mother now!' admonishments. Getting embarrassingly drunk? Getting your rocks off in public? Killing bad men with knives? No, no, no. 'You're a mother now!'

'And is it deboned, or—'

The woman had now tilted her head back slightly as the man smiled and whispered in her ear.

'Just have the fucking fish,' I snapped.

I reached for my glass to find both men were staring at me.

'Yes, the cod, please.' Fox handed his menu back to the waiter with a tight smile. 'And a bottle of the Sauvignon.'

He was the deboned one. De-backboned.

He leaned forward. 'You can't keep blaming me for the changes in our lives. We made this decision together.'

'*You* made the decision and bulldozed me into it.' I finished my glass of champagne in one gulp. I thought of how I was eight months' pregnant with Bibi when he'd hit me with the news that our rampaging needed to end. I'd been in no state to argue. My body was swollen, my head messy. I was focused on the life I was bringing into the world, not the ones I was taking out.

The waiter arrived with the bottle of wine. We sat silently as he poured us each a glass. He rushed away as soon as he'd finished.

'Don't keep thinking about what you've lost. Think about what you've gained.'

Seriously? He was patronising me now?

I'd had no role models for functional, loving relationships growing up. I didn't know what a happy marriage looked like. All I had were books, films and the occasional gushing article in the Sunday papers. Maybe my expectations were too high. Maybe just tolerating each other, just getting by, was enough. Maybe that was all we were meant to hope for. Maybe all the movies and great works of literature had lied . . . There was no great ongoing enduring love. Those happy endings always finish with the couple finally getting together. The big kiss. The embrace. The promise and anticipation of forever. It never fast-forwards to them ten years, twenty years down the line, arguing over him cutting his toenails in the bath, her hair clogging the drains, whose turn it is to get up with the baby.

Where were the great love stories of a long-term relationship? Maybe those were too complicated, too boring. Easier to end with a simple 'Happily ever after', a glossy summary of a lifetime together with no insight into how they coped after THE END. We never got to read about Elizabeth Bennett berating Darcy for always leaving his pants on the bathroom floor. We never watched Cinderella and her Prince on the carriage ride home from dinner, having a drunken row about him being a little *too* Charming with a slutty fairy from the other side of the valley. Only Romeo and Juliet went out on a high, still in love, each thinking the other was perfect . . . because they'd only had like, five minutes together. Was that the secret? Die before it fades? Before passion becomes familiarity, and the new and exciting becomes the mundane? We had no manual, no handbook for living happily ever after. We were muddling through it, and we were failing.

'Don't shut me out, Haze. We need to be open with each other.'

There was so much to say, but this was not the time or the place.

44

Fox

All I wanted was for her to talk to me. Properly. I didn't want to learn things about her by rummaging through her handbag, by hiding in the shadows and trying to help from afar.

Walking through the door this evening with my beautiful wife beside me, I had a flash of just how it used to be. The nights before Bibi. Back when a dinner out in a place that smelled expensive was more normal than not. I thought tonight would make her happy, instead I'd unwittingly angered her further. For not the first time I wished she came with an instruction manual.

Haze wanted everything. She'd grown up with nothing and it was like the rest of her life had been spent trying to claw back all the things she felt she'd missed out on. I understood that. But how could I explain to her that above everything, I was trying to give her what she had missed most – a secure and loving home? I missed our glory days just as much as she did, but I needed us to stop. It was exhausting, always worrying about what lay ahead, what detail I might have overlooked. I was older. More tired. There was more chance I'd miss something. And that would be on me. I didn't want to be the one responsible. I didn't want a mistake I made to lead to our family being torn apart.

'This is our first proper dinner out in a long time. Let's just try and enjoy it.' I drank my wine and tore at a piece of bread.

I tried to think of something else to talk about. What did we talk about before Bibi? I thought back to the endless dinners out we used to have. We must've talked about something. Ah. I was pretty sure we mostly just made out and debated where to go next, and who to kill next. Surely our relationship was more than that?

We already knew each other's life stories. Our histories of parents, schooling, lovers. We'd covered all that a decade ago. We couldn't talk about the present, as that was too . . . dull. And we couldn't talk about the future, as that wasn't looking so rosy either.

My wife. My partner of thirteen years. And I didn't know what to talk about. I needed to say something. Anything. We were one of those non-talking couples we used to mock.

'Have you . . . have you watched anything good recently?' I winced. That was the best I could come up with? The type of inane chit-chat I'd swap with a stranger at a dinner party?

She raised an eyebrow at me as she took a sip of her wine. The waiter appeared with our food and placed the plates in front of us.

'This looks nice!' I managed to muster.

Haze picked up her steak knife and examined the end of it. She pushed her left index finger down onto the tip of the blade. A spot of blood appeared. She looked at it and then sucked her finger. She started slicing at her steak.

She'd shut down on me. She was pushing me away. I

wondered how long I had before I was out in the cold for good. Haze wasn't forgiving of those she considered to have wronged her. Would my crime – of marrying her, giving her a child, whisking her away to a slower pace of life – warrant a death sentence?

'Can we talk properly? I can't—'

'Are you cheating on me?' She stabbed a large chunk of steak into her mouth as she stared at me.

I dropped my fork. 'How can you ask me that?'

'That's not answering the question.'

'What are we doing here? If you need to ask me that, what's the point?'

'We don't talk anymore.' She leaned forward.

'And whose fault is that?' I hissed back. 'I'm trying here!'

'What are you hiding?' Her eyes flicked all over my face.

'What are *you* hiding?' I leaned back in my chair and stared right back at her.

This was a dance we'd never done before.

'I'm done.' She put her knife and fork together. 'Let's get back to our daughter.' She finished her glass of wine and stood up. 'You can get the bill.'

She didn't even want to wait for me. I got up to follow her. Before I'd even made it three steps past our table, I felt a hand on my arm. I turned to see Griff standing there.

'Griff! What a surprise. How are you?' I smiled at him. Out of the corner of my eye, I could see Haze reaching the door.

He did not return my smile. 'How are you doing, man?'

I shrugged. 'Good. Here for a nice dinner with the wife. How about you?' I looked over his shoulder. His table held an array of men in suits. A work dinner – no wonder he looked so stressed.

'I know what's happened.' Griff sighed. 'God wanted me to be here for you. I just don't know why he didn't let me see you until it was too late.'

'Okay, I guess?' Griff was always so intense. 'Fun seeing you, but I need to go. My wife's waiting.' I motioned at Haze, who was standing by the door. But he wasn't looking at the door, he was staring at our table. And . . . my empty wine glass. Aha.

'I know what you're thinking, but don't worry! It was just a small glass of wine.'

'No, man, that's not how it works.' Griff put both his hands on my shoulders. 'I'm here for you, okay? It's a big thing, losing your sobriety. But we're going to get you back on track.'

Christ. Was he going to make me give back the chip? I'd earned that chip. I glanced over at Haze. She was coming back towards us. I held up my hand to stop her.

'We'll talk about this at the next meeting, Griff, but I've got to go. My wife doesn't know about AA.'

'Your wife doesn't know you're an alcoholic?' Griff frowned.

'No. Yes . . . I mean, she knows I have a problem, but she doesn't know I've been going to meetings.'

'She knows you're an alcoholic and she still ordered wine and let you drink it?' Griff shook his head. 'Wow. I thought *my* marriage was bad.'

'It's not her fault. She loves to drink. I've tried getting her to stop, but you know, it's hard giving up something you love.' I looked across at Haze, who was frowning at me. 'I really must go.'

'She's clearly got a problem too. You enable each other.' Griff gripped my arm as I tried to walk away. 'You're trouble together. You must see that?'

45

Haze

I watched Fox as he drove us home. His eyes straight on the road. I thought this man knew me. That he understood all the intricacies of me.

I am woman. Hear me roar. And also cry. I love you, but I hate you. I feel the cold and I feel the heat. I am rarely the right temperature. I might not always know what I want, but if you love me, you should know. You should decide for me, but not in such a way that you take away my power – you need to make me feel like I chose it myself. If you want to be with me, you have to be steady enough to feel like I can always rely on you, but flexible enough to roll with whatever comes next. Stable enough to give me security, but not so straight that you bore me, as then I won't listen to you – and I really won't want to fuck you. Love me, hold me, look after me. Be vulnerable but also strong. Always be there for me, but don't suffocate me. God, it was so easy. How could he not get it?

What the hell was going on with us? Had we really forgotten who we were? Did I even love him? The real him? Or did

I just love how he made me feel? Correction. How he used to make me feel.

In our glory days, he'd made me feel like the most beautiful, funny, intelligent, exciting person he'd ever met. He'd hold me close and tight, and make me forget all about the lowlights of my past. He was home and safety and comfort. Who wouldn't love someone who made you feel like that? I knew without a doubt I was the person he most wanted to be with in the whole world. He was a walking, talking ego boost.

Even years later, long after the honeymoon should've worn off, whatever party we were at, wherever I was standing, his eyes would find mine. He was always watching me, needing to know exactly where I was. He made sure I knew that he was at his happiest when he was with me, talking to me, holding me, fucking me. It was all about ME.

Now he found any excuse to spend as much time as he could away from me, and the only way he made me feel was bad.

I knew I was guilty too. I didn't make the effort anymore. I used to make him laugh until he snorted. I used to dress up for him. I'd find new, different things for us to do, things for us to try. I would revel in us.

Our spark may have gone, the flame may have dulled, but I had dulled too. Becoming a mother had both made me and broken me. We had both changed, and we just needed to work out if the new us could ever work anywhere near as well as the old us.

By the time we got home from dinner, I was drunk and tired. I didn't have the energy for a high-octane fight. While he was locking up and checking on Bibi, I took two Nurofen to fend off the inevitable hangover, pulled on my eye mask, and went to sleep.

I woke to a text from Jenny. Finally. Emojis asking if I wanted to do a picnic lunch at the park. I replied saying I only did picnics if a table was involved. She replied with a crying-laughing face. I didn't understand why she thought I wasn't being serious.

Fox walked into the kitchen just as I was scooping some things out of the fridge and straight into my handbag. He peered inside it.

'Why is there a whole cucumber, a block of Cheddar, a jar of pesto and a half bottle of rosé in your Louis Vuitton tote bag?'

'Picnic.'

'How is that a lunch for either of you?'

I whipped out my penknife. 'You forget how good I am with a knife.' I grabbed a loaf of bread out of the bread bin and stuffed that on top.

'We must have a cooler bag around here somewhere.' Fox started opening cupboard doors.

'No need,' I trilled. 'This is fine.'

Without agreeing to it, we'd decided a truce was needed. A totally healthy decision to avoid talking about our problems and act like everything was normal.

'You meeting Jenny?' He turned on the coffee machine as he looked at me.

'Yes.' I made a show of looking at the clock above him. 'And we're going to be late.' I turned around and shouted to Bibi. 'Shoes on! We're going.'

She bounced into the kitchen holding a headless Barbie. 'Oh! Yayyyy.' She shot out again.

'Why aren't you at the office?'

He made a show of looking at his watch. 'I do actually need to go now. Client meeting in Windsor.'

'Great,' I said, heading for the door.

'Great,' he replied as he gulped down his coffee.

'Bye,' I called over my shoulder.

'Bye,' he called after me. A pause, and then, 'Bye, Bibi!'

'Bye, Dada,' she shouted as she yanked on her shoes.

We were tiptoeing around each other. A steely politeness. Things were shit, but neither of us could really face dealing with it. What did that say about the state of our marriage? That we couldn't even be bothered to fight?

Part 3
Hardship

'Together you are strong enough to get through any hardship. Whatever life throws at you, you just need to hold his hand and say, "Babe, we got this." You are married. You are invincible.'

– Candice Summers, number-one bestselling author of *Married Means Life: How to Stay Happy, Fulfilled and Together Forever*

'Grit your teeth and get through it. If you're both still standing, high-fives all round. Then brace for the next round of shit, because hell yes – more will be coming.'

– Hazel Matthews, married woman

Creative Culture Club Magazine, June 2021
Lost at Sea by Hazel Matthews
Mixed media, 80cm by 200cm

This piece features a woman standing proudly astride the deck of a boat. Her head is down so we can't see her face. She's holding a sword but the tip is pointing down. The seawater is murky. Has she defeated her fears and banished them to the sea? Or is it her own mind that is her enemy, from which there is no escape? This is a new direction for this artist, but very powerful. There seems a vulnerability and fear that has been absent from her previous works, where the overriding focus was rage and domination. Here, she's in the shadows; warning us of the fear of the unknown.

MATTY MOBILE *Sent 06:23 8 November 2021*

I'm having a baby. It's starting to sink in now. I'm really having a baby. And it's going to change everything. Fox is making me give up something I love doing. This is why I never wanted to get married. It was always meant to be me in charge of my own destiny.

MATTY MOBILE *Sent 06:23 9 December 2021*

You'd laugh if you could see me now. A huge preggo belly. Living out in the sticks. And I just spent hours researching which organic cotton sheets I should get for the designer cot that cost us as much as a small car. Who even am I? I wish you were here to tell me. To remind me that underneath all this suburban shit I'm still me.

46

Then

Haze

Nearly a decade of us. Haze and Fox. Fox and Haze. Recurring seasons of a hit show with enticing lead characters. We had not just found our groove; we were moving to the beat of our very own music. We were perfectly in sync. We moved as one. We understood each other with a nauseating togetherness. Conversations could go like this:

'What about . . .'

'Ah yes, we could . . .'

'But there is the . . .'

'Right, and the . . .'

'Okay, so maybe?'

'Best not.'

'Could try the . . .?'

'Love to.'

We were like this on anything from what we were going to eat, to who we were going to kill. One look, one touch, one raised eyebrow. It was hard not to believe we were made for each other when we fitted together so perfectly.

We were happy. So fucking happy.

Every day was a new adventure.

Every day I was excited for what would come next.

Every day I was living my best life.

Right up until we were stabbed by two pink lines.

Pregnant.

Yes, I was sketchy on remembering to take the pill, and yes, we fucked all the time. But it was still a horrible shock.

I looked at all the fun, the chaos, the death we'd been revelling in and sobbed, *No. I'm not ready.*

But Fox was.

Maybe it was a remnant of that staunch Republican upbringing that made him think all foetus's lives mattered. Maybe it was because he was six years older than me. Maybe it was him not being the man I thought he was.

He held me tight and talked me through it. 'I never thought I'd get married, but you made that fun. Why the hell not a baby? We'd make that fun too. Look at us. We have everything. We can do anything. Of course we can raise a baby. We can have it all.'

I didn't know how to tell him that I knew better than most that some people just weren't meant to be parents. That they lacked that innate desire to protect, nurture, love.

We were good people. I believed that. But what if we weren't as good as we thought? What if whatever we had inside us that allowed us to kill without remorse could also stop us being the type of parents capable of loving a child the way they needed to be loved?

We loved each other, sure. But we were self-sufficient

adults that made each other's lives better. Children were hard work, annoying, fucking ungrateful, rude, always there, in your face, wastes of space, so needy, crying at anything, always hungry, life-ruining. This was some of the feedback I'd been given growing up as one. Maybe some people weren't born monsters; maybe becoming parents is what turned them into them.

'I was always meant to find you.' Fox had cupped my face and stared deeply into my eyes. 'You are brilliant and clever and wonderful and complicated and exciting and funny and goddamn beautiful. The world needs more people like you.'

He totally gamed me. Showered me with such deep love and so many compliments, that he had me believing it'd be a disservice to the human race to not try and create more perfect specimens like me.

And then there was a part of me that did want this baby too, really quite desperately. The thought of a blood relation to claim as my own. Having a baby with the man I loved. It all felt so weirdly natural, this urge to bear his child. I knew it was down to hormonal, chemical, biological, social conditioning . . . but I couldn't fight it. I wanted this baby, but I was scared. Scared of everything it could do to me, to us.

Fox convinced me it would all be okay.

He helped me ignore the voice in my head telling me it would be a tragic end of life as we knew it. He had me believe it would be a new, brighter beginning.

He brought out the best in me. He helped me drown out the voices screaming about how bad a mother I'd be. He helped me believe in myself, the good parts.

By the time we had our first scan, I had started to embrace the little bean growing inside me. When I felt her first kick, I gasped and wept at the miracle of life, at how my body, which I'd so often ignored and always been so deeply unimpressed by, was capable of such an incredible feat of nature.

She had gone from alien concept to my very own flesh and blood. Before she was even born, my love for her was already there.

As my due date approached, I started to plan. Nursery. Cot. Changing table. Nipple shields. Nappies. Logistics of being parents-by-day, killers-by-night . . .

I tried to imagine our future. With the right planning, the right juggling, we should be able to carry on nearly as smoothly as we did before. We could easily find a babysitter for those nights out that would be unsuitable viewing for a kid, or really for anyone without a strong stomach. I was sure that, together, we could make it work. We were a team.

And then Fox dropped the real bombshell. 'We're going to have to make some changes.'

47

Haze

It was a beautiful day. We had managed to secure the one remaining picnic table overlooking the playground. We watched as the kids launched themselves down the slide while we sipped rosé out of the *Finding Nemo* paper cups that Jenny had brought.

'I've had lunch with Gerald a couple of times.' Jenny smiled at me. 'And now dinner as well.'

I remembered that Gerald was the French guy she'd met at Morrisons.

'He knows all about Felix. And he didn't run for the door.'

'That's great. I'm really happy for you.' And for me. If she was finally getting some, then there was less chance she'd be focusing on trying to find the neighbourhood serial killer.

'He's very respectful. I'm actually not even sure if he thinks of me as anything other than a friend and a British snacks expert.'

'A what?'

'You know, he loves all our chocolate and stuff. Big foodie. Always snacking.'

He sounded overweight.

'Are you really into him?'

'He's nice. Very nice. I'm just enjoying the attention and having someone to talk to. I can't . . . I'm just not sure about another relationship.'

'We're not talking about a relationship. I'm asking do you want to fuck him or not?'

'Haze!' Jenny actually blushed. 'I don't think so? He's a big guy. Not that there's anything wrong with that. But you know . . . And there's everything going on with Bill. It's really just put me off men.'

I wasn't surprised.

'How's all that going?' I asked. 'Any more response to the lawyer's threat of court?'

'He's gone a little silent. I can't work out if that's good or not.'

'Get the lawyer to push him again. He needs a deadline. He owes you that money. You and Felix. Don't let him get away with it.'

Jenny getting the money from Bill was important for her and Felix's future happiness, and it was absolutely the right thing to do. But yes, getting embroiled in a messy dispute with her ex was also a good thing to further distract her from all her mad ramblings about the Backpacking Butcher being in town.

After looking inside her bathroom cabinet, I knew the names of the variety of different medications she was on. Now I had the location of her parents' house hidey key and their alarm code, it would've been very easy to swap them all out . . . Going cold turkey on all three of them would surely mean any thought of ongoing cold cases would sail out of her over-stimulated head. This was my emergency plan. If it looked like she was getting too close to piecing it all together.

I did not want to act unless I really had to.

I liked Jenny. Once you got past her neediness and deep-rooted insecurities, she was just a good person who wanted to put away bad people. In another life, we might have been real friends (a life where I was also more open to and actually interested in getting to know other people). I wanted her to be okay. I just also wanted her to be a bit mad so no one would ever take her theories seriously.

For the last few weeks, I'd been chipping away at her confidence in herself. This was all in the hope she'd be left with so little self-belief that she wouldn't share any of her theories with anyone else. If I'd had more of a conscience, I'd feel bad, as really she was so down on herself already, it wasn't hard to make her feel worse.

'How's everything else? How are you feeling? Calmed down about . . . some of your wilder ideas?'

Jenny looked down. 'Sorry. I know I've been coming off a little nutty with all the Butcher chat. I guess I'm just stressing out as I have my review in a month.'

'Your review?'

'HR have given me a date to come in. Before they entertain the idea of me coming back permanently, they want a formal interview and a refresher of standard practices, blah blah. Just a humiliating box-ticking exercise for them to remind me of everything I've done wrong.' She was shredding the napkin in her hands.

'I'm sure it's just procedure.'

'No, it's not. Technically, I just went on maternity leave. I should be welcomed back with open arms and not have to go through all this. They're nervous about me coming back. After Bill, they clearly think I'm a total liability. I just need to show my bosses, show them all what I'm capable of. Remind them how great I was. And then maybe they'd be more sympathetic when it comes to understanding how Bill forced me into lying.'

The hope I'd had earlier was fast evaporating. Jenny still wanted a big, splashy return to glory. She wasn't going to let things go. If anything, she was going to ramp up her efforts the closer her review date got.

Time to bite the bullet. Chew on it a little. And spit it out.

'You still think the Backpacking Butcher is back and killing around here?'

Jenny shrugged. 'I haven't ruled it out. But you can relax – I don't think it's your husband anymore.'

'Ha ha ha!' My laugh was hideously high-pitched.

'Talking to you did really help, though. It made me think that maybe he isn't a backpacker. Maybe he's rich. Maybe he's not using trains and hostels, but yachts and five-star hotels.' Jenny tapped her chin. 'A rich man could easily leave hostel stubs and other stuff to imply he's just some seasonal worker. And rich men always get away with everything. Which would explain why none of the police forces ever had a single decent lead.'

Fuck.

I'd made it worse.

I pictured her walking into her review and announcing her new theory to her bosses. They wouldn't listen, surely? They weren't going to muddy the waters with some random link to a European serial killer? Knives were a popular murder weapon. I did tend to leave a distinctive stab pattern, more out of habit than anything as tacky or dumb as a signature. But Fox had always checked the bodies. Made sure there was nothing linking them. So even if they noticed the pattern on the Cobham Common man, they wouldn't have anything to compare it to. Would they? If it was something I could actually talk to Fox about, he would be able to tell me everything. He probably even had it logged in that special spreadsheet of his.

God, it was pathetic how reliant I was on him. This was my mess. I had to clear it up myself. And I was doing fine. Murder weapon safely hidden. No traces of his blood or DNA on any of my clothes. Alternate suspect already in the frame. And there was no one – apart from Jenny, a lone, unreliable voice – even considering that he could be another victim of the Backpacking Butcher. I was nearly home free.

'Are there any other cases you're looking into? I'm sure there must be something closer to home that you could breathe fresh life into and get your bosses' attention?'

Jenny took a sip of rosé. 'There are a few. I don't know. Maybe I could look more into them. I'd have better access. My Interpol contact has gone quiet, anyway.'

Aside from hoping she'd get laid, hoping that her ex would start threatening her again, and hoping that she even questioned her own sanity, I needed to try and get her thinking that she could crack the Nicky Blaine case. If I could wave a big, bad predator in front of her with enough evidence to put him away, she'd soon forget about the European serial killer potentially on the loose in her home county.

48

Fox

I was still being followed. It was no longer the man in a suit. This new man had on a baseball cap, black T-shirt and jeans. There was 'just a coincidence', and then there was being spotted at a kids' café, a playground and a toy shop – all without a kid. He was better than the suit guy, though. He tried to avoid eye contact.

I paid for the small soft penguin that Bibi had spotted in the toy shop window and decided she couldn't live without.

'Come on, Bibi, let's get home now.'

Bibi took my hand and skipped alongside me, swinging the little bag with her penguin inside. I knew I shouldn't spoil her and that I shouldn't just buy her whatever she begged for, but it was a hot day and seeing her smile was so much easier than hearing her cry. I'd do better next time. Being a good parent was meant to be hard work.

I looked over my shoulder. Baseball cap guy was waiting on the corner, watching us go.

I didn't know what his orders were. He could have just been tasked with following us. But what if that wasn't it?

What if he'd been told to try and take Bibi? I wouldn't put anything past my parents when it came to making sure I fell into line.

'Dada! Too tight.' Bibi tapped my hand.

'Sorry, petal.'

It was time to stop being afraid of my parents. I needed to face them head-on.

When we got home, Haze was on her laptop at the kitchen table. She slammed the lid closed as we walked in.

'What have you been looking at?'

'Just shopping.' She stood and picked up her laptop. 'Hello, baby girl.' She walked up to Bibi. 'Shall we do some painting?'

My phone pinged. I took it out of my pocket and looked down at it. An email from my father. '*What is taking you so long?*'

'Who's that?'

'Just work stuff.'

Things had got decidedly worse since our dinner out. So much for the old romantic in me thinking a night out attempting to recapture our old magic would help fix us.

I needed to come clean to her. About everything. Before things fell apart so badly there'd be no coming back. I just needed to formulate a plan to counteract any threat my parents could ever pose. They might have the trump card when it came to evidence of my crimes on US soil, but they couldn't just idly mention custody of Bibi and then expect me not to be prepared to go to battle against them. I didn't want to be constantly looking over my shoulder, wondering who was following me and what they were going to do next.

The minute I signed those papers, I would lose any bargaining power I had. That's why I couldn't bring myself to do it. Right now, they needed me. Who was to say they wouldn't still interfere in my life once I'd done as they asked?

I needed to do something they wouldn't expect.

They thought they'd given me a black-and-white choice. Do as they say or suffer the consequences. I needed to find another option. One that wasn't on the table.

And then it all became very clear.

I needed to speak to Julian, my right-up-until-recently-perfect brother. We'd always stayed out of each other's way. Circled each other's lives with the skill of sparring boxers, keeping enough of a distance that the other could never land the knockout punch. My parents' overt favouritism towards Julian had created a rift between us that eclipsed the shared experience of growing up together. There was a time when we'd catch each other's eye at a particularly unpleasant thing they said, or share a wince when we saw them be rude, yet again, to a member of staff. There was definite hope that he was more like me than he was like them.

I'd never reached out to him before. My parents had always encouraged our separation, and I was starting to wonder why.

49

Haze

I went to Bibi's bedroom and opened the door a crack. She was fast asleep, her nightlight of rotating mermaids illuminating her face. I walked up to her, stroked her hair and gave her forehead a kiss. She smelled of bath soap and sleepiness. Clean innocence. I was lucky to have this in my life.

I tiptoed from her room. It was time to get ready for my big night out.

I'd spent the last couple of days scoping out Nicky Blaine's two clubs in preparation for attending the masked party at Labyrinth tonight.

From what I'd witnessed, both establishments were shady as hell. They might open their doors at night to paying customers who really did want nothing more than to rock out to questionable Euro pop, but what happened there in the daytime was a different story. Women were marched in and out, some looked out of it, some looked far too young, some had bruised faces. The men accompanying them were all a type I recognised. Ones that weren't used to hearing the word no. I saw men like that for what they were. I understood how their minds worked. I could predict their moves, their plans, their bad intentions.

Watching how they operated made me realise that, in another life, if I was another type of person, maybe I would've chosen a different path. Maybe I'd be the one with the badge, chasing down the bad guys and locking them up, not slicing them up.

I shuddered at the thought. All that red tape, all that having to get sign-off. Watching bad men slip away as the system failed the victims. I couldn't have coped with that. I'd have ended up like Jenny – obsessing over a wall of crazy, desperate to find another way to get them.

I pulled a short black dress out from the back of my wardrobe and put it on. I hadn't worn it in years; not since Fox had told me it was 'a bit *Love Island*'. I teamed it with a pair of chunky strappy heels that I had bought drunk thinking they were fun, and in the cold light of day had decided were tacky.

Nicky Blaine was likely to be at Labyrinth tonight. I didn't really have a plan other than to get my measure of the man, and try and find an opportunity I could use.

I wasn't going to kill Blaine – although the more I learned about him and his business ventures, the surer I was he deserved to die. I knew without a doubt that many lives would be saved if his ended. I thought of the resigned, hardened faces of the girls being led into his clubs.

The greater good was a perfect get-out-of-moral-jail card. You could justify so much with it. Kill one man, kill a thousand. It was all fine if you could argue you were saving more lives by ending theirs. If there was a God, when my time came, I'd look him straight in the eye and say, 'What? What's your problem with anything that I've done? This world was filled with so many shitheads, I couldn't just sit around and wait for you to smite them all with lightning. I've been a good soldier, I've worked hard. Now give me a fucking halo and let me enjoy my retirement.'

I looked at myself in the mirror. Perfect. Hot enough to be allowed unrestricted access, and tacky enough to make sure I didn't look out of place. I pulled my hair down and applied red lipstick. War paint was on.

I tottered downstairs to find Helga in the sitting room with an ironing board and a pile of laundry. I wanted to weep with happiness. No more would we have to suffer through my 'once the duvet is on, you can't really tell how crumpled the sheet is' logic.

I hated to admit it, but Fox had been right. A nanny was exactly what we needed. She was a godsend. She looked after Bibi, she kept the house tidy, she cooked, she ironed. She was the perfect wife for us. I understood now why all our neighbours were so protective of their nannies and always talking about pay rises and perks. They were the only gateway to getting glimpses of our old lives back. I was so grateful to Helga for giving me the chance to hang around dodgy nightclubs, stalking potential prey.

'I'm just heading out.'

'Wow. Big party?'

Fox was due back before me. I didn't want him having any idea what I was up to.

'No . . . Book club.'

We observed each other.

'Book club,' she parroted back to me with a straight face. 'If you're back late, maybe take this with you.' She handed me one of my jumpers from the laundry basket. 'Fox might worry seeing you come home like that.'

'Worry?'

'That you'd be cold, coming back from book club in something so . . . small.'

So not only did this wife keep the house perfect and help with my kid, but she also knew how to help cover for me. Whatever we were paying her, we needed to double it.

Just as I was leaving, I realised that I had no mask, a vital part of my outfit both to fit the theme of the night, and because I sure as hell didn't want to be seen at a skanky nightclub in Slough. I quickly went to Bibi's dress-up box and rummaged around, looking for options. The Chewbacca mask definitely gave me the best facial coverage, but kind of gave off the wrong vibe, so I settled on a cat one with a pink sequin nose.

The club was heaving. The music was terrible. I wanted to leave immediately. The women outnumbered the men. It was hard to tell how much of this was down to women being offered free entry, and how much was down to those who worked the floor at Nicky Blaine's strip club being encouraged to attend. There was a lot of contouring, cleavage and fake nails.

Blaine was on the other side of the club. I got a Diet Coke from a leering barman and watched him operate.

One of the women next to him looked like she could be anything from fifteen to twenty. I really hoped it was twenty. Her eyes were glazed. Blaine was talking to a big man in a suit who was standing next to him. Blaine reached out a hand to the woman's back and she flinched. He didn't notice. He was now stroking her arm. Her shoulders were raised and her jaw was clamped as she just stood there.

I looked around. There were so many men here whose lives

I could end without losing any sleep. I felt like an alcoholic surrounded by vintage champagne. I must not take a sip.

This club was a scumbag magnet. And I was starting to see why. Everywhere I looked, I kept seeing it: men were touching women, just reaching out and groping them . . . and the women weren't complaining. Fake smiles and leaning in to talk to them. Hushed conversations. A lot of these women looked young. Very young.

I felt a hand grip my right butt cheek. Really grip it. I spun around and kneed the short man to whom the hand belonged in the balls. Instinct had taken over my need to not make a scene. I pushed away through the crowds, but too late . . . a man in a black suit gripped my arm.

'Get off me!'

'The owner would like to find out what your problem is.'

I weighed this up. If I wanted to, I could get out of his grasp, make it outside and disappear into the night without being identified. I could walk away from this.

But a chance for a face-to-face with the King Scumbag himself?

Couldn't waste that opportunity.

I allowed the man to lead me to Blaine, who gave me a very obvious once-over.

'What's your problem, sweetheart? Who sent you here?'

'No one sent me. I'm my own boss.' I put on my cockney-gal-done-good voice. I looked around. 'I have some girls in London looking to move out. I'd heard of you. Of your establishments. Thought I'd see if this was an avenue we'd like to explore.'

I saw a flicker of interest. Of course, he was always looking for more women.

'You mean they're not good enough for London, so you're shipping them out?'

'All my girls are excellent.' I gave a small smile. I was very loyal to my imaginary flock. 'So where's the VIP area?'

'You're standing in it.' Blaine motioned to the threadbare red velvet rope that separated this seating area from the club floor.

'I mean the real VIP area – the private one. What's your set-up?' A place like this would always have a separate location where the pretence of being an above-board business could drop away and anything went.

We assessed each other.

'I don't give away information to masked strangers.'

I laughed. 'You think I'm a cop? You think there's space in this dress for a wire? Keep your secrets, doesn't bother me. I'm sure there are plenty of other establishments who'd like to hear what I have to offer.'

I walked away, hoping for a tap on the shoulder and a full rundown of his whole business model.

It didn't come. Damn it. I needed to find a new way of obtaining a nice, juicy piece of evidence to gift-wrap and give to Jenny.

I headed back towards the main club.

A drunken man wearing a feathered mask stepped into my path.

'You're just lovely, aren't you?' he slurred.

'I'm wearing a mask.'

'I can see enough to know I'd like what's underneath. What you been talking to Nicky about?' He was holding a large beer. The liquid kept sloshing slightly as he swayed.

'Just catching up. We haven't seen each other in a while.'

'You coming to his party this weekend?' He took a glug of his beer.

'He mentioned it. Saturday, right?'

'Friday. His house is pretty amazing. Worth coming just to nose around.'

'Where is it again?'

'The jewel in Virginia's Water crown. He calls it a "willy-waver" house. One to really show off how much fucking money you've got. Big white house with the stupid over-the-top columns.' The man chuckled to himself. 'I just love what he did with the gates. His up-themselves neighbours would shit a brick if they cottoned on.'

'You know him well, then?'

'We go way back.' The man swayed towards me. 'I knew him back when he just filmed girls on his phone. Pretty funny when you think of his fancy set-up now.'

In all the research I'd done on Blaine, there was no mention of him ever venturing into porn. If whatever filming he was doing wasn't for commercial reasons, then it must be for personal ones.

'Oh yes, Blaine likes to watch, doesn't he?'

'Wait until you see the home cinema!' He drained his beer. By the time he turned around, I'd melted into the crowd.

On the way out, I spotted two swaying men by the bar being propped up by a couple of women. One of them pushed his mask back as he did a shot, and I recognised him as a dad from Bibi's nursery school.

I needed to get out of here. I wanted to be back home with my clean, sweet-smelling child and forget places like this even existed.

50

Fox

Julian expressed no surprise when I rang him. He said he'd come and see me, as casually as if he was down the road and not sitting in his penthouse in Manhattan. He arrived by private jet the next day. We met at a luxury hotel close to Farnborough Airport.

The restaurant was serving high tea. I spotted him sitting in the corner near a large window as soon as I walked in.

Julian was two years younger than me. We didn't do Christmas cards or catch-up calls. There had been no violent falling-out, just a disinterested drifting apart. The last time we saw each other was at a particularly strained Thanksgiving lunch when we were twenty-something-year-olds.

We shook hands when I reached him. We observed each other for a beat longer than was really socially acceptable. Like me, he had aged well. I had always been able to see that we looked alike, although he had paler skin and a skinnier, shorter frame. An ex of mine had once described him as being an anaemic version of me. Despite rebuking her for her unkindness (only I was allowed to insult my brother), I could see what she meant.

A full cream tea was already laid out, along with a pot of tea. Julian was already on his second scone. I noted he'd put on the jam before the cream. Haze would've been horrified. She couldn't care less about politics or global warming or any big world issue, but 'fucking up scones' really made her blood boil.

'Sorry to hear about the divorce.'

Julian frowned. 'What divorce?'

'I recently had the privilege of spending some quality time with our dear mother and father. They mentioned you and Martha were ending things?'

Julian laughed. 'And you believed them? I'm not splitting up with Martha, I'm splitting up with *them*.'

My head spun a little, and then everything fell into place.

The hostile takeover. It was being led by Julian. This explained their panicked trip across the pond to threaten me into doing their bidding.

'I have to say I'm surprised. I always thought your goal in life was to please them,' I said.

'My goal was to keep my head down and hope they left me alone.'

'And that didn't work?'

'You did the right thing, moving to the other side of the world. Controlling parents don't stop being controlling, even when you become a parent yourself.' Julian had twin boys. They must be around thirteen now. He'd met Martha in college, and they'd married straight after. 'Especially when you work for the family company.'

'You're trying to take it over?'

'Times have changed. They can't expect things to stay the way they always were. It's a good business – it just needs to be run better. And I can do that.'

I realised that I really didn't know my brother. I'd never had him pegged as someone with the balls to take them on like this. Maybe always pitting us against each other had been part of my parents' game plan. It was easier to control us when we were individuals rather than a united front who might join forces against them.

'I want to help you. But they have certain things on me.' I spread the cream on my scone. 'Things that could really harm me if they were to come out.'

Julian nodded. 'Devon. I hate that guy. They have things on everyone. That's how they've always operated.'

'I want to vote with you. I absolutely want to screw them over.' I drizzled jam on top of my creamed scone. 'But unless you can find a way to destroy his files on me, I have a very big problem. I have a family now. I need to think of them.'

Julian reached into his pocket and took a USB stick out. He laid it on the table between us.

'There are seven files on you dated from the late 1990s through to the early 2000s. Then nothing until one final eighth file dated a month ago.'

Haze's file. After years of leaving me to it, my parents unleashed Devon as soon as they met her.

'The server I took them from has been destroyed. If you have a tech whizz on payroll you can confirm this is the only copy.'

This explained why he'd insisted on flying over.

'Did you look at the files?'

'I did not.'

'Too moral to violate my privacy?'

'Too moral to discover anything that could force me to have nothing to do with you.' Julian shrugged. 'I need your vote.'

I looked down at the USB stick. I was impressed. 'How did you get to Devon's server?'

'I've been planning for this for a very long time.' Julian smiled.

I picked up the USB stick and put it in my pocket. 'They aren't going to take this well.'

Julian leaned back in his chair. 'I'm forty now. I want to start living my life the way I actually want to live it. I'm done with pretending.'

I looked at him and waited.

'I love Martha. She's my best friend. But . . .' He took a large bite of his scone. 'I'm gay.'

'I'm presuming Devon informed our parents of this fact before you did?' Things were becoming much clearer now.

'Of course. Why speak to your son or wait for him to open up to you when you can just have him followed and get all his correspondence hacked?'

'How old were you?'

'Seventeen.'

That would've been the same year I stabbed Cornell outside a boathouse. I wondered which they'd found more horrifying: a son sleeping with a man or killing one. With my parents, such a choice would not be clear cut.

'I'm sorry, Julian. That must've been . . . awful.'

Haze and I may have had very different upbringings, but I felt we could use them both as references on absolutely how not to parent.

'They made it pretty clear what kind of life and what kind of support I could expect from them if I wanted to pursue what they called "being a freak".'

'And Martha?'

'We met in college and became close friends. She doesn't like being touched. We realised we both still wanted children and that if we could play being the traditional married couple, we could have a good life, with more money than we could ever spend. It seemed . . . a perfect solution.'

'And has it been?'

'We are happier than nearly all the married couples we know. Our boys are thriving. Everything is as it should be.'

'So why now?'

'Call it a midlife crisis or a wake-up call to the need to be true to myself. But I came to realise that if we bring up our boys to abide by the status quo regardless of who they are or how they feel, Martha and I would be just as bad as our parents.'

I nodded to myself. You could live your life perfectly contained in your bubble of self-involvement. But parenthood popped it. You had to look around and see everything for what it was. What you were. What was good enough for you was not good enough for your children.

'You'll take over the company, cut all ties, and then come out?'

'Exactly. On my own terms. I've spent over twenty years toeing the line, doing exactly as they wanted. Now I get to live how I want and run the business as I see fit. We're one of the largest pharmaceutical companies in the country. We can afford to start initiatives for lower income families.' Julian shook his head. 'Some of the decisions our parents made have been sickening. I presented them with options that wouldn't affect our bottom line and could actually save people's lives, and they still said no.'

I could now see why my parents had initially been so eager for me to move back to America. Julian and his family were about to be vanquished from their lives completely. No more father-and-son rounds of golf where investors could be charmed by their double act. No appearing at the country club with the suited-up twin grandsons and all that talk of the next generation of Cabots. They had wanted to show they still had at least one son in their lives, someone they could show off at society events to imply they weren't such poisonous monsters that both their children had chosen to have nothing to do with them.

This falling-out with Julian was not going to be a temporary one. He was doing the unthinkable: taking the business from them. They had worked so hard to try and shield themselves from scandal, to protect their reputations, that they had never stopped to think about how trying to control Julian's life could lead to them losing control of theirs.

It might have taken him some time to rebel, but he was really going full throttle now.

'You're doing the right thing.' I nodded at Julian. I wanted to say something gross like I was proud of him. He knew what they were capable of, the depths they'd sink to, and he was prepared to take them on.

I stood up and we leaned towards each other and patted each other's backs. It wasn't quite a hug, but it was close.

'I'll send you the documents that need to be signed.'

I looked out of the large window. 'Do you think they know we're meeting today?'

Julian shrugged. 'It doesn't matter. They can't stop us now. Once they're out of the company, they lose any control they have over it.'

'The trust fund?' I wanted to believe I'd do this regardless of whether or not I lost my nest egg, that I could prioritise doing the right thing over access to unlimited funds.

'It's protected.'

I could do the right thing, screw over my parents, and still end up rolling in cash? The stars were aligned.

On the drive back home, I thought of everything that had happened in our lives to lead me and Julian to this moment. The two of us united against our parents. They might have given us everything we could've wanted in a material sense, but I wondered how much better we'd have turned out as people if they'd been capable of actually parenting us. It was hard to establish a good sense of right and wrong when the adults in your life simply believed they were always right.

Until I had Bibi, I had never really troubled myself with how terrible they were as parents. It was amazing I was so well-adjusted. If Haze and I had been loved the way we should have been growing up, would we still be the way we were now? A question I could never know the answer to. And I was happy with who I was. It didn't matter what had made me like this; it was who I was meant to be. I clenched the steering wheel. I missed feeling like I was making the world a better place. But I was guaranteeing a better life for my daughter. That was what I had to focus on.

51

Haze

I drove around Virginia Water looking for a gaudy house that could be considered the 'jewel' of the area. I was on the road that had the largest houses. It had to be one of these to be in the running. The fourth house down was white. It also had large stone columns that held up a wide balcony above the oak front doors.

I looked at the ornate iron gates. It was an unusual design. The right- and left-hand gates weren't matching – they had similar yet different patterns. I drove forward a little bit more. I looked back at the gates. And then I saw it. Tits and cock. From this angle, the left gate design was a buxom pair of breasts with pointed nipples. The right gate was a large penis.

I had found Nicky Blaine's house. In case the tacky gates weren't enough of a sign, a catering truck was parked inside the drive. Preparations were under way for the party tonight.

My phone pinged. 'Client drinks tonight. Back late. Give our girl a kiss from me.'

Fox staying out late using some bullshit work excuse, did at least mean I could make the most of his absence by attending Blaine's party without worrying about returning to awkward questions.

When I got home, I went up to the attic to the big trunks in which we'd stored all our disguises. I was sure I'd always kept both locked, but one of them was open. I lifted the lid and rummaged around until I found the wig and contact lenses I was looking for.

Tonight, I was a blonde with green eyes. I did my make-up carefully. Blue eyeshadow and thick black eyeliner. I looked at my reflection and was glad Bibi was already asleep. She'd barely recognise me. I'd needed to choose an outfit in which I could be agile enough to break into a house, while also looking like I belonged at a party. I had opted for a fitted black jumpsuit and studded pumps. I knew I could run in these shoes. A sheathed knife was secreted in my pocket, and on my right index finger was a large ring that functioned as both a statement piece of jewellery and a useful eye-gouger.

I walked downstairs to a waiting Helga. She looked at me. 'Book club?'

'We . . . we have to dress as one of the characters.'

'I won't ask what book.'

I paused, then: 'Thank you.'

I parked a few streets away and walked to the park opposite Blaine's house. I hovered behind a tree and watched as a slow stream of cars started dropping off guests. Men in gaudy shirts and women in tight dresses. A lot of women. The gates seemed to open automatically as the cars approached, and I didn't see any security checking the car or the guests until they got to the front door. Seeing as some men were arriving with a few companions, I doubted there was a list anyone was checking them all off on.

I walked up to the ornate metal gates of Blaine's front drive just as a taxi arrived. The gates opened and I walked in behind it. I slipped to the left as the gates closed, my hand clasped around a vape. If I was found in the grounds, I was just a drunk party guest who'd got lost while getting a nicotine fix. The front doors were opened by a man in a suit. A couple got out of the taxi and he spoke to them briefly before waving them through. I got a glimpse of the hallway, which was all white marble and gold wall fittings. I walked round to the side of the house, avoiding the spotlights. Hearing the clinks of bottles rattling together, I followed the sound to the back. A waiter was lugging a bin bag of empties out to the bins.

'Hiiiiiiiiiii!' I stumbled past him and through the open kitchen door, brandishing my vape above my head. The kitchen looked busy. I took out my phone and held it to my ear as I walked past the various suited waiting staff. 'Darling, yessss, you have to make it here. It's so fun. So, so fun.' Once I was out of the kitchen and in a lengthy corridor, I put the phone away.

Blaine had applied for planning permission for an extensive renovation of this house three years ago. The detailed architectural plans on the council's website meant I had at least some idea of the layout. There was a study on the ground floor. I doubted I'd be able to get in there. It was right on the other side of the house, and too close to the main reception room where the party was in full flow. The cinema, however, was in the basement. The stairs were just up ahead. All I needed to do was slip down them without being seen.

I caught a glimpse of the party taking place in the reception room. There was a pole in the middle of the space. A blonde was gyrating round it, just out of time with the music.

I walked fast down the stairs.

In the basement, the pumping music from above was barely audible. The cinema should be the second door down. I reached it and pushed it open. The room was just as over the top as the rest of the house. There were twelve plush red velvet armchairs, laid out in rows of four. On the very front row, instead of armchairs, there was a huge bed. I grimaced at the thought of Blaine entertaining down here.

He was a man that liked to watch. Judging by the loose lips of the drunk man at the club, I was convinced that he filmed the women he had sex with. From what I knew of Blaine, there was every chance he had an extensive library of footage showing him committing some of the crimes of which he'd been accused. I went to the back of the cinema, where there was a large cupboard. Inside I found an extensive amount of hardware. Considering I could barely work out how to get our sound system to work, I doubted I'd be able to get to grips with the five different remote controls. I couldn't risk turning on the system – and even if I did, there was every chance it'd need a password. I looked at each device in the cupboard. The third one was exactly what I hoped it'd be. A DVD player. Hopefully this meant he still kept some of his old footage on discs instead of a hard drive. I pressed a button on the drawer next to the DVD player, and out slid a tray of DVDs. They were labelled with just first names. I recognised a few of these names from police reports, and took out three of the discs. I put them down my jumpsuit, which was fitted enough to keep them snugly in place.

It had been eight years since Blaine had had a case built against him. Eight years was clearly long enough for him to think he was so invincible that he could have his very own viewing parties down here, and that he didn't even need to hide his library.

I heard footsteps. The unmistakable sound of high heels on resin flooring and a man laughing. Shit. I looked around. Nowhere to hide except behind the back row of armchairs. I dropped down, quickly smeared my eye make-up. Looking blind drunk was the only hope I had if they found me.

The door opened.

'And this here is his cinema room. Can you believe it?' said a man with a gruff voice.

'Oh my God.' She had an Eastern European accent. 'It's bigger than my flat!' She sounded young.

'Nicky is a very important man. We work together, so I guess that makes me important too.'

'Imagine watching James Bond in here. So cool!'

I heard her walk toward the big screen.

The door closed.

'Shouldn't we get back to the party? I don't want to be rude. I haven't even met Mr Blaine yet!'

'I meet all the girls first. A preliminary interview.'

The hairs on the back of my arms stood up. I felt a chill. I knew what was coming.

'Oh. Okay. What do you need to know about me?'

'Let's just see how we get on.' I could hear he was slurring a little. Drunk and on a power trip.

I heard the thuds of his steps as he went down to join her by the screen.

'What are you . . . I . . . I didn't think . . .'

'What? Do you want the job or not?'

There was a pause. And then. 'No.' Quiet at first, and then again, steelier this time. 'No.'

'Fuckin' time-waster!' There was a crack and a squeal. He'd punched her. 'Fuckin' slut. You want it, don't you?!'

'No! Please!'

There was the sound of a rip.

'Get off!' And then a muffled scream.

He must have pinned her down on the bed.

There was a ringing in my ears as the rage took over. I couldn't just leave her. The door was so close, but I had to stop him. The knife in my pocket was screaming out to me. But I couldn't. It'd be too obvious. I looked around for something, anything I could use. In the corner behind me was a standing metal ice bucket. That could work. I risked a peek over the back of the armchair I was hiding behind.

He had his back to the stairs. The bald top of his head glinted in the dim spotlight above him. She was struggling as best she could, but he was a big guy. I didn't have long. I crept over to the ice bucket and picked it up. It was heavy. Holding it in both hands, I charged down the stairs and whacked him over the back of the head with it as hard as I could. He immediately went slack and slumped on top of the girl. As his hand slipped off her mouth, I went to her before the scream came out.

'Quiet!' I pushed the man off her. I felt his neck. There was a faint pulse. He was out cold.

'You okay?' Which was dumb, as she clearly wasn't. But she looked back at me and nodded with wide eyes, tears still streaming down her cheeks. The strap of her thin blue dress had been ripped and half her bra was showing.

'Help me?' I motioned to show I was trying to roll the man over onto his back. With her help, we were able to shove him over. 'Hopefully he'll wake up with a sore head and just think he was blind drunk and passed out.'

'What . . . what if he doesn't?' She was still crying. 'What if he remembers?'

I put a hand on her shoulder. 'Does he know your name?' She shook her head. 'Does he know where you live? Where you work?' She shook her head again.

I tucked the ripped strap around the top of her bra. Her handbag was by my feet. I gave it to her. 'Fix your face.' With a shaking hand, she got out a compact and dabbed at her face, covering up the tear streaks and smudged make-up.

'Get out of here and never come back.'

She took several deep breaths. 'Thank you,' she said eventually. Then she headed for the door. She paused a moment when she reached it, then straightened her shoulders and opened it.

I looked down at the unconscious man. He didn't deserve to live. There was no doubt about that. My hand was itching for my knife.

I clenched my fist. I couldn't do it. I was having enough trouble covering up the man I'd killed last month. Once was a slip-up. Twice was a pattern.

I picked up the ice bucket and put it back in the same spot I'd found it.

The adrenaline buzz I felt leaving Blaine's house was like the one I used to get in the lead-up to a kill. Injuring a man. Neutralising him as a threat. It was the amuse-bouche for the main course – a salmon blini topped with caviar before a big, sumptuous steak. Tonight, though, it was just foreplay with no follow-through. All the teasing with no satisfaction. I hated this. A pathetic little head wound was not enough for a bad man like that.

I'd just closed our front door to a departing Helga when I got a text from Fox. 'Back in twenty.' I went upstairs and scrubbed off my make-up, then returned the wig and coloured contacts to the storage trunk in the attic. I hid Blaine's three DVDs in the bottom of my art supplies box in the spare bedroom. I wasn't sure if I could ever face watching them, but if I was going to use them to try and get Jenny off our case, I needed a clear idea of what I was dealing with. By the time Fox crept into our bedroom, I was tucked up in bed, feigning sleep. I'd become pretty good at bypassing awkward conversations.

As I listened to him getting ready for bed, I couldn't work out which was pushing us further apart: the fact I'd killed a man behind his back, or everything I was having to do to keep it from him.

52

Fox

I had signed the papers, voting in favour of my brother taking over the business. I'd checked over the USB that Julian had given me. The evidence Devon had collected on my slip-ups back in America was not exactly enough for a slam-dunk conviction, but it was definitely enough for some very awkward questions to be asked. I had to trust Julian when it came to whether there were any other copies of these files still in existence. Now that I was tied to him with my vote, our interests were aligned. My downfall would disadvantage him.

For Julian to be so confident moving forward, he must have been sure that everything Devon had on us, and any other useful contacts, had been obliterated.

I looked out of our large living-room window. Was there anyone out there watching us? Until recently I hadn't realised just how much my parents were still trying to influence my life. What would their next move be now? Julian had neutered them by destroying Devon's files. Would they still try and come after my little family now that it was too late?

'I'll drop off Bibi at nursery today,' I announced as I entered the kitchen.

Haze frowned. 'Helga is working today. I've got some errands to run.'

'It's fine. I want to.'

'What about going into the office?'

'I don't need to be in until later.'

'I suppose they owe you some time off, considering all the late nights you've been doing.'

'That's just socialising with clients. Doesn't even really count as work.'

'Really?' Haze took a sip of her coffee. 'I was thinking the same.'

I gritted my teeth. 'What are your errands today?'

'Shopping. Yoga. The usual.'

Usual for who? For bored housewives around here, maybe. But not for Haze. I wanted to believe she was embracing suburban life, but I knew my wife better than that. I wished I had time to follow her. But considering I was having to keep watch over Bibi today, I couldn't factor in chasing Haze around town too. Maybe I could put an AirTag in her car or even her handbag – it was such a mess in there, she'd never notice. I shook it off. She was my wife, I needed to trust her. When she was ready to tell me her secrets, maybe I'd tell her mine.

It was all clear at Bibi's nursery. An hour ago, I'd dropped her off with a long hug at the door, handing her over to a painfully perky Miss Flora. There was no sign of anyone watching the building. I had a coffee at the small café round the corner, then headed back to the car park – and that's when I saw him. Baseball cap guy. Standing next to my car.

I walked up to him. 'Go on then, deliver the message.'

'You've made a mistake.'

I sighed. 'Can you remind my parents we're not part of some mafia family and that all this' – I motioned towards him – 'is a little embarrassing.'

He pushed me with his right hand. A shove against my chest. I clenched my fists. 'They told me to take your daughter.'

I felt the prickles of the red mist starting to swoop over me. Thirty feet from my car was an alleyway leading off into a side street. I could drag him there and end him. That would send a pretty strong message back to my parents. A great big bloody 'leave me the hell alone'. They would soon see the error of angering me, they would— and then it clicked.

That's what they wanted me to do.

I looked at the gormless face of the hired muscle standing in front of me.

He had no idea just how dispensable my parents considered him. They knew what I was capable of, and yet they had got this man to stand here and dare to threaten my daughter. It was all so very clear to me. They wanted me to kill him, to hurt him. I swung around looking for the cameras. There were two in the car park alone. Positioned just at the top of each side of the wire fencing. They looked brand new. I was betting the alleyway had its own camera, too.

'Leave us alone. For your own good.'

He shoved me again. Harder.

He had been sent to tempt me. Bait to make me slip. I wasn't falling for it. I reached for the driver's seat door handle. In the corner of my eye, I caught a flash of light as he raised his arm. I slammed his hand against my car. I felt a sharp sting and then the clatter as the knife hit the ground. I punched him in the stomach and watched him keel over, groaning. Considering the vast amount of money my parents had at their disposal, I'd have thought they would've been able to find someone of higher calibre to start a fight with me.

I got into the car and looked down at my hand. It was bleeding; the tip of the blade had cut me. I took out my handkerchief and wrapped it round my hand, then screeched out of the car park before Baseball Cap had even got himself off the ground.

I clicked on my father's cellphone number on loudspeaker. He answered on the second ring. 'Et tu, Brute.'

'Let's save on the dramatics, Father.' I pulled out into the main road.

'You cast the first stone, Nathaniel.'

'My whole life you've told me Julian's better than me, so when he came to me with a proposal, of course I listened.' I checked my rear-view mirror. There was no sign of Baseball Cap or a colleague in pursuit.

'He will destroy that company.'

'I don't believe that. You don't believe that, not really. You just didn't want to lose control of it. Just like you didn't want to lose control of us.' I made a sharp turn. 'I got your message. From one of the men you've had following us.'

'I don't know what you're talking about.' I could hear the smile in his voice.

'I don't want to see anyone around me or my family again. You think Devon didn't keep files on all your dark secrets too?'

There was silence on the other end.

'There could be a lot more humiliation ahead.' I came to a halt at a red light. 'Now that you have two estranged sons, people will talk. They'll wonder what it was about you that drove us both away. Anything we have to say will be listened to.'

'What are you proposing?'

'I just want to be left in peace. Enough with the spies and people meddling in my life. If you don't come after us, I won't come after you. Do I make myself clear?'

'Crystal.' My father hung up.

I was the first to arrive at nursery pick-up. The kids were all lined up in the playground. I saw Bibi's little face light up at the sight of me and my heart swelled. I felt sick at the thought of her ever being in danger.

I crouched down as she bounced into my arms. 'Oh, Dada blood.' She pointed to the cut on my hand.

'It's okay, just a little ouchie. Lucky I'm so brave.' I smiled at her and straightened up.

Helga tapped me on the shoulder. 'I thought I was picking up?' She looked between the two of us.

'You are! I . . . just thought I'd say hello. Before I headed to the office.'

'Cookies?' Bibi jumped up and down in front of Helga.

'Yes, Bibi, we're going home and making cookies, just like I promised,' Helga said.

I handed her Bibi's backpack. 'No need to tell Haze I was here! She'll get worried I'm getting in the way and confusing things.'

Helga looked at me. 'Right. Okay.'

'Call me if there's any problems.'

'What problems?' Helga frowned.

'You know, like, if you're worried about anything. Or anyone.'

Helga folded her arms. 'I not report on your wife.'

'No! I didn't mean that. I meant if any strangers, you know, bother you.'

'Ah, you don't need to worry about that. I have taser.' Helga tapped her handbag. 'Come on, Bibi, let's go.'

'Bye, Dada!' Bibi waved at me as they left.

Did she say taser? Was that normal? Did all nannies carry one? I guessed it made sense for them to feel protected. As long as it had a good child lock. Should I check that it did? No – I couldn't be one of those helicopter parents, always second-guessing everything.

Bibi would be safe at home. I could keep checking the security cameras to be sure, but I doubted my parents would risk another confrontation. I'd shown I was perfectly capable of keeping my temper in check, and for all they knew, I had every slimy detail of every crappy thing they'd ever done. They could take a hit to their millions, but I knew they'd find a hit to their reputations – and the good Cabot family name – too much to handle.

I just had to hope they were now done with me. Done with us.

53

Haze

I'd practised my story to myself in the mirror three times, even down to the nonchalant shoulder shrug. If Jenny was a good detective, which I was pretty sure she was, despite her personal issues, she might still be able to sniff out an elaborate lie. Now that the moment was fast approaching, I was getting what felt suspiciously like butterflies in my stomach. Ridiculous. I had faced down far greater threats than a doggedly determined single mother.

We were eating éclairs in the park. Sunglasses were on, the sun was shining, and Felix and Bibi were busy in a sandpit. Altogether a very tolerable Tuesday afternoon.

'Here, have another.' I thrust the pastry box at her.

'I can't. I'm full. Is that your third one? Look at you! I don't understand where you put it.' She motioned at my skinny jeans and cropped T-shirt.

'It's just food, Jen. I crap it out like everyone else.'

'I meant . . . okay. Never mind.'

I looked out at the playground. A seven-year-old boy was running around, getting a kick out of hurting other kids.

I watched him push over two girls on his way to the slide. His nanny was sitting on a bench nearby, staring at her phone. I wanted to step in, but I was just about to start my spiel with Jenny. Unless the little shit went anywhere near Bibi and Felix, I'd just have to hope someone else had the balls to take him on.

I tapped the pastry box. 'Had a bit of a drama on the way back from the bakery.'

'What happ—' She stopped and stood up. 'No, Felix! Not in your mouth!' She kept watching him as he tried to rub sand off his tongue.

'What happened?' I finished for her. 'I was coming out the bakery and there's a bus stop right outside it. A girl was crying. Sobbing, really. And not really a girl. Eighteen, I think. I felt bad for her, so I asked if she wanted an éclair.'

'That's really kind of you.'

'No, that's not the end. I gave her the éclair, and then she started telling me about this awful man who'd hurt her.'

'I wonder why she opened up like that?'

I shrugged. 'I guess people like talking to me?'

'Really? I'm surprised at that. You give . . . quite strong fuck-off vibes.'

'Do I?' I clasped a hand to my chest. 'I don't think so. Anyway, it was funny – okay, maybe not *funny*, but for half the conversation I thought she was saying the famous American magician David Blaine had assaulted her. I kept saying she should go to the press, and she said no one would care about some nightclub owner. And then I was all, "Why does a famous American magician own a nightclub in Slough?", and then she looked at me like I was insane. Turns out her creep is called Nick or Mick or something Blaine. Anyway, so that's why I won't ever make it as a counsellor; she's opening up about her traumatic experience, and I'm going on about magic.'

Jen had stopped waving at Felix. She swung around. 'Nicky Blaine? Was that his name?'

'Yes!' I reminded myself to reel it in. 'That's it. Is he famous around here or something? His club sounded shit. Like one of those skanky ones you wouldn't be seen dead in.'

Jen sat down next to me. 'What was her name? What did she say, exactly?'

'You all right, Jen? Why so much interest? I didn't get her name.'

'He's someone I'd been looking into.'

'Don't tell me you think he's the Butcher?'

Jen shook her head. 'No! He's been on my radar for a while. Sex offender.'

'Oh yes, that would track. She said he tried to rape her, and she managed to fight him off.'

'When did this happen to her?'

'I'm thinking last night, early hours. She looked like she was still in her party clothes.'

'Do you know how to find her again?'

'I don't think so.' I took another bite of éclair. 'Oh! Actually, I think she said something about a Saturday job at Josie's Jewels. Not sure which branch.' I got up and moved towards my daughter. 'You want any water, Bibi?' Playing it cool. Totally cool.

Jen followed me. 'Haze, this is really important. Sorry to ask you, but do you think you could try and find her again?'

I looked confused. 'You going to try and get him for

attempted rape? She said she didn't want to report it or anything.'

'I just want to find out more about what she knows.'

'I don't think she'd be much help.' I counted to five, then went in for the kill. 'It's her friend who's trying to bring him down. Says she's got tapes or something.'

Out of the corner of my eye, I saw Jenny's jaw drop.

I did my best, 'Oh, wow, really?!' as Jenny proceeded to talk at me at about a hundred miles an hour. She wanted to immediately march me round every Josie's Jewels in a thirty-mile radius. I had to talk her down. I said that we didn't want to freak the girl out, and that Jenny gave off strong police vibes (if that were only true, I never would've found myself in this situation). I told her I'd do a county-wide Josie's Jewels tour tomorrow morning when Bibi was at nursery, to see if I could find the girl.

It was all coming together rather nicely.

Jenny's review was in a few weeks. I could hear her mind screaming at the thought of being able to show up there with tapes that proved Blaine's guilt. From what I could tell on Google, although the chain of evidence had been broken by the whole me-stealing-it thing, there was scope for Jenny to say that an anonymous informant had handed over the tapes to her. All this due process blah-blah-blah was so tiresome.

Later, when Jenny had taken Felix to 'poo corner' to relieve himself, the little bully from earlier ran past me. I stuck out my leg and watched as he tripped over it. He barely touched the ground, but the shock was enough to make him snivel.

I went to help him up. 'Oh, it's okay, little man!' I said loudly. I leaned down and whispered, 'Every time you hit someone, something bad will happen to you.'

His eyes widened as snot dripped out his nose.

'Just remember that.'

If you couldn't get people to think about others, you could always get them to think about themselves. I could only hope this would trigger an association between hitting others and being harmed. Good to start the conditioning young; it might save me having to come after him when he was old.

The nanny came rushing up. 'Benedict! There you are!'

I straightened up. 'Poor little thing went flying.'

'Thank you for helping him!' She leaned down and helped Benedict to his feet. As she led him away, he looked back at me. I death-stared him, and he started crying again.

It was good to know that there was no minimum age when it came to getting a kick out of exerting my power and instilling fear.

54

Haze

'I found her,' I announced to Jenny. I had taken her aside after music class to give her the big news that there might be hope for her floundering career.

I had watched the tapes – on fast-forward. I didn't need to properly see what Blaine was doing. I saw enough to know he was everything I thought he was. There was sound on the videos. I was sad for the women who did not get justice. I was sad about the fact that I had a bad man in my sights, yet I couldn't end him myself. But this was sacrifice. I was protecting my family. I had to do what was best for us.

'And? What did she say? Does her friend have tapes? Will she give them to me? Will she meet with me? You think she'll trust me?' Jenny talked fast.

I knew I needed to make it realistic. To try and explain why this imaginary girl and her imaginary friend would be so eager to hand over horrific tapes to a stranger they'd just met.

'She doesn't want to go to the police. She's been arrested before and thinks they'll find a reason to lock her up. She's also terrified that if she goes on the record, Blaine and his men will track her down.'

Jenny was chewing on her lip. She kept clenching and unclenching her fists. Her big chance at redemption was within her grasp.

'She wants to know if you'll be able to get him locked up without her having to testify about stealing the tapes from his house?'

Jenny nodded. 'I will do everything in my power to make it happen. Within the lines of the law. If we can verify the tapes are real and that it's definitely Blaine in them, we have a good chance.'

'Okay, well, let me talk to her again. I'll see if I can convince her.'

Jenny leaned forward and gripped my hand. 'Haze, you don't know what this could mean for me. If you can make this happen, I'll be forever grateful.'

I smiled at her. I was a genius. She was so into getting Blaine behind bars, a bona fide local criminal, that her thoughts of the Butcher would be long gone.

I was doing it. I was saving my family.

I got home to a reminder text from Fox. 'David and Georgie's party tonight. 8pm.'

That was the last thing I needed. A night out celebrating the fact that the neighbourhood's most-in-love couple had reached ten years of marriage.

I put Bibi in front of the TV in our bedroom as I went to paint. My canvas was nearly finished. With snatched hours here and there while Bibi was napping, at nursery or with Helga, I was working faster than I ever had before. Maybe becoming a mother had helped my work after all. The need to fit it into whatever moments I could made me focus properly. No getting distracted by my phone, no staring into space – no time for that. On top of this masterpiece, I had a dummy canvas going too. It had nothing more than a few brushstrokes on it, but that was what I left on display on my easel – just in case Fox happened to pop his head round the door when I wasn't there. I hid my real one behind a stack of blank canvases. My hidden treasure. I knew I really had the dead man to thank for it. All artists had their muses; mine just happened to be bloody corpses.

I painted and painted until everything else faded away. Time. Worries. Regrets. I was oblivious to all. I paused mid-brushstroke. It felt so good to be back doing this, but I was already dreading finishing this canvas. Then what? Back to the stagnant artist's block?

Bibi came in. 'Mama? TV stop.'

I wondered how old she'd have to be before she could work out how to click 'yes' on Netflix's 'Are you still watching?'

I checked my watch. Half an hour until Fox was home.

'Okay, bubba. Let's get you in the bath.' I put my paintbrush down.

55

Haze

I thumbed through my dresses, stopping at the bright red of the dress I'd been wearing the night Fox and I first met. I took it out and looked at it. How did we go from that, all that potential, all that passion, to this? When did we stop enjoying each other? I put the dress back into the wardrobe.

I settled on high-waisted trousers and a black silk shirt. I did my make-up carefully, applying a rose-pink Chanel lipstick – a sales assistant in a Monaco boutique had convinced me to buy it by effusively exclaiming that it really made my eyes pop. Although, come to think of it, I had been wearing blue contact lenses that day.

'Haze?' Fox shouted up the stairs.

I came out of the bedroom and onto the landing. 'Shhh!'

He frowned back at me and tapped his watch as I walked down the stairs. 'Helga is in the kitchen. Let's go.'

'Hello, little one. You look nice! How was your day?' I mouthed the imaginary conversation to myself as I went.

We walked down the street to David and Georgie's house. I didn't know what the traditional presents for certain wedding anniversaries were (Fox and I stuck to watches and jewellery, regardless of the year) but now I had a good idea what ten years was – outside their front door was a life-sized tin man holding a heart.

There were more scattered hearts on the grass, leading towards the side gate and into their large garden, where the party was being held. Strolling through a honeysuckle walkway, we had to admire a photo montage of David and Georgie looking loved up over the years before we could even get to a glass of champagne. I took one from the uniformed waiter, downed it, and handed him the empty before taking another.

Fox looked as though he was about to say something, then thought better of it. The first thing he'd done right this evening.

I saw Caro and Raquel waving at me from the other side of the garden and headed over to them.

'You look amazing!' Caro cooed.

We launched into the usual pleasantries about how delightful the garden looked (fairy lights wrapped around all the trees), how perfect the music was (romantic songs sung by a singer with a quivering voice), and how in love the happy ten-years-in couple were (retch).

Caro took a sip of champagne. 'Have you heard about this stuff going on with the homeless community?'

Raquel frowned. 'Can we still call them that? Homeless? It sounds a bit like a slur, don't you think?'

'Persons without a home? The property-disadvantaged?' offered Caro.

'What do you think, Haze?' asked Raquel.

I'd already popped a smoked salmon canapé into my

mouth. I gave a few chews and then spoke with my mouth full. 'Homeless is fine.'

Not long after we'd moved here, when at a dinner at Caro's house, I'd given one explanation for what the + in LGBTQIA+ stood for and just like that I'd been established as the neighbourhood expert on anything 'woke'. Over the last couple of years, I'd got used to out-the-blue text messages asking anything from 'When does the b in Black have to be a capital B?' to 'If a man is in a dress are their pronouns "she" or could they still be a "he" just in a dress?'

They were at least trying, but every question was a reminder of how I was different to them. I was the outsider, the cuckoo in the nest, the one who didn't belong in this sanitised version of life. I might be a useful guide, but I wasn't one of them. For someone wanting to fit into this world this knowledge would've been shattering, but for me it was liberating.

'Have there been any more fights or anything?' I asked. If I was really lucky, a couple of them would actually kill each other and further confirm the police's theory.

'No more fights or murders, thank God,' said Caro. 'Denni from number seven mentioned she'd seen a few of them hanging out at the Shell garage just before our turning.'

Raquel frowned. 'I just don't understand why it's suddenly such a problem. It never used to be.'

I plucked another smoked salmon canapé from the tray that was being offered to the people behind us. 'I think homelessness has always been a problem. Perhaps you've just never noticed it before because it wasn't on your doorstep?'

Raquel put a hand to her mouth. 'You're totally right, Haze. I am so sorry I didn't check my white privilege.'

I drained my glass and motioned to the waiter for another.

The next hour passed by in a whirl of small talk and canapé-chasing, and then the big moment arrived. The string quartet started up and Georgie reappeared, having changed into a white lace dress. The waiters and waitresses gently parted the crowds until there was a clear walkway to the grinning David, who was standing under a flower-strewn gazebo at the end of the garden. Georgie walked down towards him – admirably regally, considering she was in white Louboutin heels on grass. Their three children trailed behind her, sprinkling flower petals.

After a brief welcome from the female celebrant who had a big smile and purple hair, David and Georgie began their vow renewals. They'd gone the traditional route. We'd been less so.

Nearly thirteen years ago in Chelsea Registry Office, I had stood there in a slightly crumpled white dress, clutching a bouquet of red roses, facing Fox, who wore a blue suit with an open-neck white shirt. We'd giggled together as the very stern registrar kept a straight face throughout our vows, which included a pledge 'to love you as much as I love an ice-cold rosé on a balcony on the Amalfi Coast', a promise 'to always convince you you're looking beautiful even when you're sure you're not', and a commitment 'to never say annoying things like "It is what it is" when you're facing a difficult problem'.

I stared across the garden at my husband. He wouldn't meet my eye. Was he remembering too? What else could be on his mind other than the freefall of our marriage?

56

Haze

I had woken up alone. I hadn't seen Fox in three days. Battleships in the night. He'd leave before I got up and return after I was already asleep. The only evidence he'd even been there was a wet toothbrush and, last night, a vague memory of an arm being flung over me in the small hours before being swiftly retracted. He didn't even want me in his dreams.

If I'd known marriage was just having a housemate to share childcare with, I would've at least picked someone with the same taste in TV.

Bibi and I were on our way to meet Jenny and Felix at The Post Room, a small café near the park that had outdoor seating overlooking a climbing frame that had seen better days. Today was the day. I'd hand over Blaine's tapes to Jenny and let her go skipping into that performance review with something great to offer them.

I could see her staring at my tote bag before we'd even sat down at the rickety table. I handed over the lumpy A4 envelope as she handed me my coffee.

'The girl has repeated several times now she doesn't want

anything to do with the police. I don't even know her real name. She just hoped this was enough to help you put him away.'

'I don't know how to thank you.' Jenny clasped the envelope to her chest.

'Let's not make it weird. Rape videos are not meant to be the perfect present.'

We both laughed. Properly laughed. I couldn't remember the last time I had. The gurgle in your throat, the ache in your stomach. It felt good to have that again. With a stab, I remembered how long it had been since I'd felt like that with Fox.

Jenny was staring down at the envelope. 'How is this my life?' She carefully put the envelope in her backpack.

'I ask myself that a lot.' I looked out at Bibi, who was at the top of the climbing frame.

I could feel Jenny observing me. 'You didn't expect to ever have kids?'

I shook my head. 'Honestly, it never even crossed my mind.' I chewed on my bottom lip. 'I worship her, but I never wanted to be a mother. I don't really know what I'm doing.'

'Me neither.'

I swung to look at her. 'Is that normal, then? To feel like you're winging it?'

'We do our best.' Jenny shrugged. 'And mum guilt always makes us feel like it's never enough.'

I watched Bibi whizzing down the slide. 'I love her more than anything. I would die for her. But some days, I just . . .' I trailed off.

'Want to only think about yourself and not the pressure of keeping another human being alive?' Jenny shook her head.

'And not just alive but making sure they've eaten vegetables, drunk enough water, properly brushed their teeth, that they're hitting developmental milestones, and are happy and well-balanced and not addicted to screens?'

'Yes! That's it! It's exhausting.' Loving someone so much was terrifying. From the moment I looked down at a newborn Bibi, it hit me – she was mine to worry about forever. A life sentence. I would never stop wanting the best for her and doing whatever I could to make her happy.

It felt good to have someone to talk about this with, someone who understood. I wanted to keep going. 'And our bodies. Why is it *our* bodies that have to deal with the growing-a-whole-new-human-being? It's not fair.'

Jenny sighed. 'Periods, childbirth, breastfeeding – and then, just when you think you're done, you're hit with the menopause. Men go through puberty and then that's it.'

No doubt about it, we got the raw deal. No wonder this rage, this rage that so often needed to bubble over, was not abating with age.

'Mama!' Bibi was shouting for me. She was pale and clinging on to the side of the climbing frame as a golden Labrador sniffed at her. I went over to her.

'Bibi, it's just a dog. A nice dog.' I reached my hand out to pat his head. The good boy's tail started wagging. We'd met this dog several times before. Every time Bibi's reaction was the same. 'Just try touching him? For Mama?'

She shook her head and kept clinging to the climbing frame. I wanted my daughter to be a fearless warrior, to charge through life and not ever cower. If I could face down bad men, why couldn't she face down fluffy golden retrievers?

'Bibi, if you confront your fears and overcome them you will be tough. Like Mama.'

She reached out a shaking hand. Nearly reached the top of the dog's head. And then snatched it back.

We still had work to do.

When I met Helga in the park, Bibi immediately went bounding over to her. I'd got over my jealousy. I was just enjoying having someone around to help – someone Bibi enjoyed spending time with, so I didn't even feel guilty about leaving her. Helga did all the fun stuff I couldn't face doing. No matter how much I loved my daughter, I wasn't about to chase her around a public place, pretending to be a growling monster.

I was looking forward to getting home and painting. But as I pulled up onto our drive, I saw Fox clearing the gutters up on the roof. A large metal ladder was propped up against the wall. His hair was wild. He was wearing a muddied T-shirt with tracksuit bottoms. Until this moment, I'd been pretty sure he didn't own anything without a collar. Even all his pyjamas had one.

I looked at him again. He hadn't even shaved. What the hell was going on with him?

My calm, ice-cool man was now a burning hot mess.

Had he fallen for the investment banker curse of cocaine?

He wouldn't do that to Bibi. I was sure of it. So what, then? A mental breakdown? Maybe he missed killing even more than I did. How did we get here?

It might only be 3pm, but I needed a drink. People had wine at lunch, after all. This was just a late lunch – one without food.

As I walked towards the front door, the ladder came crashing down and missed me by inches.

'Fuck!' I jumped and stared at the fallen ladder.

'Haze!' shouted Fox. His head popped over the edge of the roof. 'Are you okay?'

'Did you . . . did you just try and kill me?'

His eyes widened. 'Come on. Please. You're serious?'

I stared up at him, unsmiling.

Fox clenched his jaw. 'You know for a fact that ladder wouldn't have killed you. It would've just given you a nasty head wound.'

'Should I be comforted by that information? Do you just want me out of the way for a few days?'

'You're sounding like a crazy person!'

'You're *looking* like a crazy person!'

I stormed into the house, trying to focus on how a nice, crisp Sauvignon was waiting for me in the fridge.

Fox's phone was on the kitchen countertop. It was ringing. I got to it just as it stopped. Missed call – Petra. Who the hell was she? I picked up the phone and stared at it. My fingers hovered over the passcode entry. I finally had it in my hands, but now what? Did I really want to be the clichéd wife going through his phone? Or was I just too scared of what I'd find? I went to put it back down, but as I did, an email preview popped up on his home screen. It was from a Jacqui Shuttleworth. *'Dear Mr Cabot, I hear you're due to exchange on a townhouse in Mayfair. Lesley suggested I get in touch so we could discuss your ideas for the building. We would love—'*

The email preview cut off. I tapped in Fox's passcode. Bibi's birthday. Error. He'd changed his passcode? When? I threw the phone back down on the countertop. What the fuck was happening? He bought a whole house without telling me?

I tried to think straight. I clenched and unclenched my fists. I wanted to go out there and drag him off the roof and kick the shit out of him.

What was this house? Or really, *who* was this house *for*? Some harlot he'd been fucking? Was it this Petra? Fuck! This wasn't meant to happen to me. I was never destined to be a dumb wife in the suburbs who could be lied to and ignored, while the charming husband lived the good life in the big smoke. He'd forced us out of London with his claims that it would be best for our family, when really it was about what was best for him. I went to the fridge and got out the bottle of wine. It was already open, with the cork pushed back into the top. I pulled it out with my teeth and poured myself a glass. I needed to wait. I needed to calm down and wait. I needed my own plan of action.

Over what could've been a charming family dinner, I wouldn't talk to Fox, and he wouldn't talk to me. Instead, we talked through Bibi.

'Tell Mummy to slow down and leave some wine for me!'

'Tell Daddy he can always open another one!'

'Silly Mummy is going to feel ill tomorrow!'

'Silly Daddy drove me to this!'

Bibi kept giggling at how funny we were being. It was a blessing she was too young to understand the undercurrents of hatred.

We went to bed separately and fell asleep back-to-back. Certainly no kiss, but not even a goodnight. I couldn't remember the last time he'd touched me. Yet I could remember a time when he used to not be able to stop.

I needed to do something. Things couldn't go on like this.

I was the master of my own destiny. That's what I always told myself. I was in control. I could make decisions about how to make my life better. How to make Bibi's life better.

As I drifted off to sleep it came to me in a flash.

57

Fox

Haze's side of the bed was empty when I woke. Her car had gone. She had still not appeared by the time Bibi was finishing breakfast. I started to wonder at what time I should start to worry, or start to believe that was it – she had upped and left us.

I was losing control. I hadn't been paying enough attention to Haze as I'd been so caught up in my own dramas. I knew my parents wouldn't back away easily. I should've seen it coming – everything they've been doing. I needed to think of my next move. I had to protect my family and our future.

With everything I had going on it felt like the fates were conspiring to make me break my sobriety for real. A couple of days ago I'd taken out yet more money for Cal telling him it was the last time. He'd better respect my decision, or he'd become the victim I was looking for.

'Bibi? Where are you?' Haze was calling from the hallway. I hadn't heard her car pull in. Bibi bounced up off her chair.

'Here, Mama!' She skipped through to the hallway. A beat, and then: 'Ohhhhhh, Mama! Ohhhhhh, so cute!'

Clearly Haze had clocked her new penguin and was playing a game of one-upmanship.

Bibi came rushing into the kitchen. In her arms, she was clutching a small, black . . . real live puppy.

'Look, Dada!'

Haze walked in and dropped her handbag on the island. I stood up. 'Haze? Whose puppy is this?'

'Ours,' she replied. 'She's a rescue. Bibi can name her whatever she wants.'

I gritted my teeth. 'Don't you think we should've talked about this?'

'I don't know. Do we really need to discuss all big decisions with each other?' She looked me straight in the eye. I was in trouble. But what for? There were quite a few options on the table.

'Sausage!' shouted Bibi.

'Really, baby girl? That's what you want to call her? She's a French Bulldog. She's four months old. She's had a bad life so far, but we're going to give her a really good one.'

Bibi giggled. 'Love! Love Sausage.' She snuggled into her.

'If you love Sausage, does that mean you like dogs now?'

Bibi nodded and kissed the top of her head.

I understood that Haze wanted our daughter to face her fear head on. I just wished she'd thought it through a little more. What did either of us know about dogs?

I leaned closer to Haze. 'Do you really think we can look after a puppy?'

She shrugged. 'How hard can it be? We've managed to keep Bibi alive.'

'Is she house-trained?'

'About as much as Bibi is.'

Great.

'Puppies need things. Like beds, toys, food.'

'Wow, thanks for that information. I had no idea.' Haze stomped out of the kitchen and came back a few moments later holding two enormous bags. She unloaded everything onto the kitchen table. She'd bulk-bought dog food, what looked like three beds in different materials, a folding cage, or should I say playpen, numerous toys and what looked like . . . outfits.

'Are those . . .' I pointed to a couple of pink and leopard-print items. 'Clothes? For a puppy?'

Haze picked up the pink one and went over to Bibi and Sausage. There was a little manoeuvring, and then she held Sausage out for us to admire. The puppy was now sporting a bright pink hoodie.

Bibi squealed with delight and plucked Sausage back into her arms, cuddling her even more.

'See? If we're going to have a puppy, we're going to do it properly.'

I looked at Bibi's enraptured face. Of course it was a good idea. I just would've preferred it if it was something we'd actually talked about. But judging by the firm line in which my wife's mouth was set, she wasn't interested in talking to me – about anything.

'Shall we take her for a walk, Bibi?' Haze picked up a diamante collar from the table.

Bibi bounced up and down and ran to the door, Sausage still clamped in her arms. Haze swiftly followed.

'I'll just stay here, then? And get lunch organised?'

The only reply was the slamming front door.

My phone pinged. Suzanne. 'Tomorrow night?' I sent back a thumbs-up.

By the time Haze and Bibi came back from their walk, lunch was on the table. I'd rustled up gnocchi with fresh pesto, baked garlic bread, put together a green salad and cut up carrot sticks and cucumber to make a smiley face with gnocchi hair. They had walked into the kitchen laughing together. There was a light in Haze's eyes I hadn't seen in a long time. Sausage was doing circles round them in her little pink hoodie, her stubby tail wagging. I guessed I had three girls now. It might take me some time to take to her – I'd never really been a dog person – but maybe this was all we needed. A band-aid puppy. Maybe we were going to be okay. Haze looked up at me and her smile faded. Or maybe we weren't.

58

Haze

Sausage had settled in perfectly. She might have started out a little unsure, but now she had the full run of the house and three humans who worshipped her. Despite Fox's initial shock at our surprise new arrival, I'd seen him whispering sweet nothings to her when he thought they were alone. I'd even seen him feeding her bits of leftover steak off a fork.

It soon became clear that Sausage really did not like to be cuddled unless it was on her terms. If you tried to pick her up, she'd wriggle out of your arms, then run off and stare at you, furious, from the other side of the room. Then she'd trot over to your lap an hour later to let you know that now she was ready. But even then, she wasn't always sure. Sometimes she'd allow you to pet her, sometimes she wouldn't. She was a grumpy bitch who didn't know what she wanted. I understood her. I loved her.

Above all, she was a wonderful distraction from all the shit I had going on. A lying husband. A secret house. Yes, I had my own little misdemeanours to hide. But really . . . killing a bad man, then covering it up, accidentally befriending and incriminating us to a police officer, then breaking into a rapist's house and stealing tapes of their crimes . . . These were all things that had just spiralled out of my control. None of it was my fault. Not really.

I was unpacking Bibi's backpack after nursery. Inside, I found a large, bulky envelope. I opened it just as Bibi came running up to me, informing me exactly what it was for. Fox's birthday was in a couple of weeks, and the nursery not only knew this fact but had sent Bibi home with materials to make 'an extra-special birthday card for Daddy'. I wondered how much extra I'd need to sling them to actually make it on the premises so I wouldn't have to let a two-year-old loose at home with red food dye and glitter.

'Now? Make now?' Bibi plucked the envelope out of my hands, bouncing up and down.

I thought of one of the Pinterest mum accounts I liked to torture myself with sometimes. Imagining a craft room and plenty of newspaper and aprons and perfectly labelled plastic boxes. I had none of those things. But we did have a garage with a floor I could pressure wash afterwards.

'Come on, Bibi, let's go downstairs.'

I moved my car outside and we spent a whole hour and a half trashing the garage. We started by making the card. A lot of the materials seemed to end up on the floor, and poor Sausage was now very sparkly, but Bibi was thrilled with the end result. Then we built a fort out of old Amazon boxes and, in case that wasn't enough fun for one morning, I finally let Bibi use her dinosaur excavation kit, which involved chipping away at a solid substance to get to the bones underneath. It took fucking ages. I got impatient and used a hammer.

Helga was really making me up my game. Seeing how

good she was with Bibi, and how much she enjoyed playing with her, had made me think I could do it too.

The doorbell rang. I looked around at the annihilation of the garage – I couldn't leave her alone down here. 'Come on, Bibi. Upstairs now.'

She trotted up the stairs behind me. I went to the front door as she ran into the kitchen.

I opened it. Standing there was a tall Black man with a grey beard – he looked slightly familiar, but I couldn't place him. He was in a suit.

'Yes?'

'I shouldn't be here. I know you're Nathaniel's wife, and I just wanted you to know I'm worried about him.'

'How do you know him? What are you worried about?'

'He's on a dangerous path.'

Who the hell was this guy? A Jehovah's Witness, or something more sinister?

'My husband is fine.'

'You don't think he's hiding things from you?'

Was I hallucinating my subconscious?

'I know he is. But I'm waiting for him to tell me in his own time.' I hadn't realised that was what I was planning, but saying it out loud made me realise it was true. I wanted Fox to tell me himself. If he didn't, then there was no hope for us, no hope at all.

The man nodded his head. 'I understand. But he needs support. He's on a difficult journey.'

In the background, I could hear Bibi calling me, asking for a snack.

'Aren't we fucking all?' I said. I honestly did not have time for mysterious men giving me cryptic messages.

The man looked taken aback. He clearly didn't like swearing. 'Please don't tell him I was here.' He leaned towards me. 'I just wanted you to know that he needs your help.'

'My husband is capable of helping himself.'

I slammed the door closed.

Things couldn't go on like this. Everything was coming to a head; I could feel it. We were going to need to show our hands and thrash it out, or this was going to blow up in our faces.

59

Fox

I pulled into our driveway and looked up at our house. Home. When was I last happy walking in and not dreading what lay ahead?

As I got out of my car my phone rang. Suzanne. I looked around. No sign of Haze. I answered. 'You shouldn't be calling me.'

'Don't we need to talk about the other night? You were pretty amazing.'

I pinched the bridge of my nose. 'This is our secret. Remember?'

'I know that. I just wanted to check in and see—'

'I've got to go.' I hung up. I thought Suzanne had understood. Clearly not.

The garage door was open. I walked inside.

A large red stain. String and duct tape. And a hammer.

'Haze, come down here!' I called up the stairs to her. 'Alone!'

There was a beat and a scuttling sound, and my wife's legs came into view as she descended the stairs. Sausage was in her arms, wearing a leopard-print vest top.

'Do you want to explain what happened here?' I motioned towards the garage floor.

She looked over at it and shrugged her shoulders. 'I was playing with Bibi.'

'You expect me to believe that?'

'What on earth . . .' She trailed off as she looked again at the floor. She shook her head. 'Really, Fox? That's where your mind goes?'

She stomped over to the shelf at the back of the garage, pulled back the tarpaulin and retrieved an item, which she thrust into my hands.

'Happy early fucking birthday.'

I was holding a very red, very glittery card with a big heart on. In the centre was a photo of me holding Bibi at the aquarium. We had matching goofy grins. I think we were trying to mimic one of the fish.

'Now we'll always remember it as the one where you accused your daughter's mother of killing someone behind your back.'

Even Sausage looked disappointed in me.

'I'm sorry . . . I just . . . I'm tired. I saw all this and . . .'

'As well as your card, we built a fort' – she motioned towards another corner of the garage and a questionable cardboard structure – 'and excavated some dinosaur bones.'

'It sounds like you had a great day. I'm glad that—'

She talked over me. 'Who was the man at Scott's?'

I blinked a few times. 'What are you talking about?'

'The man who you were talking to when we were leaving. Black guy. Beard. Suit.'

Where was this coming from?

'Just a man I know from work. I don't know him that well. Why?'

She stroked Sausage's head. 'And how is work?'

'Fine.' I tried not to swallow. I held eye contact. I could do many a bad thing, including lying to my wife with a straight face.

She continued to stroke Sausage's head as she stared at me. 'Have you remembered it's my talk at the art college tomorrow?'

'Of course!' How had I forgotten? I thought of where I was meant to be tomorrow and wondered how I was going to do both. 'I'm looking forward to it.'

60

Haze

I was dropping Bibi at Jenny's house. I'd got a message from Helga early that morning saying she had to go in for an emergency dental appointment. Thankfully, Jenny had answered on the second ring, and before I'd even finished explaining the situation, she'd told me to bring Bibi over, as she and her mother would be in all day.

'Thanks so much for having her. Helga will come and get her as soon as she's finished at the dentist.'

'It's no problem, and I'm happy to help. It's what friends are for!'

'Is it? I . . .' I looked at her and blinked repeatedly. 'It means a lot.'

'Where are you going?'

'I'm off to Kingston. I'm giving a talk at my old art school.'

'Wow, that's so impressive. I bet you'll be brilliant.'

I chewed on my thumbnail. 'I'm not so good at talking in front of people.'

Jenny shrugged. 'Well, you know what everyone says. Just

imagine them all naked. Meant to knock the nerves right out of you.'

I nodded. 'Okay. Right. I'll remember that.'

Jenny looked at me more closely. 'I've never seen you nervous before. You're always so together.'

I took a deep breath and lifted my chin. 'Remember, Jenny: no one is ever how they appear.'

My old art college looked exactly the same as it had when I ran out of it sixteen years ago. I was standing outside, looking up at it.

This should be a triumphant moment. Sweeping in, sunglasses on. A big star in the building. I had made it. I was in that tiny percentage of people who'd left here and gone on to make an actual living from their art. I had beaten the odds. Proof that I had some semblance of talent.

I took my phone out of my bag and texted Fox. 'Where are you?'

Things with us were strange right now, but I needed him for this. He knew that. A familiar face in the room to help me through this.

I checked my watch; ten minutes until my talk started. I'd cut it fine on purpose, to minimise the cringey schmoozing beforehand.

I took a deep breath and went through the doors. A woman in a large gold necklace was waiting for me in reception. She was in a stylish orange-and-red print dress. I felt a little understated in my ripped skinny jeans and black shirt. I'd agonised for hours over what to wear. Something that didn't look too arty try-hard, but also didn't look too styled. Now I felt like I was trying too hard to appear ten years younger.

'Hazel!' She held out her arms. 'I'm the head of the college. Mercedes Remuinan. I'm so glad you could do this. I'm a huge fan of yours.'

'Thank you. Where are—' I stopped. A familiar face had appeared besides Mercedes – but not the one I wanted I see.

'Long time, Haze.' My old tutor Dan Richards gave me a little wave. I wasn't surprised. I'd known from the college's website that he still worked there.

'Hi Dan.' I'd never felt any guilt about Dan's effusive efforts to help me with my career. It really was the least he could do for a girl he'd touched up just after her best friend died. I should try and find out how his life had been since I last saw him. I should check I hadn't been naïve in thinking he wasn't a truly bad man, just one who'd badly misread the signs.

'We've got a great crowd in there.' Dan motioned towards the lecture hall. 'Everyone really wants to hear you speak.'

'We start in five minutes,' sing-songed Mercedes.

I looked down at my phone. No message from Fox. 'I just need to make a couple of calls and I'll be right in.' I took a step away from them as I rang Fox. It rang and rang. Where the fuck was he? His voicemail kicked in, and I hung up and rang again. I wasn't sure how long I'd stood there, or exactly what I said in the message I eventually left him, but then Mercedes tapped my shoulder and said it was time to go in.

I walked into the lecture hall and stood to one side as Mercedes gave me an introduction. On the large screen behind her was a slideshow of my work.

Dan gave me a nod from the front row.

I just needed to grit my teeth and get through this. Fox hadn't turned up. Matty was dead. And all men were arseholes. I could only rely on myself. And I was pretty awesome.

I was a serial killer. An avenging angel. What was a little speech when I once killed a man with nothing but roaring aggression and a broken plate?

Jenny's advice had been to look out and imagine everyone naked, but I would just look out and imagine everyone dead. The snarky-looking guy with the neckerchief. Picture him with his throat slit. Not a problem. The eye-rolling woman in the front row. Decapitated. Totally fine.

The door opened. I swung to look. No Fox . . . But Jenny. She gave me a little smile and quickly went to an empty seat in the third row.

I blinked repeatedly as I took this in. My husband hadn't shown up for me, but my friend had. At least the fury I had at him was a little abated by the gratefulness I felt for her. Back when Matty and I would talk about this big moment of glory, it was always cackling over how the other would be in the crowd, whooping with pride. It might not be his face smiling out at me from the audience, but at least I had someone here for me. Someone who cared.

'. . . And now I hand over to Hazel!' Mercedes motioned towards me, and I stepped forward. She handed me a microphone. I fiddled with the bottom of it as my heart raced. My eyes found Jenny's. She gave me a thumbs-up.

I looked out at the crowd. 'I know what you're all thinking. One day, it'll be me up there – it *has* to be me up there!' There were giggles. Thank God there were giggles. 'That's what my best friend and I always used to think when we sat through these talks. But let me tell you, you don't find it any easier or feel any more successful when you're up here; there's a whole heap of new shit that'll bog you down. I think . . .'

I continued into my carefully prepared speech, my heartbeat slowed, and it felt like it was going to be okay.

It all passed by in a blur. I read fine, my voice was level, they laughed and frowned in the right places. The floor was opened to questions, and I actually enjoyed answering them. Talking about my process, my work. I didn't delve too deeply into my inspiration, but I did make reference to the 'simmering rage women experience because of the way men feel they can treat them'.

I enjoyed Dan squirming in his seat at that one.

When it was all over, I stood and took the applause. It felt good. Many students came up to me as they were leaving. A brief chat, thanks, questions. I was gracious and charming and really everything a visiting dignitary should be.

After effusive thanks and praise from Mercedes and a tight smile from Dan, who couldn't meet my eye, I went to Jenny and hugged her.

'How did you find me?'

'Haze, if I couldn't work out which Kingston art school you were giving a talk at, I don't deserve my badge back!' She took my hands. 'You were amazing! It was so inspirational and honest, and really all I can say is I'm so impressed.' She looked around. 'Did Fox not make it?'

'He got held up at work.' I hadn't yet checked my phone, but he was going to need a far better excuse than that.

61

Haze

'Nathaniel Cabot doesn't work here anymore.' I kept replaying the UBS receptionist's voice over and over in my head.

I was sitting at the kitchen table with a plate of chocolate cake. A full glass of red wine was next to me. I was waiting for 5pm to hit.

I heard the front door open. 'Haze? Haze, you in here?'

My husband was home.

He came barrelling into the kitchen and came to a stop when he saw me. 'I'm so sorry I couldn't make it. I wanted to be there for you so much.'

I stabbed at the cake with my fork. 'If I need you to show up, you fucking show up.' I kept my voice calm.

'What can I do to make this better?'

I took another forkful of cake. 'I've always trusted you with my life. When you do the type of things we've done, trust is everything. I always believed you'd be there for me if I needed you. No matter how big the man, how sharp the knife. You'd be there.'

'Of course! I will always—'

'But you weren't there for me, were you? You couldn't even make it across London for me!' I pushed my plate away. 'I can't trust you; I can't rely on you. What's even the point of you?'

'There was a big crisis at work. I couldn't leave, I had no choice!'

I took a deep breath. I wasn't going to play my trump card. I wanted to hear him lie until he couldn't dig himself out.

'Held up at work? Really? That's what you're going with?' I stared up at him, willing him to crumble. To be honest.

'Life doesn't just revolve around you, Haze! I have things going on in my life too! You never think about what I might be going through, do you?'

I clenched and unclenched my fists. 'I don't want you here. If you stay, I won't be held responsible for my actions.' I downed my glass of wine. Fuck 5pm.

'Is that it? You're threatening me? You think I can't take you?' Fox's voice was rising.

'You really want to play this game?' I stood up sharply and the chair fell to the floor. 'Let's go. I'm all fired up.'

We stood facing each other.

We knew how to fight. We knew how to kill. Our rows weren't like other couples'.

I tensed. If he was coming for me, I'd be ready.

We stared at each other. His eyes were dark. I did a sweep of the kitchen. I could make it to the knife block in five strides. It would take him seven. But I didn't know what he might have in his pockets.

He caught my eyes locking on to the spade by the door out to the garden.

'You're being ridiculous,' he hissed at me.

'That's just what every woman who's been let down wants.' I eyed my cake fork on the table. 'To be told it's all their fault. That they're overreacting.'

'I've apologised!' He flung his arms up in the air.

I flinched. And caught a scent of something. Acrid smoke? Where the hell had he been? 'It's not fucking enough!' I shouted at him.

'What do you want from me?!' he shouted back.

'The truth! But you're not giving it to me, are you?' I stared at him. This husband of mine. This father of my child. I knew what needed to happen, for all our sakes. 'Pack a bag and get the fuck out.'

I was pretty sure that you couldn't ever get a marriage back on track if you'd stabbed your husband in the thigh with a fork. And right now, for Bibi's sake, I wanted there to still be hope of some kind of future for us.

'Fine. I'll leave. Gladly.'

I stared at his back as he left.

Was this it? The white flag of surrender? The beginning of the end?

I might not have known where he'd really been during my talk, but it sure as hell wasn't a boardroom. What was he hiding? Where was the man I'd married? Where was my bright, brave Fox who worshipped me and told me everything? I remembered all too clearly, the peace of lying naked in each other's arms and feeling that there was nothing separating us, nothing we didn't know about each other. We belonged together. We belonged to each other. We were one.

Did I dream it all? Was it all a lie?

Maybe he'd never been right for me. Maybe we'd both got blinded by the joy of a mutual passion – a rare, and hard to understand, mutual passion. Maybe that overrode any other feelings, any other questions about our suitability. We fell hard and fast, without ever really knowing each other.

We were first bound together by a love of death, and now we were bound together by a love for our child.

Maybe the whole trouble was that I had been expecting too much of him.

After all, he was a man.

Part 4

Hiatus

'Sometimes a little reset can be needed. A little time apart, perhaps at a spa or on the golf course. This pre-agreed quality alone time is important to help revitalise you and focus your mind on how you can be a better spouse. It will make you all the more appreciative of the love that's waiting for you when you reunite.

– Candice Summers, number-one bestselling author of *Married Means Life: How to Stay Happy, Fulfilled and Together Forever*

'Sometimes you need a fucking break, before you break his fucking neck.'

– Hazel Matthews, married woman

62

Haze

England had been hit by a heatwave. It was already getting clammy, and it wasn't even 9am. Summer in the suburbs was a type of hell I had never wanted to face. I was driving over to Jenny's house and had ramped up the car's air-conditioning to full blast.

I'd left the house just as Fox arrived. Communication over the last few weeks had been limited to curt messages about seeing Bibi and me trying to be out of the house whenever he was in it.

I still wasn't totally sure how we'd ended up here. I didn't know what I wanted. I just knew it couldn't carry on like it was. He didn't get to let me down so spectacularly and not tell me the truth about why.

Last night, the doorbell had gone at 9pm – Ocado. The delivery driver handed over one plastic bag and left. I looked inside it. Nothing but a bottle of champagne. I stared at it for a minute, and then I realised. Last week, while I was trying to get to grips with a Fox-less life, I had booked a delivery slot in an attempt to be organised. I'd clicked on the bottle of champagne to meet the minimum delivery fee. And had then failed to replace it with the long list of groceries I actually needed. It was like the universe was reminding me how badly cut out I was for this. Bibi had had waffles from the freezer and a flat glass of Appletiser for her breakfast this morning.

I parked the car and rang Jenny's doorbell. She was still in her pyjamas. At least I hoped they were her pyjamas: a tank top with a hole in it and pair of shorts with pineapples printed on them. I handed her a bag of pastries.

'Haze! What's this for?' She peered inside it.

'I know it's your review today, so wanted to wish you luck and make sure you had plenty of energy.'

She clasped the bag to her chest. 'Thank you, Haze. This is so kind of you.'

She had showed up for me, for my big day at art college, so this was the least I could do. I felt guilty that she'd been nothing but open and honest with me, and I'd lied to her more than I'd told the truth. I could at least comfort myself with how I'd given her evidence that would not only help her get her job back, but with any luck, get a bad man locked up for decades.

'I've been trying to concentrate on getting ready for today, but all this stuff with Bill keeps creeping in.'

'What's he been doing?'

'He's been ignoring all the letters we send. Or sending them back with just "fuck you" scrawled across them. My lawyer says we're going to have to sue him. It's about to get really messy.'

'But she's hopeful you'll win?'

'Very.' Jenny nodded. 'Says the evidence is a slam dunk. And his constant abusive messages have made it even easier for us.'

'Mamaaaaa.' Felix was shouting from inside.

'Do you want to come in?' Jenny turned round to the hallway. 'I'm coming!'

'I need to get back. Let me know how it goes.'

'You'll be my first call!' She reached for me and hugged me close. 'I'm so glad I met you. You've helped me so much with Bill, and getting me the Blaine tapes.' She pulled back. 'And most of all you've made me feel more like myself.'

'Me too.' I squeezed her shoulder and walked away.

To my surprise I meant it.

When I first met Fox I felt like I finally understood my place in this world – I was a lover, a partner, a killer. I didn't fit neatly in a box until I found him, and we made our own. Everything I was suddenly made sense as now there was someone else just like me. And we were perfectly in sync until we weren't.

Parenthood rocked us so hard that I was lost once again. Until Jenny. She'd helped me find my place as a mother. We were doing the best we could and that was all that mattered. It was boring, exhausting, rewarding, beautiful. And I'd discovered you didn't need to be an actual serial killer to want to enact serious bodily harm upon anyone who threatened your child.

I could never have predicted any of this. Without it ever being, at any point, my main objective, I had made Jenny's life better. I'd always thought I was poison. That spending too long with me was dangerous. I spoiled things; I spoiled people.

But maybe I wasn't cursed. Maybe I could live a good life and let people in, and they wouldn't disappoint me, destroy me, or die. Maybe I didn't have to live with this dread of what was going to go wrong next.

Somewhere along the last few months, despite my frequent lies and occasional attempts to get her to second guess herself and her sanity, this had become a real friendship. Jenny was now someone I could rely on. If I needed her, she'd be there for me, and I knew I would do the same for her.

I smiled to myself and then it hit me.

My best friend was a police officer.

63

Haze

When I got home, Sausage jumped up and up and licked me over and over. It must suck to be a dog; never knowing if the person you loved was leaving for an hour or forever. I covered her in kisses and watched as she trotted off through the kitchen and out into the garden, on to her next task of patrolling for squirrels. We could all learn a lot from dogs – they didn't let the devastation of potential abandonment get in the way of the rest of their day or their sunny outlook.

I walked into the kitchen and felt my good mood seeping away. When I wasn't looking at Fox, I could nearly forget the ramshackle state of our relationship.

He was, at least, looking more like himself, in chinos and a polo shirt, although the stubble was still there, and judging by the *Peppa Pig* oinks I'd heard on the way in, Bibi was watching TV in the sitting room. What happened to his regimented screen-time limits?

'I want to explain,' is what he greeted me with. 'I know how important that speech was to you. Not just because of Matty, but because of everything it symbolised. Your success despite everything, how you'd made it all on your own.' He touched my arm. 'I really wanted to be there for you.'

I stared at him silently.

'I'm sorry it's taken so long for me to tell you where I was.'

I crossed my arms. 'It's another woman, isn't it? Just admit it.'

Fox's eyes widened. 'What? No! How did . . . Are you talking about Suzanne?'

'Who the fuck is Suzanne?' I hissed. Who even was this man and how many secrets did he have?

'No one! I don't mean . . . You've got it wrong. Just let me explain.' He took a deep breath. 'I've been involved with Petra for five months now.'

The name from the call log on his phone. I tried not to let my eyes stray to the kitchen knife on the island countertop.

'Who is she?'

'It's not just one woman. It's forty-two of them.'

I took a breath in. 'Are you fucking kidding me? Have you got some kind of addiction? Is it—'

'A domestic violence women's shelter. The charity that runs it is called Petra. It's Greek for "rock" and the work we do is all about resilience and building foundations for a new life.'

'Petra . . . is a charity,' I said slowly.

Fox nodded.

I tried to breathe and process what he was telling me. One thought shouted the loudest. 'Are you going after the men that hurt the women there? Are you . . . hurting them back?' I clasped my hands against my chest. All this time, he'd been undertaking vengeance without me? Had he been using some kind of loophole – not killing, just maiming?

'No, of course not! I'd never do that without you! I'm just . . . helping the women with their financial planning. Getting their lives back on track. That kind of thing. I'm volunteering.'

Not maiming, volunteering. 'Oh.'

'I've sometimes threatened the men who were trying to find their girlfriends and wives. But I've never hurt them – just strongly insinuated I would. It was more effective than involving the police and another restraining order.'

I took this in. He claimed he wasn't fucking anyone, he wasn't killing anyone – but he had still been lying to me.

'Why the hell didn't you tell me?'

'I thought you wouldn't understand why I needed to do it, and I didn't want you to know how much I'd been struggling with our pact when you were doing so well.'

I tried to keep my face neutral.

Fox ran a hand through his hair. 'It wasn't just the killing I missed. It was the feeling of doing something good. Something to make the world a better place.'

I grimaced. He was so male in his need to be the hero. 'Why did you have to volunteer, or whatever helpful thing you were doing, on the day of my speech?'

'It was Petra's big annual fundraising day. We had speakers there, and sponsors. A lot was going on, but I'd made sure everyone knew I'd be leaving early.'

'So what the hell happened?'

'During the speeches, one of the women's husbands broke into the basement and started a fire. The whole place caught alight. It was chaos. I did what I could to help everyone get out.' He had the good grace to give a humble shrug. 'And then I saw the guy who did it, watching from across the street. You know . . . we know bad men. I went for him and had to be pulled off him. I'd knocked him out. Then the police had to talk to me. I had to give a statement. They took my phone.'

I tried to take this all in. 'You missed my speech because you went into a burning building to save people? Did you get any little puppies out alive too?'

'You don't believe me?' Fox tapped at his phone and showed me his screen. There was a news report, shaky video footage of a man rushing out of a smoking building with an elderly woman in his arms. A flowery scarf was tied across his face, but I still recognised my husband.

'Why didn't you tell me this on the day?'

'You were too angry! How could I tell you I didn't make it there for you because I was helping other people? I thought there was more chance of you accepting my absence if it was something to help our family, like working on not losing my job.'

'Your opinion of me must be pretty low.' Fox had always acknowledged my selfishness, but in an understanding way – I put myself first, because no one else ever had. Now he made it sound like a bad thing.

'I wanted to wait until you'd calmed down. Explain things properly. But things just . . . escalated.'

'You not only lied about where you were that day, but you've also been lying to me for months about what you've been doing?'

Fox sighed. 'You see? I knew telling you the truth would've led to the fact I'd chosen to never tell you about Petra.'

'So why are you telling me now?'

'Because look at us! I've been living somewhere else. Things can't really get much worse! I'm alone in a hotel room while you're getting champagne delivered late at night. Partying while I'm in purgatory!'

I forgot he got the Ocado notifications. I felt a little comforted that my poor organisation skills had given him a night of agonising over what I was up to.

Fox looked down. 'Everything I did was with the best intentions. Petra became part of my coping mechanism for not killing.'

'Don't you think it would've helped me? To know you found all this' – I motioned around our gleaming kitchen, our supposedly perfect suburban life – 'difficult too?'

'I was the one who led the way with the pact. I knew you didn't want to stop. So no, I didn't want you to know that I found it hard.' He bit his lip. 'I've had to try all kinds of things to help me keep control of myself.'

'Like what?'

'Poker. High stakes.' He shrugged. 'I'm pretty good at it. I'm up 300k and only had to suffer through one punch-up from a group of heavies. Turns out gangsters are bad losers.'

His bruised face. The supposed bike accident.

A name kept niggling at me. 'Who is Suzanne?'

Fox sighed. 'Suzanne is a woman at UBS. She's American. Her parents are friends with my parents. She'd been tasked by them with spying on me. Trying to stir up trouble. It didn't click for me until recently that we'd met years back. That's when I figured it out.'

'Why didn't you tell me?'

'I was trying to protect you! I didn't want you to get freaked out about all the dark stuff my parents had been doing.'

I shook my head. 'You should've been honest. About it all.'

I let the silence linger between us.

'They got me fired as well.'

He took a couple of steps towards me.

'A few weeks ago. But you don't need to worry as I've already got a plan in place. I've bought a property in Mayfair. I'm going to set up my own firm.'

I stared at him. 'Anything else?'

Fox ran a hand through his hair.

'The man at Scott's. I know him from AA meetings. I figured they help people stay off booze, so why not a different addiction?'

I couldn't judge. He'd used ways to help him deal with missing the kills. I hadn't. And look where that had got me.

Petra. Suzanne. His face. His job. The Mayfair house. All his secrets unmasked. I had thought the worst of him and he had an explanation for them all.

He attempted a smile. 'Can you please let me try and make things right? We could do a night away? Neutral territory? A chance for us to properly talk.'

I didn't even know what I was meant to feel now. Hiding everything from him was easier when I thought he deserved it as he was betraying me too.

'I've found a beautiful place, just an hour from here. I've already checked, and Helga can babysit tonight and sleep in the spare room.'

'I'm not sure. It feels like a lot. I'm—'

He frowned. 'Don't you think our marriage is worth putting time into? For Bibi's sake?'

I took a beat. 'Yes, honey, of course I do.'

'Great!' Fox attempted a smile. 'It'll work wonders, I'm sure.'

He was right. We needed to do something to try and reset. I just wasn't convinced a mini-break would fix the gulf between us.

64

Haze

I took Bibi out for lunch – me not cooking was a treat for both of us. After big bowls of pasta, I got her an enormous ice cream sundae, and tried not to think about how this would be the first night I'd ever spent away from her. We went to the park to feed the ducks. Sausage was furious they were getting food she wanted. She kept barking at them, and then barking at us. I watched Bibi laughing and thought about how the older she got, the easier it was to hang out with her without it being an effort. She also hadn't shat herself in weeks, which really helped me enjoy spending time with her.

I was wearing shorts and a knotted T-shirt. I still felt overdressed for the heat. I bought us both ice lollies, not so much as a treat but out of sheer necessity. This clamminess was unbearable. Weather like this was for pools, cocktails and air-conditioning – not for trying to entertain a hyperactive toddler.

Walking back slowly from the playground, I kept feeling

like someone was following us. Twice, I caught a glimpse of a large man in a baseball cap. It felt like he was watching us.

Were my senses attuned to a potential threat? Or was I just being paranoid? I looked back just as the man disappeared behind a tree. He was probably looking for a quiet place to piss. I had to get a grip.

My phone rang. Jenny. I quickly answered.

'My review went great!' She was out of breath. 'I'm just heading back to my car now.'

'I'm so glad. You think they'll let you have your job back?'

'They're going to let me know in the next two weeks. But I have a good feeling about this. I really do.'

'What did they make of the Blaine tapes?'

'There was a lot of bluster about needing to review them and chain of evidence, etc. But they're desperate for a break in that case, I know they are.'

I heard the bleep-bleep of her keys as she unlocked her car.

'Even if they can't use them in court, they can somehow use them to get him. Or get someone else to turn on him.'

I smiled to myself. It might not be as satisfying as a slit throat, but really, the idea of him suffering the indignity of being locked up was a good thought. Any punishment was better than him walking around and getting the chance to hurt another woman. 'This all sounds really positive.'

'I'm going to get my job back, get money off that shithead Bill and finally move out of my parents' house. See, Haze, you've changed my life for the better!'

When it had looked like she was frighteningly close to discovering our secret, a knee-jerk reaction could've been to kill her. But with a little careful thought, planning and genius acting on my part, I had solved the problem before it ever became a real issue.

This was the type of shit even Fox wouldn't have been able to pull off. Next time he lectured me about my hot-headedness and my inability to think things through, it would take an iron will to not lay out everything I've done in the last few months as an example of just how brilliant I really was. I'd found a violence-free solution and made my first proper friend in decades.

Helga was in the kitchen, unpacking shopping bags. She'd noticed all the essential grocery items we were missing. I wanted to hug her.

'Thank you for this, Helga.'

'A storm is coming.' She looked at me with a straight face as she held a large bottle of Fairy Liquid.

I looked back at her. 'Oh, the weather? Yes, I saw the forecast. I'm leaving in an hour, so I'm just going to go pack.'

'Do you know what time back tomorrow?'

'I think we'll be home around lunchtime. The place we're staying isn't far away.' Fox had messaged me the details earlier saying he'd meet me there. It was a beautiful modern lodge set back within what looked like a small forest. It had that glossy sheen of rentals where everything looked brand new, no clutter to make it feel real.

'Oh,' said Helga, 'you're going away together?'

'Yes.'

She nodded. 'Okay, I didn't realise going same place. Together.' We had been making a half-hearted attempt to hide our marriage problems from Helga, but clearly they were too obvious to miss. 'He just left here. He said back morning time.'

I frowned. Fox had been back here without telling me? I shook it off. This was his house, too. And we were trying to make things work, weren't we?

Upstairs in our bedroom, I opened up my Louis Vuitton weekend bag. I looked at it and thought of all the times I'd taken it around Europe, stuffed with high heels, strappy dresses and silk negligées. I'd taken it to the hospital too, when I was in labour with Bibi. Then, it had been full of breast pads, nipple cream and sanitary pads.

I picked out a black cotton dress and a pair of sandals. It was too hot for heels. It was too hot for anything. I chucked in my washbag and a pair of clean pants.

I stopped and looked at my bag. Could I really believe this was it? That he was genuinely trying to get us back on track? That all his secrets were out in the open?

I thought of Fox and the ladder crashing to the ground by my feet.

I went to the drawer in my bedside table, took out my favourite knife and added it to my bag. Now I had protection covered, what else to bring for a romantic mini-break with a husband who had a questionable agenda?

Protection. That word jogged a memory. *'This is for our protection.'* Fox's stock response whenever I complained over the time he was taking tapping into his spreadsheet about our kills.

I went downstairs to Fox's study. I never went in there. Fox barely went in there. It was more of a showpiece. A large room to store his laptop and briefcase, decorated with shelves of books he'd never read. I headed straight to the corner next to a small filing cabinet. I moved it to the right and pressed the floorboard where it had been standing up and down. It wobbled. I reached for the letter opener on his desk and prised at the corner of the floorboard. It came up easily. I looked down at the lockbox underneath. I took it out and tapped in the code. It clicked open. Inside were an array of fake passports in both our names. I emptied the box onto the floor. One item was missing.

His encrypted hard drive.

The hard drive that contained all our secrets. His spreadsheet. Where we were when, what man we'd killed, how we'd killed him, what disguises we'd been using, what passports we had entered the country with.

It was always here. Always. Was he hiding it because he knew I might think to use it as leverage? Leverage. Evidence. The dread hit my stomach. He wouldn't . . . would he?

I ran back upstairs to the spare bedroom, my makeshift studio. I'd hidden my current work-in-progress under an old bedsheet in the corner.

As soon as I opened the door, I could see that it was gone.

Fox knew.

Fox knew everything.

He had always questioned my insistence on incorporating blood, hairs, fibres and anything else from a kill that took my fancy into my work. I'd always said it was so unlikely anyone would ever find us, let alone think to check the paintings, that it was worth it. And the materials I used were so important to my creativity, they often became the very focus of the painting itself.

I'd taken flakes of blood from the knife I'd used to kill the man in the park and mixed them into the smear of paint in the top right corner of the canvas. I'd used the piece of fabric I'd ripped from his T-shirt to make a black heart in the centre of my piece.

Fox had the painting. Fox had evidence of my involvement. Was he going to confront me with it? Or was he going to deliver it to the police and let them take me?

Why this charade of a mini-break? Was it a trap?

He had let me go off at him about honesty and hiding things from me, all the while knowing I was hiding a much bigger betrayal. Was he trying to save us, or kill me? He wouldn't do that to Bibi. Surely?

I'd put us all at risk. Betrayed his trust. Whatever he had planned, it wasn't going to be a reward.

I tried calling his mobile. Voicemail.

I had to stick to the plan. Not give any indication I knew.

I finished packing and headed downstairs to Helga and Bibi. Helga was making homemade fishfingers. Bibi was helping. She had on a little apron and a chef's hat. She looked picture perfect.

'Mama, look!' She motioned towards the breadcrumbed fish. 'Not out box!'

'Wow! Aren't you clever?' I picked her up and showered her in kisses. I held her tight.

'Mamaaaa.' Bibi wriggled to get back down. I kept gripping her.

'It's hard leaving for first night away.' Helga nodded, holding up a spatula. 'Don't worry. She's in good hands.'

I put Bibi down gently. 'I love you so much. Never forget that, okay?'

Bibi grinned at me. 'Love you, Mama.'

65

Haze

I drove fast. Too fast. I got to the rental house in under fifty minutes.

There was a long drive down to the house. The white bungalow with clean, modern lines had looked impressive in the photos. In reality, it looked dwarfed by the trees surrounding it. Naïve of me to think it was romantically remote – it was *worryingly* remote.

I parked outside the front door and checked my phone for the garage code. I tapped it into the keypad. Nothing. I tried again. The buttons were stiff. Still nothing. I double-checked the code and entered it for the third time. Finally, the large double doors rolled back. I drove inside as all the garage lights came on. I checked my watch. Fox would be here any minute. No point closing the doors.

I let myself into the house, having retrieved the key from the key box in the garage.

As soon as I stepped inside, I could see why Fox had chosen it. It was the type of place we would've loved to live in before Bibi. Concrete floor. Large wrap-around windows. All the latest modern appliances. Huge, sprawling sofa in front of a cinema screen that came down with the press of a button. A huge master bedroom with views of a wildflower field leading towards a natural swimming pond.

It was the type of kitchen that was made for padding around in bare feet with bed hair, wrapped in one of his shirts. A quick check of the cupboards. No food. No wine, either. What the hell did he have planned? Was this going to be a romantic reconnecting or a heated interrogation?

I was getting a lot of mixed messages here.

I checked my watch: 6.30pm. He was late. He should be here by now.

I rang him. No answer.

At 8pm, there was still no answer. And my stomach was rumbling. Was this part of his plan? To torture me by making me sit and wait for him in a house with no food?

He knew how grumpy I got when my blood sugar dropped.

I rang him again. This time, it connected.

'Hello? Fox?'

It was a bad line. I could barely hear him. Some mumbling and then, 'I'll meet you there . . . real pain. Okay?'

'Fox? Where are you?'

His phone cut out.

Then I got a text with a location pin.

He wanted me to meet him in the middle of a forest, half an hour from here. It felt unlikely there'd be a romantic pop-up restaurant there for us to dine at. It looked like a body dump site.

Was this the surprise? That he wanted me dead? And he'd found the perfect location to do it?

I shook it off.

This was the father of my child. My husband. If he wanted to kill me, he didn't need to lure me out into the middle of nowhere.

We were supposedly on a mini-break. An attempt to recreate our lost magic. Yes, he knew I'd broken his trust by killing a man behind his back. Yes, he had proof that could be shown to law enforcement agencies. But he also loved me. He would give me the benefit of the doubt, wouldn't he?

I thought of the wild-haired, stubbly Fox. The untamed Fox. Did I really know this version of him? What he was capable of?

I looked down at my wedding ring, a thick diamond band inset with rubies. I didn't like wearing my ruby engagement ring as it was so big (I know, I know, cry for me) so Fox had insisted that my wedding band be a bit more special than average. I thought of the day we chose it together. Fox holding a jeweller's loupe as he inspected each stone. 'Gems for my gem!' he had said, grinning at me.

When it really came down to it, when you tore away all the bullshit, I knew – I one hundred per cent knew – that he loved me. And despite everything, despite all the shit we'd gone through these last few months, I loved him, even when I hated him. He was irrevocably tied to me, and me to him.

He might have some questions for me, there might be some anger, some shouting, but I could handle it. We both knew we were long overdue a serious conversation about our future. We needed to finally be honest and open about everything that had happened these last few months and see what came next for us.

I could do this. I could face him down.
He was my husband.
And I was a strong, independent woman.
With a knife.

66

Haze

My weekend bag was still on the living room sofa. I had considered changing outfits, continuing the charade of us going for a romantic dinner. But seeing as my husband hadn't bothered showing up or even really explaining where we were headed, he could suffer through the slightly sweaty clothes I'd had on all day. The heat was stifling now. The intense clamminess before a storm. With my knife safely tucked into the back of my shorts, I picked up my handbag.

I walked through to the garage and got hit so hard across the side of my head that my handbag went flying across the room as I fell back and landed on the floor, hitting something on the way down. A man wearing a baseball cap came into view.

I recognised his clothes. It was the man who'd been following me and Bibi at the park.

'Fucking bitch!' he screamed at me.

I had no idea who he was.

I blinked several times. The left side of my head was throbbing. I touched my cheek; I was bleeding. I looked to my right. I must've cut it on the side of the toolbox as I fell. That all-too-familiar metallic taste was filling my mouth. The force of the fall had whacked one of my teeth.

'How fucking dare you stick your nose in my business!' He took off his cap and threw it on the ground.

I squinted at him. He was short and balding, with dark hair. I knew him. From where?

He pulled at the top of his trousers.

Bingo.

Officer Flash.

Bill.

Jenny's ex.

'Nice to meet you, Bill. You seem lovely.' I smirked. The throbbing had subsided. The anger was rising. How dare this man, this stranger, stalk and attack me? And how the hell had I not seen him coming?

'Don't you talk to me! All this lawyer shit – that's all you, isn't it?!'

I pushed myself upright. My right hand behind my back. I could feel the reassuring bulk of my knife.

'No, Bill. It's Jenny, realising she owes it to her son to get money out of his deadbeat pervert dad.'

He came at me just as I pushed myself to my feet. His hands were round my neck, his piggy eyes bulging, his face red. I saw him for what he was. A sad little man who needed to bully, flash, intimidate to feel good about himself. I dug my thumbs into his eyes. AJ would be proud. As he squealed, I kneed him in the balls for good measure. He keeled over, and I elbowed him in his back with full force. He went down hard. I looked at him collapsed in a heap on the floor and kicked him. Twice. This was the fucker who'd been so awful to Jenny. My best friend. He deserved a hell of a lot more than the bumps and bruises he'd have in the morning. I could finish him off easily. But I felt a bit icky about killing Felix's dad.

'Stay the fuck down.'

I went up to my car's wing mirror to examine my cheek. The last thing I needed was turning up to meet Fox looking like I'd been in a fight.

I heard a rustle. I whipped out my knife and I spun round to see him charging at me with a hammer.

He howled as he ran at me – and right into the blade of the knife, which he hadn't seen I was holding. I watched as he looked down, his eyes widening. He stumbled back, clutching his stomach. The blood spread fast across his torso. Very fast. The blade must have nicked his abdominal artery. He was suddenly pale. Very pale.

He was still standing as he swayed. He was in shock.

What to do? My mind raced as I tried to work out my options.

Save him. That was the loudest shout.

I had to stop the bleeding. He couldn't die. Not here. And not by my hand.

I needed to move fast. I dropped my knife, hearing it clatter to the ground. I reached into my handbag on the floor and took out my car keys. I popped open the car boot. Bibi's swim stuff was there, in a tote bag with her name on it. I pulled out her pink unicorn towel and turned to Bill, holding it.

'I just . . . I . . .' He fell towards me, straight past me and landed half in the boot, face down.

Fuck.

I felt his neck for a pulse. Nothing.

I'd killed him.

Accidentally.

I was running late to meet my husband. Who was already undoubtedly furious at me for killing one man behind his back. And now there were two.

I looked around the garage. I needed to clear this up. And fast. As remote as this place was, there was no guarantee someone wouldn't unexpectedly wander by.

Bill was lying at an angle across my boot, half in and half out. I picked up his legs and pushed them into the boot, then slammed it closed.

Blood had dripped down the back of the car, staining the number plate. I wiped it off with Bibi's towel.

He ran into my knife. He fell into the boot of my car.

No one – and I mean no one – would believe that.

It was now 9pm. I sent Fox a message. *'Running late. Should I still bother?'*

I looked at the floor of the garage. Streaks of Bill's blood were everywhere.

We certainly wouldn't be getting our damage deposit back if I left it like this. I used Bibi's towel to clean it up as best I could.

I needed to find the cleaning cupboard.

I looked at my phone. No reply from Fox. Fuck him, then. What was the point in arranging a mini-break to get our marriage back on track, and then not even turning up?

I looked down at the bloody towel.

I guessed I wasn't exactly one to talk about appropriate behaviour, but this really wasn't my fault.

67

Haze

It was nearing 11pm by the time I was happy there was no trace of Bill anywhere in the garage. I'd got into a zone and kept my head down, focused on getting out every spot and stain I could see, and even the ones I couldn't. I had been so thorough that I was pretty sure even one of those fancy CSI glow lights wouldn't pick up any blood traces. My T-shirt was drenched with sweat.

My car was trashed thanks to him bleeding out and his actual body – there was nothing I could do about that. I couldn't think about it now. I'd have to make a plan later. If only things were better with Fox – I could really have used his help.

Shit.

Fox.

I'd been so involved in scrubbing, mopping and bleaching, I'd forgotten I was even meeting him.

I checked my phone. '*You have to come now.*' It had been sent an hour ago. I replied telling him I was on the way.

I opened the garage door and walked out to the front of

the house. Darkness had settled in, and spotlights artfully highlighted the sweeping trees surrounding the building. I saw a glint of something by one tree and took a step towards it. A bicycle, leaning up against the trunk. That was how Bill had got here without me hearing a car.

I got into my Range Rover and drove out of the garage. I stopped by the bike and flung it into the boot, on top of its dead owner.

Now there really was no trace of Bill ever having been here. I took a deep breath and got back into the driver's seat.

I could work out how the hell I was going to play this to my husband on the drive there. He'd understand, wouldn't he? I was attacked by an angry man. It was self-defence.

Again.

The location pin he'd sent was in the middle of Bisham Woods. A totally normal place to be meeting my beloved at nearly midnight. My knife, cleaned of Bill's blood, was back in my pocket.

68

Haze

As I approached the signposted entrance to the nature reserve, my phone pinged.

'Ignore the signs. Drive right to the pin.'

Okay then.

I drove straight past the signposts for the car park and kept following the pin. A dirt track with a 'No Entry' sign was up ahead. The barrier had been moved back. I kept on driving. The pin was half a mile ahead.

I'd seen no other cars and my headlights provided the only light.

The pin was a straight left turn off the track and through some long grass. I couldn't see beyond it, but if this was where my husband wanted to meet, I guess I had no choice but to go see what was there.

There was a bump as I drove off the track. From the boot I heard the clank of the bike squashing the dead man underneath.

I drove for a few minutes, and then I saw it. A pair of headlights just up ahead, and a shadow of a man alongside them.

My waiting Fox.

I pulled up a few feet from him, my headlights lighting up the same patch of grass. Our stage was lit. Ready for the big show.

I turned off the engine and got out of the car. 'Hi, honey. What the fuck are we doing out here?'

Fox walked out of the shadows. A knife was in his hand.

No.

This was how he wanted to play it? Not even an attempt to play nice?

I took mine out of my back pocket.

We stood facing each other, knives in hand.

Fox's lip was bleeding, his usually perfectly tousled hair wild. What the hell had happened to him? Who had he been fighting?

A storm was brewing. The wind was picking up. Finally, the weather was about to break.

'Where the hell have you been? Have you given up on me?' Fox stared at me, his hand gripping his knife. 'Is this how you want things to end?'

'No! I'm sorry I lied to you.'

'Tell me about the man you killed without me.' Fox ran a hand through his hair. 'You knew how important our pact was to me!'

'It wasn't my fault! It meant nothing! He attacked me!'

Fox looked up to the sky and raised his arms in the air. 'You wanted him to!' he shouted. 'You wanted an excuse. You couldn't respect our vow, to do whatever it took to protect Bibi!'

I paced up and down, the long grass tickling my calves. 'I handled it. All of it! No one will ever know.'

'Because of *me*!'

I stopped and stared at him. 'What are you talking about?'

He took a step towards me.

I raised my knife. 'What the fuck are you talking about?'

'You were sloppy.' Fox folded his arms, his knife resting on the edge of his elbow. 'You left an AirPod at the scene. You stabbed the way you always stab. No attempt to hide the pattern you always use.'

'How did you know?'

'You thought I wouldn't recognise that flush you get in your cheeks after killing a man? And then the sudden need for sex? You thought I wouldn't remember how being post-kill always made you pre-coital?' He shook his head. 'It didn't take me long to find him and clear up your mess.'

'Why didn't you ask me about it?'

'I didn't know what you were planning! I thought you were getting ready to leave me!' His voice broke a little. 'You'd been so fed up, I thought you might be depressed. That you were done with me—'

'How could you think that?'

'Think about it, Haze! Think about how things had been.'

I knew I'd made my misery, my frustrations clear. But I thought he would have understood that it was just me ranting. That I wasn't actually going to do anything about it.

'I didn't know if you killing that man was you branching out on your own. A practice run to see if you needed me at all.'

I shook my head. 'No, no. It was a momentary loss of control. That was all.'

Fox shrugged. 'I didn't tell you as I wanted you to believe you'd got away with it, all on your own. And then I wanted to be able to show you that you hadn't, that you couldn't do it without me.'

It was his very own grand gesture of love. A desperate one, at that. To persuade me not to leave him behind.

'If killing him was just a mistake, why didn't you tell me about it? Why didn't you just say, "Hun, I'm so sorry, I messed up. Let's work this out together. As a team." '

He was right. I should've just told him.

'I panicked,' I said. 'I knew I had screwed up, but I thought I could fix it, that I could make sure I hadn't endangered us all.'

Fox laughed. 'Did you really think you'd just got lucky? That the police only ever focused on a homeless guy as a suspect? That there just so happened to be a witness who saw them fight? That out of nowhere there was an uptick in complaints on homeless men behaving badly in our ever-so-nice-area?'

My mouth dropped open. 'You did all that? How?'

'It's what I do, Haze! I protect us! I think of everything. You have your fun, and you think everything just falls in your lap? Money's always in the bank account. Police are never at our door. I do that! Me!'

He was right. I didn't appreciate him. 'I'm sorry, okay?! But there were other threats to us. And I solved them. I'm not totally useless!'

Fox smiled at me. 'You're talking about Jenny?'

Jesus. He really did know everything.

'How the hell – and I mean really, the *hell* – did you make friends with a police officer? You don't even like people!' Fox pinched the bridge of his nose. 'I know you live in your own little Haze bubble where you don't trouble yourself with thinking about protecting yourself, about protecting us, but that's a whole new level of sloppy! Of all the mums you could have chosen to hang out with, you picked someone who investigates cold cases FOR FUN?'

'I was as surprised as you! But I did fix that. All by myself. She's forgotten all about the Butcher. She's got her life back on track.'

'So you played nice and got her excited about some sex offender? How long before she's picking up the thread of her next cold case? You sorted out her life and made her more of a threat! The force will be welcoming her back with open arms after her little breakthrough – and then what? You've given her power, confidence, and the resources she needs to chase down any hunch she has!'

When he put it like that, it did sound a little less than ideal.

'It doesn't matter. You don't know that. She's forgotten all about our links to the Butcher. She is not a threat to us!'

'Only because I'm going to make sure of it.'

My heart skipped a beat.

'What have you done?'

'I've got her.'

'What?' I could barely get the word out.

'You know what needs to be done. For us. For Bibi.'

She was still alive? I looked at his messed-up hair. That was why he was late. Of course. He went and took her. She fought back. His bleeding lip. Where was he keeping her? His car?

I looked at his boot. Fox saw me.

'I had to knock her out.'

My best friend was unconscious in my husband's boot.

'Are you insane? You kidnapped a detective?' My Fox, the risk-averse man-hunter, had taken an unarmed woman.

'You could've been seen!'

Fox shrugged. 'She came with me willingly.'

This didn't make sense. None of this made sense.

'What did you say to her? She would never go off with a man she didn't know!'

'Oh, Haze. She knows me.'

What the hell was he talking about?

'She doesn't know you. She would've told me!'

Fox tutted at me. 'You're not thinking properly.'

The wind was whipping in my ears. My clammy T-shirt stuck to my skin. My mind couldn't slow down. Jenny. My Jenny. Locked in his boot. Jenny, who had no social life. Who only hung out with her parents, and me, and . . . No. No – it couldn't be.

'You're . . . Gerald?'

He flung his arms in the air. 'You know full well that in my big trunk of disguises, I have the means of making myself look a lot heavier. And you don't think an American can put on a French accent?'

The trunk. I knew it. When I'd gone to get my disguise for breaking into Blaine's house, it was already unlocked. Why hadn't I realised then?

He had been out there getting Jenny to confide in him, to trust him. With a chill, I realised I was little better. Our friendship was half-based on false pretences. She didn't deserve any of this. And she didn't deserve to die. I lost Matty and now I was going to lose Jenny. The voice in my head was back louder than ever, telling me I was bad luck – I brought death, I was darkness, I dragged people down.

Oh, God – Felix. I thought of his little face lighting up every time he looked at her. He worshipped her. Of course he did. She was his mother.

This was all my fault.

69

Fox

'She won't talk!' Haze was shouting at me. The wind was rising. That promised storm just around the corner.

'Is it worth the risk? What if one day she suddenly has another flash of inspiration? Another reason why we fit the bill for the Butcher?'

Haze chewed on her lip. 'Do you really think she will?'

'It's only a matter of time. She's a good detective. I've seen her record. And she knows far too much about us.'

'I'm sorry. I know this is all my fault.' Haze closed her eyes. When she opened them again, she stared me right in the eye. 'I'll do it. Let me do it.'

'It's best I do it. I know she's not our usual type. But just this once, I think we can make an exception.' I shrugged. 'It's for our protection.'

'I want to do it! I don't want to think less of you for killing an unarmed woman. Let me take the guilt. This was my mess. Let me clear it up.'

I'd been worried that she wasn't going to be able to get on board with this. I had waited for her here, knife in hand, to see which Haze I'd get when she arrived. If she'd somehow had any indication that I'd taken Jenny, I knew I needed to be braced for a fight.

It was promising that I'd got her to see my point of view, to understand how important it was. We had to come first. Our family trumped everything.

'I don't think you'll go through with it.' I held up a hand before she could speak. 'I'm not saying that in a negative way. It's a lovely character trait to have. To not want to harm women. I really don't want all this to change you.'

'I want to do this!'

'You've done enough damage, don't you think? Just trust me to finish this!'

She stared at me as she shouted at me over the warm wind that was whipping both our faces. 'Do you even still love me?'

'How can you ask me that? Of course I love you. I would've killed you in your sleep months ago if I didn't!'

She winced as she touched her cheek. It looked as if a bruise was appearing. She'd been fighting. Was she going to tell me about it?

'What about me?' I shouted back. 'Do you still love me?'

'Till death us do part.' She spat blood onto the ground.

The sound of thumps carried over the wind. We both turned to look at my Audi.

'We need to make a decision,' I shouted. 'You or me?'

We stood there, staring at each other. Both still holding our knives.

'How about we do it together?' I offered.

'Something to bond over?' She managed a smile.

Finally, after weeks and weeks of lying to each other, of

secrets and betrayals, we could come clean. We could tell each other every last dirty detail, and decide if our future was still with each other. She just had to pass one final test.

I headed towards the back of my car.

'Wait!' she said. 'Before we do this. There's something I need to show you.'

She led me to her Range Rover and popped the trunk.

Inside was a very dead bloodied body and a bicycle.

'You ran over a man on his bike?' I peered closer. 'But how did it slice his abdominal aorta?'

'Ignore the bloody bike! I was removing evidence he'd been there.'

'You can see why I thought that. You do hate bikes, you—'

'I hate bikes because I can't bloody ride one!' Haze shouted. She looked down. 'No one ever taught me. Obviously.'

I felt like an idiot for not realising this earlier. It was just one of those things everyone presumed adults could do.

Haze motioned towards the dead man. 'Before you accuse me of betraying you again, it was self-defence. He attacked me!'

The heavens opened on us. Warm torrential rain.

Seeing as she was finally being honest, it was undoubtedly my turn to follow.

'I know he did. He was a present for you.'

There was a flash of lightning and a crackle of thunder. We stared at each other, as we got wetter and wetter.

Haze frowned. 'What are you talking about?'

I peered closer at the body. 'That's Bill, right? Jenny's psycho ex?'

'How? How do you know that?' Haze was staring at me.

'We've been hanging out a little, good old Bill and me. We

got talking at his local pub. Real woman-hater, that one. I got it into his head that Jenny must've been led astray by someone. Someone who was encouraging her to pile on the pressure.'

It had been very easy to do. I'd only followed him a few times before his routine became obvious. Work, then pub. Every day. One evening, I sat at the table next to him. Bill liked to talk. He felt hard done by. That everyone had conspired to ruin his life. He was not to blame, of course. Not for flashing his work colleague. *She led me on.* Not for being a useless father. *She had the kid to spite me.* He was so full of hate. For anyone female. *Snakes with tits.* Anyone not white. *Coming over here, stealing our jobs.* He was a deeply bitter and unpleasant man. Some of the vitriol I'd had to sit through had made me feel so dirty I'd want a shower afterwards. But I needed to have these drinks; I even enjoyed them, to a degree, as they were getting me one step closer to my endgame. Saving Haze, saving us. Just like when I was being Gerald with Jenny. These innocuous nights out were all part of a greater plan. And that helped give me the buzz I'd been missing so much during my killing retirement.

Bill enjoyed showing off about the many things he'd done wrong as a police officer, as a human being. The women he'd intimidated into doing things they really didn't want to do. The innocent men he had framed, deciding 'their kind' needed to be taught a lesson. If Haze and I were still in the killing business, he would've been a prime target.

That was why I had no problem unleashing him on my wife.

'I told him last night that I'd found out who was egging Jenny on.' Haze didn't take her eyes off me. 'I told him where you'd be tonight.'

'You set me up? He was lying in wait? He could've killed me!' She screamed at me through the rain.

'Come on, I know you and what you're capable of. Never crossed my mind you wouldn't be able to handle an overweight five-foot-seven man with a drink problem.'

Haze took this in. She knew I was right.

'I chose that location as I just wanted it to happen away from our house. Away from Bibi. And away from any witnesses.'

'But why? Why did you want him dead? How was you getting him killed, not a threat to our family?'

'Him being dead is going to save our family!' I pushed my wet hair back out of my face. 'To get us cleanly out of the mess you've made, we're going to need a fall guy.'

I strode over to my car and flung open the boot. Inside was a bound and gagged Jenny. Her eyes widened at the sight of Haze as she struggled against her ropes.

'He' – I pointed back towards Haze's car – 'is how we get away with it all. It's a perfect plan. The threat of Jenny is eliminated. And everyone will just presume he killed her, then himself. It's such a predictable domestic murder-suicide, no one would ever come looking for anyone else. You've already seen how easily led the cops here are.'

'Just because we got lucky once doesn't mean it'll be as smooth this time around.' Haze was soaked through. She was shivering a little.

'I've already told you! It wasn't luck! I paid this homeless guy to be a witness, and to stir up trouble in the area.' I thought of Cal and the numerous cash withdrawals I'd had to give him. 'Everything I've been doing has been for you, for us!'

Cash for Cal, drinks with Bill, dinners with Jen . . . all

while trying to keep the threat of my parents at bay. No wonder I was exhausted.

Haze took a step back. Jenny was thrashing around, trying to get her to look at her.

'What's your plan? What are you thinking?' Haze asked eventually.

'Remember Sicily? That lifeguard? Exactly the same play. It'll work even better, because look at this weather!' I motioned around at the apocalyptic storm. We were both drenched.

I took out my knife at the same time Haze took out hers. We were back in sync.

'Don't look at her, little one. It'll just make it harder on yourself.'

Part 5

Happy Ever After

'If you follow my advice, I'm sure you too will get to live happily ever after. Marriage is what builds us up and what makes us stronger. It can be hard work, but it's worth it. Someone chose to spend their life with you. Don't let them down!'

– Candice Summers, number-one bestselling author of *Married Means Life: How to Stay Happy, Fulfilled and Together Forever*

'Life isn't a fucking fairy tale. A happy ending is a story that hasn't finished. We're all going to die. That's the real end, and it's not very happy, is it? Living with the same person for decades is wholly unhealthy. They're going to annoy the hell out of you. But with any luck, there'll be some good bits too. Do what you can so that when your time comes (and it will) you look back and go yep, I did okay – I spent a lifetime with that man and I didn't kill him.'

– Hazel Matthews, Married Woman

The Berkshire Bulletin, 7 August 2024
OFFICER FLASH DEAD!

Bracknell-born man Bill Grundy (45) came into the public eye three years ago when CCTV of him flashing a work colleague at Slough Police Station was posted online. He lost his job on the force and became known by the moniker 'Officer Flash'. Two days ago, Grundy kidnapped his ex-girlfriend Jennifer Needham, with whom he was in the middle of a legal battle over child maintenance. Grundy was involved in a solo vehicular crash out by Bisham Woods. Witness James Wright, on his way to work, was first on the scene. He said, 'You could tell immediately the driver was dead . . . Mostly because the whole car was on fire. No one could have survived that.'

Police sources confirm that a search of Grundy's home uncovered a trophy cupboard of mementos, and even a very disturbing flash drive detailing his crimes. Rumours are rife that the evidence links him to potentially being the Backpacking Butcher – a prolific serial killer whose victims, until now, were mostly found in European hotspots.

Alistair Littleton, MP for Windsor, gave this statement: 'It is becoming apparent that Bill Grundy committed heinous crimes while serving as a Thames Valley police officer. Our police forces clearly need more stringent measures in place to weed out the bad apples.'

Sarah Seldon lived next door to Bill Grundy and described him as 'often drunk' and 'ranting'. According to another neighbour who wished to remain anonymous,

'He was the neighbour you crossed the street to avoid. He just gave off bad vibes.' Daisy Browne, from the house opposite Grundy's, added, 'I didn't even know he was that flasher chap. But saying that, he never closed his bathroom blind.'

Harriet Pugsley, who works in his local pub, had this to say: 'He was always hassling women in here. He was generous, mind you. Always buying us all drinks. It's quite something knowing a serial killer got me a G&T.'

Jennifer Needham is still missing. Needham has been on an extended maternity leave from Thames Valley Police Force, where she worked as a detective.

Will McKegney, Chief Constable of Thames Valley Police Force released this statement: 'Regarding the actions of former officer Bill Grundy and his suspected involvement in historic murders abroad, we cannot comment on an ongoing case, but we are working closely with Interpol. We are continuing our search for Detective Needham and are working tirelessly to bring her home to her family.'

70

Haze

I walked into the kitchen in my dressing gown and headed straight to the coffee machine.

'It's all over the news now.' Fox nodded at the television, where Sky News played on mute. Bibi was playing with her dolls just underneath the TV, muttering to herself as she brushed the smallest one's hair.

I didn't turn to look. I jabbed at the buttons on the coffee machine.

Fox walked up to me and wrapped his arms around me. I leaned back into him. We stood silently as the coffee beans ground.

'Felicks' mama! Felicks' mama!' Bibi pointed up at the TV. A photo of Jenny was now on the screen, alongside a photo of Bill.

Fox reached for the remote and turned it off. 'You need to go get ready. You can't be late.'

I took a sip of coffee. 'Do you think it'll be okay?'

Fox nodded. 'Of course. We've thought of everything, right?'

'I feel bad for Felix. I can't—'

'He'll be fine. You know how resilient children are. Look at you.'

I gave a half laugh. 'Exactly.' I put down my coffee mug and shuffled out of the kitchen.

Slough Police Station. Somewhere I'd hoped I'd never have to visit. I walked up to the front desk. 'I'm here to see Detective Mike Andrew? He asked me to come in.' I was in a flowery Boden dress and ballet pumps. Innocent yummy mummy. My right foot was tapping on the floor. Pumped up on caffeine.

The man behind the desk looked down at the book in front of him. 'Right. Yes. Follow me.' He led me down a corridor and opened a door marked 'Interview Room Three'. Inside was a small table and two chairs. I took a seat. My heart rate was just fine. I was just fine. I would get through this. I'd been up prepping all night with Fox. We were ready. And I would walk out of here.

A dishevelled man in a suit came bumbling through the door. 'Hazel Matthews?'

I nodded. He shut the door behind him and sat down opposite me. A small, tatty notebook was in his right hand. 'Thanks for coming in. The car Bill Grundy was found in was registered to you. Did you know him?'

I shook my head. 'I'd never met him. His ex Jenny is a great friend of mine.' I looked down at the table. 'It's just such a terrible thing. So terrible. It's just such a shock to all of us in the community.'

He checked his watch.

'Jenny asked to borrow my car,' I went on. 'Her little boy

Felix gets on so well with my daughter, and we just spend so much time together. Jenny doesn't have her own car, and that day her parents were with her son at Alton Towers, they—'

He cut me off. 'Detective Needham had told her parents she was going to meet a man she'd been seeing.'

'She mentioned that to me too. They'd been talking mostly online.'

'Do you think it's possible this man didn't exist? That it was Grundy pretending to be someone else?'

I nodded. 'I did warn Jenny about how she could be getting catfished. She'd never FaceTimed him, and his messages were a little . . . *off*. But you know, she was being careful. I think it's why she wanted my car. So she could make a fast escape if he was a weirdo.'

'Do you know where they were going to meet?'

I shook my head.

'We're trying to piece together Grundy's final movements. His state of mind.'

'I know Bill was very distressed that Jenny was going after him for money. He was not in a good place. If you speak to her lawyer, she'll no doubt have all the awful voicemails he was leaving her.'

'Yep, we have them.' He checked his watch again.

'He sounded horrible. I know Jenny was afraid of him. She was worried that getting lawyers involved would make him angry. But she had no choice. She needed the money, and he is Felix's father. Oh God, he's done something to her, hasn't he?'

'The evidence we have found so far points to Grundy and Detective Needham meeting up. Their movements after this are unknown.'

'Can't you police do something clever with tracking her mobile?'

'Detective Needham's mobile phone and handbag were discovered in the passenger seat of your car.'

'But she definitely wasn't—'

'Only one body, identified as Bill Grundy, was found inside the wreckage.'

'She could have been injured and got out of the car? And got confused? I hope you've got people out there searching! Poor little Felix, this is just so—'

'We're doing all we can to find her.' He stood up. 'Thanks for coming in.' And he rushed out the door.

I smiled to myself. I was just a witness he barely had time to talk to.

I rang Fox as soon as I got into the courtesy car grudgingly provided by my insurance company. I'd parked just opposite the station.

'It's all fine.' I heard him breathe out. 'I'm just Jenny's friend who had the misfortune of getting my car nicked and totalled.'

I started the engine.

'They had no other questions?'

'Nothing. Just told me they were still searching for her.'

'What if they find her?'

'They won't. But I think it's time.' I watched as people walked in and out of the police station.

'Do you? Not another day?'

'Let's ask her.'

71

Haze

Two days earlier

We stood over a bound and gagged Jenny. Fox raised his knife first. Jenny gave a strangled scream through the cloth tied round her mouth.

I gripped his arm and held it back. 'We're better than this. If fixing things means having to kill an innocent woman, I'd rather just turn myself in. I want to be an example to our daughter.' My voice broke. 'We've always been proud of what we do – punishing bad men is a worthy mission. If we fuck up, we should have to pay for it, not an innocent.'

'What are you saying?' Fox stared down at me.

'I know all of this is my fault. I never should've tried to hide anything from you. I just . . . it's taken time for me to adjust. I took it all for granted before, but I can see it all clearly now. I want this life. I want us.' I tucked my knife into my shorts. 'We are good people. But we won't be if you do this.' I could feel his arm tensing. 'Let Jenny live, or our marriage will die.'

I stared at him, waiting for his response. Braced for having to do the unthinkable; if my words couldn't stop him, my knife would. I'd already squared it away in my mind. I couldn't let him hurt her. I couldn't let my mistake leave a little boy without his mother.

'Please, Fox. Please. For me. For us.' The tears were coming now. The impossibility of our situation, of everything we had hidden from each other, of how we were ever going to find our way back to each other. It all hit me. The sadness of all we had lost and what I was going to have to do if he didn't listen, if he didn't see why he could not harm her.

Fox looked at Jenny and then back to me. He dropped his knife and pulled me to him. We clung together as the wind whirled around us.

Everything we'd been hiding from each other all came flooding out. A babble of sobs and truths. We forgave each other, apologised to each other, and both of us promised to do better.

Months of pent-up anger and lies – all vanquished.

'Mbummbbmmhhhh.' Jenny's attempts at shouting brought us back to the present. And the difficulties of our current situation.

Together, we helped her upright. I took the cloth away from her mouth.

'What the fuck, Haze? What the fuck?!'

'I'm sorry, Jenny. I'm so sorry.' I put a hand on her shoulder, which she shrugged off.

'I can untie—' Fox came towards her with his knife.

'Get the fucking fuck away from me!' Jenny leaned back into the boot.

'We want to untie you. Let me . . .' I reached for her bound hands and, with a flick of my knife, cut the ropes.

Jenny rubbed her wrists. 'What the hell is going on?' She stood up and turned to Fox. 'I was bloody right about you! Wasn't I? You're the bloody Backpacking bloody Butcher! Ha – I've still got it!' She turned towards me. 'And you knew? How could you not . . . How . . . Oh!' The moment where the last piece clicked into place. She looked between the two of us and sat down hard on the edge of the boot.

Fox approached us with his hands held up. 'I'm going to give you ladies some space to talk.' He looked at me. 'You take my car. I'll take yours.'

I nodded. 'Still the Sicily lifeguard play?'

Fox gave me a thumbs-up. We agreed how to deal with Bill.

'What are you . . .?' Jenny looked between us.

'I'll explain everything.' I helped Jenny to her feet and led her to the passenger seat of Fox's car.

She stopped suddenly. 'How the hell can I trust that you won't hurt me? How can—'

'Clearly, if we wanted you dead, you'd be dead by now.' There was another crack of thunder as the rain continued to pour down on us. 'So will you just get in the car?'

She flung open the passenger door and stumbled in. I went round to the driver's side. We sat there, not speaking, not even looking at each other, as the rain belted down on the windscreen.

A minute passed.

And then another.

There are awkward silences, and then there are the 'My husband and I are serial killers' kind of awkward silences.

I took a breath. 'Okay, so things have got a little crazy. But you must know the whole Fox pretending to be an overweight

Frenchman, kidnapping you, wanting to kill you . . . That was all him. I had no idea!'

'You might not be guilty of that, but everything else? Who even are you? I . . . I thought we were friends.' Jenny swung round to look at me.

'We *are* friends!'

At this, Jenny motioned towards the rope indentations round her wrists. 'This is how you treat friends?'

'Look, I'm kind of new to this whole friendship thing.'

'You don't say!'

We sat in silence for another minute.

'Okay, so Bill is dead.' I looked down at the steering wheel. 'I don't know how you feel about that, but you of all people must know the world is better off without him.' I turned to look at her. 'Fox and I, we only ever kill men like him. We aren't, you know . . . *bad* serial killers. No chasing after innocents. Just administering justice to those who deserve it.'

'Bill is dead,' Jenny repeated.

'Very dead.'

'And you're *good* serial killers.'

'Yes!'

'Bill is dead,' Jenny repeated again. She looked across at me. 'I'm okay with that.'

'That's great. Really great. He attacked me. It was actually self-defence.'

'*You* killed Bill.'

'Yes.' I paused. 'Chances are you'll get his money now. So that's a plus. And it's not like Felix had any relationship with him anyway. Oh, and his house! You'll get that too. It'll need a lot of work, though.' I grimaced at the memory. 'A full refurbishment needed inside.'

'You've been to Bill's house?' Jenny was staring at me.

'Ah, yes. A while back. I wanted to check he wasn't planning on hurting you.'

She didn't seem as touched by this as she should have been. 'And how are you planning on getting away with his murder?'

'Fox will put Bill in the driving seat of my car, and with the help of a branch wedged onto the accelerator, set it on course to drive into a tree at high speed. He'll make sure the car explodes. The police won't be able to tell the body was stabbed first.' I paused. 'We have done this before. Worked a treat.'

'I hope so.' Jenny closed her eyes. 'Neither of us can be tied to the scene.'

I nodded. 'But it's my car.'

'And he's my ex.'

I thought of all the lawyer's letters and his angry voicemails. 'If they think I'm involved, they'll think you are too. You put me up to it. I was the great friend getting rid of a shitty ex.'

Jenny looked at me. 'Then let's think of a plan together. Get us both free of this. And then I'll work out what the hell I'm going to do next.'

I started the engine.

I knew that the decision I'd made to save her was the right one. I also knew it meant that I would lose her as a friend – and that I'd probably lose my family and my freedom, too. With everything she now knew, Jenny held our lives in her hands.

The Berkshire Bulletin, 9 August 2024
MISSING DETECTIVE FOUND ALIVE!

Detective Jennifer Needham walked into her former police station last night having managed to escape from the abandoned house where her ex-partner Bill Grundy (aka Officer Flash) had been holding her. Needham had been missing since last week, when she was abducted by Grundy in the midst of their ongoing dispute over child maintenance. Grundy died in a solo vehicular car crash the same evening he abducted her. The inquest is scheduled for next month, but unofficially sources have reported that it will be ruled a suicide. Interpol are continuing their investigation into Grundy being the Backpacking Butcher, but sources are saying they are likely to confirm he was indeed the man they've been looking for. Detective Needham is currently recovering from her ordeal at home. Thames Valley Police released this statement: 'We are delighted that Detective Needham is safe and well, and we look forward to welcoming her back to work as soon as she is back to full health.'

From Hamish.Graham@redfern-gallery.co.uk
Sent 10:40 9 August 2024

Dear Haze,

Your husband dropped off your latest piece the other day. We love it! He said you'd titled it 'Deception' – bravo, a perfect choice. It so beautifully illustrates the domino effect of lies and hidden truths. Delighted your maternity leave is over and you're painting again. Any idea how long it will be until you have enough new work for a big exhibition?!

All the best,
Hamish

72

Haze

Me. Fox. Jenny. The three of us were sitting around our kitchen table. Bibi and Felix were playing next door. Fox was pouring us each a cup of tea from a large blue teapot that I'd always hated. It was silent except for the noise of our children's laughter, punctuated by the sounds of a singing *Frozen* doll.

Jenny cleared her throat. 'I'd like to say a little something.'

Fox sat down next to me and reached for my hand.

All it took to save our marriage was a mini-break.

For other couples, it would be the reset of a change of location, the luxury of child-free lie-ins, good food on fine china and great sex on luxury Egyptian cotton. For us, it was a dead man, a tied-up woman and a Berkshire wood. It may have been an unusual combination, but it saved us. And we felt together, stronger than ever.

The irony now being it was, most likely, about to be the end of us. But at least we were going out on a high.

Jenny was a do-gooder. She was no doubt about to lay out a timeline for our confessions. I wondered if she'd already planned the outfit she was going to wear when she marched us into Slough Police Station. All I was hoping for was that she would allow only one of us to take the fall. Mother to mother, I felt this was a plea she'd have to understand. And if that didn't work, there was always money. Thankfully, we had a limitless amount to throw her way to beg for her silence.

Jenny took a deep breath. 'Let me help you.'

Fox and I looked at each other.

'I think you should get back to doing what you do best. You guys are an amazing team. And all the men you killed, I know they were bad men. They all deserved it.'

Fox started to speak, but before he could, Jenny stood up and lifted up her top, exposing a slightly greying M&S cotton bra. She did a twirl. No wire. She wasn't recording us to dob us in to her colleagues. Did that mean she really meant it?

'I'm officially back at Thames Valley Police, and as much as I'm really happy to have a salary again, and be back in the office, I've become a little jaded with the whole law-and-order process.' Jenny shook her head. 'All those unsolved cases, the ones where we know the men are guilty, but we can't nail them? They keep me up at night. Those men don't deserve to live!' Her voice shook with anger. 'Just like Bill. He didn't deserve to live.'

'What do you mean, you want to help us?' Fox asked. I couldn't get a read on what he was making of all this.

'I can do research for you. Pinpoint exactly who needs to be targeted and help you track them down. I'd be your back-office grifter, doing all the work that needs to be done to free you up to do what you do best.'

Fox and I had spent the last few days preparing for the

worst. Preparing for the fact that one of us was going to have to pay the price for everything we had done. We'd focused solely on enjoying being with Bibi, being with each other. Appreciating our little family unit, scared about how long we'd have it for.

The subject of killing again had never crossed either of our minds. And now here was Jenny, dangling it in front of our faces. She didn't want us punished; she wanted us reinstated.

I was trying to hold it down, but a prickle of excitement was forming. This was better than anything I could've hoped for. But it was down to Fox. If these last few months had taught me anything, it was that we both needed to be on the same page. We had to work together, or we didn't work at all.

'What's in it for you?' Fox asked.

The high-pitched screech of the *Frozen* doll grew louder as Bibi and Felix careered into the kitchen brandishing it.

'Snacckkkkkkk!' Bibi demanded.

I got up and went to the cupboard, handing them each a packet of Pom Bears. 'Back to the sitting room. The grown-ups are talking.'

We waited until they were safely back next door.

'I want a better life for me and my son. I can forgive all the . . . you know . . . catfishing me, kidnapping me, wanting to kill me, and so on. All that stuff. Because I can see the bigger picture.' She turned to me. 'I know the circumstances were . . . less than ideal. But planning how to help you get away with Bill's murder was the most alive I've felt in years.'

I knew it! I thought I'd picked up on a vibe. She had been very thorough in thinking of everything we needed to do to throw the police off our scent – it had been her idea to hole up in an isolated location to lead the narrative that Bill had abducted her. Her parents had been sworn to secrecy and Felix thought Mummy was on a lovely spa break.

We had all worked hard to cover our tracks. It had been a busy night. Fox had edited his kills spreadsheet to make it sound like Bill – he'd spent enough time in his company to be able to make it sound believable. He implied he was jealous of successful men and that was why he'd killed them. He'd bigged up escaping capture through his expert police skills (which his old colleagues might find a stretch), and did a lot of ranting in caps lock (which they definitely would've found believable). I had broken into Bill's house once more and planted the USB stick in his spare bedroom cupboard, along with a couple of trophy items that linked him to our previous victims. We'd killed Bill and we'd killed the Backpacking Butcher. A clean slate.

'I've dedicated my life to the police, and for what? They tried to get rid of me! They didn't appreciate how Bill coerced me and they certainly never appreciated just how good I was at my job. I've lost count of the number of men they promoted over me!' Jenny looked between the two of us. 'You're clearly excellent at covering your tracks but with me helping you further, you'd be untouchable.'

Fox cleared his throat. 'Let's talk more about your terms. What exactly are you thinking?'

'You help me with cases I'm finding tricky. If I have an impressive solve rate, that will increase my chances of promotion. The higher up I am, the better access I have, and the easier it will be for me to cover up anything we want hidden.'

Fox frowned. 'You want us to help you punish men with prison? How?'

'Just like Haze did with that creep Blaine. You find evidence that I otherwise wouldn't be able to get. You'd be like my own private investigators.' She turned to me. 'I'm guessing there was no helpful girl with the tapes? You just stole them?'

I shrugged. 'You've got to make your own luck.'

I knew helping Jenny would come easily to us. We'd have no problem getting inside the sick heads of the men she was after. We could easily work out where they were likely to have screwed up and where we could find actual evidence to help get them locked up.

'I know there are certain men you target both because of what they've done, and because of the financial benefit they can give you.'

I smiled to myself. She really had done her research on us.

'I'd also want a ten per cent cut of whatever you pull in from a kill. This would cover my time, and the additional risk I'd be exposing myself to by helping you.' She turned to me. 'You're right about Bill's house. Total renovation needed.'

'Ten per cent?' Fox guffawed. 'That's a lot.'

'I think I've been through a lot.' Jenny stared at him pointedly. 'And I will offer you a lot. I will be taking the pressure off you. When you're out on a job, I'll be your HQ. We'd keep in radio contact, ensuring you won't be disturbed or seen.'

Fox nodded. I knew he'd always seen this as our weakness: the chance of someone interrupting us.

'I'll be the one doing a sweep after you've left a scene, making sure it's clean. And afterwards, I can easily track all the chatter in law enforcement agencies. I'd be like an incredibly efficient PA. I could even do itineraries and little reminders.' She paused. 'I know how much you love a spreadsheet.'

I was finding it hard to sit still. This all sounded perfect. Magical. The dream. I looked at Fox. He was the one who would need convincing. Jenny and I looked at each other. Together, we could surely make him see this was going to be great. A no-risk, efficient way of eliminating bad men without any fear of capture? We could go back to our glory days, back to how it was; reaching our full potential, going to bed at night high off a kill, content in the knowledge that we'd made the world a better place. Surely, he had to see it made sense?

73

Fox

Today had been interesting. Just before Jenny had walked in, I'd received the email I knew was coming. My beloved parents had managed to find a legal loophole that allowed them to dissolve mine and Julian's trust fund. It was official: my safety net was gone. For the first time in my privileged life, I was going to have to stand on my own two feet. With no limitless credit card, I'd now have to actually check bills before I tapped my card. Would I have to readjust my whole attitude to grocery shopping? Was organic food really that much more expensive than regular food? I bit my lip. I'd make savings elsewhere; I couldn't have Bibi ingesting God knows what kind of chemicals.

From the moment I was unceremoniously fired from UBS – courtesy of my father and his impressive contacts list – I knew they weren't going to stop. Cutting me off from my employment was the first step. Thanks to Suzanne they'd had a large amount of information on my movements at work. Her parents had pressured her into forcing herself into my life, she wasn't clear on whether they'd asked her to also attempt getting into my bed or if that was just her going rogue. I rang her parents one evening, with Suzanne on the line, to tell them that my parents were monsters. I said they never should've allowed a beloved daughter to be used as some kind of pawn in a sick game just to gain social cachet. Suzanne was thrilled. I don't think anyone had ever dared speak to them like that before.

I'd predicted they'd come after the trust fund next. I realised I needed to make a hefty purchase as quickly as possible. Putting a good wodge of cash into a Mayfair townhouse seemed a sensible plan and considering my lack of employment it would make the perfect headquarters for setting up my own firm.

These last few days might have meant uncertain times for everything else in our lives, but I was still basking in the relief of having a clean slate with Haze. Everything we'd both been doing was now out in the open. I felt lighter. Until now I hadn't realised how deeply it was affecting me, keeping everything to myself.

I'd woken up this morning prepared for life as we knew it to change beyond recognition, but it was at least with a certain peace knowing that Haze and I were closer than ever. I'd been prepared for Jenny walking in here with colleagues from her police station, ready to take us away. I had already prepared myself for an elongated negotiation through lawyers to make sure only I took the fall; my girls kept together at home, waiting decades for me to return.

Today was going to be a dark day. But to be blessed with this instead? The offer of a risk-free way to restart our little sideline in bad men? No more having to choose between the happiness of my wife and the safety of my child? The things we could achieve with a police detective in our corner . . .

Over the last few years, I'd succeeded in supressing that dark side within me. I'd compartmentalised all my desires to kill. I had become Nathaniel through and through. Had this helped me grow as a person? I thought back. I'd spent hours and hours at AA meetings, I'd had several near-misses at high-stakes poker games, my investment portfolio had taken a nosedive, and my marriage had gone to crap.

Nathaniel could be retired, and I would not miss him.

'Okay.' I looked between the two women staring at me. 'Let's do this.'

74

Haze

Six Months Later

I parked up and sat staring at the house. I let a few moments pass and then I got out, walked up to the front door and rang the bell.

The sound of footsteps and then the door opened.

'Hi,' I said. I didn't know how this was going to go.

'Haze!' Matty's mother exclaimed. She smiled. 'Come in.'

I had met her once, sixteen years ago, but as she led me through their hallway, still decorated with so many photos of Matty, it was as if I popped over all the time.

'I'm sorry to just turn up.'

'It's lovely to see you.' She bustled around the kitchen, putting on the kettle and getting out two mugs. 'Tea or coffee?'

'Tea, please.'

I sat down at the kitchen table.

'How are the exhibitions going? And your husband and daughter, is it?'

I tilted my head as I stared at her. How did she know?

She looked down and wrung her hands together. 'I have a confession to make.' She took a deep breath. 'I kept Matty's number. I lost my phone not long after he died. And I just thought . . . Well, his had all of his photos. I spent so long going through them whenever I missed him, I figured I might as well have it with me all the time.'

I tried to ignore my creeping heart rate.

'I'm sorry if I sent anything bad . . . I guess I just really missed him, and missed having him to talk to.'

The kettle boiled and Cathy turned to fill up the mugs. 'I loved getting them. I'm sorry for invading your privacy. You thought no one would read them.'

Over the years I had been guilty of texting Matty's number a lot when I was drunk. Just how honest had I been?

Cathy brought the mugs to the table and sat down opposite me.

'It really meant something to me, to see how much you missed him. Of course, I'm so sorry that losing him hurt you so much. But it helped me. Knowing someone else out there was still mourning him.'

I nodded. 'I understand.'

'It's so good to see you. I've been worried. You haven't texted anything in months.'

'I figured it might have been time to stop.' It wasn't a conscious decision I made. It just happened.

Cathy leaned towards me. 'I hope you've never blamed yourself for what happened. That's what I meant to say the first time we met. I guess I never got the words out. It was all still so raw.'

I looked down at my mug of tea. I didn't trust myself to speak.

'His depression had been there for a long time,' she

continued. 'I want you to know having you in his life probably kept him alive for longer.'

I took a breath. 'I just . . . if I hadn't been a self-obsessed twenty-year-old, I might have been more helpful. I might have got through to him.' I had known Matty had bad days. I'd just thought everyone had bad days. I knew I did. But I didn't stop to think how everyone's pain was different – as was how they handled it.

'If he'd died of a brain tumour, would you have beaten yourself up over that? As if helping him wasn't down to the doctors, but down to you?'

I shook my head slowly.

'His depression was every bit as dangerous as a tumour. It took over his mind completely. There was nothing you could've done.'

Black dog, black spot. Both potentially deadly.

I took a breath. 'Thank you. That helps.'

She squeezed my hand.

I reached into my bag and took out a small object. I placed it on the table.

'I took it. Just after he died. I'm sorry, it belongs with you.'

Cathy smiled as she picked up Matty's bird sculpture. 'It's beautiful. Are you sure you don't want to keep it?'

'I've had it for long enough. It's time for you to enjoy it.' I was never going to forget Matty – I didn't need his bird to remind me of him. Turning it over and over in my hands while staring at a blank canvas had helped me wallow. And I was done with all that.

'I hope your husband is letting you paint again? You were clearly very upset about not getting to do what you love.'

I was thankful that even in my text rants I'd managed to rein in exactly what it was I missed doing.

'He was being overly protective . . . he knew it caused me a lot of stress, but he realised I wasn't myself without it. I'm painting more than ever now.' Hamish at the gallery was back to being overwhelmed by my productivity.

We sat there for a long time, drinking far-too-weak tea and telling and retelling our favourite Matty stories. Eventually, I hugged her goodbye on the doorstep.

'Please keep in touch.' Her voice broke a little.

'You've got my number.' I smiled and rubbed her shoulder.

Back in the car I looked over at the house.

I *had* been a good friend to Matty. Just like I had been a good friend to Jenny – and her life I had been able to save. I could be there for the ones I loved and not worry it was all going to blow up in my face. I wasn't bad luck. Life could be messy, unpredictable, unfair and beautiful. I couldn't control it. The hardest part of loving people was losing them. I couldn't let that fear hold me back.

I thought of yesterday. Bibi had gone skipping up to a Labrador in the park while holding Sausage's lead. 'Look, Mama, friend for Sausage!'

I was proud of her, proud of me.

75

Fox

My firm already had a big name first client. The mighty Algernon Lockwood III, an American bigwig I'd been schmoozing, had decided my golf game was good enough and my handshake firm enough to trust me with his investments. When Haze kicked me out, he'd joined me at my otherwise lonely dinners at the club and we'd bonded over us both having overbearing parents. There was no doubt he enjoyed knowing that using me would be a big middle finger to mine.

The Mayfair townhouse had needed a small refurbishment and a change of usage permits, and we were all set. While the plan was to eventually let out some of the smaller offices, the top two floors would belong to Cabot Matthews Investments. A small private stockbroking firm with a little off-the-books sideline in eliminating bad men.

Jenny, Haze and I now used the meeting room to discuss, plot and plan our next kill. We'd really upscaled operations. There were slideshows, maps, planning. I felt more secure than I ever had. Our small-time couple's hobby had been upgraded to a slick vigilante killing operation. We were going after bad men whom I previously would never have dared to try and take – the ones so powerful and rich, they felt cocooned, out of our reach. But not anymore. With Jenny's police access, all our efforts had been expedited and our tracks hidden.

I found it addictive, knowing that the bigger the villain we eliminated, the more people we saved. Recently, we'd killed a man who was in charge of an abuse network that procured women and children for his clients' depraved sexual requests. His death had thrown the network into disarray. Despite knowing that the gang funding them would soon ensure someone else took his place, I was able to comfort myself with the knowledge that we'd kill the next leader, too. We'd keep going until it was a job no one wanted. These people didn't know who we were, but I wanted them to be afraid of us.

As we often worked weekends, we'd sometimes install Helga in one of the empty offices to entertain Felix and Bibi. Then, once we were finished for the day, we would take them around the Science Museum. We really took flexible working seriously. 'Having it all' was very much our mantra.

Jenny had fit in so smoothly, it felt like she'd always been with us. She had somewhat taken over my role as the voice of caution. Sometimes she disapproved of my ambitions; she was wary of drawing too much attention from the wrong people. It was helpful to hear her reservations, but I thought she was underestimating just how good we were at all this.

Post-Bill's death, she'd had one hell of a glow-up. Haze had taken her to an expensive Knightsbridge salon to give her a makeover. She'd made it clear that upgrading one's physical appearance wasn't anti-feminist, as it was all about self-confidence. If Jenny was going to succeed in living the double life of police officer by day, Killer HQ by night, she was going to need all the swagger she could get.

Back when I had been encouraging Haze to try and make a 'mum friend', it was because I'd thought it'd be nice for her to have someone to share the trials and tribulations of motherhood with. I was thinking more shared playdates, not shared kill dates.

But then, this was us. The traditional, expected path was always one we'd deviate from – and in fairness, Jenny was a support system (an incredibly efficient one). Knowing her had made Haze happier. She might not be the mum friend I'd envisaged, but she was the one Haze needed.

Now and again, I caught Jenny looking at me funny. '*What? It's just so weird getting the odd glimpse of Gerald.*' I look back on that crazy time as things were falling apart with a kind of terror. How did we ever let things get so bad? I'd lost control for a little while back there. At some point, while I was making myself appear fifty pounds heavier and putting on a French accent, I should've considered just putting the disguises back into their box and talking to my wife.

But she was pretty frightening back then. She was either bored on autopilot or full of rageful indignation. There was no in-between, no happy medium – just an all-time low.

And now look! That fire I'd so missed was back in my wife's eyes and we were back in sync. Happy. Satisfied. Passionate. Turns out that feeling unfulfilled and keeping secrets from each other did not make for a hotbed of hot sex. You needed to feel connected, to want to . . . connect.

Life together was better than ever.

We'd found a way to be out there doing our best work, while still getting home for bedtime. We took our responsibilities seriously – both to our daughter and the female population as a whole. We were out there fighting the good fight, taking down men who were a threat and making sure they could never hurt anyone else again.

Whether my wife and I were out for dinner, or out killing a man, I'd look at her and think about how ours was a true love. We had skirted around rock bottom, and now we'd built back bigger and better than ever. We were invincible now; I was sure of it.

76

Haze

'Target is on the move.'

Jenny had made us get headsets. I think she really was living out her secret agent fantasies.

We were in Vienna for a long weekend. Jenny had discovered that our latest target would be attending a black-tie ball at the Vienna State Opera house. She'd planned everything, right down to the red Alexander McQueen dress I was wearing. Not only did it suit me to perfection, but she'd found it in my size at sixty per cent off. She'd grinned at me. 'You can buy matching shoes with the money you saved.'

Jenny was my first ever female friend. Until her, I didn't really understand the point of them. I'd seen movies about the strong bonds of gal pals, eye-rolled at the gushing Instagram 'Slay, queen!' posts. It sounded nice, but not really for me. *You go, girl!* All that shit was beneath me. I had always been a loner who mostly only really liked hanging out with people I could have sex with. I was happy killing bad men to help women, but I didn't want to actually talk to them. I'd purposefully shut myself off. I realised now I had been missing out.

When people talk about friendship, they might use platitudes like 'I'd die for them'. But I thought 'I didn't let her die' was just as special. I had stopped my husband killing my best friend. I was a hero. A woman-supporting woman.

Last year had been rough. People did always say it would take some time to adjust after becoming parents. But look at us now. Our daughter was thriving, our marriage was back on track. We had got better at communicating openly, outlining our fears and frustrations, and above all realising it was better to kill bad men rather than each other.

The opera house was a grand building in a pedestrian boulevard. This ball was one of the highlights of the season. There must've been over five hundred people in attendance. A heady combination of black tie, the occasional fur stole, and glittering diamonds. Inside the auditorium, an opera singer with an elaborate headdress was belting out a classical aria, her voice reverberating round the ornate domed ceiling.

I moved out towards the main reception area and saw a short man with white hair heading up the marble staircase.

'I have eyes on the target.' I raised my glass of champagne to my lips as I spoke.

Fox's voice in my ear: '*The private room is ready.*'

I headed up the staircase, half listening to the conversations of those I passed. I heard French, Italian, German and English. A very international crowd.

Most people were downstairs, listening to the singer. As I walked along the corridor, I noticed only a few men slowly making their way to the staircase.

I felt a brief flash of something. What was it? A jolt of feeling unsure. I shook it off, smiling to myself. With Jenny and

Fox's thorough reconnaissance and detailed operational security measures, we were totally protected. My subconscious was clearly freaking at the idea of getting blood on such a beautiful dress. I would have to be extra careful. It'd be a crime to ruin it.

I spotted the white-haired man I was looking for just up ahead. I caught up to him. 'Luca?' He turned to look at me as I touched his arm. 'I've been looking for you. Can we go somewhere private?' We had tracked down the missing paedophile teacher from Jenny's wall of crazy. Fox had been grumpy about us killing him next – he'd become quite grand with his ambitions and now considered a run-of-the-mill paedophile too small-time.

The man looked very little like the mugshot of him that was in circulation. No wonder the authorities had found him so hard to locate.

His eyes widened and a grin formed.

He wouldn't be smiling soon.

I led him towards my Fox's lair.

Our marriage wasn't like other marriages. There was no handbook for couples like us, no way to understand how we were meant to be. We could only go by our instincts. Love hard and fight harder. We had each other. And we had our knives. Our future was bright and bloody. There were no limits to what we could do together. Who could possibly stop us?

Acknowledgements

I loved writing this book and I don't think it would've been anywhere near as fun without my exceptional editors Jack Butler at Wildfire and Jenny Chen at Bantam. Inspiring, insightful and a dream to work with – I am so incredibly grateful for everything you have done for Serial Killer.

The team at Wildfire have consistently impressed with their imagination, enthusiasm and downright hard work. Standout thanks go to Oliver Martin in Publicity, Katrina Smedley and Alexia Thomaidis in Marketing, Assistant Editor Areen Ali and Cover Designer (of dreams) Caroline Young.

Alice Lutyens, my "Super-Agent" – it is truly great having you by my side. Thank you for always pushing me (even when I really don't want to be) and for constantly telling me what an amazing, fun, low-maintenance client I am (okay you don't, but I know you think it).

There are far too few opportunities in life to immortalise in print the people that make your life significantly better – so I take full advantage of this Acknowledgements to do just that . . .

In TV land – a big thank you to my most excellent agents

Camilla Young and Katie Battcock for being the best support system and relentless cheerleaders.

To the legendary Ileen Maisel – until we can honour you on screen, I hope you'll accept a mention here. I was so lucky to work with you and even luckier to call you a friend. I'll never forget everything you did for me – including introducing me to the brilliant Michael Duggan. We'll do our best to make you proud.

Rebecca Thornton. This book is for you – a small token of the mountain of thanks I have for you always being there for me and keeping me sane (well, sane enough).

Theodore Backhouse. My brilliant, kind, loud, impossible, much-loved friend. I'm keeping my promise of raving about you in one of my books. Twenty years of having you in my corner was nowhere near long enough and my world is much sadder (and quieter) without you in it.

Georgia Tennant. I don't think all those many years and children ago, we could've predicting this happening - you reading the audiobook of this, a book I have somehow written. Thank you for the amazing job you and the very talented Kyle Soller have done bringing Haze and Fox to audio reality. I'll always be grateful that fate and our hungry babies brought you into my life and I can't imagine you not in it – especially as I'm now so reliant on your wise and informed counsel I can't even choose a paint colour without you. *(Pause here as your eyes fill with tears and your voice wavers at how much you love me and how special our friendship is).*

Caroline Barrow and Lara Smith-Bosanquet. A huge thank you for always reading whatever I send you with reassuring enthusiasm, and handholding me through everything from the very big to the very very small.

Special mentions also to George Backhouse, Chris Blackford, Will Callewaert – for helping me through the bleakest of days with dark humour and sloe gin.

Further thank yous to Lou Hill for everything you do. To Zoe Flower and Simon Byrt for being core Team Chiswick and always being on hand for drinks and encouragement. Lastly Neil Frame, who only just slips in for a mention, for occasionally being useful in responses to my random inane questions.

To make my kids feel involved in my writing (and to apologise for the vast amount of time I'm chained to my laptop) I let them choose character names . . . so if you're a teacher of theirs who made it in here, I hope you take this little nod in the good spirit and affection it was done with. I'm very grateful my children have adults in their life that can offer more educational answers to their questions than 'dunno, just Google it.'

As always, enormous gratitude to . . .

My parents – for everything. Love is referencing a carrot cake I made in 1991 whenever anyone mocks me for not being able to cook. Extra special mention to my beloved Dad for being the very best first reader of my every draft – a habit that started when I was five and has never stopped.

My partner-in-crime, Andrew Trotter, for taking the flack of me writing a book about killing and marriage and coping with the side eye at the school gates. And for being the fun parent who does all the stuff I won't (rollercoasters are the devil's work).

Tavie, Arlo, Gus and Silva – you are the best of me, and I am forever proud I get to call you mine.

To all my other loved ones who didn't make it in this time, I encourage you to try harder and remember this potential accolade when debating birthday present budgets for me.

Finally, to anyone who read this all the way through to this very last sentence – did you know that every time you rate a book five stars on any public forum rainbows light up the sky, fluffy bunnies leap with joy and a writer ecstatically cries how it was all worth it?!

©Claire Menary

Asia Mackay is a Chinese Scottish author and mother of four based in London. Asia studied Anthropology at Durham University and began her career in television. She moved to China, presented and produced lifestyle programmes in Shanghai before returning to London where she worked for the likes of Ewan McGregor and Charley Boorman, and subsequently completed a Faber Academy course. Her debut novel *Killing It* was the Runner Up in Richard and Judy's Search for a Bestseller competition and Runner Up/ Exceptionally Recognised for the Comedy Women In Print prize.